MARGE PIERCY

FLY AWAY HOME

A NOVEL

SUMMIT BOOKS
NEW YORK

Copyright © 1984 by Marge Piercy
All rights reserved
including the right of reproduction
in whole or in part in any form
Published by SUMMIT BOOKS
A Division of Simon & Schuster, Inc.
Simon & Schuster Building
1230 Avenue of the Americas
New York, New York 10020
SUMMIT BOOKS and colophon are trademarks of Simon & Schuster, Inc.
Designed by Karolina Harris
Manufactured in the United States of America

1 3 5 7 9 10 8 6 4 2

First Edition
Library of Congress Cataloging in Publication Data
Piercy, Marge.
    Fly away home.
    I. Title.
PS3566.I4F55   1983   813'.54   83-18026
        ISBN 0-671-49419-8

I would like to express my gratitude to the many people who answered my endless questions as I wrote *Fly Away Home*.

I would especially like to thank Anni Waterflow for sharing so many of her adventures in organizing, for sharing the terror and the energy of all she went through; and for showing me the ins and outs at the Registry of Deeds.

I would like to express my thanks to Mark Zanger for his generosity as an expert and as a raconteur. His being equally a connoisseur of arson and of cookery was a surprising coincidence.

Ruthann Robson has my gratitude not as the fine poet she also is, but as my legal adviser, especially in courtroom procedures.

I would like to thank my dear friend Penny Pendleton for searching the relevant psychological literature for me.

I'd like to express public as well as private gratitude to Woody, who drove me round and round and round and round neighborhoods in glaring heat and in ice-rutted glacial blizzards, and who walked with me all over greater Boston as we chased together the patterns that lie behind this novel. As ever he is my shrewdest critic and text editor.

Marge Piercy

Ladybird, ladybird
fly away home.
Your house is on fire.
Your children will burn.

1

LIKE many women, Daria both loved her mother and prayed not to become her. Often Daria felt helpless before her mother Nina's woes, yet her first impulse was to reassure herself: I am different. I have a good and faithful husband, I have my own work, I live in a beautiful house, I like my life. Misery was not hereditary or contagious. Since the plane had taken off late from Chicago, Daria had been dividing her time between worrying about her younger daughter Tracy, who had gone away to college for the first time, and Nina, who had sounded more depressed and lonely than usual on the phone last night. Was Nina really sick? Or just unhappy?

Grey murk enclosed the plane, clouds on which it bumped and slipped and veered as if bouncing over a shifting sea of children's marbles. Daria felt a little sick. Four-thirty on a Friday, Boston's Logan Airport was embroiled in its customary traffic jam. On the invisible ground hidden in some random direction, cars would be backed up through the Callahan Tunnel, while here in the lumpy air, planes circled like blind boxes.

Daria had a fatigue headache. For ten days she had been rushing through seven cities. She had been kept up past midnight, then forced to rise at five-thirty for morning television shows or to catch early planes to other cities. Everywhere she had to put on exhibitions to plug her cookbook in an unfamiliar studio with no rehearsal, no backup, no repeats and a technical staff she had never seen before. In the canvas bag wedged under the seat in front of her was that minimal equipment she needed for the two to four minutes she was given.

Still once she was on camera or in front of a crowd, she got excited and involved, no matter how many times she had given the same spiel. Since studios and department stores generally lacked stoves, she cut up local vegetables, showing how to slice and display crudités for hors d'oeuvres or a first course, with her patter. "People always feel virtuous when they eat raw veggies, it's almost as if they're dieting by eating. You have them in a good mood, especially if you want to serve something more fattening, such as a delicious pasta next." The knife and honing block, the platters, the spices for dip all had to accompany her on the plane, because at least once every tour her luggage went off to Juno while she was heading for Houston. There was usually that little scene at the metal detector when her knife went through, and sometimes that pouch was taken by the flight attendant until landing. Her carry-on luggage always rattled in spite of how well she packed the platters. She was an old pro. Her index finger was still infected from the cut she had given herself on camera in Atlanta, but she had simply carried on smiling. Demonstrating with flash was fun, even the twenty-eighth time.

Closing her eyes against the dismal cabin, she saw Ross's face. She had not been able to reach him the night before, but finally she had caught him in his law office while she was waiting and waiting to board the plane at O'Hare. She missed him, a raw loose feeling in her. They had married so young they had formed each other. She had come to him not fully human, a fish-girl, half jelly and half bones. He had been raw, bright, idealistic and entirely unsure of himself, spiny as a sea urchin, shy as a feral cat. Home, please, home, she begged, concentrating on the murk and the plane. Slowly she spun her wedding ring round and round on her finger as if rubbing a lamp that could emit a genie.

Somewhere under the grey sludge, Ross was waiting, watching the clock. Maybe Robin their older daughter would be with him. Tomorrow was Daria's forty-third birthday. She had discharged her last obligation to promote the new book, except for cooking schools and demonstrations around Boston. Did the engines sound funny? She caught herself breathing through her mouth like Torte, their dog, when he was scared. The day after her birthday she could go back to work on the new cookbook she was writing. That would be paradise: to be home, her place, her peace, her husband—alone for the first time since Robin had been born. She would talk to Ross about bringing Nina north for a visit, even if Pops wouldn't come. That would cheer Nina up, seeing her children and grandchildren. She would call tonight and make sure Tracy was coming home for the weekend.

Suddenly the sound of the engines changed as the flight attendant rapidly recited that landing litany, make sure your tray tables are upright. Daria hugged herself, glancing around her seat for stray items. Home. Her stomach was stripped raw, her complexion mottled with poor food. She had suffered from bad dreams. But almost immediately she was being returned to Ross, her love, and things would be better between them. He would have missed her. Now things would be just fine.

The next morning, Daria's birthday present from Ross was more intimate and frisky than had been true in years. He tended to give her safe gifts, leather pocketbooks, cardigan sweaters, or if he was feeling truly flush, small classically set jewels. This present was a nightgown and peignoir set in black satin and handmade lace. The trouble was that it said Small. She wore Medium.

"The idiot salesgirl must have mixed it up," he thundered. "Damn Lord and Taylor's."

He had not actually bought the gift, she assumed. Nowadays he sent his secretary Lorraine out to shop, but Lorraine knew Daria's sizes and would never have made such an error. She had a reassuring image of Lorraine in one of her beige fitted suits poking at the word processor or shunting calls around the three-man law office. For an instant she wondered if through the size Ross was obliquely chastising her, for he had been dropping hints that she was overweight.

Daria found fluctuations of her body difficult to take seriously. She had never been thin and she had never been fat, but always more or less pleasantly rounded and very slightly plump. At the moment she was within five pounds of her weight the day they had married, twenty-two years before. She was not in the habit of worrying about her body, viewing it as accessory; sometimes lighter, sometimes heavier as their habits together dictated. Men were silly to attach importance to the momentary shape or style of a female body, when inside and outside everyone was always changing. Yet she went on being the child who had squatted one day under the grape arbor of her family's home in East Boston and thought as the wasps buzzed in the ripe black grapes, I am Daria Porfirio, only me, there's only one of me. I am seven today, yesterday I was only six, someday I'll be old like Mama and even like Grandma, but there's only one of me: an insight she had had to work toward in her large family.

While she remembered, Ross was talking and she was emitting soothing sounds, those maternal chirpings she could give off in sleep, to indicate that the mistake was all right. "But I love it, really. It's such a romantic present. I'll trot down there Monday and trade it in for my own size."

He looked dubious, rocking on the balls of his slippers, in his old navy bathrobe. She had bought him a beautiful cashmere robe last Christmas, but it only came in camel and he had never worn it. Blue, blue, blue. "You can get something else," he said.

"Never. I love my present, really! I'm only sorry I can't try it on for you till Monday." She imagined herself stuffed into the nightgown, bulging out of it like a double-dip ice-cream cone, and smiled ruefully. When they had first been together, Ross had used to ask her what she was smiling at. She would try to describe the images, but they were not transmittable.

Their terrier Torte was barking at the door. Ross let him in, kneeling to give him a big hug. "There's my boy, there's my bundle of joy." When he had fussed up Torte enough, he asked her, "Want a cappuccino, birthday girl?"

While he made the coffee, on impulse she went into the garden, taking her basket and clippers. Bronze chrysanthemums, yellow, lavender. Bronze had the strongest scent. She had read that chrysanthemum leaves were edible; she must check that by asking Alice, her botanist at MIT. People liked pieces on cooking with flowers as much as she enjoyed writing them. She picked monkshood, dark velvety blue. Oh, and the last Dr. Brownell rose, buff washed with pink. She tilted her head to look up at the maple behind the garage, a brilliant torchy shade between orange and yellow. Before she had left on her publicity tour, the tree had been blotched with cooking apple green.

She could hear Ross singing in the kitchen "La donna è mobile." He had caught a passion for opera from her own father. It was about the only field on which they could easily meet. Perhaps Ross had picked out the present himself and simply not noticed that nightgowns came in different sizes. It could be a sign of his caring.

At the sink she deftly sorted her flowers into two vases, one for bronze and yellow, one for cobalt and lavender, then for the rose a tiny old pale lavender bottle from the days of their antique hunting together.

He handed her the cappuccino, finishing his song with a flourish and a bow to Torte, who sat thumping his tail on the tiles, his eyes gloating on Ross. Torte was nine years old and beginning to show his age. The machine that made the cappuccino had been her Christmas present two years before. She did drink a lot of coffee. Perhaps he had considered that the machine appropriately touched her ethnic base, for Ross thought that way sometimes.

She carried her coffee and the vase of bronze chrysanthemums to the narrow table in the bay window facing south to the garden, her favorite spot downstairs. Although her kitchen was efficient and large, it was darkened by the maple. Even if she was only having a quick cup of coffee, she carried it into the dining room to the trestle table by the windows facing her garden.

Of course the room centered on the big table for company and more formal family dinners under the chandelier. Now that Ross was so successful, they entertained a little less aggressively than the five nights a week that had been typical. What she liked about dinner parties was planning the menus and then cooking. The people themselves often were dull, but she had used them as guinea pigs for whatever she was working on: Indonesian, Mexican, Provençal, Hungarian, New England, or whatever new dishes she had invented.

He sat staring into his cup. She asked, "You're having it black?"

"Diet."

She had the impulse to tell him the maple today was just the color of his hair. She was not sure what held her back. She felt a little shy. "You know, I had to go on this tour—it's written into my contract," she said tentatively. He did not answer. His nickname among men was Rusty, but that did not suit. His hair was the prettiest color she had ever seen on a man. The years had thinned it somewhat but the color was undimmed, the feature by which she could pick him out in a crowd. Redgold was the name of a floribunda rose. She had planted three in a bed set in the lawn against the backdrop of the granite grey ledge—a little homage she kept to herself, for he would have found it silly. He was still staring out the mullioned windows, perhaps at the flock of juncos that had just arrived. He was whistling softly the same song from *Rigoletto* and drumming his fingers in time to the music. Ross had so much energy that rarely was he completely at rest: usually some appendage was jiggling or tapping or swinging.

"They're early this year," she offered.

"What? Who's early?"

"The juncos. I noticed them for the first time this morning."

"Early winter maybe. Snowbirds. If they do know." He was looking at them now. "Did we send in those forms from Audubon?"

"Yes, love. Next Saturday we make the pickup. I found the form on your desk and sent it in with a check—six fifty-pound bags of sunflower seeds, five of wild bird mix, five pounds of thistle and two bags of cracked corn, right?"

A phone rang as they both waited to see which one. It was hers and she rose to take it. "Mama, Mama," Tracy bubbled. "Happy Birthday! I didn't take the bus. I got a ride but I'm in Dorchester."

"Dorchester?" Daria winced. The southern part of Boston was miles from Lexington.

"Because that's where Betsy's boyfriend lives."

"Aren't you coming home?"

"Can't you or daddy come for me? It's gruesome to get there on the T, particularly on the weekend. First the Red Line, then the Arlington bus and then change again at the Lexington line. I'll be all day, Mama. I got you such a great present, I can't wait to give it to you."

Daria covered the mouthpiece. "Tracy didn't take the bus from Amherst. She got a ride, but only to Dorchester. I think we'll have to pick her up."

"Dorchester? That's almost as far as Amherst. What's she doing in Dorchester? That girl is completely unreliable. You can't count on her for a thing but trouble."

She gazed at Ross, standing now at his full height, his long face pinched with annoyance. Tracy had guessed the outcome, since she had chosen Daria's phone to call in on. "I'll come get you, ducks. Just give me good directions. You know how I hate getting lost."

Mostly the separate phones worked out. Four years before, Ross's irritation over the number of times he answered the phone to be asked for her had mounted to critical proportions, around the time she began writing the regular food column for the *Globe*. The summer book *Cool as Cucumber Soup* was just out and she was in demand for appearances and speaking engagements and demonstrations. Now she tried to confine business calls to weekdays, when he wasn't home; with her separate listing, the problem had diminished.

Other problems loomed. "Ross. . . . Don't start the weekend angry at Tracy. You're not fair to her. If Robin's more responsible, Robin is after all four years older. Try not to be so hard on Tracy."

"You didn't say one word of reproof. You encourage her."

"It's her first visit home from college. I miss her. Let's make it nice."

Not wanting to labor the point further, she ran up to get her purse. A suspicious lump in the big bed. Reaching under the covers, she found the kittens, brother and sister twisted in a double **S** and sound asleep. She dragged them free and carted them in a drowsy bundle, still clutching each other, out to the dooryard garden and dumped them. "Go play! Sleeping till eleven A.M. No wonder you want to run up and down the stairs all night." Their golden eyes regarded her from their little black heads as with disapproval they watched her around to the garage.

As she backed the Rabbit out, she thought the drive wouldn't be such a bad idea: she would have a chance to talk to Tracy alone. Tracy and Ross had been fighting a lot during the past year, but Daria felt close to her younger daughter. Tracy needed her, whereas Robin didn't seem to need anyone, or wouldn't admit it if she did.

Tracy took more after her in appearance, in emotional temperature, in sensual nature. Tracy was the family enthusiast, although that was less marked now than when Tracy had gone through her religious phase.

Then Tracy had been Teresa, the name on her birth certificate and Daria's grandmother's name. The newly pious Teresa had prayed on her knees for long hours at a private shrine to Saint Teresa in her bedroom. Then she trumpeted she was about to become a nun. Daria had never been religious after first communion. She had formally lost her faith in public high school—which she attended after parochial grade school—but she had never owned much. Nina, for all her martyrdom, was a long-lapsed Catholic who attended Mass only on the main holy days for the socializing and the pomp. Nina's father had been an anarchist who hated the Church; Daria's had not been a religious family. Her parents had made little fuss about her marrying a Protestant.

The girls had been raised Unitarian, which had seemed a nice sensible compromise to Ross and Daria between having no religion at all and having to lie to the children about what they believed, enough religion to be respectable but not enough to get in the way. Daria had been as appalled as Ross when Tracy turned Catholic with such fervor. That was how Tracy experimented: she tried new things by diving in over her head.

Daria made a wrong turn only once, finding the triple-decker without difficulty. Two buildings on one side of it had been burned to the ground, although the row then marched on over a hill undaunted. When Daria rang the bell, Betsy came out on the porch with Tracy but the boyfriend was nowhere to be seen and Daria was not invited in. She stood on the porch waiting, staring at the sinister ruin of the house next door, boarded up and marked with an official warning against trespassing. A charred smell hung in the air still.

Covertly she examined Tracy as they sped off. Her auburn hair, a shade redder than Daria's, was tightly curled all over her head in a new style Daria found attractive. "Have you been missing Nick a lot?"

"Some, of course. . . . I guess I'll see him."

"Didn't you call him to tell him you're coming home?"

"I wrote him a couple of weeks ago I might. I never had a chance to call. It's been so frantic at school, Mama. So much work!"

Daria shut up about Nick. Nick and Tracy had gone seriously steady the last two years of high school. Their senior year they had been sleeping together, a situation Daria had read long before Tracy had been silly enough to let Ross figure it out. Tracy had announced they were going to be married right after high school (in the Greek Orthodox Church) and that she had no need of college, which was a waste of time. One wave of trouble at a time, Daria thought, slamming on her brakes as a typical Boston madman ran a light.

"I met this guy Gordon in my psych class—he's intense," Tracy was saying.

Tracy was intense. Enthusiastic. All the way on or all the way off. She would cool with time, and perhaps Robin would warm. They had in some underhanded way been played off each other, the sisters, each scrambling to occupy turf the other had not claimed. Robin played field hockey? Tracy would sit out gym. Tracy studied piano and sang with Ross? Robin would claim to be tone-deaf.

"And he says I'm beautiful, Mama. Nobody ever said that before—"

"You've always been beautiful to me."

"Sure, Mama. I suppose deformed babies are beautiful to their mamas." Tracy stopped abruptly, as through both their minds Frederick Jonathan Walker briefly passed. Tracy had been too young to remember Freddy in the flesh. Daria said nothing.

"Anyhow, Mama, when somebody like Gordon says it, it counts. Know what he said, Mama? He said I look like a Raphael madonna."

Daria laughed out loud before she could stop herself; then she was ashamed. With Tracy glaring, she had to explain. "Darling, that's an old line." Tracy had Daria's own dark deep-set huge brown eyes and her rounded face, passed on from mother to daughter during the four generations she had witnessed in person and in photographs. "Every guy I dated in college used that line. One reason I liked your father right off was because he didn't."

"He probably didn't know who Raphael was."

"But he has a wonderful feeling for music," she said, automatically defending. "Your father's been under a lot of stress lately. I don't know what it is—something at work. You know how he hates me to pry. But he's been on edge, sleeping poorly. Ducks, try not to set him off. Not this weekend, please."

"I won't say a word. I won't even talk to him, for fear of bugging him, the way I always seem to."

"Teresa, you don't have to sulk about it. Just don't go out of your way to irritate your father."

"I never go out of my way. It's my way he can't stand. It's me."

"Sweetheart, I want you and your father to make up. To be close again. You used to share so much, with your music—"

"Why should I have to give a damn performance for him to like me? Robin doesn't have to. She makes fun of music, and she's the one he adores."

"Promise me you're not going to fight with your sister all weekend."

"Mama, it'll be a wonderful birthday, you'll see. . . . Did they really give you that madonna bit?"

"Afraid so. Doesn't mean he wasn't telling the truth about finding you attractive."

"They said the same thing to you?" Tracy was staring at her mother in alarm.

Daria understood. She had never relished being told she looked just like her mother. All the women in Daria's family were pleasant-looking sweet-faced women who retained an aura of girlishness into old age, with soft round chins, round arched brows, immense rounded eyes and perhaps too-round bodies. A touch of red in their dark brown hair, a touch of olive in their skin: the family look handed down from mother to daughter. The men might turn out otherwise, but no matter who the women married, mothers gave birth to daughters who resembled them: except for Robin, whom Ross had wanted to be a boy and who took after Ross. Daria loved Nina with an unsatiated dogged yearning that never felt fully returned, as she felt sure Tracy loved her more happily, but she had never wanted to become her mother and she had never enjoyed being told how close was the resemblance.

Describing her classes, her roommate Betsy's habits and clever sayings, Gordon's every shining word, Tracy stopped suddenly, drawing up. "And how have you been keeping, Mama?"

Daria thought of her friend Gretta who would talk about herself with scarcely a pause for breath for forty-five minutes, keeping Daria on the phone fretting over all the things she was not getting done. Then in the last minute of the call with melodious insincerity Gretta would warble,

"And how about you, Daria darling. Is anything new?" But with Tracy, she was touched. It was very adult to turn polite with your own mother, to recognize the social contract as reciprocal even to the extent of bothering to ask. She wanted to hug her daughter but confined herself to tapping her near knee. "That tour was draining. I'm so glad to be back home I can't say it often enough. . . . Let's see, your father wants me to go on a diet, and I suppose I must. It just seems boring and trendy, and I don't want to look like a fourteen-year-old boy. Does James Beard look anorexic? Does anyone demand that Julia Child resemble Brooke Shields?"

"What's for supper tonight?"

"I'm not cooking, not tonight, not on my birthday. But I'll make an early dinner tomorrow before you go back. What do you want? Anything."

"Duck! Flamed, and I get to light it. Or a Chinese feast with the pancakes. Let me think about it. The food at school is dreary, Mama."

She never gunned her car up their hill, negotiating the twists and turns to her house, without a pang of satisfaction. Ross would add that the best houses were on top of the hill around that artificial little pond, but she did not covet those mansions. They were too grand to live in, and she had better soil. No matter that here in the winter they had twice the snowfall of Boston; no matter that the streets collected ice and were gutted with potholes, kept in disrepair out of a kind of snobbery, she loved the hill. To her it represented both luxury and adventure.

Her own house gave her the deepest pleasure. It was one of the oldest houses on the hill, of a pale yellow clapboard contrasting the weathered slate of the paths and the grey shingles of the roof, with dark grey shutters and trim. Instead of the common expanses of lawn broken only by hedge, she had put up a picket fence enclosing a dooryard garden rimmed with old-fashioned perennials, including hollyhocks in a row at the west end where they got just enough sun.

Tracy smiled at her, knowing her mother's satisfactions, and for an instant they touched hands. Ross's Mercedes wasn't in the garage. Where had he gone? Perhaps to pick up Robin, who drove an old Honda that often refused to start. That idea pleased her; so symmetrical, she picked up Tracy while he fetched Robin. But Robin arrived on her own within the hour, dressed in bright blue running clothes that set off her strawberry blond hair, just a shade lighter than Ross's own.

"Where's Dad? He was going to run with me today." Robin paced the downstairs peevishly, stepping over Tracy who lay on the floor playing with the kittens while Torte watched with an occasional uneasy thump of his tail.

"They're such special cats, Ali and Sheba. I'm glad we took them in." Tracy was snuggling Sheba under her chin. "Aren't you glad now?"

"Asshole names," Robin muttered, pacing. She had her father's nervous energy, part temperament, part imitation of him. "There's Annette." Their next door neighbor.

"You're back, Daria!" Annette was holding out a package almost at arm's length. "The UPS dropped this at my house yesterday, since no one was home here."

"Is it a birthday present?" Tracy sat up, arranging herself gracefully.

Daria took the box, profusely thanked Annette, who could not stay as she was preparing a dinner party. "No, it's addressed to your father. Ugh. No wonder Annette was carrying it that way."

"Why?" Robin leaned close and then leaped back. "Gross. It stinks."

"I can't imagine what it is." The return address was illegibly scrawled so she could read only Allston MA and the zip code. She carried the package into Ross's study and set it on center of the green blotter he liked kept immaculate on his neat walnut desk. The wastebasket was overflowing. Monday she must tackle the house.

Torte was barking, running into the kitchen. He always heard the car before she did. She shut the door of Ross's study and met him carrying a Lord and Taylor box. "Happy Birthday, old kid," he said with a big grin. "I straightened everything out."

"Ross, what a sweet thing to do! I can't believe it." He didn't like shopping any better than she did, so his trip verged on the heroic. He knew she would put off the exchange. Department stores confused and overheated her so that she was always deciding once inside them that she could get on perfectly well without whatever she had come for.

"First a little extra to make up for the mistake. Ta dum!" He fished out a golden packet of Godiva chocolates.

Robin grimaced. "You know what a chocolate freak she is." Robin considered chocolate a cut below heroin as a habit.

Tracy said, "But I thought you wanted her to go on a diet."

Sometimes she could wish for a little silence from the girls. Were they jealous when he did something caring for her? "Not today. I'm opening it right now and everybody have a piece. Ross?"

Ross succumbed. "One won't hurt. Now open the big box."

It held a pastel paisley shawl. "But, Ross, what happened to the gorgeous nightgown?"

"They didn't have it in your size. They seem to be wearing shawls again."

She cooed over it, angry with herself for missing the nightgown, a gift that had seemed to hint of a renewed sexual interest. Oh well, the shawl was pretty and in the winter to come, it would serve. "This kind of fine wool paisley, they used to call a wedding ring shawl—it would fit through a wedding ring." She worked her ring off to demonstrate for Tracy. Robin and Ross were chatting about running and football. The shawl would not fit through.

While Robin and Ross jogged, Tracy brought out Daria's present, a quarter ounce of Madame Rochas perfume. "Tracy, I adore it. You know I love perfume. But this is beyond extravagant!"

Tracy agreed giggling and followed her out to the garden, a procession of animals behind them. There Daria knelt to put in a row of early blooming Kaufmania tulips, rimming a new bed where she then dug in bronze Darwins for May. She would keep it coppery all year: marigolds later, calendula, nasturtiums. She was a little nervous about Ross's new habit of running a couple of mornings a week and then weekends with Robin. Annette had told her horror stories of husbands dropping dead suddenly in the driveway, expiring dramatically on street corners. All the local men had taken up jogging at one time; Ross was simply the last to start. Perhaps she resented jogging because she had the idea it was something he was doing instead of making love with her. Today, her birthday, surely they would. How could she object to a healthy habit? He could have taken to drinking too much like Gretta's ex-husband or womanizing like her own father. Would Nina call today? Lately Nina seemed especially miserable. Pops had begun spending a great deal of time at Joe's restaurant. Joe was their oldest surviving son, who had moved down to Florida too. Kneeling to tuck the bulbs into their neat holes with the maple glowing over her, nonetheless she sensed something wrong she could not identify. "Is school really all right?" she asked Tracy sharply. "Are you keeping up? You're not too lonely?"

"Mama . . ." Tracy said slowly. "Some of the girls at school, they've heard of you. I mean, I never realized you're famous. I always thought your books were . . . kind of a family joke. But they've seen you on television."

"Well, does that bother you?" Daria felt a little pang of guilt.

"*Bother* me? No. I'm proud of you. But, like, it was a surprise. Do you know what I mean?"

"Are there any of the girls you've met that are your special friends?" Daria quickly changed the subject. Talking too much about her work or the modest measure of celebrity it had brought felt dangerous around the house, even if Ross wasn't in earshot.

When Robin returned tousled and sweaty, she brought a package from her Honda that turned out to contain an oversized apron stenciled in big red letters *I AM A KITCHEN WITCH/HOT STUFF*. Daria tried very hard to admire it. Robin dressed Ivy League to her job at an insurance company, but otherwise she had no taste at all.

"Dad and I did five miles today. Don't you feel great, Dad? How many are you doing on weekdays?"

"Three. I'd like to do more. I need a running partner."

"Can't you get one of your buddies from the neighborhood to run with you?" Robin urged. When she was excited, her voice always rose, reedy.

"I'm trying. If I could only run with you every morning, when you run anyhow, I know I'd keep up my pace."

"But Dad, I'm not that far from your office. You could come in a little early and run with me."

He stopped halfway up the staircase, hanging over the bannister. "My smart daughter. I knew I could count on you. You just may have an idea. If you'd put up with me."

"Of course I would, Dad. It'd be super."

"I'm going to ponder that. We might be on to something." He clumped on up to their bedroom, whistling an air from *Don Giovanni*.

Daria frowned, made her forehead smooth and turned away. Mornings were the time they had traditionally made love. Why did the conversation sound staged to her? She brought her hands up to her eyes and rubbed. She was still tired from travelling, a little crazy with fatigue. The day was slipping rapidly away from her.

They all dispersed to dress or make phone calls. She laid out the baby blue chiffon on the bed so that she could wear the shawl with it, then dabbed on Madame Rochas. In the bathroom he was singing loud and clear above the force of the shower. Robin had tickets to a basketball game with friends from work and Tracy was going out with Nick after all. She would miss the girls, but lately she had been missing Ross more. He had been busy, harassed. Then she had been gone ten days. A romantic evening out would do them good, for once a Saturday night without six to ten other people to feed and entertain, to dazzle and impress. My wife, the great chef. She curled up on the queen-sized bed, not putting on the dress just yet, facing the wall of photographs.

Ross had a darkroom in the basement; for years he and his Nikon had commemorated every family event, every trip, every holiday. He had taken portrait studies of each of them including Torte. The bed faced a wall of mounted eight by tens on the matte paper he preferred. He had put them up in his own arrangement, not chronological, so that Daria pregnant with Robin and wrapped in a white and blue Moroccan kaftan looked toward Robin holding up a striped bass she had caught surf casting. The wall was full and no new photographs had been added since that summer, three years before.

He had not photographed the kittens, she realized, which was odd because he adored young things, puppies, babies, the unprotected. There was Orville regarding her, the pet crow they had when Tracy was still in middle school and Robin a sophomore in high school, a nestling they had found and raised and finally freed. There was Miss Muffet, the grey cat who had died out front, hit by a car that had never stopped. She remembered Ross holding her as she died, crying himself as the girls cried. He had that sweet tenderhearted core she loved. He would not hurt a living thing. He would never strike an animal with his car and then speed on.

As he swung out of the bathroom he glanced at her arranged on the bed and his singing faltered. Then he started rummaging in his closet. Embarrassed, she slipped off the bed to dress. As they went down together, she remembered. "A package came for you yesterday, but it was left at Annette's."

"A package? From where?"

"I put it on your desk."

When he opened his study door, the smell came out at them, stronger in the small room. "Pee-you. What is that? Something rotten?" He peered closely at the package, looking at the return address.

"Who's it from?"

"Ummm. Daria, I think I left my car keys upstairs. Beside the bed or on my dresser. Could you run up and get them for me?"

She thought she heard them clinking in his pocket, but obediently, she looked for them. Then she leaned over the railing. "I can't find them, Ross."

He did not answer. When she came down he was outside by the garbage can. Dusting his hands he came into the kitchen and washed them. "Let's get going."

Apparently he had his car keys now because he got into the Mercedes and waited for her. "What was all that, Ross? What was in the package?"

"The package? A cheese. It was a present from a man I did some paperwork for on a building closing. That's all. The cheese had spoiled."

The package had not smelled like cheese; it had smelled like something dead. Really, she must be off her stride completely, because she had the ridiculous feeling that he was lying.

They ate at Chez Claude in Acton, an old favorite of hers, in the front dining room of the old house. Sitting across the small table from Ross, she counted her satisfactions. It was an old habit, touching bases, reminding herself how far she had come, how much she had to be grateful for. First she always put Ross. Unlike Robin and other women she knew who wanted to marry their daddies, she had always wanted to escape hers. To that end she had compiled a mental list of admired characteristics, the opposite of what her mother had to endure. She was happy in her choice of Ross, who exemplified every virtue her wandering father had lacked. She adored his solidity, his straightness, his rectitude, his tenderness, his capacity for feeling about the domestic. He was no hit-and-run expert, as her father was. He never needed to play macho. He was bright, he was sweet, he was good. No children could have asked for a better father. And he had as many buddies as her father did. He would always go the extra distance for a friend.

She had her health. She had two delightful daughters, lively, not shooting up drugs or flunking out of school, not moping around the house like Gretta's son waiting for someone to appear and beg him to take a good job. Her daughters had never had to fight for attention, as she had after four preferred brothers had taken the lion's share. All but one of her books were still in print. Why hadn't Nina called today? She wanted to talk to Nina, but she was too proud to call on her own birthday.

She made a decent income from the books, from the *Globe* and other papers, women's magazines, talks and demonstrations. As she looked into Ross's cornflower blue eyes, she concluded her stocktaking. I have not wasted my life. I have almost nothing to complain of. Yes, I am happy. It was a duty, not to waste her life, not to wail and mutter along as Nina did. Yes, I am happy, we have a good life together in our good home, yes.

2

When Daria could not sleep, she had a few standard routines. Lying alone the next night, Sunday night, in the queen-sized bed, with Ross sleeping across the hall in Robin's old room, she took herself back to the first eleven years of their marriage and called up all the places they had lived. As Ross had earned more money and as they had another child and then as the children grew, he was always becoming discontented with their dwellings and moving them on. They had trekked from Back Bay to Brookline to Arlington to Cambridge apartments and then to their first house in Newton, a move every two years. To put herself to sleep she would summon each apartment in turn, sketching the layout of the rooms, bringing them to life with their hues of paint, their windows, their view or lack of it, furnishing them with the right pieces in the right places.

Tonight she kept being distracted. She knew how to read his signs of discontent. Lately he had been dropping remarks about the house being too large for them. His restlessness frightened her, for she loved the house. It didn't feel too big to her, for every room had its purpose, its aesthetic. She had put enormous effort into house and garden, her treasure, her artwork, her outer skin. Nina had told her often enough that she was house-proud. She rolled over in bed. In the hall she could hear the kittens scuffling.

Why hadn't Nina called? She always called on Nina's birthday. Why couldn't it be reciprocal? Any particular girlchild in a family of six children, four of them boys, never feels cherished enough. Never had she considered she was given enough time, attention, money, privacy or love. In April Nina had announced she was very ill, and Daria had flown down to Florida. When she had arrived, Nina had seemed to be suffering from nothing more dramatic than bursitis. She had had enough trouble getting Nina to a doctor for that. She had cancelled two cooking demonstrations, turned in a piece on pumpkin entrées for *The Cook's Magazine* late and had to have a friend fill in for her at cooking school; then Nina had simply not been ill enough to justify summoning her. It had been annoying. Now Nina was complaining again of mysterious pains.

She was never going to sleep, never. She was used to company in the bed that now felt too huge. Ross and she had always slept together, and some time during the night Torte would sneak out of his dog basket with the old braided rug in it and climb on the foot of the bed. Now he had followed Ross into exile in Robin's room where Ross let him sleep in his bed all night. She felt deserted by her dog as well as her husband. Ross had been sleeping in Robin's old room occasionally since August, but while she was gone, he seemed to have settled in there more permanently, across the stairwell.

She rose and opened the door, looking across. At once the kittens came to her, their pointed black faces and round yellow eyes staring up. Sheba understood at once and dashed past her, straight for the bed. Ali hesitated, skeptical, then followed his sister in a flying leap. The kittens had been Tracy's idea. She had found them in August along with a third who had died, abandoned in the alley behind the Stop and Shop in an instant pudding packing box. They had entered the house on sufferance. Whenever they were mischievous, Ross would threaten them with expulsion.

As she lay down again they curled with her, Sheba fitting herself into her right armpit and Ali turning and turning and finally laying himself down pressed against her thigh. Purring, kneading, trying occasionally to suckle, they were warm against her, comforting. The bed did not feel quite so vainly large.

Her birthday had passed, Sunday had drained away with a quick gurgle, and they had not made love: an absence like a presence. She stroked

Sheba, still cuddled into her. If only he would speak to her: I don't feel well; I feel too anxious; I'm worried about something, and tell her for once what it was. Not being touched, not plunging in that hot private mutual turmoil made her feel papery, shadowlike, as if her body were vanishing.

When she woke, she reached out to touch his back, but her hand encountered the sheet, the quilt chilly from the night. She missed waking with him; every day she missed him. Morning had been the time they usually made love, before the girls were up. She had loved mornings in this house, to wake and have it hers again, a light house, a trim house, well proportioned and comforting in its age, having witnessed many generations and survived handsomely. It dated to 1840, although the type of architecture was older than that, Cape Cod cottage with a gambrel roof, two dormers in front, two dormers in back. The garage wing had been added in the thirties.

Monday morning: was that why she felt so blue? Sheba sat on her shoulder, purring into her neck. Ali, Tracy's pun on where he had been found, stared into her face. She felt older this morning, in a grey twilight of the soul. Forty-three was middle age. How many women had lain in this room during the last century and a half wanting their husbands to love them again?

As her bath water ran she laid out a simple cotton blouse and an old skirt. Intentionally she had made no appointments today. Tomorrow her secretary Peggy would be in, as usual. Today she would slip back into her life and tidy it up. She let the kittens out to run down to their box in the little lavatory off the kitchen. In the mirror she saw herself, shoulders drooping. After Gretta's marriage had broken up, Gretta announced she never missed sex. Making a fuss about it was like creating a mystique around brushing your teeth. Daria could not agree.

When they had first married, she had enjoyed sex for the contact, the expression of love, the holding. She did not think she had experienced a full orgasm until after Tracy was born. In fact she associated coming to want and need sex with moving into this house. Then the privacy, the knowledge that the girls could not overhear them since their master bedroom shared no common wall with either of the girls' rooms eased her into strong sexual response. She could give herself leave to move, to speak what came into her mind, to moan, to sing out. Ross had been delighted and for some years, they had shared an intense sexual life together.

Gradually it had diminished. Several times before, his sexuality had gone into abeyance and then he had flared into passion again. Only this time was much too long. Perhaps work was taking him over. Once she had tried to bring up the matter with Annette, her neighbor, but Annette just said that she didn't think anybody made love much after they'd been married awhile. Daria didn't want to believe that all the joy could be worn out forever. She read a few books from the library. One suggested that males peaked early and women later. It felt sadly unfair that she should be receptive, sensually alive to him as he gradually shed his passion for her, slowly, a little at a time as imperceptibly as skin sloughs off. Never was there a moment she could grasp: I did that wrong. He would say he didn't think most people were that into it after twenty years of marriage. He would say she simply could not understand the pressures on him, and that he was tired. He would suggest she take up some new interest or hobby.

The only conceivably useful comment Ross had made was about her weight. In puzzlement she stared at her body flushed and wavering underwater. She liked her body as it was. But she must diet. If he wanted skinny, she'd give him skinny. She couldn't think of another ploy to try, in spite of all the boring and unctuous if not actually disgusting books she had read. Books about sexuality were the best arguments for chastity. Cookbooks were her preferred bedtime reading, so she always kept a couple on the telephone table. She found the illustrations in good cookbooks—those perfectly glazed turkeys, those feathery chocolate mousses, those terrine confections decorated with bits of truffle like slices of IBM stock—far more erotic than photos in the sexual manuals of position fifty-seven with his feet in her face. They suggested, those books on winning your husband back, that she dress up as a geisha or as a hen packed in plastic wrap from the Stop and Shop; that she learn to perfect all the little tricks the best call girls knew about oral sex. They didn't suggest what to do if she brought herself to wriggle around and try some of those meretricious maneuvers and the result was that her loved one went limp as a wet sock and inquired in icy tones just what the hell she thought she was doing?

Instead of her old skirt, she put on the flounced cotton Tracy had bought her last year and marched down. Ross was on the phone in his study, door shut. At eight o'clock? Really his work was taking him over more and more. Finally he emerged for a hasty breakfast. Perhaps he had forgotten his scheme to pare away even this rim of their day together by running early with Robin. She hoped so. "I'll make that Western omelette you like?"

"Just boil a couple of eggs."

"I'll have the same." Not that there was any pleasure in providing a clutch of three-minute eggs. Lately he would not be seduced through his stomach, always the surest way of commanding his favorable attention.

All his attention now was fixed on Torte, standing with front paws on Ross's lap whimpering with pleasure. Ross could at least smile at her for half a minute. He had a slight paunch but more from lack of exercise than from overeating. Now he was dieting just like Robin, who always wanted to be thinner than she was.

Daria gave herself an hour to straighten in a rush before she went upstairs to work. When Ross and Daria had bought the house, he had decreed she should stop substitute teaching and stop making desserts for Mario's and stay home. Then she had launched into her first cookbook. Before the children began school, she had never been alone for longer than an evening in her life. After college she had moved from her parents' crowded house in East Boston to a small apartment in the North End with two other girls, and from that crowded nest she had married Ross. She could remember first savoring the tangible huge quiet of this house after Ross and the girls left for the day. It was hers, all of it, splendid, beautiful, sublimely quiet making her dizzy with freedom. She could organize her days however she pleased, so long as she picked up the children on time, took them to their various after-school events, kept the house prepared for the evening's entertaining for Ross's clients. Everything except cooking and gardening she did in a blind rush, so that she could saunter through the heart of her days in that rich fecund plain of space and choice.

Her office was what was called the maid's room still in family parlance, as if to create images of luxury and bourgeois domestic ease that amused her, because if there was a maid it was herself. Growing up in East Boston where several of her mother's friends cleaned the houses of people who had seemed rich to her then, she could not bring herself to hire someone to clean her house. She felt all people were morally obligated to deal with their own dirt. Furthermore she knew exactly how cleaning ladies talk about the filthy pigs they work for, rendering her incapable of taking on that role. It was a sticking point between Annette and her, Gretta and her, because everybody thought they had a special relationship with their own cleaning lady, who naturally adored them. Since the house had been an extravagance when they moved in (low though real estate prices had been compared to now, as Ross never grew weary of reminding her), she had justified the lack of domestic help financially.

Her office, then, was over the attached garage, with a steep narrow staircase going up from the kitchen. She could also reach it through a stark little hall off the far side of the master bedroom. The coldest part of the house, nonetheless the room had a dormer window opening on the garden. The room did not look chilly, for she had painted it in peach and pale leaf green. She sat at the library table overlooking the garden and picked up the pages she had laid down two weeks before. She had arranged her work on this book so that each month she was writing the correct chapter, seasonally focussed to use whatever a home gardener would have in abundance and whatever would be cheap and plentiful in the stores. They were going to market a calendar with it. On her table stood a butternut, an acorn, a buttercup and a Hubbard squash, the latter two grown by Alice. She winced at the drawing she had made two weeks before and crumpled it. She would not draw them together as she had planned, no, but she would do each separately with no attempt to draw to scale and then work them into the text. Realism was not her forte. Her agent Laura said her vegetables all looked like character actors.

As she went over the pages Peggy had prepared in her absence, her depression began to lift. She felt proud of the summer's work. She wished she had shown September to Tracy, the only person in the family who took any kind of interest in Daria's work. Her method in all her books was to introduce a basic recipe, the process set out in detail, and then present a list of variations, each with a flashy name. Then a woman following a variation (she imagined her readers as women although she knew better from book signings) would feel each time that she was making something special for her family. A catchy name made a cook feel better about her work. Beef in bread lacked the panache of Beef Wellington. Similarly her Chicken for Remembrance sounded much zippier than chicken sautéed with rosemary, garlic and some white wine added. Queen Anne's Veal suggested delicacy better than breaded veal slices baked with a light cherry sauce. She was selling the reader on trying something, and the reader had to sell her family on eating it.

At two she broke and went down for her mail. A note from Laura about an Australian adaptation of her working mother cookbook with a reminder they needed new publicity pictures for that edition. Ross always took her pictures. Lately he had been putting off a new session, but she had used the last of the most recent batch and had to have new ones. Her phone bill. Ross's American Express bill. Rather high, although the charges from her recent trip weren't in. She went through and checked off for him her business-related expenses, grouped under her card number toward the end of the list. A birthday card from Nina two days late with a note stuck inside, that scrawl she moved her lips to decipher:

. . . cold here so what's the use being in Florida when we freeze. I wish we were Home where we belong with old friends and Family except of course your Father wants it this way. . . .

Of course. She was always saying that herself, from her mother's lips. Of course it's raining today, we planned a picnic. Of course the car won't start. Of course he lost it. That sour assumption of martyrdom was what she liked least in Nina and what she fought hardest to stave off in her own life.

. . . grapefruit now all over the trees in the yard. It has a black rot on it but they taste good anyhow. But I can't seem to grow roses down here, remember our roses. Liz always said I could grow roses out of asphalt but no luck here . . .

. . . headaches and my back keeps me awake . . . worry about water they say we may run out. . . .

. . . your Father's habit of disappearing when I have lunch on the stove and then expecting everything perfect when he pops in from nowhere. He is eating six nights a week at the Restaurant I am home here alone . . . worry with Joe working so hard he will get a heart attack like his Brother. . . .

Nina's letter depressed her and she put the rest of the mail aside unopened. She rose and went out under the slow drizzle. Fetching a trowel, she moved the anchusa from its spot too far forward in the border for its height. A shovelful of compost, a touch of bone meal.

When she stuck her hand in the pocket of her corduroy gardening jacket, she found a rolled packet of radish seeds left from her late August planting, some plastic ties and there, damn it, the key to the lock on Tracy's bicycle she hadn't been able to find for her yesterday.

Weighing the big key in her hand lifted the depression from her. Years ago, that key in her hand. When Robin and Tracy had been tiny, she had made a little money by preparing fancy desserts for her brother Joe's restaurant in Revere. Then Mario's had hired her at far better wages. She remembered going to the North End at ten in the morning and letting herself in. She had a key to the outer door and then that odd-shaped key to the cabinet where liquors were kept. Mario's had only a wine and beer license, so the liquors were just for her to make rum chocolate mousse, brandied peach torte, zuppa inglese. She had loved the stale but intimate smell of the empty restaurant. She had loved taking out her keys and moving about in the huge kitchen. Her first book had been ghostwritten for Mario, who was still proud of her.

When at home for special occasions she would make the treats she prepared for the customers of Mario, Ross and the little girls would Ooh and Ah twice as much because they knew she was paid to do it for others. Ross was still working for the Johnson antipoverty program in Boston, in the housing office. His job had been exciting, in spite of the frustration, the graft, the level of corruption in the state and county and city government he simply could not believe. Patronage hacks with their hands in the till, the rake-offs, the kickbacks, the payoffs. He carried his anger home to her. That year he almost got an ulcer, yet he had been passionately engaged. Then he had been able to talk over his job with her the way he no longer could. Somehow the details of real estate trusts and drawing up deeds, all that legal paperwork did not provide him with material to share with her the way he had used to share his stories of skirmishes, advances and retreats in the war on poverty—and on the politicians.

He had used to come home boiling with words. Always they played with the children together. Always he helped put them to bed. He sang them songs for the bathtub, songs for the ride to bed, songs for putting on jammies, songs for tucking in. Abruptly her eyes filled with tears.

How silly she was being. Torte was sleeping in the sun where it hit the granite ledge. Reluctantly she turned from the garden to the house. The robins and blackbirds had gone south, to where her parents lived.

She sat down to run through the rest of her mail quickly. An invitation to attend the twenty-fifth wedding anniversary celebration for Chuck and Irma Petris. Clients of Ross's? He received most of his mail at his office, but probably they had sent it home since they were inviting her also. Mr. and Mrs. Walker. Letter on General Foods stationery asking her to judge a baking contest. The last piece of mail for Ross was a rather good quality linen weave envelope addressed in a little crawling hand. She was curious about it as she carried it in with the American Express bill and his other mail to rest on the blotter of his walnut desk. His room on the northeast corner of the house with its forest green carpeting and beige draperies always felt somber. She usually scuttled in and out. Now she noticed his wastebasket still needed emptying. He had made a few sarcastic comments lately about her housekeeping, so she took it to tidy up. His room still smelled of something dead.

As she dumped it into a trash bag, she noticed a crumpled piece of notepaper on the same stationery as the envelope she had just carried in. From idle curiosity, she straightened it:

Dear Rusty,
You can expect our little visitor Tuesday night. I won't disappoint you.

Yours,
Lou

She stood very still, one hand on the doorjamb. She must be crazy, she must be a raving paranoid, but a little visitor to her was a euphemism for a woman's period. And what woman, Lou, would be writing to her husband about a period? She fished through the trash and found the envelope, identical to one that had come today, down to the Belmont postmark. Her brother Tony lived in Belmont, but she did not think this note had anything to do with him.

The phone rang and she leapt to pick it up as if it were the answer to what ran through her mind. It was the president of a Weston women's club wanting her to give a little talk, a demonstration. While she negotiated date and price, she was still mulling over those few words: You can expect our little visitor. Won't disappoint you. Twenty-two years she had lived with Ross and knew him if she knew anybody living. Her suspicions were absurd.

When she finally got off the phone, she raced downstairs and took the letter from his desk. Without giving herself time to think, she carried it into the kitchen and put a kettle on to boil. She had read about people steaming open envelopes in detective novels, but she had never tried it.

Steaming an envelope proved more difficult than she had anticipated. After the water finally boiled, it took her a full twenty minutes to pry the envelope unstuck, and then it was limp as cooked spinach. Quickly she unfolded the note.

Dear Rusty,

Too noisy this week. Visitor now set for Tuesday after next.

Yours,
Lou

Carefully she returned the note to its envelope. As she was trying to reseal it, the kittens chased each other across the kitchen floor. She jumped, dropping the packet. Finally she put it back on his desk, shut the door and crept out, limp as the envelope with shame. She felt as if someone had been running a Robot Coupe in her midriff. What did it all mean? The second note sounded far less as if a woman were worrying about being pregnant.

She checked the date on the envelope that had held the first letter. Not last Tuesday, then. The Tuesday previous, the night before she'd left for her trip. Where had Ross been? Actually right at home. He had insisted on entertaining that night, his two partners in his law office, Carl and Nancy Johansen and Roger and Barbara Kingsley. She had had two arguments with Ross about that dinner party. First, she had not wanted to have it at all the night before she set out on a ten-day promotional tour. It meant having to pack the morning before leaving, and not getting a full night's sleep, as she had to set out for the airport at six-thirty. Ross had also insisted on including their neighbors Pierre and Annette in that dinner party, although she preferred to see them with real friends rather than with business associates. The evening had worked out awkwardly, with her talking to Pierre, Annette and Nancy, who seemed as out of the men's brisk chitchat about real estate as Barbara was hot to engage in it. Usually Daria managed all right on these business evenings on a diet of bored wives, but Pierre and Annette clearly wondered why they had been invited.

There, that should fix her soap opera imagination. Tuesday had come and gone that week—or was that what was meant by noisy? But Ross had insisted on the dinner. He could have seen Lou, whoever Lou was, in perfect ease with her on the road. Had he? Was Ross the visitor? Was it a rendezvous? Who was Lou anyway? She swore she had never heard him mention a Lou.

Something was very wrong with her to allow her to entertain such a notion even briefly. She had always trusted Ross; she had picked him out for his rectitude. He was a good man and she was crazy. She made herself go down in the basement to iron. She loathed ironing shirts. Ross was right; she was becoming obsessed with sex. Next she would start questioning her daughters for prurient details. She was ashamed of her snooping, her fervid imaginings. Ironing his shirts was fitting penance.

Nevertheless she did not throw the old note back in the garbage but kept it in its envelope folded in a tight wedge in her pocket. When she went upstairs to her bedroom just before supper to change, she put it in her jewelry case, tucked under a loose flap of the velvet lining. Then she willed it out of her mind. If she did not brood about things, oftentimes they took care of themselves. She would forget and wait. All would be innocently explained, by and by.

3

ARIA's day ended up muddled and rushed. She had planned to work with Peggy until it was time to dress and meet Ross for a cocktail party some developer was giving. Although Ross had made a point of her not having to go, she wanted to please him even in the minor ways, to get back their fading intimacy. She planned to dress up far more than she usually bothered and meet him at the party in the new hotel complex just a few blocks from his office.

What altered her plan of the day was a phone call from Laura. *Epicure* had commissioned her to write a piece on Valentine sweets and she had done so last August. Now as they were putting their February issue together, some editor had decided they wanted a historical box to go with it, Valentine goodies past. Daria drove to the Boston Public Library to do some fast research. She parked under the Little Pru, taking the elevator up to Saks. Although Christmas decorations were going up all over the store, outside it was balmy, the air soft, scarcely a breeze and the sun rebounding off the pavements and the granite walls of the library.

Inside the library she kept her coat buttoned over the black cocktail dress. The BPL was a good library, but since funds for social services had been sharply curtailed, working there was like doing her research on the back ward of a mental institution. The homeless dozed in chairs, sponge-bathed with wet paper towels in the bathrooms, eyed her purse longingly.

Sometimes when both her hands were occupied, she had to clutch it between her knees. If she let go of it for a moment, one of the librarians would come over to issue a warning.

By five she had everything she needed. She had slipped off to a pay phone a couple of times to call Ross, but Lorraine had said each time he was with a client. She would simply go directly to his office and they'd head for the party together, an entrance she strongly preferred to wading into a bunch of strangers alone and having to search for him.

Walking briskly in the crowd of workers pouring out of the offices and shoppers heading home, she did not see the pickets until she was almost upon their skimpy ragged flock winding across the raised plaza on the east side of the Little Pru, formally named One Huntington Avenue. It was called the Little Pru by just about everybody because it was near to and smaller than the Prudential Building; she had always found it more attractive, warmer with its brick-faced pillars among the banks of glass. She first noticed the pickets' wavering line with a prick of pity. It must be embarrassing to parade around in front of strangers with homemade hand-lettered signs. They seemed a mismatched bunch, an attractive dark-haired woman with a pretty little girl by the hand, both in new-looking coats in shades of maroon; a tall black man with a beige suede jacket zipped over hospital greens; a blowsy fat woman whose yellow hair looked incongruously freshly coiffed over a baggy green coat; a big broad-shouldered man who was twirling his sign high over everyone's head and singing out something she could not catch, acting as if he were at a football game. But it was what his garish sign said that stopped her so that she rocked back on her heels. WALKER'S BUILDINGS ARE FIRETRAPS. LITTLE BOBBIE DIED SO CONDOS MAY LIVE.

Walker? That couldn't have anything to do with her. Walker was a common name. She sidled closer through the hurrying crowd. People glanced at the pickets and glanced away, except for one man who was arguing with a curly-haired guy in a parka whose sign hung down but not enough to prevent her from reading WALKER AND PORFIRIO SLUM LANDLORDS.

Me? She felt as if someone had punched her. Of course not. Yet Walker and Porfirio must be her husband and one of her brothers. Tony

38

and Ross did some kind of business together, although she realized she had no idea exactly what. She found her face heating and imagined herself blushing conspicuously, blinking red neon, in the plaza full of people rushing past, only herself and that man, who was arguing with the curly-headed guy holding the sign with her maiden name on it, standing still before the pickets. She felt dreadfully obvious, yet none of the picketers seemed to notice her stopped there ill at ease staring at them.

If she walked past them quickly, they would not look at her. Yet she did not feel safe till she had gained the lobby and slipped into an elevator everybody else was rushing from. Lorraine was halfway down the hall carrying a shopping bag as Daria stepped out of the elevator. "Has Ross left yet?"

"Not yet, Mrs. Walker. Are you going to that party after all? I thought . . ."

"Certainly I'm going. I know it means a lot to Ross." She wanted to ask Lorraine about the pickets, but she was too embarrassed.

Ross was in his office on the phone when she knocked and then walked in. "Daria!" He jumped up, covering the receiver. "What are you doing here?"

She almost never bothered him at his office. "I had to do some work at the library, so I thought I'd go over with you." She opened her coat to show him she was all dressed up.

"No," he said to the phone. "I'll talk to you later. . . . Not now. . . . By the way, my wife is coming over too."

She posted herself at the window to kill time admiring his view, south across the city stretching away and east toward the bay. As she turned from the window she realized that the near wall was covered with extremely large photographs of the view from this window, in various stages of development. In the earlier photographs there were many streets of low redbrick buildings. High-rises bloomed in the later photographs, more in each. Some of the views must have been taken from someone else's window, perhaps one of his law partners, pointing west, where the Christian Science mother church stood in lonely splendor, having removed a neighborhood to create a long colonnade with a reflecting pool and fountains.

Ross was off the phone. "You didn't have to bother coming in for this silly party. It's bound to bore you."

"I don't mind at all. We never have supper in the city together. I thought we might make a night of it. . . . Ross, who are those picketers out front?"

He stood, thrusting all the papers on his desk into a heap, his teeth tightly clamped in a grimace of anger. "Those miserable hoodlums! You saw them. They can't annoy us in here, it's trespassing, but they can try to embarrass me outside. But they'll get bored parading back and forth. My best strategy at this point is simply to ignore them, and that's what I intend to do. They'll get damned tired and footsore."

"But who are they? They have signs with our names on them."

"They're nobody. Nobody at all." He sighed, walking from his desk to the windows and then turning toward the photographs. "They blew up nicely, didn't they?"

"Are they yours, Ross?"

"Certainly are." He beamed at the wall. "Look professional, don't they?"

"Ross . . . is it some case you're involved in? Those pickets?"

"That's it. Some petty case. Forget about it. It'll all blow over in a day or two."

"I think there was something on the evening news, wasn't there, about a child named Bobbie—Bobbie Rosario, wasn't it?" Daria frowned, trying to recall a story she had noticed at the time only because of the death of a child. "Fire, wasn't it? Are you defending his family? or are they suing somebody?"

"Just some paperwork. It's a matter of a lot of hot air and little importance. We should head on over to the party."

"But . . . won't they try to stop us from leaving?"

"They won't even see us. My car's downstairs. If you really want to go to this party with me, we'll take your car and I can pick up mine later on. I presume you parked downstairs too?" At her nod he grinned, clapping her on the shoulder. "I doubt if they have enough manpower, those poor creeps, to watch the exit from the garage. But if they do, they don't know your Rabbit. They're just a bunch of crackpots, Daria. All lawyers have to deal with fringe groups sometimes. Forget about them."

He had not been pleased when she had walked into his office, probably because he disliked being barged in on. His work was a separate province than their life together, with sharply drawn and well-defended boundaries. But now she felt welcome. Her coming had been a good idea after all. Those pickets who had frightened and embarrassed her downstairs had unintentionally done her a service after all.

4

I was the Friday before Thanksgiving, a favorite holiday of Daria's, but she had a knife-edge headache. She had had it since early afternoon. No amount of aspirin abraded its edge. Finally she abandoned her manuscript and went into the yard to rake oak leaves yesterday's storm had torn loose.

The yard rose toward Annette's in terraces until a granite ledge broke the surface splotched with lichens, the rock a note of the wild on the well-planted and well-tended hill. The maple in Daria's yard had long since been stripped, but until this storm, nothing had torn the rags of leaves from Annette's massive white oak.

"Getting chilly. Do you think we'll have snow?" Annette called from her back door as she let her marmalade cat Fox inside. If Daria had not still worn her spiked helmet of headache, she would have crossed over to drink coffee. She could not talk; furthermore she felt bound to her house and yard. She was waiting for something—perhaps simply the pain to lift.

She had imagined she was waiting for the mail, until she met the mailman's little truck. In fact one of those linen weave envelopes had been among the day's letters. No more of them had shown up in Ross's wastebasket, but since she got the mail first every weekday, when a note appeared she read it, resealed it and put it with his other mail on his desk. This one read:

Dear Rusty

That was some party the other night, all right. Meet me with the usual at the usual. Now is that service?

Yours,
Lou

An earlier note had talked about a party postponed. She presumed he burned the notes. A large bronze ashtray on his desk sometimes held ashes, after having been clean for years. He never smoked. The notes remained mysterious, but she had mentioned them to no one. The last time Nina called, Daria had almost told her, but what was there to tell? Ross was a lawyer who carried out complicated business for many of his clients, she supposed. Sometimes she remembered those pickets, but as he had said, it seemed to have all blown over.

Crows were perched in the denuded maple on the downhill side. She found them oddly decorative, oversized and hulking, seven of them arranged in the branches in a rough arc like a candelabrum. The kittens were overawed and stayed close to her; they had become her cats. Every night she waited in hope that Ross would return to their room and her bed; every night when he had gone to sleep in Robin's old room, she opened the door and let the kittens in.

When he got home that night she asked him, "Do you have everything you need for a photography session? We really should take care of those new publicity shots soon."

"Tonight Chuck and Irma Petris are coming over."

"I know, love. But soon. Please."

About an hour after she had loaded supper dishes into the dishwasher and rejoined the dinner party sitting over liqueurs in the living room, she found out what she had been dreading. Dinner had not been a glorious success. The pumpkin soup had been a little peculiar, perhaps the yogurt added at the end too acid. The mustard lamb had been excellent, but the flageolets from her garden although carefully stored had been mushy.

Everyone else had eaten heartily, so perhaps it was her continuing headache that made the food taste off. The guests were Roger Kingsley, one of the partners in Ross's law office, his wife Barbara, who unlike

Daria, was very involved in her husband's business, and Chuck and Irma Petris, two chubby middle-aged and grey-haired dumplings who looked like brother and sister. They even wore the same aviator-style glasses, popular ten years before. She had trouble following the conversation, which centered on an office complex the Petrises were involved in near Alewife Brook in Cambridge, and the market in condos in Brookline and Allston. Her eyes glazed over. She kept circulating, making sure glasses were filled and putting more cookies out. Nevertheless when the phone rang, Ross jumped up to answer it, disappearing in his study to take the call.

He came swiftly back. "It's for you. Your father."

They never could remember to call in on her line. She took it in the kitchen. "What's wrong with Mama?" came out of her mouth.

"She had a stroke this afternoon."

"A stroke? Mama?"

"It was . . . a massive stroke, a massive stroke." Pops was echoing some official pronouncement. He sounded bemused.

"Where is she now?"

"In the county hospital. It's a good hospital. The rescue squad came and they worked on her. Then they loaded her in the ambulance and went off with that funny siren they use nowadays. She's unconscious there in the hospital. In intensive care."

But she is conscious, Daria thought. She could feel Nina, aware even though unable to see or move, imprisoned deep in her own body. "Can she speak?"

"Naw, Dolly, how could she? It's a coma. You should get down here as fast as you can. You, Ross and the girls. They say she won't last long."

"Pops, when did she have the stroke? When did it happen?"

"Right after lunch. She made a good lunch too. Manicotti, just right. We both had a glass of wine. Then I lay down to take a snooze. I woke up, I heard something. Like something fell, you know?"

"Did she say anything?"

"I called out, 'Nina, go see what that is.' Like maybe it was the newsboy throwing the paper against the door again the way I told him not to. I heard her say something but then I dozed off again. I figured she was taking care of whatever happened. When I got up, there Nina was on the floor. What I heard was, the dishes in the rack all fell down when she went over. She was still speaking a little then but she was out of it before the rescue squad came."

She wanted to ask him how long her mother had lain there but she did not want to seem to be accusing him. On the other hand, he wasn't prone to guilt feelings she had ever noticed.

"You come down here, Daria, right away. They say there's no hope. You get the girls and Ross and hop on a plane."

As she walked toward the living room, Ross came to meet her and pulled her aside in the hall. Numbly she told him.

"Poor kid. That's hard news. Just let the evening pass. No point dumping our troubles on our guests. We'll get them out the door early, and then we can talk."

Afterward she had no recollection of the social evening except that an ashtray broke, a big ugly one in the shape of a deformed swan Ross's other partner Carl had given them and which must therefore be constantly on display. With faint relief she watched it fall and break. While Ross was saying good-bye to his guests, she started calling airlines. She made reservations on a one o'clock flight the next day. An hour to Logan, an hour before the plane: they'd leave the house at eleven. Tracy would have to follow them. In spite of what Pops had said, the situation was uncertain. She could still feel her mother. She could feel Nina's conviction of hanging on till they arrived, at least. Nina was not ready to let go.

Ross followed her into their room to spend the night with her. Before he fell asleep he kissed her, while Torte, back in his old dog bed, thumped his tail. She was deeply grateful for his company, even of his gently snoring body on his back and then silently on his side, a parenthesis facing away. She could not sleep.

She had no idea how many aspirins she had taken, to no effect. The most she could do was float in half-sleep and worry. The full impact had not hit her and she tried to stave it off. She fussed instead about what she should take. Must call Palm Beach weather. Her parents lived in Hobe Sound near Fort Pierce, but West Palm Beach was the closest major airport. Take the big blue suitcase? Who could guess how long she might have to stay. Appointments to cancel: dinner engagements, her gynecologist for her annual checkup and pap smear, the talk to the women's club in Weston, book signing at the Harvard Coop, her class at the Cambridge Adult Education Center where she was teaching pastry skills, Crisp and Crusty 101 she called it. Peggy, her secretary, was due in Tuesday and Wednesday, because Thursday, when she usually came in, was Thanksgiving.

Thursday was Thanksgiving. Should she call her butcher Leo and cancel the goose? Or would she be back? In the hall the kittens hurled themselves against the shut door. She could always cancel Leo later.

Suddenly at three-thirty—she looked at the bedside clock-radio—her headache lifted. As the pain receded, she could not feel her mother. Nina was gone. She's dead, Daria thought. No, she can't be. She's just unconscious the way they thought she was before. She can't be dead, I won't let her be dead. But she just isn't there!

In the dark she wept, slow tears that trickled over her cheek until the pillow was damp. Torte arrived at the foot of the bed, settling with a deep sigh of contentment. Soon he too was softly snoring, man and dog. As the dark finally began to dilute, she longed to rise and tackle some of the multitudinous tasks flipping through her mind, but she did not want Ross to wake and find her missing. The opportunity was too precious. Out of sad events, sometimes people grew closer and a marriage was reknit.

"I can't charge off suddenly," Ross said. "We're in the middle of negotiating with HUD about rehabbing some properties. Neither Carl nor Roger understand the feds' ways well enough to handle them. I'll join you if it's necessary. You see what's really going on, and we can work out the proper family response. You know I'll get on the next plane if you really need me."

"It's the weekend. Tracy could go with me."

"Daria! You're not going to pull her out of college because her grandmother is sick. Robin can't go rushing off either. Those executive trainee programs are hard as hell to get into. She's a woman, she has to be twice as good—you've said that yourself. When we run today, I'll tell her."

"With both of you running together all those mornings, you see Robin five times as often as I do. I want to get closer to her again."

46

"Give her some rope, old kid, give her some slack. She's out on her own. If you want to be close, you have to do it on her terms."

For Ross to give her advice on the girls was disconcerting. Always she had explained them to him. Always she had explained their needs, their fears, their feelings. Then she had in turn explained Ross to the girls. Daddy didn't mean that, he was upset about work. "You mean I should run with her too?"

He laughed, patting her shoulder. "You couldn't keep up with her. I slow her down some myself. She's good, Daria. We can be really proud of Robin."

She didn't want to go south alone. She did not relish dealing with Pops without Ross to mediate. Pops could make her feel inadequate, even at forty-three, for no other reason behind his bravado than that he was male and her father and she was female and his daughter. All the little successes and pleasures and strengths of her life seemed to wither in his presence until she felt like a bloated middle-aged child about to be punished for some obscure deed of omission.

She called Gussie in East Boston (for Augustina: Pops had given every one of them grandiose names—Anthony, Cesaro, Franklin, Daria— except for Joe named for Pops' own father) to try to persuade Gussie to fly down with her.

"No way," Gussie whined, "Jackie has an earache again and Angie's got a fever. They all were soaked in that storm. I can't run off and leave my children. You go down and you call me and tell me how Mama is. You don't have children at home anymore. You can afford to take planes and all that."

Next she tried Cesaro at home in Lincoln. "You're kidding, Daria. My office is piled with paper four feet deep and I'm giving a speech at the Chamber of Commerce. I can't go anywhere unless they carry me out feet first. Pops called last night. He has her practically buried, but I bet Mama surprises them all and pulls through. You see what's what and let me know. You're my official delegate. . . . Is Ross home? I need a few words with him."

Ross did his insurance with Cesaro, though Cesaro's office was on Beacon in Brookline, one of Ross's many kindnesses to her family. Last she tried Tony, leaving a message with his new wife Monica, with whom she still felt awkward. Daria was going to have to fly down alone. She moved her reservation to five, called Florida and started setting up things to run in her absence.

"At least she's only sick." Robin seemed flustered. She patted at Daria's shoulder in a way that seemed a parody of a common gesture of Ross's toward her. "You have to hope. It's just awful for you, Mother. I wish Dad could go with you."

Daria felt better for her conversation with Robin. Robin was never effusive, that just wasn't her buttoned-down style. Ross had made Robin stand in for the son he wanted. From her birth when he had been stubbornly convinced Daria was carrying a boy, and then even more so after the death of their only son, Frederick Jonathan Walker, who had been born prematurely and deformed, with Down's syndrome. Freddy had lived ten months and then died of pneumonia. All that time Ross had been tremendous with him, had lavished love and attention on Freddy, fueled by a pity that seemed infinite. She had admired Ross immensely for the ability he had shown to love their baby, whom they had been warned would die very young, all the more so since some brake in her had held back her feelings. She had pitied Freddy and cared for him, but she had not given him the love that Ross had, and she had felt guilty. She tried. But she truly wished he had never been born.

When the doctor had told her that he could not rule out future babies with birth defects, they had fought for months about who should be sterilized. Finally Daria had had her tubes cauterized, in a laparoscopy operation, the so-called Band-Aid operation over in a day that left her with no visible scars.

When she thought of how Ross would come home every night from the JFK Building in Government Center and rush to pick Freddy up out of his crib, she felt like crying again. He was good, she thought, a better person than she was. Daria resolved to become close to Robin again, to be a better wife, to make arrangements today as best she could in the limited time and leave without complaining about flying down alone.

Ross drove her to Logan where they had a drink in the jammed bar

48

after she checked in. Ross drank martinis, but Robin had taught Daria to drink a tequila sunrise, which tasted better to Daria than the whiskey sours she had habitually ordered since coming of age. However, this time Daria remembered she was supposed to be dieting and had only a glass of Perrier. The conversation was studded with silences she caught on like burrs, when she would begin to obsess about Nina, and why she couldn't feel her mother's consciousness any longer, and what a stroke meant or felt like. Mostly they got through the half hour till she had to go to her gate by running over the two dozen things that still had to be arranged, cancelled, taken care of.

"I put out food for the kittens on the left of the counter and for Torte on the right. I cooked three suppers. One is in the refrigerator for to-night. You just have to put the casserole dish in the oven, all the directions are taped to it. It's chicken divan, just heat it through. Two more meals are in the front of the freezer, plainly labelled."

"Don't worry about it. I'll probably eat out."

"Not every night. It upsets your stomach."

"Annette will feed me."

"That's another thing. I forgot to tell her. Would you give her a call? I left a message on my answering machine, so you don't have to answer my phone. But nobody was home at Peggy's. Would you tell her she doesn't have to come in this week? Unless I get back. We can make up the days next week."

"Providing you're back."

"Oh, Ross, I can't stay down there forever. I have a contract to fulfill, deadlines to meet."

"If she does, you know, die or anything, I'll take a plane down. I'll call you at your father's—or should I call Joe's house?"

"I don't know. Let me call you. Tonight after I know. I'll call around nine. I'll miss you! Terribly."

Right after he left her, she called Tracy from a pay phone. At four-thirty Tracy was almost always in her room at the dormitory. "Mama, that's terrible. Should I go along?"

"I wish you could, but your father thinks we shouldn't ask you to miss school. I don't know how long I'll be down there."

"I wouldn't mind, really. I love Florida. Here it's snowing."

Daria sighed. Tracy was young, after all. "Just try to get caught up on your classes, in case you do have to fly down."

"Mama, I'm going cross-country skiing tomorrow with Mac, so if I'm not in my room, I'll be back later."

On the plane she had an aisle seat. Mac? That wasn't the Raphael madonna: that was Gordon. The plane was almost full, so the middle seat beside her was occupied by the wife of the man in the window seat. Daria picked at her cardboard supper and succumbed to a glass of white wine. She believed she was a good mother. She had given her girls love, attention, good schooling, firm guidelines. They always had tasks to do, even if none of their friends did. She felt she had done as good a job as she could with the society threatening to inundate them with its violence, its casual nastiness. She had tried.

When she reviewed her parenting, she never thought as Ross did when he toted up his contribution, of the good school, the advantages, as they were called. No, what she felt she had given them was her attention: her love, her caring, her willingness to listen. A wholehearted being there for them had been her own private criterion for good mothering and then, a loosening at the right time, a lightening up, a relinquishment of the need and even the right to control. Ross, she thought, had not gone that extra step, which was why he was so hard on Tracy nowadays.

But had she been a good daughter? She tried to feel Nina but sensed nothing but silence. How pleased Daria had been when she began to make enough money so that she could afford to be extravagant in small ways, so that she did not feel fully accountable for buying her mother pretty things, a woven silk shawl, a gold necklace, a pin the shape of a silver rose delicately detailed. Did Nina like the gifts? She thought so. It was difficult to be sure, because Nina had the habit of misery. Perhaps Nina thought if she rejoiced in anything wholeheartedly, if she relaxed her litany of complaints, her plainsong of martyrdom, then something far worse would penetrate her defenses, just waiting its chance to rend what was yet endurable in her life.

Daria had called Nina regularly, she had written her faithfully and sent appropriate cards at appropriate times. Every year since her parents moved to Florida, she had flown down with Ross, or if he was too busy for a winter vacation, with the children. Often she would fly down when the girls had their February recess. Since she disliked Florida at Christmas with carols booming over the flat hot parking lots, she vastly preferred going in February when the New England winter had begun to wear on her and the girls usually suffered a string of colds linked by periods of sniffling.

She never stayed more than three days, that was true. It was expensive. They also had to visit Ross's family, in South Bend, Indiana. They visited Indiana in June, before the Midwestern heat bore down. One year they had gone at Labor Day, because of Ross's nostalgia for picnics of his boyhood when his father had managed a department store. The temperature had been 101 degrees, the girls had fought continuously and Ross had come down with heat prostration.

Why did a sense of failure haunt her tonight? Because she had never made Nina happy? Only Pops could make Nina happy, and he made her unhappy. That was an oversimplification, but it held more truth than not.

When she was little, the third born after Franklin and Joe, she had conspired, she had striven mightily, she had plotted to please her mother. She also wanted to please her father, of course, but so many things and so many people pleased Pops and were pleased by him. He was a widely social man with inner and outer circles of pals from the neighborhood, from the bar, from his various jobs. Her father was what far too many women had always called a fine figure of a man. Maybe that had made Daria fairly immune to appearance. Ross was not conventionally handsome. He had his features: his glorious red-gold hair, his intensely blue eyes. However, he moved always on the edge of awkwardness and he had an underslung jaw. His posture was poor and his cheeks still pitted to the touch from acne he had barely overcome when she met him, in his second to last year of law school. One of Daria's roommates had said something cruel about Ross: "He's so good looking when you see him from behind, and then what a comedown when he turns around." She had been furious, protective of him. She had immediately preferred him to her more conventionally handsome boyfriends for his character, his sense of social and personal responsibility. She had learned from watching her mother's troubles, her mother who had married the tall dark handsome corner boy.

Yet Nina's approval was the hope she could not kill off, the fantasy she could not quite resist: that Nina would turn and say at last, "Daria, what you've made of yourself! What a good daughter! What a good mother! What a good wife! And people respect you. All those books! Your name in the papers . . ."

She had the intermittent fantasy that standing beside Nina in the intensive care unit, she could penetrate the fog of the stroke, reach with her mind into her mother's consciousness. Either she would bring Nina back to consciousness, defying them all, or she would at least say a personal farewell. She wanted to believe that still, but the scene was no longer credible to her.

She dozed, the wine making her sleepy. She woke only as they landed. Stumbling through the small West Palm Beach airport, whose name always suggested visions of luxury that its reality belied, resembling as it did the seedy bus station of a medium-sized city, she felt disoriented by the heat and the humidity. The hour of sleep had simply made her groggy. Joe called to her as she was waiting for her bag to appear on the carousel. "Where's Ross and the kids?"

"I came down alone because I was the only one who could get away immediately."

"Everybody's working weekends now? They must be in my business." Joe loomed over her, the tallest of a family in which she and her mother were considered short at five six. If his nose had not been broken in high school and reset poorly, he might have been as handsome as Pops. As it was, his hair was receding fast. "They sent you down alone? When are they planning to arrive?"

"When I've checked out the situation, I'll call them."

"You get on the phone right away and tell them to move their butts down here." Five minutes in her company and as usual he was issuing orders, trying to bully her.

"Tracy's in college and Robin has a new job at John Hancock. Ross can't just fly off whenever he pleases." She tried to sound calm and confident. "So, how is Mama? If you wouldn't mind letting me know." She grabbed her suitcase as it rode past.

He took it from her and carried it out to his station wagon, double-parked outside with his oldest kid Junior at the wheel. "Did you eat?" he asked, bumping Junior over.

Daria climbed into the back. "Not really. But it doesn't matter."

"He said you wouldn't eat the crap on the airplane. *He's* waiting for you at the hospital."

He said with emphasis in her family always meant Pops. "I'm not hungry. I want to see her."

"Sure. Not that there's much to see. She's got a nice nurse. It's a real modern hospital, first-rate. All the new gadgets. Every room a private room. Nice for Mama. A quality place."

"So tell me. Mama, how is she?"

"She's in a coma. They did an EEG on her this morning and it was flat. Two flat readings in a row, and they shut off the respirator."

"Why?"

"Because that means she's dead."

"They could make a mistake. Everybody makes mistakes."

"Daria, you're being silly. They handle strokes every day. There's six other stroke victims in there right now."

"How far is it?"

"Another half hour, relax. You'll see her, plenty of time. Then you and him eat at the Lobster. He must be starving, he hasn't had a bite since lunch."

Joe had moved his family to Florida a few years after their parents retired there. The restaurant he had owned in Revere had done poorly. After a fire, Joe had given up on Revere and moved his family south on the insurance money, where they opened a restaurant in a shopping plaza two towns away from where Nina and Pops were living.

When she entered the hospital room, she was astonished at the small heap Nina made under the hospital linens. Nina had been a plump woman most of her life, but now she was girlishly slender. Daria took Nina's cool papery hand. The respirator made its horrid sound while glucose hung down in a bag into Nina's limp arm. Pops rose from a chair by the window and came to embrace Daria. He looked well: tanned, unlike most old men she saw around the hospital, unlike Nina who was as pallid as if she had spent the year up north. He had his full bushy head of black hair streaked with snow. Now he had grown a pepper-and-salt moustache, with longer sideburns. He pinched her cheek, calling her Dolly, as he had pet names for every one of his children, drawing her into a massive hug against his paunch.

The nurse was adjusting the machine as Daria moved close to take her mother's hand again. She pressed gently. Nothing.

"They took another EEG. Flat. Stone flat," Joe was explaining. "You should say good-bye to her and then we should take Pops to supper."

"I was waiting for you," Pops said. "Sad thing. There was nothing they could do for her. But she didn't suffer none. We can be glad for that. It hit her like a bolt of lightning, and that was it."

"What's going to happen?" She wriggled between her father and Joe to address the nurse. Daria was forty-three with her own family and a career: how could her family make her feel immediately eleven, awkward and a misfit?

"The EEGs measure whether her brain is still functioning, you understand? Whether it's still on, if you follow me." The nurse avoided her gaze. "We can start a heart again and we can put a patient on a kidney machine, but once the brain is turned off, that's it. Legally that's death in this state."

"Suppose the machine isn't working?"

"It's functional. It's working on the other patients. That's why we do it twice to be sure, dear. She didn't suffer. She never knew what hit her."

During those two hours or more of lying on the floor, she didn't know? "You were with her all day?"

"I come in for the evening shift. I kept talking to her last night because naturally I always do that just in case the poor dears can hear, even if the doctors say they can't. Why take a chance? Nobody really knows."

"I'm glad you talked to her. Thank you."

"That's what I'm here for. Go ahead. You can talk to her if you want to."

She stepped close to the narrow bed. Nina looked asleep. It was hard to believe she could not be awakened. That was still Nina there, palpably.

She bent over to kiss her mother's forehead. "It's me, Daria, your daughter," she said. The presence of the others inhibited her. "Mama, it's me, Daria, come down to be with you." Gently she laid her cheek on Nina's breast.

When she finally let go of Nina, the men were waiting in the corridor. The nurse said, "Your father is such a wonderful man. Such a lively gentleman. He doesn't miss a thing."

"What is going to be done now? Exactly what?"

"We turn off the respirator. That's all that's keeping her body going. Her own breathing had stopped." The nurse drew her aside, lowering her voice. Why, Daria wondered, because only Nina was there to overhear. "Dear, it's only a matter of time, a short time, even if your father hadn't decided. She's only on the respirator. Either her heart or her kidneys will malfunction over the next two days. It'd be uremia or heart failure. Her pressure's critically low. You can let her lie there on the respirator till her kidneys fail, but she can't come back."

She had a fierce and irrational desire to force them to leave the machine going, but as she clutched again at Nina's limp chilly hand, she knew she was wrong. Nina was no longer present. Daria also knew she had no power here. She was only a daughter. Decisions were being made by Pops as usual, and any he left unmade, Joe would clean up. Nonetheless the sleeper was Nina, still some kind of mother. She did not want to give her up. Surely her lashes were lightly quivering. She did not want to leave. "Come on, Daria, come on! Visiting hours are over." Joe took her arm and dragged her away.

At first Nina and Pops had lived in a vast dusty trailer park. Then Ross and Cesaro had bought them out of the old house in East Boston, so they could purchase a garden apartment in cluster housing for old people. One more kindness Ross had shown her family over the years. She begged Joe to drop her at the garden apartment, where she would be staying, but Pops insisted she come along to the restuarant. In the kitchen a big table was set with room for twenty. The kitchen staff and the waiting staff ate there every night before the restaurant opened—many of them family. Pops sat in the head chair while everyone fussed around him. Pops worked in the restaurant as a sort of greeter-headwaiter, for his style was mellower than Joe's, who annoyed many people, herself included. She tried to call Ross from the restaurant phone, but there was no answer.

She picked at her minestrone and her salad. She knew the food was probably good, but she could not eat it. She wondered if they had turned off Nina yet. The very way that Joe wanted the soup made was their mother's recipe. After the third attempt to reach Ross, she tried Annette's number.

"What? Where are you? No, I didn't know. He must not have had a chance to tell me. No, I haven't seen him over there. Oh, poor dear, is there any chance of recovery?"

Daria could not bring herself to tell the truth, to speak it, when somewhere she hoped still it was not real. "Not much."

Joe and his wife Marie were taking turns calling the rest of the family, summoning them down. The restaurant, the Blue Lobster, was doing a brisk business as usual. She had always considered the Blue Lobster a stupid name. Joe did in fact serve some Maine lobsters, not blue, although frozen so long they tasted of iodine and only a fool would order one for $18.95. Daria was glad to leave, finally, for her parents' garden apartment.

There she tried her call again and again, without success. Ross must be having a late supper with friends or a colleague. She would catch him in the morning. She kept imagining the hospital room with the small body under the sheet. Why could they not have let her stay? Nina had been even thinner than in April. Ever since Pops had begun working at the restaurant and taking his evening meals there, Nina had been losing weight. When he took his evening meals out, she would not cook for herself but simply would open a can or nibble a piece of fruit. Although it was less work for her, Nina had felt deserted, passed over, as she complained to Daria. Now Daria felt as if Nina's loss of weight were some secret practice at vanishing. She could not accept that Nina was dead. It was more as if she had lost her, allowed the hospital to hide Nina from her, allowed alien rules to come between them. She could not accept that Nina was not someplace, hidden, hiding. She felt as if she had never in her life wanted anything so intensely as to talk to Nina again, even if all that happened was that Nina complained.

5

THAT night Daria crept into Nina's bed to lie rigid and unsleeping while the quiet death was accomplished miles away at the hospital. The grief she felt was so pervasive it seemed a part of the thick air she was breathing. No one really cared, she kept thinking, all those years married and who really cared? What did Nina get out of it? I can't live like that, she thought, I can't. I can't stand the emptiness.

After a while she switched on the light. Nina's room was ugly, pastel green with old stains from a leak in the roof showing through, a dampness that never left the walls. The brightest spot was an afghan Grandma had knitted. Grandma had lived with them until she died. Daria could remember her making a square at a time. Daria had pointed out that the squares were all different, that they didn't match exactly.

"But why should they be the same?" Grandma asked in her heavy singsong accent, grinning with bad teeth. "Why keep doing the same thing?" Grandma sent her out into the yard to look at the roses. Sure enough, none were the same when she looked at each carefully. That had impressed her. Grandma knew things that other people didn't: that the pigeons puffed like ruffled balloons were the men pigeons courting the lady pigeons; that the sparrows who hopped around in the street used to eat seeds from horse dung; that the flowers of the summer phlox had sweet nectar at the base of each floweret that she could suck.

Nina's dresser was a jumble of clippings, spilled powder, hairnets, safety and bobby pins, postcards and letters from her children and grand-children. Several clippings concerned strokes. SEVEN WARNING SIGNS OF STROKE. Nina had suspected. That upset Daria so much she lay down again and switched off the light, as if to dim her discovery. She wanted to throw the article away and forget. Why hadn't Nina told her she was afraid of stroke? Nina had taken up their last phone call with complaints about Pops flirting with a waitress at the Blue Lobster and how lonely she was when he didn't come home till after midnight, and how at the restaurant he was gaining too much weight, which was bad for his heart.

They had wasted their phone calls; they had wasted their letters, and now there was no time at all. Nothing more could be said; nothing could be added; nothing could be given. She remembered that last call. Those strange notes had been on her mind as she wondered whether or not to tell Nina about them; then she had thought, What a lot of fuss over nothing at all. After all, Ross was a lawyer; people dealt with him every day about their private business and he was privy to many peculiar secrets. Fussing about those idiotic notes, she had missed the chance to draw Nina out about fears she must have had.

. . . her mother was sitting in Grandma's rocker in the big back kitchen of the house on Havre Street. She wanted to ask Mama why she was sitting in Grandma's chair. Mama was rocking back and forth and singing to herself about a paper moon. Her belly was beginning to stick out again Daria noticed, and wanted to strike her mother. Wanted to hit Mama right in the belly. Another one! She thought she had too many brothers already, who needed yet another? Her mother was mending one of Pops' shirts, turning the cuff with those fine, fine stitches Daria could hardly endure to look at, they were so tiny and tight, and humming her silly song. Daria was two when Cesaro was born; six when Gussie was born; ten when Tony was born. Joe was three years older than Daria and Franklin had been six years older. At the same time she was figuring all that out, she was still a little girl standing there in the kitchen glaring and pouting at her mother for taking Grandma's chair and for the belly showing she understood far too well. She smelled cinnamon and coffee and something simmering, tomato, basil, olive oil . . .

All Sunday and Monday she drove back and forth to the West Palm Beach airport in the Pinto that belonged to Joe's wife Marie—an overworked, overweight, much put-upon woman who, like her sons, worked at the Blue Lobster. Tony arrived first with his wife and baby. Daria felt a little awkward with Monica, the new wife, as his previous wife Gloria had used Daria as a confidante and still called her up on occasion to run over the troubles of her new life. Daria found it difficult to switch her loyalty from the old wife to the new.

Later Gussie flew down alone. Her children still had sore throats and Don, her husband, was staying with them. Daria felt a familiar pinch of anxiety when she saw her younger, her only sister. Gussie had been by family agreement the pretty one, as Daria had been cast as mother's helper. Daddy's little girl and mother's helper could not miss being rivals as Robin and Tracy were, but in a house with four brothers ready to cuff them, tease them, roar them down, they also drew together.

Gussie had liked boys, craving male attention, and married young. She was the only one of the siblings who had not crawled up out of the working class. Gussie still lived in East Boston and no longer looked younger than Daria, six years her senior.

"Daria, do you think Mama was in pain?"

"At first, when it happened, maybe. Then no, I'm convinced."

"It's hot here! I didn't know it was going to be hot." Gussie collapsed in the seat. "Nobody warned me." She was wearing an old black winter coat. Under it when she wriggled out, she had on a turquoise pantsuit just a little tight.

"In the winter, you can never tell. Maybe something of Mama's will fit you, something summery. Or something of Marie's?"

"Marie? That cow? She's twice my size. How would I know about Florida in the winter? The only time we ever get down here is summer when it's cheaper, and besides, that's when Don gets his vacation. You think maybe Joe will pay for my airplane ticket?"

"If he doesn't, I can give you something toward it. Off the record."

Daria ran errands all day. She was coming to hate pulling out of the parking lot by the garden apartments, so called, with their brown baked lawn with two squat scabby palms and a stand of crown of thorns, and heading over to Route One, the inevitable road to anyplace. The land was flat as a pool table, and at every intersection big enough for traffic lights sprawled not one but four shopping malls, one for each corner.

Each seemed lined with the same assortment of shops. What differentiated them from Northern malls was the presence of a broker's office, an E. F. Hutton or a Paine Webber. Fat men in short-sleeved polyester shirts and baseball caps, wizened men in golf shirts in flat plastic-looking colors wearing black sunglasses and digital watches that talked, came and went, looking self-infatuated.

Driving was hazardous. There seemed two types of people on the road. There were young blond surfers or Burt Reynolds look-alikes in pickup trucks, often with a shotgun mounted in back, weaving through traffic ten miles over the speed limit. Then there were nearly blind old people with their hood ornaments lined up with the median strip driving ten miles under the speed limit until they abruptly veered for a never-signalled turn.

She called Ross from the apartment, she called him from the airport, she called him from the restaurant. Finally Sunday evening he called her. He was very sympathetic but dealt firmly with her protests. He had an enormous amount of paperwork to complete for the HUD project, he said, that must be got out of the way before he could fly down.

Finally Monday evening Ross arrived with the girls on the same 8:05 flight as Cesaro and family. Obviously they had travelled together. Cesaro's blond wife Vinnie stumbled off first with their little boy Jay. Their horsy daughter Trish came next with Robin and Tracy, all of them giggling. Then Cesaro and Ross got off, deep in conversation. Everyone shuffled out looking dazed, then put on somber expressions upon seeing her. She was startled to see a camera around Ross's neck, but then he never travelled anywhere without one. It turned out Ross had reserved a car, so she turned the Pinto over to Cesaro and got in the rented Dodge Omni with Ross and her daughters. Ross drove and she sat back, filling her family in on events and arrangements.

They were far too many to fit into the garden apartment and Joe's split-level, so Ross immediately volunteered to take a motel room for himself and Daria. Robin and Tracy objected to staying in Nina's room, agreeing for once. Finally Ross took a room for them and for Trish, who insisted on being included. Were they afraid death would be contagious? she asked them. Their holiday mood was annoying her. Yet she did not want to sleep in Nina's room herself. It was too sad.

Except for breakfast, which in itself seemed to take two hours minimum at the garden apartment, with everyone wanting something different, meals were being handled at the Blue Lobster. Daria tried to keep herself from hanging all over Ross, but she was immensely relieved to be with him. The moment he appeared, her stock rose. Her brothers were all fond of him. In fact, he had independently friendly relationships with Cesaro and Tony.

One aspect of Ross she would never cease to appreciate was his warmth toward her family. His own parents were rotten snobs, who had cut him off for five years just because he had married her. What did they have against her? Only that she was Italian, and therefore not a twirpy suburban Wasp, not a bland Midwestern corn-fed cheerleader, blond as a palomino. Only that she had been raised Catholic, although she had made it clear to them she was indifferent if not hostile to the Church and had no intention of raising children under the power of the nuns who had lorded it over her early schooling. Only that she came from the East Boston working class, although she had put herself through Boston State. She had never figured out what the Walkers had to feel superior about. They were plain-looking unimaginative middle-class people who had seemed always to expect more from Ross than any human being could deliver, who seemed to feel superior more because of what they weren't— poor, Black, Jewish, Catholic—than because of anything they had been or done.

Ross was clear of his parents' intolerance. He had taken to her brothers just as they had welcomed him into the family. Tony had started off in the insurance business with Cesaro, but now he was a public adjuster, living with his new wife Monica and new baby boy in Belmont. Daria loved Tony, but she couldn't spend ten minutes in his house without beginning to redecorate it silently, beginning by throwing out everything in the place and scraping the walls. Sometimes when she passed a furniture store, she would notice in the window a garish and outlandishly expensive bedroom set swarming with gilt cupidons and think at once of Tony. Tony was the best looking of the boys, slender still, favoring tapered well-cut Italian suits she knew to be expensive but always found a little sleazy.

Cesaro, who like her had married a Wasp, was stolid. Chunky, thick-waisted, already balding, he wore Harris Tweeds and rep ties. If clothes from the British Isles had been forbidden, he would have stood before them naked. When Prince Charles had married, Cesaro had given a party at five in the morning for friends to watch on television eating kippers and Scottish salmon and baskets of boiled eggs. His teenage daughter Trish did something odd with horses, teaching them to dance, and was always going to obscure meets. Trish was midway in age between Tracy and Robin and got on with both. Cesaro and Vinnie had a house as old as hers in Lincoln with an immense and functional barn housing Trish's horse. Chester was what his business card read, but all his friends called him Cesaro; as he had once told her, he liked his name. From East Boston her family had spread out westward scattershot through the suburbs of Boston: Lexington, Lincoln, Belmont, and Tony's first wife in Bedford.

Daria knew she had always been Nina's favorite child to complain to, but that was not the kind of favorite she had always longed to be. She had wanted to be the pet, the way Gussie had been, or the big important one like Joe or the darling fussed over like Tony. Cesaro was most like her, in the middle, a little pushed aside in the family.

Ross was her treasure and her worth in her family's eyes. If she wanted something done or not done, she would pass on the request to Ross and he would make it. If she spoke for herself, nothing would happen. Ross made her respectable to them. Her career, which brought home a pleasant if clearly secondary income and had given her a measure of fame so that she was accustomed to people doing a double take when they heard her name and making at least some fuss, was invisible to her brothers except for Cesaro. Yesterday she had said to Joe, when she was trying to establish contact with him, "We're both in the food business."

He had looked at her blankly. "You mean you cook for your husband, you call that a business?"

Robin, Tracy and Trish were bored and a little rebellious. In the morning she drove them to a beach, insisting they not get sunburned and be ready to be picked up in two hours. The rest of the time she used TV to baby-sit them as she had sometimes when her girls were little and bored on rainy days.

Pops said to her, "You take care of Nina's things."

Marie was blunter. "That room is full of junk. She saved like a pack rat. You got to clean it out. You can't leave it for him to deal with, it's not fair."

On her fell then the task of sorting through Nina's drawers and closets, discarding the worst and bundling useful objects for Goodwill. She did not mind, for she did not want strangers or even the wives of her brothers going through Nina's things, not because they were precious or valuable, but precisely because they were not.

Nina had worn mostly floppy faded housedresses. When going out, she had put on polyester waffle knits in bright harsh shades of peach sherbet, acid yellow, Pepto-Bismol pink, laxative green. Once in a while during Daria's march through the stuffed closets, she found a present she herself had given Nina, carefully wrapped in plastic: a cardigan embroidered with birds, a dressing gown in a flower print chiffon, a woven silk shawl, all looking as if they had never been worn. What fit her she took back, for they would always remind her of Nina. What didn't fit her she offered Gussie, who was a size or two bigger than Daria.

The first several drawers were crammed with worn, stained underwear Daria discarded. But in one bottom drawer she was surprised to find a batiste and a silk slip with fine hand embroidery, apparently never worn. Laid in with them was an unopened bottle of L'Air du Temps perfume one of them must have given her and two linen handkerchiefs edged with lace. Nina was waiting, Daria thought, for a special day that never came, a day that would be worthy of the perfume, the handkerchief, the best slip. With tears running slowly down her face, Daria took the prettiest slip for the funeral home. It would be big for Nina now; no matter. Who would know the slip was too big under the fancy pink lace dress Gussie had selected in consultation with Marie?

In the same drawer she found a fan that looked vaguely familiar. Then she remembered. When she was fifteen, she had brought it home one hot August night, taking the Blue Line back to East Boston. She had gone to Chinatown with her girlfriends. The fan bore stylized birds in tones of black and pale grey against burnt orange ribs. She had bought it so Nina could fan herself, sitting out in the yard by the arbor on summer nights. Instead, Nina laid it away carefully with her best underwear, for some glorious occasion that had someday to arrive and for which she would then be prepared in clean raiment. A second coming of love?

Daria wept over the fan, then she took that too. She would give it to Tracy, who would play with it and break it, which was what it had been meant for, Daria's dollar fan from 1956. She had had a crush on a sailor that summer, but fortunately nothing had come of it, or she might well have stayed, stuck in East Boston like Gussie.

She took the afghan off the bed. She wanted it, but so did Gussie.

"I remember it too. I remember it just as well as you do."

"You were too young."

"You can't tell me what I remember and don't remember. It's still pretty. And warm. Jackie and Bobbie have a room that's always cold. With all the fires around and the old wiring, I'm scared to try an electric blanket. This would be perfect."

Daria could not stand up to a cold child. She relinquished the afghan.

"Did you notice how nice I did Mama's hair?" Gussie's own was up on enormous pink rollers. "Now I'll do yours."

"Never mind. I have to pick up the girls."

"But you need to get your hair done before tomorrow. We have the viewing tonight and tomorrow the funeral's at eleven. It isn't respectful."

Daria hoped Gussie would forget about it. Once in a while, when she was about to appear on television, she did have her hair done, but the hairdressers always made such a fuss about how she had to keep herself up, as if she were some sort of mortgage payments. If she was faced with the choice between doing her nails or cleaning up the iris bed, if she had to choose between just enough time to run to Bloomingdale's to buy a dress or make a special dinner, she would divide the irises and cook the vitello tonatto, and figure she would be herself and that would be all right.

The viewing was hard. It was Nina lying there. The problem was not so much that the undertakers had done a good job, for the lipstick was smeared and a harsh coral, but that Nina looked lovely. It was her slenderness, in part; but mostly the expression on her face—relaxed, faintly smiling. "Mama was a pretty woman, you know?" Tony said in surprise. She nodded, too choked to speak.

"Of course she was a real looker, what did you think?" Pops said scornfully.

The absence of Nina's usual expression made the difference. For years pain, disgust, depression had pulled her face downward. Now her features were relaxed and at seventy-three she looked fresher than Daria remembered her looking in twenty years. Hardest for Daria to endure was the sense of Nina's wasted life. What had Nina ever done besides produce the six of them, and how much pleasure had come of that?

Tracy was sniffling beside her, while Robin looking uncomfortable moved closer to her father. Tracy mumbled, "She was always so sweet to us. She used to let us put on her jewelry and dress up in old white summer curtains. When the planes were coming over, she'd say things like, 'Duck, here comes the San Francisco express right through the kitchen. Watch out for the wings.'"

She held Tracy's hand. "What's happening afterward?" she asked Pops. "They're cremating her, right? What happens to her then?"

"We used to have the plot up in Billerica but we let that go. They kept raising the upkeep. Most everybody goes that route down here. It's easier."

"Then what? What happens to her ashes?"

Pops nodded at the undertaker, hovering in the doorway. "They'll take care of them."

"Take care? What does that mean?"

"They disperse them. It's a service."

"No!" she said. "I want her if you don't. I want to take the ashes home."

Pops patted her shoulder. "Sure, Dolly, sure. You take them. You talk to Mr. Andrews right now. I'm sure they don't care." She made the arrangements immediately.

When they sat on the folding chairs, Ross whispered, "What are you going to do with the ashes?"

"I don't know!" The tears started again. "I'll make a new garden for her in the yard. A rose garden. I'll take up part of the perennial beds."

"I don't know if you can legally do that with human remains."

"I don't care, Ross. I'm going to take her home. I'm not going to let them throw her away or take her to the dump."

Back at the apartment they drank wine as she spread out Nina's costume jewelry on the coffee table to let Gussie, the wives and the girls pick through it. Nina had a surprising number of clunky screw-back or clip-on earrings with false pearls, glass beads, plastic twisted into the forms of flowers or animals. Pops used to bring his wife costume jewelry when the occasion called for a present or when he was making up with her after some escapade she had learned about. He had a friend who manufactured it in a neighborhood factory. The jewelry Nina wore, because it wasn't real. Whenever they entertained or went out, she was weighed down with glittery necklaces, button earrings, big brooches pinning her breasts into her dress.

While the others were picking through the geegaws on the table, Daria went back to cleaning out the bedroom. The garbage of the ages filled Nina's drawers, the brooches with missing stones, the shoes with thongs that had torn, the handbags whose clasps had snapped off, the white gloves that had lost their mates, the stockings with only one run: all waiting for a healing that would never descend, a use that would never be found. Unmercifully she threw into large plastic trash bags all the objects her mother could not bear to discard in the fervent belief that some good thing must finally be made of them. She wept and wept, quietly, hearing the loud cheerful voices in the living room. She was simply the more conscious of her relationship to Nina, perhaps, aware of how she had loved her mother, aware of how she had spent her life trying not to become her. Had Nina identified with those spoiled and mangled objects she protected and preserved?

Finally they could leave for the motel. At once she said good night to her daughters and fled into the air-conditioned room with Ross. He put his arms around her and rubbed her back, her shoulders, kneading the tension. "You bearing up okay, old kid? I couldn't believe that trash you hauled out of there."

"It's hard, Ross, it's hard. I'll be glad when tomorrow's over. I dread the funeral."

"It'll be boring, like all funerals, and then it'll be over. You don't want to stay down here to get your father settled?"

"Tony and Monica are staying on for a couple of days, and he has Joe."

"He certainly does. Daria, you have to be a little warmer to Monica than you've been acting."

That was Tony's new wife. "I thought I was nice to everybody. Under the circumstances."

"Old kid, you practically took that silver pin out of her hands."

66

"But I gave that to Mama."

"You were ten times as warm to everybody else. It's not Monica's fault you liked Gloria. Monica's a nice girl. That's the cutest damn little boy they have. Tony's done it again."

She ruffled his hair. "Just think. Robin's of an age to marry soon enough and we'll have grandchildren. Won't that be strange and nice?"

He pulled free of her. "Don't be in such a hurry to marry her off. People married far too young in our day."

"I'm not in a hurry. But it will happen." She had an urge to continuity tonight. Perhaps he was too possessive of Robin to want to imagine her marrying.

Even before the funeral at eleven, everybody was jockeying for telephone time to try to make reservations back. Joe was trying to argue the whole family into staying for Thanksgiving dinner at the Blue Lobster. Plenty of plane seats were available on Thanksgiving, but Wednesday everything was booked out of West Palm Beach and out of Fort Lauderdale too.

During the funeral, Ross was right, she did not weep. It was too polished, too generalized, too alien. Most of the local people who came had some connection with the Blue Lobster or were friends of Pops; she doubted if Nina had made two friends down here. Nina's friends were back in East Boston. Daria had packed away small memorabilia for Liz and Patsy who still lived in the old neighborhood and who were still Nina's best friends.

She found herself sitting through the service with her hands clenched in her lap, in a state of mute anger. With whom was she angry? With her father for flourishing? Nina had been a good woman by all the traditional values and rules, and what had it gotten her? The love of a daughter who had never been her favorite. A service by a priest who had never met her.

Afterward a woman came up to her, "You're Daria, aren't you?"

She was surprised by the first name. "You knew my mother?"

"I met her. Your father plays bridge with us. She was very proud of you. I have your hot weather cookbook, and your Italian one that's dedicated to your mother and grandmother. I cook that lasagna all the time for company and everybody always loves it. I saw you on the *Good Morn-*

ing America show when you made that five minute chocolate cake. Is that in one of your books?"

"*The Working Woman's Kitchen.* That's in paperback now."

"I wish I'd brought my books for you to sign, but I didn't dare . . ."

The exchange restored her. Business as usual.

Afterward she drove the girls to the beach. In between the newest malls going up and the old-age condominiums they were erecting with sky-scraping cranes, patches of palmetto scrub still stood. She could not feel that the development was spoiling an attractive landscape, although she knew she would feel differently if she were a great blue heron or an armadillo. On a sunny morning with the temperature 81 degrees, her daughters and Trish were alone on the beach except for a few surf fishermen. On the road above the public beach, however, the parking lot was crowded with trucks, vans, cars, a lively trade going on among them.

"Drugs," Robin hissed. "It's a bigger business than tourism."

If so, these were the small-time operators. With her new dry energy she drove straight to the garden apartment and finished bundling trash for the pickup. Gussie, Robin and Tracy all were taken to the airport to wait for standby, but everybody else was resigned to spending one last night. Cesaro and family were booked on the same Thanksgiving morning plane as Ross and herself. That night everyone remaining sat at the family table in the kitchen of the Blue Lobster for a very early dinner, before the restaurant opened.

"What are you going to do now, Pops?" Tony asked. "Got any ideas?"

"Pops always has ideas," Joe said, going around with the wine.

"I'm considering moving into one of those condos that provide for your old age. They give you meals, they give you maid service, they give you clean linens . . ."

"I bet they don't give any of it away," Cesaro said.

"They got a hospital right on the premises, nurse always on call. I been thinking about one of those."

Ross said, "By the way, I notice a lot of building down here. I gather mortgage money is available. What's the going rate?"

Within ten minutes Pops had brought the conversation back to his plans. He and Nina had always carried life insurance, and with the price of the garden apartment, that would buy him in for a studio. He had his

Social Security, and with what Joe was paying him under the table, that would take care of the monthly charge.

"They got a swimming pool, a sauna, a little gym. They got machines that take your blood pressure. They got cardrooms, cable TV, machines for doing your personal laundry, what isn't provided by the weekly linen service."

Obviously he had been looking over the possibilities, for he passed a brochure around the table. Ross was looking at Pops with a wry expression, in which she could read the annoyance around his mouth. As well as he got on with her brothers, he had always been skeptical about her father, no doubt an attitude he had picked up from her. They were all waiting for the inevitable pitch. She was convinced Joe had known this was coming tonight.

"Now I'm fine these days. Got years of work left in me. You know it. Healthy as a horse. Maybe I should lose a little weight, but I don't have to be a bathing beauty at my age, right? But a few years from now, I'll be getting tired. I don't want to work every day, even for such a great boss as my own son Joe. I'm going to want to sit in the sun in my old age and regard the fruit of my labors."

"Pops, the kind of place you're talking about," Cesaro waved the brochure disparagingly, "it's a bit expensive. It'll use up your whole savings and your Social Security won't cover what you—"

"Pipe down, *Chester*," Joe said. "Listen to Pops. He's got it all figured out." He roughed up Cesaro's thinning hair with a heavy hand.

"I don't want to spend my old age in a filthy dirty nursing home where they drug you and treat you like a dog sent to the pound. I could move in with Joe, but he has the right to his own life."

"Pops wouldn't have much company or any help if he needed it, with us at the restaurant six nights a week," Joe said.

"So I want to know you fellows are going to pick up the tab, what the government don't cover. Gussie, she'll never have a penny to rub on another. That Don will never amount to much. But I know my own sons have all done good for themselves and provide plenty for their wives and their children. I know they want to help their old man, and the same goes for my favorite son-in-law, who's always been real family to me, just like he was born my own son."

Ross was displeased; she could tell by his hardened chin and tightened mouth. "I have a daughter just starting college and one just out in the world. My cash flow is mostly committed. I have mortgages in four banks. I don't have that extra fluidity. Some periods I'm strapped to meet all my mortgages and taxes. I think you might consider a place with a monthly fee you can afford."

"Between you, you do all right. You come and look over this place with me, and you'll see what I'm talking about. Not some kind of dirty hole you shove an old man into just before his grave. It's nice. People can have a good time there. If you get sick, they got facilities right on the grounds."

Tony shook his head woefully. "Sounds swell, Pops, but I'm paying alimony, I'm paying child support, I'm bleeding dry. In a few years, things'll be brighter for all of us because we've got some good property nailed down, Rusty and me, but these are tight times."

Cesaro sighed as if deeply aggrieved. He hated these family councils. Out in the world he was the most successful of the brothers, with his own insurance agency, a couple of developments he had a hand in, a highly visible officer in his local Community Chest. But back in the family he was the middle son, the fat kid, the one with glasses they all picked on. "Now I'm a little more diversified than Rusty and Tony, but I can't carry you alone. Frankly this monthly fee is on the high side. Why not sit tight, get a cleaning lady and when you're tired of the restaurant, maybe by then—"

Ross burst out, "Maybe the rest of you are in favor of this scheme, but as for me, I can't swing it, I simply can't." He hadn't been listening, she realized, just fuming.

Lying in bed beside him that night, she moved closer with what she hoped was tactful slowness. "Pops made you angry tonight."

Ross chuckled. "That old pirate. Always looking out for number one, more power to him."

"Then you aren't mad?"

"Not about to agree to anything before all those witnesses."

"Ross, Cesaro and Tony weren't overjoyed either, didn't you realize?"

"I guess so. Tony's over his head. It's Joe who's been cooking this up with the old boy. He could perfectly well stay on in that apartment and get one of his pinochle-playing cronies to move in."

"That was Cesaro's idea. Pops could go on eating at the restaurant, even if he didn't work there."

"You can see the old boy figuring it out, the high-rise of his dreams. No, I'm not mad anymore—just amused."

"I guess I mind. Making capital out of her death."

"I'll settle it with your brothers when we get back home. We can work out a response between us."

She eased herself closer to the curve of his back, feeling his warmth like an aura on her skin. Sharing this strange sterile room was a different kind of intimacy, cut off from the thousand tasks and demands and interruptions of home.

"Aren't you sleepy?" he asked her.

Through the wall she could hear the girls' television set on, occasional peals of laughter. "Not yet." She rested her cheek against his shoulder. "Are you exhausted?"

"It's tiring and yet we didn't do anything all day but chatter and wait around. Funeral's are such a waste of time."

"But everything does stop when somebody close to you dies."

"She was one sad woman. For years she hadn't done a thing but complain. Don't you think she's better out of it?"

"Can you ever say that for somebody else?" She slipped her arms around him, working an arm under.

"I thought you might be stuck down here for a month at least. It went quickly for her at any rate."

"I missed you. I do feel as if I've been down here forever."

He turned and nuzzled into her shoulder, settling himself closer. "Sure you don't want to stay on and relax, like Tony?"

"Do you want to?" She was shocked.

"I have to get back to the office."

"Love, so do I. I'll ask Peggy if she can come in every day next week."

"What would it matter if you were a couple of weeks late?"

"But, love, this is a seasonal book. And my editor has scheduled it for the Christmas trade next year." She could sense by the slackening of his grip that she was losing his attention. "We're going to be cheated of our Thanksgiving too. Should we have it Saturday instead?"

"It won't hurt us to skip it one year. It's a tremendous amount of work for you anyhow."

"I don't mind. I've always liked it."

He kissed her, very gently. The shape of his long body through the layers of nylon and cotton struck her into excitement so intense she felt a vast ache, a slow painful burn. She refused to let herself remember how long it had been since they had made love, but the room had been warm and the air conditioner on, as it was tonight. The lack of easy regular habit gave an air of awkwardness to their embraces—"Sorry, my elbow"— that she associated with their lovemaking years before, when she had still been four-fifths a virgin after marriage and his experiences had been accumulated through fumbled groping and fast copulation in the backseats of cars.

They were a little tentative. She had the sense of his body as exotic to her. He was thinner than he had been in a decade, thinner than at any time since he had left the government. Then he had burned off his food in an intense work frenzy and felt frail, bony in her arms. The sharp protrusion of his ribs, his shoulders, his knees, the long bones of his body conjured the younger husband she had loved perhaps more passionately although less sensually.

The sharp bones of his body stuck into her with an angular insistence they had lacked for a long time. Any caress tonight made her breath catch and then run ragged and fast as white water. She felt as if she could come to orgasm from kissing, sucking his mouth, his tongue, his lips. She thought, It is like eating, it is nourishment and I've been starving.

For a moment as he came in she hurt a little, it was that long since they had, and then she felt fine. She imagined from what she had seen of her brothers that Ross was probably unusually large, but she had no other basis for comparison. She always prepared herself for him, often using jelly; but tonight she was so wet the lack did not matter. How beautiful it was to feel him on her, in her again, in the intimacy that was the core and the symbol of all the rest. Here was the heart of being a couple, coupling. At last. Close again, joined together. Nina would have understood, for she had deeply loved Pops. Life in death, she did not care, they were joined again.

He paced himself, moving up against her in a new way that she liked. It took her a while to come but then she did, with a great sighing of her whole body, a gusting through her and then a vast ease, as if her body were big as a sandbar and shining from within with its own soft red glow. The aftershine was with her long after he had changed his pace, building up to his orgasm, giving that deep whistling moan that seemed to issue from the bottom of his belly as he too came. They were lovers again, again man and wife, united, one body renewing itself. They were *we* again. Through the wall came Robin's high piercing laugh, her child, his child. For the first time in days she fell asleep at once, softly drifting.

Something woke her. After she reached for him, did not find him in bed, called his name and got no answer, then checked the bathroom, she realized it was probably his careful closing of the door that had nonetheless roused her.

What could be wrong? The girls? It was silent in their room, next door. Her watch on the bedside table read midnight. Putting on slippers and robe, she slipped into the night that closed around her skin like a tepid bath. Leaving the motel room door open, the air conditioner ceaselessly churning, she peeked at the room her daughters and Trish shared. It was dark. Their door was shut. She heard nothing but their air conditioner.

As she walked past the row of dark and still lit rooms toward the office, she asked herself what could have gone wrong. Had he heard something? Their rented car was safe outside. Then she saw him in a lighted phone booth by the ice machine, his tall frame constricted, the receiver pinned by a lifted shoulder.

All evening at the restaurant he had slipped away to try to call. She had assumed he was calling the airport trying for a better flight. That night she kept trying to reach him, where had he been? Something was wrong, something bad. She watched him talking in the booth and could read from his body language, the way he hunched around the receiver curling his body to it, that he was speaking personally, emotionally. His face was suffused with a kind of tender desire.

Ashamed of standing there spying on him, she turned and slipped back to their room, shutting the light off. What did it mean? Who could he be talking to with such an intimate face at ten after twelve at night? Rigid, she lay under the sheet. Those strange notes from Lou. She could not ignore her trouble any longer; there was someone else in Ross's life. He was involved with another woman. He was involved with a woman named Lou.

6

Sᴴᴇ expected the ashes to be a handful of white dust (perhaps like
the bone meal she fed her bulbs) passed to her in a funeral
urn. The ashes came out of the back of the funeral parlor in a
plastic baggie, like lettuce from the supermarket, and were fitted
into a four-by-four-by-six box with a certificate on top to the effect that
these were the remains of Nina Maria Porfirio. The box was surprisingly heavy.

Now the ashes rode in her suitcase. She kept imagining that the airline
would lose her luggage, and she would have to demand a search for
Nina. We're going north, she addressed Nina, back where you wanted
to be. I can't return you to East Boston. I can't return you to being a
young mother. You liked having babies, you liked talking to us and
playing with us as if you were our big sister. You loved cooking and
canning and baking, taking the ordinary and making prettiness. You
loved being loved and you got so little love, in the end. We fled your
unhappiness like a plague we might catch. But I can promise you going
home again and I can promise you roses.

The plane was half empty. After Vinnie moved back to the smoking
section with Trish, Cesaro spread out, put up the armrests and napped.
When Daria saw her brother was asleep, she asked Ross, "Did you
smooth things over with Cesaro?"

"I don't know why you thought his feelings were ruffled. Takes more
than that to upset him. We see eye to eye."

Just so they were back in accord. Cesaro was her favorite brother, the smartest and most sensitive. Once he had dreamed of being an artist, and he still did decent watercolors. He was easy to make fun of, Anglophile, stocky, balding, the butt of family humor when he was growing up.

Daria knew she should not start on the plane but should wait till they were home and Ross was comfortable, rested, but she could not wait. She was too loose with anguish. Besides he looked cheerful, even a little ruddy with sun, with a *Globe* propped up fencing him off. ARSON PLAGUES NORTH SHORE SUBURB. MURDERER OF TWO SOUGHT. HUB CAR THEFT CAPITAL, FBI SAYS. "Ross . . . I want to talk with you, really talk. Something's wrong between us."

He craned around to see if Cesaro was asleep. "What are you starting up about now?" He glanced at his watch.

"You know as well as I do things have changed between us. We aren't as close as we used to be."

"Oh, that again. What was wrong with last night?"

"Why did you leave the room afterward?"

He glanced at her sideways, a flash of ice-blue. "Sorry if I woke you. I was trying not to."

"Ross, who were you talking to?"

"What's this inquisition? I was trying to be considerate. There you were finally catching a little shut-eye."

"Ross, are you involved with another woman?"

"Another woman! What is this nonsense? Are you crazy?" He flung his newspaper down. "Do you know how many phone calls I make in a day? Sure, they're all women I'm having torrid affairs with. That's what I do all day when you think I'm at the office."

"Who were you talking to so late?"

"Carl, of course. He was out all evening. We had a little fire in a building and we're setting up a meeting with the insurance people, and Tony, of course, our adjuster, to work out the settlement. I was arranging everything."

She felt like a fool. It was all plausible. Of course he was calling his partner. Yet she saw him still, inturned toward the phone cupped between his cheek and his shoulder, pleading with his hunched body. His face was flushed with a tender desire she had not seen in perhaps two years, not even when they had made love just before. She knew that luminous look, she knew it well.

Ross was looking straight ahead but she could feel his controlled tension like the humming of a generator. She said nothing more. His denial felt so absolute she could not think how to go on. After perhaps ten minutes, he barked out, "It's incredibly demanding of you to make me account for every phone call I make."

"Demanding?" She bristled. He had been using that word ever more frequently during the past year. Every time they disagreed, he threw that accusation at her. "Because I wake in a motel room and want to know where you are in the middle of the night?"

"The middle of the night!" he echoed rhetorically. "See how you exaggerate? And what was I doing in that motel room? I came down to keep you company, to go through your family ritual with you. To please you. Your mother never meant anything to me. A perpetual whiner. A woman who never managed to learn how to dress, how to conduct herself. She's been a millstone around your father's neck. I was down there trying to make things easy for you at a time I should have stayed put."

"You know I'd never make a fuss about going out to Indiana if anything happened to your parents, God forbid."

"I wasn't making a fuss, you were. You're the one who's making a scene on this plane. I wonder if your father really did have all those affairs, or if he was just trying to get down to the corner for a beer."

"I've never pestered you about your work. I've never demanded an accounting of where you go and why. When I kept calling you the night I came down here when I could expect you'd want to know if I arrived safely and what was happening, I didn't reproach you. I kept trying you till midnight and all the next day. I never demanded to know where you'd been."

"You were saving it up for a good time, such as on a plane with your brother sitting right behind us."

"Ross, please, please talk to me! Something's wrong between us. Something's very wrong. Let's deal with it. Let's try together."

"What's wrong is your attitude. Slowly you've turned into a real demanding bitch. You want to own every piece of me. You want to control my whole life. You want everything to revolve around you—you and your family and your silly little claque of fans."

Ross's voice had risen. Behind them Cesaro stirred and yawned. Ross stood as a signal the conversation had ended and went back to the lavatory. He did not return until the flight attendant announced they were beginning their descent into Logan.

It turned out that Cesaro, driving in from Lincoln, had the only car at the airport, as Ross had come by cab. Cesaro offered to drop them off in Lexington. In the car conversation was forced and choppy.

The front hall reeked of dog piss. The house smelled cold and musty. An odd pile of newspaper lay just inside the door, as if Torte had had an accident and somebody (Annette probably) had cleaned it up perfunctorily and left it to be thoroughly cleaned when she returned. Annette must have forgotten to walk Torte at least once; he was generally pretty good about waiting.

He ran barking to hurl himself on Ross, who hugged him and roughed him up. "Now here's a boy who's glad to see me, isn't he?" Torte carefully avoided the paper in a way that convinced her it was his accident. Ali and Sheba crept cautiously partway down and stared, their eyes light flames in the dark of the stairwell. Then they rushed toward her mewing and led her to the kitchen purposefully. She thought they looked a little thinner, as if in her absence they had shrunk rather than grown.

The chicken divan was still in the refrigerator, spoiled. Annoyed, she threw it out. He must not have eaten there at all. The milk too was spoiled. She took out the frozen grapevine leaves stuffed with ground lamp and pine nuts to defrost. That would have to be their Thanksgiving supper. Ross slammed the door of his study and shut himself in. He was acting out a massive sulk. When she knocked on the door to bring him a cup of coffee, he was on the phone and glared at her, putting his hand over the receiver as if something might escape.

When she had fed the animals, let them into the yard and thrown out the foul garbage that had been sitting in the kitchen, she went to her answering machine to play back messages.

Her agent Laura had called: call me back Monday and where are those new photos? We need them toute de suite.

An adult education program in Worcester.

General Foods re: new contest on gourmet food line.

Mellicent Products, manufacturers of the Smo-King Home Smoker, about commissioning a booklet of recipes.

Gretta: what's this about cancelling Thanksgiving? What's going on? Where are you?

Annette introjected an occasional plaintive query between the other messages, checking if she were back yet.

Leo her butcher sounded furious. Ross had obviously forgotten to cancel the goose. She would pick it up tomorrow morning, see if it was still good and make her peace with Leo, without whom no high-quality meat would grace her table.

Gretta called again sounding reproachful.

Channel 7 called about the series they had discussed with her. A couple of years before, she had done a slot on the morning show on Channel 4. Now Channel 7 was negotiating for a feature on their magazine format early evening show.

She read the note Peggy had left. Hadn't Ross told her not to come in? She had trouble averting her gaze from the ashes on her desk. The sun had sunk beneath the curve of the hill. While they were gone the temperature had risen. Now it was well above freezing. Tomorrow she must make a bed for the ashes in the yard. She ought to do it right away, but she had not the heart yet. She must act before the ground froze.

Then she heard the sound of a car and ran to the window in their bedroom across the hall to look out into the street. It was his Mercedes pulling out. Where was he going today, Thanksgiving?

Slowly she returned to her office. She had to speak to someone. She called Peggy, on the pretext of arranging their work schedule.

"Of course I came in Tuesday," Peggy said. "No, Mr. Walker never called me. Are you okay, Daria?"

"My mother died and I just had a fight with Ross."

"When I got there Tuesday, everything was a mess! Torte had done his business all over the floor—not once but several times. He didn't mean to. I don't think anybody had walked or fed him, and the kittens were just crazy with hunger. I cleaned it up the best I could. Then I talked to that lady next door who always takes care of them when you go out of town."

"Annette? Why hadn't she come over?"

"Mr. Walker never asked her to. So I told her it didn't look to me like he was around either, maybe he'd gone south by then. She said she'd take over. Want me to come in tomorrow?"

"Maybe you'd better. I feel way, way behind." When she had put down the phone, she laid her head on her arms, cheek to her desk, and remained there too depressed to weep. Where had Ross been? Where was he now? Her trust of him was like her spine, a part of her body, the support of her life. She simply could not believe what was happening. Ross and Daria, Ross and Daria, that was who she was. For her whole adult life, her name had been Daria Walker, the name she wrote under. That was the face in the mirror. What was left to her if he turned against her, if he withdrew himself from her? How could he want to hurt her? How could he want to stop loving her, even briefly?

On Friday while upstairs Peggy typed the manuscript, Daria dug Nina's ashes into the yard. By midmorning the sky was beginning to threaten as the air grew heavy with a leaden chill. First she dug a new rose bed, putting in peat, manure, compost, bone meal. Then she dug her mother into the whole bed. The ashes were coarse, gritty, with little shards of bone, odd brightly colored and pastel fragments, blue, copper, pink, black. Good-bye, Mama, she said to the rose bed. In spring I will plant roses that are strong and hardy and fragrant. I remember when you were lovely. I remember when you were happy, when you were the rose of Havre Street. Everything I am comes from you. Whenever I cook, whenever I write, I celebrate you and the kitchen of my childhood. That is my contribution: real food women prepared, rooted in peasant cooking and bound to the seasons and the changing times.

Why did you leave me, now when I need you? That was how Nina must have felt when Grandma died, deprived of her own support in the house. Grandma never hesitated to stand up to Pops although in her own sly way. Grandma had bent and sprung back. A conspiracy of women, centered on their kitchens.

She had too many decisions to make; she felt like fleeing them. She felt like saying no to everybody: Channel 7, Mellicent Products, General Foods, Worcester Adult Ed. Whenever she was approached, she had to balance her desire to carry out a project with Ross's potential annoyance. She felt tempted to decline everything. But would he then spend more time with her? Basically she tried to defer decisions. She declined Worcester. She took the next step in negotiating with everybody else, without committing herself.

She called Gretta and made up with her. Gretta's son was going out that night, so she was spared him. She roasted the goose, putting it on in midafternoon. Supper would consist of Pierre, Annette, Gretta and the two of them. She did not feel like trying to corral an extra man to balance the table. She called Ross's office to tell him what she was doing, but he was always in conference and did not return her calls.

By afternoon the first flat discs of snow were floating down. She felt grim with determination, marching about her tidy kitchen making the quince-based stuffing, making the cheese filling for the pumpkin, making the rum maple-butternut pie. She would not live out Nina's life, she would not. She had always considered herself more practical, luckier than Nina, better able to cope. In Nina's death she felt the waste of a potential for love, the energy of a woman who opened to love like a rose. Nina had been a woman of daily strength, of strong emotions, of a yearning wistfulness. All curdled into complaining. All withered into martyrdom. As she felt her face moving into the lines of sour wasted grieving, she refused that mask. She would take back her life. She would make Ross love her again.

She managed to dash upstairs to dress with more care than usual. Ross arrived before the guests, as she was finishing the salad. He had no objections to the supper; perhaps he was glad to have a buffer between them. As they were talking, the kitchen phone rang—his line; they had never got around to changing it. She started for it but he barked, "I'll take it."

Dashing past her, he picked it up. "Hello, Ross speaking." His face changed instantly. "You bother me around here again and I'll take legal action. Don't try to scare me. You're a bunch of dirty loudmouths." He slammed down the phone. Then he went in and turned on his answering machine.

She followed him to his study door. "Who was that?"

"Oh, just some troublemaker. Nobody. . . . When's company coming?"

Saturday morning after a silent breakfast—Ross was holding to his anger like a banner, like a shield, like a magnificent steed he rode about the house—he went upstairs and began moving clothes and toiletries into Robin's room.

"What are you doing?"

"I should think that would be obvious. If you insist on staying in this oversized barn, we might as well use the space. I want my own room."

"But why? We have a huge bedroom. Why can't we share it the way we have? I love sleeping and waking next to you."

"I need space. Away from your demands, your suspicions, what you just *love* to death."

She studied him, struck by his happy appearance. He was experiencing his anger as energy. Ross's myth about himself was that he never lost his temper. Actually he rarely yelled, although on occasion he did that also. He had the habit instead of preserving his anger and slowly leaking it until it colored the atmosphere of the house to a dark murk in which she found herself suffocating. She was supposed to have the hotter temper, but as the price of losing it with him was expensive and protracted, she had learned to control it. "What do you need a room for? I liked sharing the motel room in Florida. I felt closer."

"Sure. So much you made a scene as soon as we got on the plane."

"You're putting more distance between us. How will we ever make up?" It would be harder for sex to happen between them. She could not help but feel that sex was the real motivation between husband and wife to come back from quarreling.

"I don't feel close. Why should I be made to pretend? It's important for me to be in touch with my feelings. You want me to go along being stoic and numb and just absorbing everything, taking it coldly and swallowing it. I'm getting in touch with my feelings."

"What about the good feelings? Are you in touch with tenderness? Joy? Intimacy?"

"How about them? You don't treat me especially great. Where do you see yourself showing me joy and tenderness?"

"You don't share your life with me any longer."

"You just about swamp me with yours. Your phone calls, your appointments, your dinners, your women friends, your books, your agent, your fussing and fussing and fussing around the kitchen. It's just an ego trip. I need to find out what *I* feel. I need to discover what *I* want."

"You're going to figure that out by moving across the hall?"

"It's a start. Then at least I'll have some little place that's really my own."

She felt a tug of anger. After all, he had his law office and his study, much larger and pleasanter and certainly better heated than hers. "Ross, it almost feels as if we're separating."

"By all of fifteen feet. Don't be melodramatic. It makes me feel swamped. When you overreact, I can't figure out what *I* feel. It drowns me out. . . . Is that the phone?"

He rushed downstairs to his study to listen to the monitor on his answering machine, shutting the door behind him. Whoever it was did not please him, for he was upstairs a moment later. She felt absurd chasing him back and forth across the central hall. Robin's stuff was out of her room, Daria noticed. When had that happened? Robin had left a great many objects and clothes behind when she moved into the tiny apartment in Back Bay she shared with two roommates. Had he packed up Robin's things, or had Robin?

Down the basement she went to look and there stacked against one wall were eight boxes neatly labelled in Robin's squarish script, Robin's Summer Clothes, Robin's Books, Robin's Hiking Gear. He left the house before breakfast now most weekdays to run with Robin; he had plenty of time to urge her to pack up and get out of her old room. They ran together in the city mornings and then every Saturday in Lexington. Daria felt conspired against.

After Robin and Ross had gone jogging that afternoon, she laid out a nice lunch: cold goose, leftover pumpkin casserole warmed and a freshly made salad. Robin would eat only the salad, after washing off the dressing. "I'm on a diet, Mother."

She contemplated her daughter's thin wrist lying on the table like a winter twig. "Honey, but why? You're too thin now."

Robin stared. "How can you be too thin? Don't try to sabotage me, Mother."

She studied Robin, blond with a snub nose and uncertain chin, who had no breasts, no hips, the body of a twelve-year-old boy. When Daria had been a little girl, she had stuffed pillows under dress-up clothes to look like a woman. Robin had begun dieting at puberty and never had she stopped.

"It's a matter of willpower," Robin was asserting. "You must take control." Ross was nodding. Both of them seemed to be obsessed lately with notions of control. Without realizing, she began eating frantically, stuffing her mouth with the goose, the pumpkin. Robin turned from her with a grimace.

Daria rose and fled to the kitchen, leaning against the refrigerator. Tears ran down her face. Food had always been a source of pleasure, something to be shared, something that centered the house, the family, something to give and enjoy at once. Was food love to her? Or a way to command love? Perhaps she just enjoyed it, plain and simple. Sometimes she was forced to see herself as Robin saw her, a fat middle-aged failure. Why did her daughter judge her a failure? She did not know. It was as if being forty-three in itself made her a failure to Robin. Yet Robin admired her father at forty-six inordinately. Perhaps because Robin denied herself food as a source of pleasure—being rather a source of disgust so that her favorite verb for eating anything was pigging out—she could only view her mother's professional involvement with food as a sin.

However fast Robin ran, it was never far enough; however thin Robin starved herself to become, it was never thin enough. Her very bones appeared too large to her. At the same time Robin was hotly ambitious and seemed to believe that she would be rich and what she considered a success in a matter of a few years, that executive power and vast responsibility would become hers if she but hurled herself into her job with fierce enough energy.

Sometimes Daria felt as if her older daughter had made every choice since puberty in an effort to distinguish herself from Daria as well as from Tracy. What did Robin see in her that made her daughter flee so hard in any other direction? Alone with her, Robin sat with elbows pulled in, chin lowered. With Ross her eyes grew large and her manner spirited. They both looked ruddy and cheerful, drifting from the table into the living room and turning on the TV automatically. They were having an animated chat about football and the virtues of down versus artificial fabric vests, from which she felt excluded as she had used to when Grandma and Nina spoke Italian. She never knew whether she was being denied some spicy story or whether they were just discussing the daily soaps, whose characters they gossiped about as regularly as the lives of their neighbors. Even when they gossiped in English, she could not always guess if Lydia lived on the next street or in the TV.

She called her mother's best friends in East Boston, Liz and Patsy, and made a date to deliver the mementoes she had brought for them, photographs, a dresser scarf Nina had stitched in her tiny fine hand long ago, embroidered with flowers in five colors; a brooch in the shape of a big flowered enamel heart Patsy had always admired. Monday, after a luncheon in honor of her retiring editor at the *Globe,* she would drop by.

The luncheon was difficult. She decided that she missed the old custom of wearing mourning. That would protect her from having to deal with the sally, "How was your Thanksgiving? What did you make this year, Daria?" The face asking to salivate, to envy, to gourmandize vicariously. "Rather grim really. Nothing at all. I just buried my mother."

Mourning was an excellent social signal, giving warning. She had the choice of trying to shunt people off with polite empty pleasantries or of producing that really fatal reply that dropped into the luncheon like a splat of sauce on the tablecloth. She found she had little she wanted to say to anyone except, "Fine, thank you, except my mother just died and my husband is having an affair with somebody." Ordinarily she would have scorned the lunch, five pea pods laid out as a flower with four shrimp and a slice of orange. Nouvelle cuisine had always appeared to her something invented for people who ate in restaurants too often. But she had no appetite today.

Leaving her car in the Commons garage, she took the Blue Line to Eastie. That made her feel curiously adolescent, as if the bag she was toting might be full of schoolbooks rather than keepsakes. At Maverick she marched up the wind-tunnel exit to the cold blast of air from the harbor. She remembered when Maverick had been the end of the line and she had used to wait for the trolleys. Then only the Sumner Tunnel connected Eastie to Boston, that and the old ferry to the North End they had ridden every Sunday to visit Pops' family. Liz lived nearby behind the police station on an alley named Elbow for its crooked shape, where she had the top floor of the narrow wooden house.

Liz held both Daria's hands as they sat on the bowlegged couch under the same painted velvet picture of a lady being serenaded that had hung over it all through Daria's childhood. "You look so like her, like Nina, sweetheart. She was the prettiest girl in our high school class, but she never had eyes for anyone but your dad. . . . When you were just a little girl, remember sitting out under the arbor in back of your house squeezing the skins off the grapes to make jam? Your dad used to make wine, remember? We all had such good times then. You remember my husband, Daria, you remember Bart?" With Liz, Daria had to drink tea and eat supermarket cake, of which she consumed the slimmest slice she could induce Liz to cut. Liz wept and Daria snivelled. She left feeling more lugubrious than when she had arrived.

The cold wind tried all the buttons of her coat as she walked north on Meridian to Paris. Havre was the next one over but it was cut by the toll booths at the end of the tunnel. She could hear the kids yelling in the playground at Holy Redeemer, where the Notre Dame nuns no longer wore the habits they had when she was a child there. A kid ran across the street in an Eastie jacket, the navy and gold winter version. She had had one of those. She had inherited it from Franklin when it got too small on him; of course it had had his name embroidered on the sleeve. Nina had reembroidered it for her so that it was truly hers. When she had finally agreed that she had outgrown it, it became Gussie's, and was once again reembroidered. A badge of local pride.

Just past Santarpio's pizza a caterpillar of wire at the top of poorly made cement steps stretched over the expressway. After they had built that road, when she was a teenager, she had prided herself on always crossing through the traffic instead of going safely over, she could no longer remember why. How broad and low the sky seemed over East Boston, with almost no trees on the streets to soften it, with the houses built flush to the sidewalks. Everything was white or grey or bleak pastels, so that even the occasional brick school or very occasional brick apartment building seemed harsh in color by contrast. All the lushness was hidden from the streets. Between every house there was a walkway, often barred by a high gate padlocked or bolted. No stranger could guess the secret world of the backyards, where in May the peach trees blossomed all over Eastie, where grapevines were trained to arbors and roses coiled over fences, where tomatoes offered their lush fruits, where right outside the back door a terrace of patterned bricks or patio blocks had often been laid so that it offered an outdoor table, some chairs, an external room under the flapping of the perennial multitiered laundry. Backyard barbecues and blue and white madonnas stood side by side. This was the world of her childhood.

From the passage over the expressway, she looked toward the skyscrapers of downtown Boston, the outsized jets and tower of Logan, the nearer ships. The cracked steps led her down to Havre Street. She started along the row of houses, but when she came to hers, it was a parking lot. She stared over the wire fence. Her parents' old house had burned down years ago, she had known that intellectually, but she had not been back and somehow she had expected to see it today. This was one of a chain of neighborhood lots that offered parking for the airport with a shuttle bus running to the terminals. Everything was paved over, the spot where their wooden house had stood, the patio made of bricks Frank and Joe and she had stolen, the table where they had eaten their most joyous summer meals, Nina's precious roses. Tears welled up. Coming to East Boston had been a mistake. The snow had blown away but patches of ice lay in every dip of the sidewalk. She felt robbed of her own past. A parking lot! Surely she had never agreed to that.

Patsy, their old next-door neighbor, braced her. Patsy met her at the door, one eye partly closed by a stye and her white hair shoved in a net, wearing a housedress that would have fit a hippopotamus, one of the sort Nina used to wear. Where did they find them? Church rummage sales? "Them damn hypocrites on the mayor's payroll, they make promises out of both sides of their mouths but nary a one they keep when it comes to putting back the money they suck from us in taxes. They just gave me the royal runaround on the phone . . ." Patsy had a cigarette dangling stuck to her chapped lower lip and another smoked by itself in an ashtray next to the phone. "Want coffee? Or would'ya rather have a beer?"

"Coffee." She'd had wine with lunch and it had almost put her to sleep. "Milk, no sugar. Thanks, Patsy. I brought you something."

Patsy received the enamel heart and photos as if grudgingly. Daria had no idea why Patsy should be annoyed. "Was there something else you had in mind? Something you especially wanted?"

"I'm a little surprised you coming around here. After what you and your fine husband done to us."

Was Patsy going to try to make her feel guilty for not visiting the old neighborhood? She'd done so every week while her parents lived there. "What's that, Patsy?"

"How'd you know we wouldn't go up with the old house? How'd you like to wake in the middle of the night with smoke and flames pouring in and have to go running outside in your nightie in the freezing cold?"

"Patsy, I'm sorry about that. But it was an old house. You know how many fires there are around here."

"A lot more than there used to be, you can bet on that."

"One of the tenants started it, by smoking, if I remember."

"That was the story, wasn't it? With the condition the wiring was in, it wouldn't take much. And now that damned parking lot. People roaring in and out all times of the day and night. It brings down a block. Some of us care about our homes."

"Cesaro and Ross took that house over so my parents could have the money to buy into their garden apartment. They were living in an awful trailer park, without a tree for miles. Hot and dusty and depressing. Nina hated it."

"I suppose you done what was right for your folks. But it wasn't so easy on us. You know what they say about those fires around here. They call them Instant Parking Lot."

88

"We were losing money on the house. We couldn't sell it. We couldn't raise the rents any higher. That's why we couldn't rebuild."

"That's what they all say, them that is destroying this place." Patsy stood up. "I thank you kindly for bothering to bring me the relics of my old friend Nina."

Back in the street, almost thrust out, she was still puzzled. Patsy had been their next-door neighbor all through her childhood. It was Patsy who had the key and made her lunch when Grandma was dying in the hospital. Patsy and Nina were always in and out of each other's kitchens, and she remembered Patsy's repertoire of cookies and cakes as well as her own mother's. To this day she made a spice cake and a gingerbread that were imitations of Patsy's. She stared at the place where the house had stood. Instant Parking Lot. Now what did that mean? What was Patsy hostile about?

Probably a class reaction, pure and simple: she had grown up working class and married out and by now her own work gave her an independent financial base. Yet Patsy had seen her many times when Nina had still been living next door, and always Patsy had had a warm hug and a great big grin for her. Maybe Patsy was just in a bad mood, feuding with the mayor's office. Some people got cranky as they aged. She stared at the parking lot whose asphalt buried the purple eggplants that had gleamed to her late childhood eyes potently sexual, the day lilies, the irises, the red and green peppers and tall twining tomatoes, the bones of their dead pets, Scamp, Tiger, the painted turtles, fluffy Tyrone, her special cat.

Maybe Patsy was right to be angry. The lot was ugly. Mean. It felt like a desecration. She could not remember discussing that option. She remembered the incessant worrying when her parents wanted to move south—to be more precise, when Pops decided to. They had been sick a lot. Pops had an on-and-off bronchitis that threatened to become chronic and he dreamed of his place in the sun.

She was sorry she had come to East Boston. She was sorry she had left her car under the Commons and taken the damned subway out of some maudlin impulse of returning on foot. Now she had to hike all the way to Maverick in the face of the icy wind that scraped her flesh raw. She could recall Cesaro and Ross agreeing at last to buy out her parents. She remembered a period of collecting rents. Yes, for perhaps two years she had been the rent collector. She never told Ross how often she had to return sometimes to collect a month's rent. They had put the house on the market but they could not get their money out. Then she vaguely remembered a fire. That must be seven years before. Six? How could Patsy still be angry?

The house had fallen into disrepair after her parents moved out. At the time she had been very busy. It had been a relief to stop visiting the wreck of the old house and to stop having occasional fights with Ross about fixing it up. She had felt ashamed of it.

The burning had felt more symbolic than actual to her, as if simply removing a worry. Patsy should be glad for a parking lot instead of noisy neighbors like that family they had to evict, and now her apartment received more sunlight. Daria trudged on toward the subway and toward her distant car, deciding she would stop for a brief bout of Christmas shopping downtown before getting her car out of the garage and heading home. The only time she ever willingly put in shopping was when she was buying presents. Today she would shop for Tracy and for Robin. That would fluff up her spirits.

7

THE texture of their life together had changed. She knew he would blame that deterioration on the fight they had had on the plane coming north, but she was convinced he was using his anger as pretext. In the mornings he left immediately upon rising, dressed usually but not always, she noted, in his running clothes. Was he really running with Robin? Her doubt spread out its fine threads like the mycelium of a toadstool under the ground, wanting only stimulation to sprout in a new place.

Usually he was distantly polite. She felt like a servant waiting on him. She felt like Torte, crouching to catch his eye and wag a hopeful tail. However, if Torte succeeded in drawing his attention, he could count on being caught up and hugged, the warmth lavished on him she had used to enjoy. How long was it since he had paid half as much attention to her as to his dog? Then her pain would grow until she burst out questioning, asking, trying to touch him. He was still Ross, her husband; she was still the same wife she had been. It could not be so changed. This was a nightmare that must end. She had not become somebody else, she had not altered or corrupted. She lived by the values they had shared. He had to turn at last and put his arms around her and say he loved her.

Their incessant entertaining had trailed off. When she invited old friends, he would put in his time. She did not think anyone could tell they were no longer living as a couple, but the pretense exhausted her and she stopped issuing invitations. He seemed to invite mostly his partners and the Petrises, whom she was coming to dislike, with their conversation confined to condominiums, bank gossip, mortgage statistics, who had how large a piece of what.

Three kinds of phone calls seemed to come in for him. Previously she had answered his phone as well as her own, but now he seemed to mistrust her doing so. Whether he answered his line in the kitchen or whether he took the call in his study, even through the closed door she could tell from his voice and the length of the call which of the three types he was on.

The first type was a standard business call. He sounded brisk, efficient, friendly but not overly: his office voice. He was on perhaps five minutes, perhaps fifteen. In the second type he barked into the phone and hung up almost immediately. In the third type, his voice took on a honeyed quality that turned her stomach as much as it roused her jealousy. Those phone calls could last up to an hour. He might emerge, pour himself a glass of wine or sherry and return to the same call. Occasionally he would issue from his office and go directly to his car. She would stand at the window watching him pull out.

She kept stumbling into efforts to recover that warm space that had been her loving marriage. She mentioned her agent's pressure to produce new photographs for the reissue of her one out-of-print book as well as the Australian edition. Ross had always taken her publicity pictures. "I was just wondering, if you'd have the time?"

"When do you need the pictures?"

"You know how they are, yesterday."

"I'll have to see."

"Ross, if you aren't in the mood, it's really all right. I can go to a professional. They have two they like to use in New York."

"I didn't say I wouldn't do it." He frowned. "Professionals, huh? Of course if you think they'd do a better job, that they know how to photograph you better than I do . . ."

"I didn't mean that. Not at all. I couldn't be as relaxed with anybody else." She had a sense how archaic a statement that was.

"If you really want me to do it, I will."

She was left not knowing if she should insist, in which case he was doing a favor, or if she should let the matter drop and be done professionally, which might be insulting. She decided to change the subject. "Patsy was rude to me when I brought her Mama's things. She seems to have a grudge against us because of what happened to my parents' house."

"Who's Patsy?" He examined his cuff.

He knew. "My parents' old neighbor. She seemed upset by the parking lot. I didn't know that was what had happened."

"Why should you know? And who cares what that fat old bitch thinks about it? First she complains because the tenants are too noisy next door. Then she complains there aren't any tenants next door."

Of course he remembered Patsy. "I found it upsetting. Patsy being rude. The house and yard all paved over."

He watched her narrowly. "Why are you taking a sudden interest in that property?"

"I hadn't seen it in years."

"Dragging back over there is bound to get you in a lot of trouble. That lot is a good steady earner."

"But . . . didn't we sell it to some company? It looks like a chain of them."

He leaned back in his chair and folded his arms. It was a new mannerism he had. She kept thinking he was imitating somebody, but she had no idea who. He asked, "What I want to know is, how long are we holding on to this barn?"

"Since when is this house a barn?"

"It's too big for two people."

"It's my office as well as my house. Tracy comes home every few weeks and every vacation."

"It eats money. Heating it. Having to commute into the city every time I need anything. You don't care, you just sit on your fanny transplanting bulbs and making up recipes for fat ladies in Medford. I spend two-thirds of my life commuting."

"That's because you aren't spending any time with me. I'd love to know who are you spending evenings with."

"I asked you months ago to let me put it on the market. This damned mausoleum represents frozen money. It's tying up capital for no reason."

"Where do you want to live anyhow?"

"There are extremely handsome and civilized condos down on the harbor in the city. Those renovated warehouses are stunning. You park right there. You can walk all over downtown. You can even keep a boat and dock it right outside."

"A boat?"

He grimaced, turning away. "I didn't expect you to understand."

"Understand what?"

"Everything here is for you!" He cried out. "Your office, your secretary, your answering machine, your daughter, your friends, your garden, your damn huge cash-eating barn! I'm tired of carrying it on my back. I'm tired! I want for me, *me!* I want something for me! I've been working for twenty years to keep you and your kids and I'm sick of it."

"But I work too," she said slowly. "I was working when you met me. I subbed till you wanted me to quit. Then I started writing the cookbooks."

"Fat books! That's what they are: fat books!"

His anger so stunned her that she let him walk into the living room and turn on the TV loud to a basketball game, without daring to continue the discussion. He used television as a device for silencing her, watching it far more than he ever had. Mostly he watched sports, which he knew she found boring and which he had always disdained. Vicarious jocks, he used to call his cronies. She sat through hockey games, basketball, football asking him the rules, trying to take an interest. He would answer her questions but he would not look at her. He never took his gaze off the screen.

After a while she felt invisible. The pattern of the couch would begin coming through her skin. Then she would find herself in the kitchen eating. Suddenly she seemed always to be dieting or stuffing herself. Food was becoming her solace. Standing she ate a fine terrine she had made for supper yesterday before Lorraine called to say he was tied up and would not be home for supper. She was loving herself with the terrine. She was mothering herself.

Often she retreated to her room, letting the kittens in. They curled up with her purring, washing each other, lying embraced. It was as if she shared the bed with two small lovers. They lay cheek to cheek. Each became upset if the other was too long out of sight. Brother called from

94

one end of the yard or the house, and sister came running. They slept with paws around each other, bellies pressed or head to tail and tail to head.

She had begun to keep the house colder so that Ross would complain less about bills. It would be a great loss to give up her bedroom with the slight slope of walls under the gambrel roof, the cleanly proportioned mullioned windows, the old wide boards worn satiny. She loved the subliminal contact with the many women who had lived in this house over the last hundred and forty years as she went about cleaning, as she sat looking out on her garden, as she cooked, as she worked.

She got into bed with the cats, wrapping around her shoulders the shawl he had given her in October, and read. Lately she had been going to the library and bringing home armloads of books, but she had also been rereading books she had loved twenty years before, even books from her adolescence pilfered from Tracy's shelves. She reread *Jane Eyre*. There the gruff male had truly loved under his cruel exterior. He had tormented Jane but he had loved her. She cried herself to sleep wanting to believe.

She reread *Wuthering Heights, Sapphira and the Slave Girl, The Wind in the Willows, Alice's Adventures in Wonderland*. Then she realized she was reading her way back into childhood. Up in her room she felt like a crazy old lady with her cats and her childhood memories, wrapped in her shawl and crying alone.

One evening Ross answered the phone and accepted an invitation for Sunday night from a new couple up the block because, she suspected, he was caught by surprise, expecting a different call and could not think of an excuse fast enough—generally a trick he was good at. Saturday morning he announced, "All right, all right, we'll do those shots you want. Is that how you want to be dressed?"

Of course it wasn't. She had just been out turning the compost pile. If only she had washed her hair the night before, but she had been planning to use that time alone in the house while Robin and Ross jogged together. As she rushed around her room, she tried to remember what she had put on to be photographed the last time, so that she wouldn't wear the same thing. Finally she flew across the back hall and looked at the covers of her books. Lucky she did, because she had laid out the blue wool again. As he photographed her, she felt stiff and strange and silly, smirking and posing and feeling coldly judged. The camera had never seemed more like an insect eye observing her as possible prey.

On Sunday they dutifully trudged through the new slush over old ice five houses uphill and around the bend to a stucco house put up in the twenties. She knew its long living room well because the Fergusons had lived there before their divorce. The house had turned over in the interim to a couple whose husband had then been transferred to Saudi Arabia.

The new couple, the Dorrs, had three children, one of whom was playing music so loudly upstairs that the ceiling above them heaved like a bullfrog's throat. They served cocktails for hours while supper cooked into leather. It was nine-thirty before they sat down to the sad little mummified scallops in mucilage, by which time both Ross and Daria had drunk too much and eaten far too many peanuts and cubes of art gum passing for cheese.

As they walked home, Ross was singing something she recognized as from *Madama Butterfly*. Inside he flung his overcoat on a chair instead of hanging it and followed her up and into the room that was now hers alone, still singing. "Jesus, what losers." He dropped on the bed, tossing his trousers in the general direction of the bathroom. "You'd never give Torte a meal like that. You're a good old bean, old kid. Come here."

They made love exactly as they would have on a night when they came in too late to make a production of it. Suddenly it was last spring again, suddenly it was a year before. The ugly tension dropped away like slush off a warming roof and they were in each other's arms. Over the years he had learned certain tricks to excite her quickly when he did not want prolonged lovemaking, touching her breasts hard after he had entered her, bringing his hand to her clitoris as he was already moving inside her. She was so surprised she could not stop thinking long enough to let herself become fully aroused. Rather than possibly discourage him, she faked orgasm and held him as he came. She was as delighted as if a full peacock tail of orgasm had opened in her. He fell asleep still curled in her arms. She lay beside him, too happy to sleep, almost too happy to breathe. Whatever had taken him from her must have finally released its grasp.

* * *

But the next evening he had Lorraine call and say he would not be home for dinner, not until late. No explanation, no apology. A call at four P.M. and no Ross until long after she had crawled into bed at eleven. Did he believe she had seduced him? Had she imagined last night? Had he been too drunk to remember who she was? Too drunk to care? She felt battered by her confusions. She could no longer even guess what he was thinking about her, about them. She felt worse cheated than before: she had been given for a moment what she had longed for, the reality of his love that still felt far more real to her than the mysterious coldness and hostility, and then it was as if it had not happened. To hurt this much inside, to feel this raw, this stripped, perhaps she was merely crazy.

The photos were spread on the dining-room table. Normally Ross did all his own darkroom work, but he had not objected when she suggested getting the roll commercially developed and then printed in three-by-five format to choose the best to have enlarged. "Pick out the ones you like," he said expansively, his eyes gliding over the shots laid out. "Whichever please you the most."

She felt twisted with despair. "But, Ross . . . Perhaps that wasn't the best day . . ."

"Why? What's wrong with them? . . ."

What could she say? She looked terrible in those photographs. She looked sick to herself, hunched over, her eyes too big and everything else puffy. She looked vaguely doglike. "Well . . . they aren't the most flattering."

"Now, come on, Daria, the camera doesn't lie. What's wrong with them?"

"Do I look like that?"

"Of course. Daria, what's wrong with you? You want to look the way you did ten years ago, is that it? I can't make you young for the camera. Don't act like a disappointed child!"

She selected the five she found the least disquieting and sent them off to Laura, her agent, to choose the couple she should have enlarged in quantity. That day one of the linen weave notes came, apologizing for something unnamed and suggesting a meeting, same time, same place. Had Lou stood him up and therefore he had briefly turned to her?

"But you're acting like a complete idiot! A child of ten would have more gumption." Gretta slapped down her soup spoon with a clatter. "I can't believe this passivity. It's classic!" Gretta was tall and lank with elegant bones and eyes such a light grey they looked silver.

"What do you mean?" Daria folded and refolded her napkin, her eyes seeking her familiar garden under a shroud of snow outside.

"You think he has a girlfriend. What are you waiting for? Ross to decide to marry her?"

Gretta was saying that because her ex-husband had done just such a thing. "But Ross won't discuss it. It makes him more hostile if I bring it up. I feel he's mocking me. Then I feel crazy. Maybe he doesn't have anybody. Maybe he's just tired of me."

"I have never, never known a woman who thought her husband was running around on her who was wrong. I've known twenty wives who thought their husbands weren't, and they were *all* wrong. This is delicious." Gretta resumed eating with gusto the black bean soup.

"But I can't quarrel with him every night. I'm driving him away. Yet I can't stand not knowing." Daria felt tears pressing against the back of her eyes.

"Ignorance is dangerous! You're waiting for the rest of the roof to fall." Gretta shook her bracelets for emphasis. Since her divorce she had been dressing more exotically. She had dropped weight and changed her style. If she had not exactly landed on her feet, she had managed to regain them by now, three years later. "Why not hire a detective to find out?"

"Gretta, I couldn't. I'd rather leave him than do that."

"Leave him the house? You want the house. You walk out that door and he'll have the real estate agent on the phone before you can back your Rabbit out the drive."

"I didn't mean that," Daria said softly. "I love him." Gretta was trying to make her think that Ross was just the same as her ex-husband, almost a stranger to her now.

"Besides, you can do your own snooping. You can find out what's going on if you apply your brain to it."

She buried her face in her hands. "I haven't wanted to know. I've been hoping it would pass. But it just gets worse. It's so bad now I have to know what's happening, if it kills me."

"Nothing he says or does can kill you, unless he buys a thirty-eight and pulls the trigger. You can survive him. We all do."

"I don't understand why this is happening. I don't!"

"Daria, I felt the same way. Remember? Half the women we know have gone through this. Either you beat her at her game or she'll whip you, so you have to find out what kind of hand she's holding. It's winner take all."

Gretta's game metaphors oppressed her. She kept thinking about the photos still on her desk, but she was ashamed to show them to Gretta.

"Daria, remember when I was getting divorced, I told you to check on your deed?"

Daria blew her nose. "Right. I'd always thought it was joint, but it turned out to be—what do you call it?"

"Tenants in the entirety. Just him and ux, whoever ux happens to be. You had that changed then, right?"

Daria nodded. "It shocked me to find out it wasn't half mine. I insisted we straighten out the deed. Ross was annoyed at me for making a fuss, and I had to get my brother Cesaro to talk him into fixing it."

"Is that the cute one?"

"You mean Tony."

"Anyhow, how do you own the rest of your property—stocks, whatever?"

"I don't know. That's always been Ross's affair."

"Daria, you'd better learn. That's what I mean by acting like a child. Daddy, may I have five dollars, please? It seems to me you must have made a fair amount of money over the past seven or eight years. Where is it?"

"Ross manages our finances. After all, he's a lawyer." She blew her nose, stuffing the paper handkerchief into the pocket of her suit jacket. A wad of them there, damp from earlier.

"Sure, he's a lawyer, and if he starts wanting to get rid of you, he knows a thousand legal ways to screw you."

"Gretta, he wouldn't! I can't imagine him acting that way."

"Would you have imagined last year that now you'd be sleeping in two different rooms and snarling at each other? That'd he be dashing off to whatever young bimbo he's got stashed in Boston?"

"Gretta, would you be honest with me? Have I aged a lot?"

"Aged?" Gretta stared. "You look a little discombobulated these days, shiny around the nose, but you've always had a very young face."

"We have to talk." Daria placed her hands flat on the table.

"I don't have to do anything. I don't have to do anything I don't want to!" Ross bounced up from the table.

He sounded like Robin at fourteen. Was he going through a late adolescence? She had inveigled him into having a cup of morning coffee with her, but now he was off to the city. She trotted after him to the door, feeling ineffectual. "You're treating me completely unfairly!"

"I'm not treating you any particular way. You're just complaining all the time. Like your mother did." He stopped and faced her with a knowing look. "Maybe you're imagining all this persecution because you're beginning menopause."

"Ross! I'm only forty-three. Nina was my age when she had Tony."

"It could come early because of that thing you had done to yourself." He was out the door and gone.

She found herself shaking. He was referring to her being sterilized after Freddy. How could he put it that way? That thing. He had not been willing to have a vasectomy. Had he been looking down on her for the past ten years for being sterilized?

She went to the phone and called Robin. "Yes, it's Mother. I thought I might come by and have breakfast with you and Dad this morning after you run. I have to spend the day at the BPL looking up some references."

"The *what*?"

Robin was not an intellectual. "The Boston Public Library. It's near your apartment, over on Boylston."

"But I don't eat breakfast."

"Not after your run? I assumed you made breakfast for your father."

"I have to go to work, Mother. I can't hang around! I never eat breakfast," Robin said vehemently, as if dismissing an accusation.

At nine she called his office. Lorraine answered. "Oh, Mr. Walker hasn't arrived yet."

"Of course not. I should have realized. I forgot to ask him to run an errand for me."

"He usually gets in around ten. Shall I have him call you?"

"Don't bother. I'll do the errand myself. How are you?"

"Just fine, Mrs. Walker. And how are you?"

After she had chatted with Lorraine the obligatory few minutes, fancying all the while that Lorraine was being unusually reticent with her, she called Gretta. "So already I figured out he sees her in the morning, in between running with Robin and going to work."

"A morning romance. Ugh. I don't think I could hack that," Gretta said. "I can't face the rigors of love before lunch and a wee drink."

She could not tell Gretta that the morning had been their own preferred time for making love. "This is the first concrete thing I've learned. Maybe I'm not losing my mind. He leaves here at seven and he gets to his office at ten. There's a lost hour and a half in there somewhere."

"Unless he has a long breakfast in a coffee shop."

"Gretta, if he does, I'm going to feel like a complete fool. I'll go see a shrink."

After she hung up, she wanted to run upstairs to bed. But she made herself sit still and confront her predicament. If she was crazy, she must seek psychiatric help at once. If she was sane, she must grasp her situation. But how? Follow him. How not to be seen? He would recognize her car. Today she must rent a car. Tomorrow when he left she would rush to Robin's block on Commonwealth in her rented car and take up a position of surveillance. When Ross came out and drove off, she would follow him. Her plan was absurd, demeaning and totally necessary. Before she could dissuade herself, she called the nearest car rental listed in the Yellow Pages.

＊　＊　＊

The next morning by eight she was sitting in a rented Chevette on Commonwealth Avenue with Robin's doorway in view. Although she had circled the block, she had been unable to locate his Mercedes. Now she saw Robin and Ross jogging together along the sidewalk lightly dusted with snow. At the entrance to Robin's apartment building, Robin ran in. Waving to her, Ross continued. Let him head for his office. Let him go to a health club. Please.

He ran on down the block and around the next corner, toward Marlborough and Beacon, toward the Charles River. Putting on her dark glasses and pulling the scarf forward over her head, she drove after. Once she had the light and rounded the corner, she could see him crossing Marlborough, heading for the river. By the time she came to Beacon he was trotting the wrong way. She pulled over, double-parked and watched in the rearview mirror. He crossed to the river side. When she could not keep him in the mirror, she jumped out and ran to the sidewalk just in time to see Ross walk into a large apartment building.

She had to drive around the long way to get back to him. Almost ten minutes passed before she was idling outside the redbrick high-rise into which Ross had walked. She stared and stared at the building, as if its facade could tell her something important. The first two stories went straight up but then the facade of the building was broken by bays made of two sharp angles. The windows were alternated in the bays to give a trompe d'oeil effect of staggered projections. In front a small area was enclosed by an iron fence with a cement bench inside it. She imagined it had been placed there for her to sit and wait for her husband to appear. She did not see Ross's Mercedes, but the building had a garage under it.

By eight-thirty people were driving off and she parked properly. She felt chilled sitting in the car with snow beginning to drift down. She felt colder and colder. She could not distinguish the pain she felt from the cold. At first she rubbed her hands together but then she could not seem to move at all. She sat on and on. The snow settled lightly over the windshield. Her breath steamed up the windows. Her feet turned numb.

Finally she felt she was asphyxiating in the car feathered over with snow. She did not care if he saw her. She got out abruptly and started to cross to the building. She was halfway across the street before she realized she had forgotten her purse and left the key in the ignition. She turned back to fetch the key and her purse. Why? She could not remember why she needed them.

She stood in front staring up at the bulk of the high-rise. Where was he? Was the woman beautiful? Perhaps Lou was some brilliant and successful professional woman, perhaps a lawyer with whom he discussed his practice. Daria saw her as tall, lean, impeccably dressed in a dove grey suit with a mauve silk ruffled blouse, saw her carrying a leather attaché case slim as an envelope. Lou wore real pearls and smelled of Joy. Was she married or was she available? If Ross could park in her garage, that would mean she could not be living with a husband.

She felt sure they were looking down on her out of one of those hundred windows, laughing. She wanted to scream at the building, her voice echoing off the jagged bays, her voice breaking windows. To stand and scream until he came out to her. A woman brushed past her with an akita on a leash. She wanted to ask the woman questions. She realized she had to make herself behave as if she were not crazy. Yes, back to the car. Insert the key in the ignition. Wait.

At nine-forty he emerged in his overcoat and wool slacks and set out at a brisk pace, but he did not turn toward his office in the Little Pru. Instead, glancing at his watch, he marched fast, very fast down Beacon. She could not seem to respond. She watched him into the next block. His hair shone like a flag above his coat. There was no mistaking Ross, whoever Ross was.

She made herself follow, pulling over now and then so that he could precede her. On Massachusetts Avenue he turned left. Outside a coffee shop he stopped. His girlfriend must have neglected to give him breakfast.

As she double-parked across Mass Avenue, she saw a man come out to Ross. The man was some years younger than Ross and several inches shorter, with hair and moustache of an ashy grey blond. He wore jeans and a leather jacket, collar turned up against the cold. They strolled on a few paces, arguing intently. Was Ross having an affair with a man too? Was this man a pimp for some fabulous call girl who had ensnared Ross? As she watched, Ross handed the man an envelope and then strode on without glancing back, again at a brisk trot, checking his watch. Now he was heading for his office, she felt sure. She had no stomach to follow him farther.

She stared at the blond man in the leather jacket as if she could read in his face or clothing or posture some answer to her questions. The man glanced back through the coffee shop window, looked around but not at her, then strolled leisurely after Ross, whistling to judge from his face. Ross was two blocks ahead by now. The man got into a Dodge pickup parked illegally in a bus stop. The cap was on the back, which was loaded with building supplies.

She pulled out into traffic jerkily. Drive slowly. Stop at the red light. Yes. One move at a time. Do not scream. Do not cry. Slowly. If you cry, you can't see.

Even back in her own home at last, she could not breathe. She lurched from room to room. Whatever he was doing in that building, he wasn't having breakfast in a coffee shop. He had clothes there. He was seeing another woman.

What did it mean that he would not tell her? "What does it mean?" Torte thumped his tail. The kittens, watching the snow through the many panes of the dining-room window, turned to gaze at her with their round yellow wondering eyes. Sheba rose on her hind legs to peer into Daria's face, paws holding her jacket. "Mrew?"

"Maybe it's temporary," she said to Sheba. "Maybe I don't need to know more. If I pay no attention, it will stop. It will end. It has to!" Sheba seemed to disagree, turning disdainfully to watch the flakes swirl down.

She found herself out in the yard, kneeling in her tweed skirt in the snow. "Mama," she muttered, "Mama, it's happening to me now."

"Daria?" Annette's kitchen door opened. "Did you lose something?"

"Yes." She had the urge to shout that she had lost her husband. "I dropped . . . my ring."

"Can I help you look? Your *ring*?"

"No, no." She waved her hand. "I just found it."

"How did you lose it there?" Annette took a step outside, peering at her. "You're soaking wet. Are you all right?"

"I'm just going in."

"Come over and have a cup of coffee. We haven't had a good chat since before you went on that tour."

Daria stood. She could not go into Annette's house. Annette was too happy. "I have to rush back to work. We'll get together soon, absolutely!" She lurched for the shelter of her house.

When she was safely inside she lay down on the floor. The phones rang, one after the other, but she let them go. When she finally rose to start supper and took the messages off her answering machine, the voice of Lorraine told her that Ross was held up at a business meeting and would not be home until late.

8

THE next day, Friday, she had breakfast, threw up and tried to work. On her calendar was the notation to shop for food today, but how much should she buy? Half the time she never knew if he was going to show up for supper. She was learning to live with a sense of constant pain, sometimes sharper, sometimes duller, like someone with a chronic disease. Everything in her ordinary routine could give out sudden sparks of pain like a static shock. She called Gretta. Gretta had a busy day but could fit her in at three if she came directly to the travel agency where Gretta worked now, in Harvard Square.

"I've only got half an hour." Gretta took her arm, peering at her, steering her along as if she were senile, guiding her among the cars. "The Algiers is quiet about now." They went downstairs at the Brattle Theater building. Gretta made her drink mint tea. Daria gave her report.

"Can he be paying the rent? Beacon Street on the river. That has to be pricy. No wonder he wants to put your house on the market."

"How can I find out who she is? I only know her first name is Lou."

"You could pick one of those evenings when he's late at a business meeting and follow him."

Daria made a motion as if thrusting something aside. "That he hasn't told me, don't you think that means it's all temporary?"

"Or *you're* temporary."

"But if he really loved her, if he wanted to . . . live with her, wouldn't he have left?"

"Maybe he hasn't decided. Maybe he wants to sell the house first. Maybe she doesn't want to marry him. Maybe she's waiting for a divorce."

"I think he knows it's something that has to run its course, but he's keeping it secret because he doesn't want to ruin our marriage permanently."

"Has he been putting a lot of time lately into keeping your marriage going?"

"He hasn't left."

"Yet." Gretta shook her bracelets. "I'm embarrassed, listening to you. You're lying to yourself. Can't you see?"

"If that's true, everything is a lie. I don't know him and I don't know my own marriage!"

"Marriage isn't a thing. It changes all the time. If you want him, fight for him. Or sit back and wait it out, if you think that will get you anything. But figure out your financial situation. That's the real bottom line."

The conversation was short and unsatisfactory. She felt unbuttoned, stumbling out. The Brattle had on its frequent Bogart festival. She had first seen *Casablanca* there years and years ago with Ross. Even the posters had the power to wound her. Gretta had kept scolding her. She had wanted Gretta to praise her for being bold and soothe her for being hurt and assure her Ross's silence was proof of the emphemeral nature of whatever was going on in the high-rise on the Charles.

Gretta didn't understand Ross. He was hurting her, yes, but it was a compulsion. Like his running. Suddenly he felt middle-aged and wanted his youth back. But he would realize that he couldn't be twenty-four again by changing wives. He could not throw away the riches of her love like socks that had holes worn in them.

She was so engaged in her thoughts she pulled into the drive and waited for the small procession to pass before she registered that they were in any way unusual. It wasn't until they surrounded her car and a fair fat woman in a baggy green coat banged on her fender that she realized they were pickets of some sort. What on earth? Startled, more annoyed than frightened, she rolled down her window. "What is this? What's going on here?"

"How'd you like to raise your kids with rats running over the beds?" the fat woman shrieked.

She took in the signs they were carrying. WALKER AND PORFIRIO SLUM LANDLORDS. WALKER'S BUILDINGS ARE FIRETRAPS. LITTLE BOBBIE DIED SO CONDOS COULD LIVE. WE PAY RENT FOR PIGSTIES TO PIG LANDLORDS. SCORE HUMANS 0 WALKER 2.

They hadn't even made all new signs. She remembered them now; at least she recognized those embarrassing signs with her name all over them. They must be the same people that she had seen near Ross's office in early November, although she remembered a little girl then. "There's a mistake here." She forced herself to speak with false calm, as she used to the first times on television and in front of groups, when her hands would shake uncontrollably but she would imitate the ease she wished she could feel. "Would you mind letting me garage my car?"

"You planning to go hide in the house?" That was a skinny Black man with the 0 to 2 sign.

"You've made a gigantic mistake. I have no reason to hide, if you'll just all calm down." She couldn't imagine what they were doing at her house in Lexington. Ross had said it arose from some case in which he was acting as counsel. They let her pull the car into the garage. She got out of the Rabbit and stared at them, standing huddled in the garage entrance staring back at her. Contrary to her impression on the street, there were only five of them, three men and two women. She was glad for the women; they made the scene less menacing. All were bundled in winter coats and boots and gloves, wrapped in mufflers, twined in scarves. A frail-looking girl kept blowing her nose. On the other side of the kitchen door Torte was barking in rising hysteria. She asked boldly, "Who are you people?"

The older woman was fat and the younger one thin. The Black man was the best looking of the lot, underdressed for the day in a good trench coat and long maroon scarf worn with a flourish, his boots down at heel but highly polished. But the man who stepped forward to speak was in his twenties, with curly brown hair and those glasses that turn from tinted to clear when the person wearing them moves from sun to shade. He had a rather high-pitched penetrating New England voice. "We represent the SON Association. That's Save Our Neighborhood."

"What neighborhood? I don't understand." One thing she was sure of was that they weren't her neighbors.

The other white man was the most menacing. He was big, hulking, older than the other two men although younger than the fat woman. He hung back, his black eyes glowering. With a muffler looped around his throat he seemed to have no neck at all but loomed there, a huge hostile Humpty Dumpty. He wore a glove on his right hand only, because his left was crossed with a bandage. She wondered if he were a boxer or a professional muscle man. Without him, she would have found the others unalarming in appearance.

The young man, the spokesman, was piping up in his sharp nasal voice all about their neighborhood, when she interrupted. "Allston! I don't know anything at all about Allston, honestly. I never go there. It's all a mistake."

"Mistake, your elbow!" said the fat woman. "Honey, your mistake is thinking you don't have to deal with us fair and square. Well, surprise! We're bringing your shame home to you. You ruin our neighborhood, so we're going to cause a little trouble for you in yours." She raised her sign and waved it. "Come on, guys, let's make some noise."

She did not want them parading in front of the house. Ross would be absolutely furious. Everybody on the street had doubtless seen them already and registered the information on the instantaneous gossip radar of the neighborhood. Even though no one was looking out and the only activity on the street consisted of an occasional child trudging past to supper or an occasional car pulling into its proper garage, she knew phones were ringing up and down the hill. It was her duty to defuse this scene; to explain gently and firmly to these people that they had come to the wrong place to complain.

She must get supper started and she must deal quickly with them. Ross would be pleased by her quiet and efficient handling of a potentially nasty situation. She would disarm them by showing she had nothing whatsoever to hide. She would do the last thing they expected and thus lighten the confrontation and incidentally get them out of view of her neighbors. "Look, I insist there's been a mistake, but why argue out here? Come inside and let's sit down and talk."

Both women started toward the door. The spokesman said, "Come on, people, we came to picket."

"But maybe we can get her to fix things. Isn't that the point?" The fat woman edged nearer to the door.

"People, let's caucus," the spokesman said. Grumbling the women shuffled off after him. Daria unlocked the door to take Torte into the yard. He wanted to run around the front, but she tied him up till he was finished.

She called Ross's office. Lorraine said he was with a client, should she put the call through anyhow? Daria decided that by the time she spoke to him, she would have dispelled the misunderstandings and the strange pickets would be gone back to Allston with their signs and their anger to find out who really owned their buildings.

She peeked out. They stood in a cluster arguing, their signs hanging down disconsolately. She wished they would hurry and come in and stop calling attention to her house as marked with a shame that felt to her secretly connected to the shame of her fraying marriage.

She forced herself to put on a chicken for supper. Back in the late sixties Daria had gone on a few antiwar marches and listened to speeches on the Boston Common, she and Ross and little Robin, with Tracy in a stroller. She had enjoyed all those people walking along united by moral purpose. The march had been a huge picnic on the grass, yet one with a goal.

But to invade someone's neighborhood, just the five of them, they had to feel foolish. The streetlights had come on. She heard them pounding on the front door. Torte got wild and she shut him into the kitchen, turning the flame low under the chicken. Either the men too had felt cold or the women had won, she thought, drying her hands on her apron and then hanging it over the newel post as she went to let them in.

They glared around the living room with differing degrees of hostility and curiosity. The curly-headed leader Mac simply looked it over and selected the most comfortable chair, where Ross sat to watch television. He tossed his down parka on the couch, where both women perched, shrugging off their ratty cloth coats. She did not take anyone's wraps because she did not want to encourage them to stay long. The thin one looked even thinner without her coat, dressed in a prim navy dress with a few flakes of white opaquing sticking to the skirt. Peggy used that stuff, to make corrections. The girl was Robin's age and her nose leaked like a faucet with a faulty washer. When she felt Daria observing her, she hurriedly replaced the Limoges dish she was examining.

"This is a real nice room. You got a nice home here," the Black man said. "These all antiques?"

"A few of them are. Most are just copies. Imitations."

The hulking man wandered around the room, his injured hand shoved in his overcoat pocket. "This house isn't imitation. Do you know the date?"

"It's been dated to 1842. Most houses on this hill are modern, but not this one." Surely they were going to do something besides inventory her living room.

The fat woman snorted, propping her hands on her knees, elbows akimbo. She wore baggy polyester slacks and a flowered shirt with its tail out. Unlike the thin girl, she did not look as if she had come straight from work. "Think that's as old as our apartment building? We got rats one hundred forty years old. The pipes are real antiques too. But you know that. They're your rats—probably they pay rent too." She had a loud cheerful voice. Above her baggy blouse her blond hair was carefully done, as if she had stepped out of a beauty parlor just before taking up her sign.

"I'm Daria Walker," she addressed the fat woman. "What's your name?" She would keep everything civil, defused.

"I'm Fay Souza." She went on to give an address Daria had never heard of. "That's your building."

The thin woman was Sherry Sheehan. The Black man introduced himself only as Elroy. He had unbuttoned his trench coat. Under it he wore a green hospital smock. The spokesman, dressed in a Harris Tweed sports coat with a clashing plaid flannel shirt and jeans, said he was Mac Ogilvie. The hulking man introduced himself in a deep rumbling sleepy voice as Tom Silver. "You use the name Walker, not Porfirio?"

"Porfirio was my maiden name. I haven't used it since I got married twenty-two years ago."

"Except to own buildings under," Mac Ogilvie said.

"Porfirio. . . ." Fay Souza was squinting. "Like Tony the Pony."

With a faint touch of fear she wondered if they could mean her brother. Probably they meant some notorious Mafia figure. Fay must be one of those people who thought anyone with an Italian name was in the mob. "My brother lives in Belmont, not in Allston."

Mac grinned. "We know. Oh how we know."

Tom Silver was still brooding on her. "You're the Walker who writes the cookbooks."

She nodded, surprised.

"Shit." He turned away, grimacing with contempt. "That's disillusioning. I was afraid it was you, from a picture on *Cool as Cucumber Soup.*"

Maybe he wasn't a boxer or a muscle man, if he read her cookbooks. "Look, I don't know Allston. I don't even know anybody who lives there—"

"You're looking at them now," Tom Silver said. "Meet your tenants."

"Your name is down on the deed, honey," Fay Souza said. "We looked it up downtown, Sandra María did, so you can't con us."

"There are hundreds of Walkers. You're wrong about it being me."

"Think there are dozens of Daria Walkers or Daria Porfirios?" Tom Silver was on the prowl, fingering the paneling, stooping to peer up the fireplace. He made her nervous, a bear lumbering around her living room.

"It sure says Daria Porfirio," Sherry said. Robin's age and just as undernourished. "I wouldn't mistake a funny made-up name like that."

"Do you think Sherry is an old-fashioned name? It came off a wine bottle," Daria snapped and then was ashamed of herself. She must keep everything smooth, civil.

"Do you ever sign papers your husband hands you without reading them?" Tom Silver loomed over her.

"Of course. He's a lawyer. Do you read forty pages of legal nonsense? Ross—my husband—handles business. Look, he represents a great many people who own property. Maybe one of them owns the buildings you're concerned about."

"Concerned! Lady, people have died in those buildings," Mac piped in his nasal high-pitched voice. "They're intentionally being allowed to fall into decay. They're turning into firetraps."

"You better be concerned too," Sherry said, fingering the upholstery. "No smoke detectors, rotten fire escapes. They're so old and rusty you'd break your neck." Her gaze never fixed on Daria but went round and round the room pricing, counting, deploring.

"Last week in 219 they were without heat for five days—without heat and without hot water," Fay Souza said. "Those furnaces are antiques too. We got lots of antiques. You want to trade?"

"Would you mind giving me a list of addresses you're talking about?" She stood. "I'm going to call my husband at his law office. . . . Why didn't you picket him there?"

"We did." Tom Silver was poking at the fireplace. "You have a leak in your chimney that's undermining the wall here."

"If you go inside an office building, that's trespass," Fay said. "Out front doesn't get the point home hard enough. Tom, what are you doing, looking for work? Get out of there."

"We want to bring your shame home to you," Mac announced, following her to the phone.

"Yes, Lorraine, put me through to Ross anyhow. It's important."

"What is it now, Daria?" Ross sounded annoyed.

"There are people here from an organization called SON. They came from Allston to picket this house because of grievances about buildings they say I own."

"Christ. Call the police. Talk to Captain Devon. No, I'll do it."

"The police? That's a little extreme. They're perfectly rational people. I'm talking to them now."

There was a stiff silence. *"Where* are you talking to them?"

"I thought it best they not remain out front making a scene. I invited them in to talk. You said those pickets had to do with some case. Why is my name on those buildings, Ross? Whose buildings are they anyway?"

"It's merely a legal convenience. Never mind. Get them out of the house."

"But why? If we haven't done anything wrong. Are they our tenants? Do we own those buildings? Why can't we explain things to them?"

Why can't you explain things to me, she wanted to add. Why don't you tell me anything?

"You let those animals in the house and they'll tear it down. They're probably stealing you blind while you're out of the room."

"Ross, I think you should come home right now and talk to them. It sounds important to me."

"You're crazy! I'm not coming anywhere near the house until they're cleared out. They're a bunch of troublemakers. They don't represent anybody but their own big mouths. And that Black queer Elroy isn't even in our buildings."

"You do know who they are!"

"They've been causing trouble since March. I'm getting an injunction."

"Darling, why escalate this? I did invite them in. Please, Ross, come home and talk to them face-to-face and fill me in on what we've gotten involved in. I'm sorry if I did the wrong thing, but—"

"You clear them out, Daria. I'm not coming home tonight." He hung up.

"She just finessed you, Bro," Elroy said. "She got to warn him right in front of you that we're on deck here."

"Yeah." Sherry blew her nose again. "Come on in, sit down real nice while I warn my husband."

"Whatever I do seems wrong. To you and to him. If I'm the owner of buildings I never heard of before, why don't you give me a list of grievances? If I do turn out to have *any* connection, maybe I can change things. Wait a minute, I'll get my recorder." She reached for her purse, which always held the little cassette recorder she used for dictation.

"We prepared a list." Mac produced a sheaf of pages, neatly reproduced from good copy typed on a Selectric, like the one Peggy used upstairs. She thought they were supposed to be living in a slum. There were also copies of letters to and from New Age Realty, Walton Management, Red Robin Trust, Walkan Trust and an article from the *Globe* about a fire in which a child had died. Clippings from a local paper covered various SON protests and activities.

"New Age. Red Robin. Walton. I never heard of any of these."

"New Age is who gouges my building," Elroy said.

"On the phone my husband said he didn't own your building."

"Who does? Santy Claus?" Elroy laughed theatrically.

"Don't take my word for it. I seem to know less than you people do," Daria said self-pityingly, fumbling with the heavy sheaf of papers. "It's hard to be hated by people you never met before for things you didn't do and know zip about."

"It's hard to live in buildings that haven't had a cent put into them for fifty years," Sherry said. "The wiring could blow up in your face. The heat keeps going off. We've had seven fires—seven!"

Fay sighed, her hands propped on her knees, spread wide in old polyester slacks. "I knew little Bobbie Rosario from the night he was born. I used to take care of him for his mother when she was at work. He was the brightest little kid. Could tell you every player on the Red Sox and the Celtics too."

That was the little boy who had died in a fire in October. What that had to do with picketing she could not guess. They might as well blame their landlords for floods and lightning. She did not want to raise the emotional pitch by trying to reason about a child's accident. She remembered how much guilt was attached to Freddy's inevitable death. She said slowly, "I know it's hard for you to believe I'm ignorant of these buildings. My husband seems to have business connections I know nothing about. What I need to straighten things out is for you to lay off picketing this weekend."

"Oh, sure," Mac squeaked. "Why should we call it off? Everybody's hot to trot now. We work during the week, and weekends are the best time for maximum exposure. We're planning to picket Friday night through Sunday night."

She had received one directive from Ross, to get rid of them, and she would. "If you don't call it off, I doubt if my husband will return here. Then I can't talk to him about the buildings."

"Where is he hiding?" Tom asked.

She had a wicked urge to tell them. She imagined the pickets marching up and down outside that high-rise. "He didn't say."

Tom stared. Eyes black as ripe olives. "You must have some idea."

She would not answer but turned her head away, saying to Mac, "What I want is to make a date with some of you. I want to see what you're talking about on Monday. Those buildings."

"You want a tour?" Fay leaned forward. "Great. I don't ask for anything better. I'll show you around."

"I can come anytime, just so I'm free by two."

They arranged she would go to Fay's apartment at eleven on Monday. She wrote the address and directions on top of the sheaf of photocopied material—broadsides, articles, letters to the editor published and unpublished, lists of violations, letters to the fire marshal's office, requests to various city agencies and departments—Mac had handed her.

They had all come in a VW van parked up the hill. She watched them pile in, Elroy giving Fay a boost. Tom was driving. On the side of the van a somewhat faded sign read Aaron Aardvark Carpentry Collective. The van rattled around the curve and down, out of sight.

She was holding herself by her arms across her breasts and smiling slightly. That in itself surprised her. It felt like weeks since she had smiled spontaneously, not that forced smirk of appeasement. She ought to be frantic. Ross was again angry with her and had seized the pretext to run to his mistress. She had felt leaden with depression when she arrived and found the pickets. Now she faced trouble. Why was she smiling?

Maybe it was the company. She who was used to seeing many people now was alone a great deal. Who would want to see her? What did she have to offer except tears, confession, pain? She was boring Gretta, as Gretta had used to bore her. Perhaps she had become so lonely that even a group of angry pickets provided some kind of company.

Perhaps she enjoyed having a slight shred of power over Ross, the power to go and view the buildings he would not inform her about. The power to loose the pickets on him at his girlfriend's. She felt quite virtuous that she had not done so immediately. She still could.

She wandered around the living room, putting the rocking chair back in its corner, idly straightening. She would comb out the tangle with those people who thought they were her tenants. Ross could not speak to them, but she could. They did not put her off. Fay reminded her a little of Patsy, who was always on the phone fighting for her neighborhood, taking on the mayor's office. Fay she thought she could reach.

Suddenly she became aware she was smelling the chicken. It was ready to eat, but Ross was not coming home. She must turn it off. She wished she had someone to eat with. For an instant she thought of Cesaro and felt a stir of empathy with him. He was easy to mock in his Anglophile tweeds, but actually both of them had been aspiring in the same direction, toward what they had perceived in adolescence as gentleness and civility. Both of them had married Wasps, both had bought and adored old houses, both loved to putter around inside and outside. She and her next youngest brother would have made a highly compatible couple. That also made her smile.

If she actually did own those buildings—which she doubted—she could take a hand in managing them. She couldn't see why Ross always felt they were short of money. Surely they could afford to fix up those buildings, however they had come to acquire them. Probably some client had defaulted on a fee and turned over to Ross some worthless building instead. She was curious, yes, and she wanted to show those people how they had misjudged her. It was Fay she saw herself talking with, making everything clear, Fay who looked a little more like Patsy the more she imagined speaking with her intimately, woman to woman. If they had been causing trouble since March as Ross had said, she would make peace. In a way she had always been Ross's social arm, explaining people to him and him to people. He would see how valuable she was to him. But she would not mention yet to Ross that she had made an appointment with Fay for Monday, unless he was very, very nice. That would be her own private excursion.

9

B Y suppertime Saturday, Daria felt crazed. She had not heard from Ross since the phone call the afternoon before. She had called his office repeatedly, leaving messages with the answering service. She stood in the kitchen wringing her hands. Torte had been irritable all day, barking at nothing, hurling himself at the kittens whenever they ventured down onto the floor. The kittens would arch their backs and spit or simply leap up on the counters to peer balefully down at him.

She could not reach Ross. She could not reach him physically, she could not reach him emotionally, they could not communicate and now she finally could not even pick up the phone and call her husband.

At once she felt herself swelling and withering. She felt gross far beyond what she knew to be her weight. Her flesh had turned to mounds of cold mashed potatoes. It was vast and watery and all of it hurt. At the same time she felt shrunken to the size of a mouse. She was someone other people could walk through. She was Nina. She was her dead mother whom she had brought home and planted in the yard, for whom she had ordered rosebushes the night before from Pickering's catalogue, wanting old-fashioned hardy bushes that would last for years, with strong fragrance and bushy growth. She wanted to honor and cherish the memory of Nina; she did not want to become her.

Yet she saw Nina wringing her hands with that some gesture, yes, the same gesture, standing in the kitchen that opened into the yard and crying to her own mother, "Perchè? Perchè?": Why has he done this to me? She saw Nina hurrying to the living room to peek out the window over the couch, to see if he was coming back to her. She saw Nina turn her head away in the street, grasping Daria hard by the shoulder and rushing her past some woman who wore in memory ever after the lurid aura of mysterious shame. She was not supposed to look. If she did, Nina would slap her afterward. "Why did you shame me? Why did you look at that whore?"

But she knew Nina had wanted to look too, for even when she was little she understood that Nina was not really angry with her, that in a few moments Nina would gather her close and kiss her, tender, solicitous.

She held her hands against her thighs to forbid them to twist around each other in that gesture of despair, of entreaty, of futilely washing her hands as if to rid herself of the dirt of misery.

Had Ross left her? Had he simply walked out? She did not even know. She picked up the phone and put it down, picked it up and put it down. But Robin was not a helpless four-year-old. Robin was an official adult and Ross was using Robin to see his girlfriend. She had to know if Robin was conspiring with him. She could not endure suspecting her own daughter, yet she found herself angry with Robin. She could deal with that: at least she knew where Robin was.

She called her. One of the roommates answered. "Oh, Mrs. Walker. Robin! It's your mother."

She decided to wade right in. "Robin, I need to reach Ross. I know where he is but I don't have the number. It's essential that I reach him."

"Why would I know? You leave me out of this."

"Because you know he isn't home. You didn't arrive to run with him today. This is Saturday and you always run here."

"I don't want to get involved in this, Mother! It's your fault! You keep making scenes and a fuss."

"We both know where he is. On Fairfield and Beacon. Perhaps we can go over there together—"

"You're crazy! On a weekend? He's in Hamilton . . ." Robin broke off.

Hamilton? That meant exactly nothing. "Is that where he called you from?"

"It's your fault, Mother. You don't appreciate him. He's got to grow and change and everything, just like me. Now you just leave me out of all this! I can't stand this mess." Robin hung up.

She was lying on the floor weeping. She had lost her husband; she had lost her mother; now she had lost her daughter. She wanted to fall asleep and never wake. It felt like dying. She could feel the organs of her body being slowly ripped out of her.

She wanted to talk to Nina so badly she was blankly furious for a moment. Damn Nina for dying. Why couldn't she talk to her mother? She was an orphan, a motherless child. Of course she wasn't an orphan, but her father would hardly receive her sorrow with interest. She sat up. What a fuss she had made about the matter of whether she called Nina or waited for Nina to call her. She had been ridiculous. It would be a sublime luxury to be able to pick up the phone and talk to Nina.

She could not lie on the floor like a sick dog. She grasped a chair and pulled herself up. Hamilton, Robin had said, Robin the daughter who had turned on her. The daughter who did not love her. Was Hamilton a town? In the corner cabinet in the dining room, she looked through the drawer of maps. Southern New England. She tried H under the index of Massachusetts towns. N-2. She found it, a small town north of Boston, a few miles outside circumferential Route 128 near Cape Ann, located between Ipswich to the north and Prides Crossing to the south.

Did he have two girlfriends, one in the city and one in the country? Had they gone there together? Did her family live there? Friends with a large house? What friends? She saw Ross smiling as he used to, hand resting lightly on the shoulder of a slender faceless young woman, chatting with friends around a fire in a secret life, an alternate parallel social universe excluding only her.

Perhaps because of talking to Robin, she imagined Lou as just a few years older than Robin, blond like Robin, aggressive and ambitious like Robin. Perhaps a young executive. A woman fresh out of law school. Moved from a small town to the city to share an apartment with other girls—unless Ross was paying for that apartment. What did she know? She was the last to find out anything. Ross and Robin, laughing together at her.

She could no longer stand still. She wandered the rooms of the ground floor. Torte was pulling himself stiffly upstairs. Could dogs get arthritis? He really should go to the vet. He had not been since his shots in February. She could not tell if Torte was feeling ill or simply protesting Ross's absence. She stood looking after him, worrying.

She called Tracy, the daughter who was still hers. The dormitory switchboard operator told her the room did not answer. Then she realized it was Saturday night. Of course Tracy was out. Did she really mean to unburden herself on her eighteen-year-old daughter?

She wandered through the formal living room with the carpeting Ross had insisted on and the small Oriental laid over it, to the dining room with its braided rugs on the wide floorboards, to the kitchen back through the hall to the living room. Everywhere her glance took in a sideboard, a pitcher, a set of andirons they had found together on a September Saturday, on a June day sweet as a plum. The early years in this house, Ross and she had driven off to New Hampshire many weekends to auctions, to sales, to little shops. Everywhere photographs beamed at her. It could not all be lost! Ross had taken the pictures except for a few where she had snatched the Nikon briefly and caught him off guard.

Four summers in Dennis Port. Then Boothbay Harbor. The girls pranced in shorts, suntanned and wet, grinning. Torte was a puppy leaping high as Ross's arm after a proffered tennis shoe. There she was in black bathing suit stretched out with her eyes shut. He had crept up on her to take that picture, saying it was the soul of sensuality. How sweet her flesh had been to him then.

She heard herself sighing, sighing as she passed from picture to picture, little portholes to a sea of shared joy. In Boothbay there they stood on the deck of the Fergusons' boat. Fergy was a lawyer too, but he dealt in divorce. She passed on quickly. That wife, Moira, those twin boys: Fergy had divorced them five years back. The last time she had seen Moira, Moira had been working as an Avon lady while the boys were in school. The conversation had been embarrassing.

That landed her. She took out the chicken held on low in the oven. She waved a drumstick cool and ate it standing. Then an idea came to her. She went to his study. The door was locked, but in an old house, locking a door had only a psychological function. She slid a dinner knife between jamb and frame and popped the bolt of the lock. Then she walked in.

She wanted the bills, the recent financial records. As she paid monthly bills, she laid them in his basket and he filed them. First she found the folder of Department Store Charges. Lord and Taylor, the November bill:

October 20 Dept 18 Women's accessories: $89.95

That must be her shawl. Purchased the Friday before her birthday, not the day of her birthday. Immediately below it:

October 20 Dept 54 Nighttime lingerie: $99.95

He had bought the shawl for her and and the beautiful black peignoir set for his girlfriend, spending about equally for both. How thoughtful and balanced. She was furious. Somehow the boxes had become confused. Perhaps Lorraine had bought both and mixed them up?

She found other purchases not for her and certainly not by her: perfume, September 14; pet accessories, August 29; sweaters, November 30. Bloomingdale's yielded nothing. Too far from his office? Saks revealed gloves; houseware (she could not remember his purchasing anything for the house) and back in August, a man's robe she had not bought. She could scarcely recall Ross buying himself clothing. The robe must be for that apartment on Beacon. Therefore in August that relationship had been well enough established for him to be needing a robe to wear there.

Next she tried American Express. They both had cards, but on the same account. Of course he ate out frequently with clients. However Ross's means of keeping track of business expenses aided her work: he checked off his business-related expenses to simplify deductions for his accountant when their taxes were prepared. After she marked her own business expenses in green, he went through and circled his in red.

Last August while she and the girls had stayed in the rented house near Newport, work-related matters had required Ross to spend several days—and nights—in the city each week. One of those weeks he had obviously gone to Maine, for there were lots of suppers for two at Down

East restaurants. Her time on tour had been particularly busy also. Obviously Lou did not cook for him, as that trip was represented by a dinner out every night. She now knew where he had been when she could not reach him from Florida: there was a chit from a restaurant in Magnolia on Cape Ann for that night.

They had their favorite restaurants, certain ones which began to appear regularly in July. During August the lunches became more frequent. During September they met at least twice a week. Thursday seemed to be the day they never missed. She seemed to remember Thursday sometimes figuring in those notes. Weekend chits often came from north of Boston, Ipswich, Rowley, Rockport. She could mark every trip she had made (to New York to see her agent and publisher; to Hyannis for a bookfair; to Chicago to judge a contest, and that tour) by the flurry of nonbusiness activity. Ross was honest in his income tax returns and apparently did not try to deduct *her*. Maybe Lou wasn't a lawyer.

Daria almost wished he would walk in and find her going through the bills, for then they would have to talk. But she grew fed up with her detection without being interrupted. She abandoned her search from a sense of despair. She knew when his affair had begun—tentatively in July and then seriously in August—but what good did that do her? At least it had not been going on for years and she, too dense to have noticed. Before July she could find little out of the ordinary reported by American Express or MasterCard.

Her job was to pay monthly bills. Ross's parallel job was to balance the checkbook. For the first time she realized that gave him an automatic review of what she had spent ("You really poured it out this Christmas") while she remained ignorant as to whom he wrote checks. The drawer the checkbook stubs and bank statements were in was locked, but she found the key in his top drawer. First she went down the basement and found a bottle of a good well-aged Bordeaux—1970 Montrose—carefully carried it up and uncorked it. Then she ate the other drumstick and shut off the oven. At nine she doubted Ross was coming home.

She spread out their bank statements from April on, to establish a pattern. She could deduce little from the checks. Most of his were written to one or another trust: Robert Realty, which she recognized, remembering Ross explaining years ago to his daughters that it was named half for Robin and half for Teresa, making Robert. Revco Realty Trust. Checks to Red Robin Trust. Walkan. Walton Management.

Then there were the banks. South Boston Savings Bank. Baybank. And then again and again, the Allston Savings and Loan.

She was astonished to see how much money poured through the account. Not much remained, but in the course of a month, a lot came in and a lot went out. Probably running the household averaged about a thousand a month. Beyond that she had business expenses, travel, her secretary, telephone, office supplies. But most of the money that came in from both of them did not go for Ross's private suppers and lunches, nor for Tracy's tuition and clothing. It simply vanished into the maze of trusts and banks.

In the early days of their marriage, money had been a topic of frequent discussion, especially how it went. The money they managed to save was in an account collecting its three and a half percent interest toward the purchase of a car, a dream house. Freddy's brief life had left them severely in debt. In recent years Ross and the accountant did her taxes. She had no clear idea how much she made in a year. It had never mattered. In fact it had been tactful not to care, although the amount had risen from a pittance to comfortable to well paid. What had it seemed to her to enquire: unfeminine? unwifelike? untrusting?

If he were paying that woman Lou's rent, Daria had no idea how to differentiate that from all the other real estate trusts he wrote checks to. As she sat sipping the good wine with her lap full of kittens and seven months' worth of cancelled checks spread out on his desk, it struck her forcibly that this hectic torrent of money out seemed to have little to do with running a law office. These must be their investments—but in what? Old houses in Allston? That seemed bizarre. She had always thought of investments—in the few minutes of her lifetime when she had thought of them at all—as having to do with brokers, stocks and bonds, annuities.

She returned the checks to the drawer, locked it and put the key back. Then she reset the lock and shut the door. Her head felt full of mud. The kittens had begun chasing each other in and out of the fireplace. Torte lay with his head on his paws growling softly, occupying Ross's favorite chair as if to protect it from encroachment. His sandy eyes were open, brooding. She stood at the windows pulling aside the draperies to stare into the street. Snow was falling idly onto the old packed-down snow. Soon it would be Christmas. She imagined the five pickets marching in the dark with hand-lettered signs: MERRY CHRISTMAS, SLUMLORDS.

How could Robin have turned against her? Robin's adolescence had not been as stormy as Tracy's. In high school her fierce competitive urge focussed mostly on sports; in college she attacked track, tennis and her classes. She had majored in business administration. Before Robin had moved into an apartment with two other girls in Back Bay, she had filled the house with books about being a successful woman executive, books about networking, magazines called *Savvy* and *Women Working*, books that coached aggressiveness and talked about "the edge." Robin was so earnest and fierce that Daria often felt a special raw soreness in her. Robin needed intensely to win. At times Daria thought victory was a kind of drug for Robin, addictive as any other. But she knew women of her own generation had feared open competition, had feared winning, and what had that gotten them? Contempt. Perhaps Robin's was the right way. She had always experienced a different kind of fearfulness for each of her daughters. With Tracy, she worried about men. With Robin, she worried about Robin's ever higher standards for herself and her own performance. She worried too whether what Robin had chosen would satisfy her in the long run.

Now Robin had turned on her. Daria could not move from that, as if impaled. She had always identified with her mother, even in trouble, in defeat. She wanted to have a better life, but she was on Nina's side. Maybe her sin was a silent bargain with Ross. After Freddy, she had not wanted to try again for the missing son. You can have Robin and I'll keep Tracy and you can turn Robin into whatever you wish: was that the silent treaty? If so, perhaps Robin was right to hate her. Perhaps she had sacrificed her older daughter.

That was ridiculous. Ross was a good father who adored Robin as Robin adored him. All children prefer one parent over the other. Why should she demand both her daughters side with her? She tried and tried to be rational, to tear herself free from the pain. She was like wolves she had read about who were killed by putting a little blood on a very sharp knife. The wolf would lick the knife and keep licking it until it had cut off its own tongue because of course the knife would continue to be covered with blood. The wolf would then starve to death or bleed to death. She must tear herself from the cold bright knife and walk away.

Torte was deliriously happy, lying on his back kicking with his stiff paws and whining with pleasure. Ross was home. Sunday around one he appeared to finish the leftover chicken for lunch, with good appetite and a bottle of the same 1970 Montrose he went into the basement and brought up after he eyed the bottle in the trash. It seemed they were competing to drink up their small stock of very good wines. Cesaro had given them that case; he knew wine and gave generous presents.

She had an agenda. She had even made a list upstairs; not that she was about to read it to him, but she was prepared. The trouble was, he had his own agenda.

"When are we going to put this barn on the market?"

"And if we sell it, will you then live someplace else with me? Or will you live with your girlfriend?" She stood, her hands on her hips facing him.

He was sprawled in his favorite chair, foot tapping, hand on Torte's head. "How do I know? How do I know anything about myself? When have I been allowed to have any feelings?"

"You've always had plenty of feelings, Ross, and you've expressed them in a variety of ways."

"I act out of guilt. I act out of obligation, compulsion. I act out of habit. I'm dying inside! Can't you see that?"

She hated it when he got rhetorical. When he made speeches, she found it hard to penetrate the busy surface of the words. "We've gone through many changes in our life together. We moved and moved and moved because you wanted to. It wasn't good for the girls, and you knew it. They were always being uprooted and starting again in a new school. That made Robin superaggressive and Tracy overly dependent. If you're really tired of this house, you know I'll miss it—but we can look together for something exciting. Then I'd be in favor."

"Too many years of compromise and habit are choking us. Gritting

126

my teeth and buckling down. Fulfilling my responsibilities and commitments, again and again and again and again!"

"What do you want, Ross?"

"I want to want! To feel again. I'm increasingly cut off from the deepest, strongest part of my being."

"Maybe that's because you've cut yourself off from me. When we met, you had trouble feeling. Remember how stifled and locked in yourself you felt? Remember how we celebrated when Robin was born? Remember when we had our first garden party here, you said you'd never felt so proud and peaceful?"

"I need to find myself! I'm trapped. This house is a noose. This marriage is a noose. I want to feel the joy of being alive again!"

"You mean, infatuation is fun. I remember that. But I put that aside for our marriage."

For a moment he gave her a look of cold fury. Then he laughed, dryly. "Do you encounter many temptations, Daria?"

She felt as if he had punched her, only words instead of wind were knocked out of her. She stared back. What she remembered was the temptation to tell those pickets where he was Friday. To gain time she seated herself in the rocker beside the fireplace, noticing as she kept her face averted from him a little water on the grate. A leak, that big sinister looking Tom Silver had said. "If you mean, do I wish to have sex with individuals whom I meet on the road," she said with flat clarity, "no. I don't know if the opportunity is even there, to be honest, because I never let it arise. Why on earth should I want to? I don't feel much for people I meet casually."

"What do you feel for me?" He forestalled her as she started to answer. "I know you'll say, love, love, love, but I doubt it. You're not interested enough in me to feel love. You depend on me, you lean all over me, you use me. I'm the one who balances the checkbook and brings home the bacon. I'm the one who takes both cars in whenever anything goes wrong with one of them. That's who I am."

"I want us to have a good time together. Ross, we haven't taken a vacation alone together in years. You won't take the time off. This summer, you were in the city in August more than you were with us. We've gradually stopped doing the nice things together, the—"

"The seeds of discontent were planted long before." His voice was resonant. "In neglect they have grown tall. Will I forever feel I have negotiated an unacceptable compromise for myself?" Something about the phrase he really liked. She could see him listening to the sound of it. "An unacceptable compromise," he repeated sonorously, rolling his voice in his head like brandy in a snifter.

She thought he was speaking for that woman, as if she could overhear and applaud. "What compromise? Ross, isn't it possible that what's getting at you is that you've been doing a kind of law that doesn't excite you? You felt burned out by what happened with your advocacy work in HUD. Maybe it's time to turn back to public interest law. That would give you the passion in your work—"

"You're living in the past. I am involved in my work, Daria, it's simply that you take no interest in it whatsoever. How can you imagine for five minutes the kind of pointless treadmill hotdogging I was doing then compares to the work I'm doing now? My work has one hell of a lot more to do with the real world and what the Greater Boston area is going to be like in ten years. How viable life here is going to be for the people who create jobs and pay taxes."

"I haven't refused to take an interest in your work. You don't talk about it."

"You cling to old ideas. The compromise I'm talking about has gone on from the beginning, anyhow, and time has only deepened it."

"A pity you never got to use your courtroom manner," she said, feeling herself grow tight. "What compromise are we discussing?"

"Our marriage was a compromise from the beginning—"

"That's the worst retroactive nonsense I've heard! You wanted to get married, if I may refresh your memory, you wanted it a lot!"

"If I may refresh yours, you weren't exactly intact."

"I was perfectly . . . intact! I wasn't afraid of an operation. I'm not a practicing Catholic and hadn't been since I was twelve. Nina knew I was pregnant. Please don't make over my past as well as your own. I wasn't suicidal or dependent on you. I was working, Ross."

"You were a kid with a teaching certificate and no experience at all. I felt responsible, the way I always have, to my own hurt."

"Ross, what you felt was lonely. You were in love with me. You sure did act as if you were."

"It's the recent years. I'm sick of gritting my teeth and pulling the load. I can come back to life, I know I can. I want to feel alive!"

She wondered why he sounded like an ad for some product offering instant youth, a face cream, a cigarette, a brand of jeans. "You're saying your new girlfriend makes no demands—yet—lays no responsibilities on you and thus makes you feel unmarried. To be twenty again, this time without pimples." The edge on her voice astonished her. This was the first fight they had had in which she had not quickly blundered into tears. Something about his rhetoric distanced her, as if he had been rehearsing speeches.

"I didn't expect you to understand." His face drew in, his shoulders hunched. "I need to find myself! If you won't help, I'll do it alone."

"Alone? Have you been spending a lot of time alone?"

"And you leave Robin out of this. You made her feel dreadful."

"I would imagine she'd have a few qualms about being used by you as a cover for seeing your girlfriend."

"And you leave Gail out of this too! This has nothing to do with her."

"*Gail?* Who's Gail?" Daria asked blankly. If his girlfriend was Gail, who was Lou? Did he have two girlfriends?

But Ross hurtled from the room and crossed the hall to his study, yanking futilely at the door. He had forgotten locking it. "You bitch!" he hurled over his shoulder. "That's all I'm saying about her, so forget it."

"Ross." She came up behind him as he rattled the knob, finally remembered and fished out his key ring. Many keys, she noticed, very many. "I know we have to talk. We must change our marriage. I believe in your anger and your pain. But spending every night with . . . Gail? . . . is no way to work out problems between us. Can't you see that?"

"You think you can coax me back into a little box. But you can't." He slammed the door of his study. Torte sat down outside and began to howl. She had a feeling of victory in that for the first time she had not broken down, and in that he had finally admitted there was another woman (two other women?); but it was a Pyrrhic victory, for he was furious with her. At least, she thought, trying to quieten Torte, she knew now she was sane. Nothing of what had beset her had been imagined and he was currently involved with a woman named Gail. Perhaps the peignoir had been for a previous girlfriend, Lou. She would watch and see if any more of those notes came. At least he had finally admitted to one involvement, and that at least was a place to begin trying to talk. Maybe this would be a turning point.

10

On Monday Daria arrived early for her appointment with Fay Souza, so she drove around awhile, tempted to turn and go home. The only thing that made her keep the silly appointment was the fear that having promised and then reneged would make matters worse. She was surprised to notice that the neighborhood to which she had been directed was near Brookline, where one of the many apartments Ross and she had occupied still stood, six large sunny rooms in a yellow brick courtyard building. More clearly than that apartment she remembered the food shopping, the best she had ever enjoyed. Brookline looked as prosperous as ever, the bakeries and butcher shops as inviting.

While she had lived in Brookline, she had never been sure where it left off and Boston recommenced. She realized she had in fact spent time in Allston; she had simply thought she was still in Brookline. The wide boulevard of Commonwealth was in Allston, she discovered. Some of the apartment houses that lined it had been refurbished into flashy condominiums with gaudy canopies out front; others next door seemed to have slid into disrepair, four names to a buzzer.

The streets were tree-lined. Fay's street curved uphill in a neighborhood that seemed an uneven mixture of three- and four-story brick apartment buildings and two- and three-story frame houses. Like all of Boston it looked bleak with the snow heaped up, but her gardener's eye could pick out fruit trees, rosebushes, arbors in yards. It looked like a perfectly decent place to live, not beautiful like her own hill, but pleasant. They must have very minor complaints.

Fay occupied the ground floor of a three-story wooden duplex painted a faded but vile green suggesting mold. Fay's own apartment centered around the kitchen, obviously the family room. Fay slept on a convertible couch in the living room, set up as a beauty parlor with two chairs with dryers over them. Fay had a worn gold band on her ring finger, but Daria did not believe her to be married. There was something a little too direct and unbuttoned about Fay. Whoever had fathered her children was long gone. However, Daria was surprised to observe that while in her memory Fay had taken on Patsy's face, she was not at all Patsy's age. Rather she was Daria's—or considering that her boys were both in high school, perhaps she was even a little younger. Daria caught a glimpse from the kitchen of the sons' bedroom: an enormous poster of the Clash and a chart of martial art positions. A bicycle leaned awry. Would a son side with his father? She tried to concentrate on what Fay was telling her, statistics about heat and water, apartments intentionally left vacant, repairs unmade.

The kitchen reminded her of ones like it where she had spent much of her childhood, but she had no time to relax before Fay led her off on a tour, gripping her firmly by the arm as if afraid she would suddenly run away. Down basements they went to peer at furnaces and piles of rubbish, at aging boilers, at boxes of wiring. Suppose she looked through the negatives in Ross's darkroom, would she find Gail's face at last? Fay pulled a flashlight from her knitting bag. She also had a clipboard in it to which she referred, pausing to catch her breath and cursing softly as they climbed. Panting, Fay would recite lists of violations as they ascended stairs, as they descended stairs. Some of the stairs themselves were broken. Daria began by writing notes diligently, but soon she gave up. She kept thinking about Ross sleeping, eating breakfast across the table from another woman. She assumed Fay or Mac Ogilvie had it all written down and probably photocopied in the hundreds. They marched through three-deckers, through sprawling eccentric houses put up in installments by mad carpenters, past rows of identical cheek by jowl brick apartment buildings spanning the hill like a wall. Daria was lost. Their trek was bizarre. Fay must be giving her a tour of every multifamily dwelling for blocks, but what was the point? Was she standing in for every landlord owning property in the entire area?

Some buildings were unlocked and some Fay had keys to, fishing them out of her knitting bag with address tags attached. Sometimes they knocked on a particular door or rang a bell. Then a tenant let them in, usually adding a litany of complaints to Fay's list, dogging their footsteps down to the cellar, along dingy corridors, up to the roof, sometimes into individual apartments to view a leaky pipe, a falling ceiling, a hissing radiator or broken window.

"I'm Sherry Sheehan's mother," the pale invalid in the wheelchair announced proudly. "This is the lady Sherry visited in Lexington?"

The woman was small-boned and thus seemed round and pale as a mound of cotton batting in the chair. "How's your case going?" Fay asked without obvious interest in the answer, a polite greeting.

"Our lawyer tells us it's looking good." Mrs. Sheehan turned to Daria eagerly. "I'm suing the MBTA," she began, and launched into a meandering account of what sounded like six or seven years of legal maneuvering as she wheeled after them through the rooms.

"And suppose there's a fire?" Fay asked dramatically.

"How do you usually get down the steps?" Daria asked Mrs. Sheehan.

"When I have to go the doctor or to my lawyer, then usually Tom Silver comes over and carries me. He says it's easy."

Fay glanced at the kitchen clock. "That reminds me, we're running late. Take care."

"Sherry will be so sorry she missed you. She's at work. Sherry's a secretary in the uniform factory over on Brighton Avenue."

"Sherry supports her mother," Fay said quietly as they climbed the hill. "She can't even look for a better job out of the neighborhood, in case she has to get home in a hurry."

As they approached a big three-story yellow house near the park at the top of the hill, they saw Tom Silver sitting on the stoop. "It's locked," he said mournfully. "The Wongs aren't home and the workmen aren't here." In his pea coat and jeans sitting on the stoop, he looked like an overgrown boy without a key waiting for his mother to come home.

She peered at the house. While the grounds had been trampled and neglected, the house itself seemed handsome, well-built and in the midst of being remodeled. "What's wrong with this one?"

"Last July, this is where Bobbie Rosario died," Tom Silver said watching her carefully. "He lived on the third floor. That fire got the Rosarios out and now it's being renovated. By you."

"Aren't you glad we're fixing it up, if it is us, or my husband, anyhow? I thought you wanted things fixed up?" She stared at them and they stared back at her, each of them seeming equally puzzled by the other's response.

With Tom along she toured more sites of fire, including the fancy condominium she had parked in front of. Tom said there had been a fire there a year ago. They crossed Commonwealth and showed her two boarded-up buildings with visible signs of scorching. They took her by another that seemed empty, although she could see workmen busy inside. They dipped into another with violations. Her feet hurt and she carried around a dull ache in her vitals. Lately her stomach always seemed upset. She threw up as often as she had during her first pregnancy: with Robin, who had turned on her. She plodded along between Fay and Tom, feeling small between them, hemmed in. Fay turned and peered at her.

"It did smell bad in there, didn't it? It's the rats."

"Are you sick?" Tom Silver asked.

"It's fine," she said automatically but sat down on the cement step at the end of a front walk. She felt disoriented. She had no idea where she was or how to get home. Why had she come? It was a meaningless nightmare.

"You look green." He was looming over her. "It's pretty depressing, I guess, but isn't it interesting to find out where your money comes from?"

That snapped her back. She sat up straight on the stoop. "Don't be so moralistic with me. I know where my money comes from. I earn it. Whoever owns these buildings, and I wouldn't expect you pay enormous rents, that isn't what runs my household. Maybe my money is going into these buildings, although I can't imagine why. But I'm not getting anything from them, so don't dump on me like that."

"Adrenaline rush." Tom was grinning, although she could not see why. "Maybe you're just hungry. Did the two of you eat lunch?"

"I didn't even eat breakfast." She had, but she'd thrown it up after a brief unpleasant scene with Ross.

134

"Come on, I might as well make lunch for you."

"Me too?" asked Fay. "Or don't I rate? How come you're going to be nice to *her?*"

"I'm hungry. I have to eat before I go back to work anyhow."

"I don't think I can," Daria began, but she was moved along between them, Fay's hand on her elbow. It occurred to her that she was dreaming. Everything lately was a bad dream. But could a nightmare continue for months? Maybe she had been struck on the head and was lying in a hospital in a coma. None of this had happened. If only she made an effort, she could pierce this imitation grey sky and come to in her real life. She did not want to eat with these strangers. She wanted to be home, waking up to her life a year before. She felt dizzy. Maybe it was all the up- and downstairs, maybe it was throwing up breakfast, maybe it was the accumulated fatigue of sleepless nights bleeding into sleepless weeks. She had not the strength to break free of her captors. Passive, on the verge of tears, she let herself be dragged along. Would they poison her? She was being absurd. All they wanted was their buildings brought up to reasonable standards. Violations. The word suggested sexual pain. She felt violated by Ross's rejection.

Trundled up the steps into yet another frame house, she paid no attention until on the stairway she looked up in surprise to notice it was paneled and carpeted. There were two apartments, a downstairs duplex and Tom's flat on the third floor. "There doesn't seem to be anything wrong with this one," she said cautiously but hopefully. She had seen enough broken windows and dripping pipes to last her. "It seems well maintained."

"That's because you don't own it." Tom unlocked his door and stood aside for them.

"Yeah, he's his own landlord." Fay dumped her baggy green coat on his leather couch and dropped beside it with a deep sigh, massaging her calf.

"You own this?" The living room was as big as hers in Lexington with many windows, a lot of greenery, a red enamel Danish stove and a sleeping loft. The rugs were Native American work from the Southwest, desert colors.

"With the couple downstairs," he rumbled as if apologetically.

"You've done a lot of work on it," she offered. In fact he must have torn out almost all the walls.

"That's my job."

"Aaron Aardvark, of the carpentry collective. That's you?"

He stared at her. "Oh, the truck. You noticed." He seemed pleased. Among his plants and rather arty environment, he appeared less menacing. He was a big man, big boned, big shouldered with something of a belly and a slump that exaggerated it. His lids, usually half closed, gave his face a dark sleepy look. A grey cat leaned out of the sleeping loft, then came tumbling down, twisting around his jeaned ankles and boots into the kitchen.

"If you're a homeowner yourself, what are you doing in a tenants organization?" She raised her voice to be heard.

Fay put down on the coffee table the kachina doll she had been playing with. The table was made out of heavy handsome wood carved into an arc. "We're not a tenants organization. We're a neighborhood organization."

Tom peered around the doorway from the kitchen. "I put a lot of work into this house. I don't fancy being burned out when some torch sets fire to the wrong house one summer night, or when the wind gets a bit too brisk. I also don't fancy being the last house standing for five blocks."

"We roped him in." Fay wriggled back luxuriously on the couch. "He's an old war-horse. He knows how to do what we have to do."

"Yeah, sure." He groaned from the kitchen. "Drafted."

"You got nothing better to do," Fay called. "You were bored."

"I wasn't bored. I'm never bored."

"You and Superman. Never bored, never lonely, don't need nothing or nobody." Fay winked at Daria, startling her. "Just your stereo, your cat and a six-pack."

"You going to sit on your behind insulting me? Will you set the table, or should we just eat on the floor the way you do at home?"

She saw herself saying to Ross, "Oh, you'll never guess who I ate lunch with today."

"With Gretta," he'd say, sounding bored.

"Not this time," she'd say coyly.

136

"Your agent came through Boston." He sounded even more bored.

It was dreadful. Even in her fantasies, she had difficulty capturing his attention. Then she set off her firecracker. "No. With our tenants in SON." Then there it was in the room with them, his new temper like a fancy attack dog, like a big bright cadmium yellow Doberman, slavering and growling and crouching to leap for her throat. He was always slamming doors nowadays and indeed seemed to have forgotten how else to shut them. He was always hanging up the phone on her, storming out of the room. This morning he had thrown his breakfast coffee against the wall, mug and all, and stomped out grinning. Afterward she noticed it was *not* his favorite mug.

"What?" she asked and felt herself blushing. The strangers were staring again. Tom was standing with a platter in his hand beckoning them through an archway to a table Fay had set. Frowning, Fay exchanged glances with Tom.

"I'm sorry," Daria said. "What did I miss?"

"Depends on how long you been gone." Fay shook her head dolefully. "Honey, are you all there?"

She felt tears burning the back of her eyes. She could not sit and bawl before these people, it would be too humiliating. She was disintegrating. She could not even manage a polite social facade. "I'm terribly sorry. I didn't mean to be rude. I'm trying to deal with a number of problems, and sometimes they overwhelm me for a moment."

Fay looked her over carelessly. "What is it, water spots on your glasses? Ring around the collar? I bet you don't have rats and heat that goes out in every cold snap. Or wake up scared your house is on fire."

"What do you want?" Daria stood. "That I have cancer of the bowel, my daughter is dying of leukemia and I married a dope fiend? Anybody's problems are big as a mountain to you if they're yours. Today I'd change places with a leper with shingles."

Fay looked at herself in the shiny side of a coffee carafe and gave her hair a pat, wrinkled her nose. "I think our tour depressed the lady," she drawled.

"I think the lady was depressed before our tour. I think we should eat while my omelette's still warm." Tom beckoned them in.

"Where's the ketchup?" Fay bellowed.

"You ask for it only to drive me crazy. You want chocolate syrup for it as well?"

Daria had the sense of them as old friends with a set of routines designed to bang their differences against each other. Fay flirted some with Tom, probably out of habit. For a woman who was certainly fat, Fay had a frankly sexy manner, as if she had never doubted her own attractiveness.

"How is the omelette?" Tom asked her with a somewhat shamefaced air, as if he didn't want to ask but couldn't stop himself. This was a familiar situation.

"Very good."

"Honestly. How is it really?"

The truth was, she only then began to taste it. She who believed in savoring every mouthful and eating only what tasted fresh and right now spent little time in her kitchen and ate at odd hours food she might not be able to keep down. He had made a fine classic French omelette with fresh herbs he must grow inside, as she did. "It's delightful to have lunch made for me," she forced out. "I'm always cooking for everybody else. When I do eat somebody else's cooking, often it's a formal occasion and I'm serving as judge and can't enjoy."

He had made a green salad and put out a loaf of bakery rye bread and some cheeses. She stopped with the omelette and salad. Perhaps her stomach had shrunk or perhaps dieting had become habitual, although she scarcely ever remembered to weigh herself. She knew she had lost weight because she could wear everything in her closet and even the tightest pants fit. But she could take no pleasure in her thinner self, as held in contempt by Ross as her rounder self and not her idea to begin with. She had only dieted to please Ross, and nothing she did pleased him. How odd that Tom could cook; Ross found it exasperatingly difficult to heat a dinner she had precooked for him. Although she often met men at book signings who claimed to have used her cookbooks, no men in her family ever cooked.

Fay finished her omelette and then plunked her elbows down on the table. "What are you going to do about what we showed you?"

"I don't know," Daria said. "I have to find out what we own, first."

The lunch had been intended to bring her into bargaining, she thought, to relax her into concessions. They still thought she had some power.

"You could try asking your husband," Tom suggested.

"I could try."

"Why wouldn't he tell you?" Tom watched her narrowly.

"Perhaps he doesn't think it's any of my business. Up to now I've never interfered. He's not thrilled by my new curiosity."

Fay tapped her arm. "We can put some pressure on. We're thinking about coming back with our signs this weekend."

"I don't know if he'll be there. If it's only me, you don't get much mileage out of it."

Tom leaned back in his chair, his lids half lowered but under them his eyes were observing her like a cat watching a bird, she thought. "Where would he be?"

Daria simply shrugged.

"Are you going to play dumb with us?" Fay wagged her finger. "Where does he hide out? In his office?"

Daria shook her head. "He's been spending weekends on the north shore. A place called Hamilton. That's all I know. It's a little town between Prides Crossing and Ipswich. I found it on the map."

"You're married to the guy and you don't know more than that? Baloney." Fay was rummaging in her knitting bag.

"You don't know Hamilton?" Tom raised his thick eyebrows. "Princess Anne rode there I believe when she visited the States," he drawled with a put-on accent. "Horsy people. The right sort, you know."

"Rich people?" She tried to grasp the situation. Was he involved with some rich heiress? She could see her: blond, beautiful, dressed in a jodhpur outfit leaping her horse over a fence like the Olympic team she had watched on television. On the other hand, why would a rich heiress want Ross? A married forty-six-year-old real estate lawyer with two grown daughters?

"You could say that." Tom sat bolt upright. "Hey! What are you doing?" He was glaring at Fay.

Daria turned to look at Fay, surprised by his panic. Fay had lit a cigarette. As far as Daria could tell, it was an ordinary tobacco cigarette out of a True package.

"I forgot, I forgot. I'll take it on the porch." Fay shook her head at him, sauntering out through the kitchen door onto a porch.

Tom waved her out, fluttering the door to clear the air.

"You don't like smoke." She was glad to change the subject.

"I'm allergic." He made a face of apology and disgust.

"Really allergic?"

"Why do people always ask that about smoke? If you say you're allergic to ragweed or roses, nobody ever asks if you're lying." He was talking more softly now as if embarrassed.

"I don't like it—it gives me a headache when Ross has people over who smoke all evening—but I'm not allergic."

"If it gives you a headache, you're probably mildly allergic. Anyhow, I smoked for years and years, so it's worse for me."

"Then how did you get allergic?"

"I got chronic bronchitis. For two years I was damned sick. A lot of people who have to stop for medical reasons develop allergies."

"Maybe it's the body protecting itself."

"But it's a damned nuisance." He rubbed his dark hair. It was thick and glossy and black, moderately long, with a little sawdust caught in back. "I can't go to bars anymore. Most restaurants I can't go to. Most parties. And I'm always having to explain, explain, explain. I just can't deal with people who insist on smoking. And if you try to explain how you got this way, they don't want to hear it. It scares them. . . ." He glanced toward the kitchen door. "Fay's okay, she just forgets. . . . How come your husband disappears weekends and you don't know where he is?"

"How come you imagine it's any of your business?"

"We have to be detectives. If SON hadn't done . . . actually it was me and Sandra María. If we hadn't gone through a paper chase down in the Registry of Deeds, we'd never have figured out *who* owned those buildings."

Sandra María must be his girlfriend. The apartment was too neat for a man living alone, although she saw no signs of female presence. She said coolly, "I don't know if you've found out yet."

Tom looked at her, his eyes sleepy, skeptical, "You won't acknowledge yet that you own Fay's building?"

"No. It's too . . . unlikely." As he turned his head toward her when she spoke she noticed that in one earlobe he had a stud earring. She could not take her eyes off it.

"Because you think of yourself as a nice sweet liberal lady and not a slumlord?" The black eyes glinted anger under the heavy lids.

"I wouldn't call this any kind of slum," she snapped. "I don't know where you come from, but this seems like a perfectly decent neighborhood to me." She kept staring at the stud winking at her. Maybe he was gay; that would explain the cooking and the ear jewelry. "The house I grew up in was in worse shape than any of these."

"But I bet it didn't run any danger of burning down."

"Oh yeah? That's what happened to it." Mr. Know-it-all.

"Fancy that." Tom grinned. He had a big flashing grin but this time without warmth. "How your buildings do burn."

"Boston's built of wood. Wood burns."

Fay came in shivering theatrically. "Cold out there."

"Our lady of injured innocence is asking about fires. She noticed we have lots."

"There's violations of the building code everyplace. You saw the conditions in those basements," Fay rapped out.

"Fay and Mac still think fires happen. I say it's statistically improbable. In the past four years we've had far more fires per block than areas just as old."

"Don't get him started on his conspiracy rap." Fay pointed her finger at him. "He's one of those types who know just how to organize a picket and dig up the facts of who owns what, but they all grew up on Kennedy Comix and they think everything's a plot. It's the CIA, right, sweetie?"

The grey cat after long contemplation landed precipitously in Daria's lap. Its fur felt like plush. "This cat is gorgeous."

"You can laugh till you get burned out too," Tom was saying when he turned to investigate the motion that had caught his eye. "Look at the tramp come on to her. He doesn't care how many buildings you own, he likes the way you smell."

She stroked the grey velvet. "He knows a soft touch. He looks like a very special cat."

"Russian Blue. Scheduled to be offed because his eye color is wrong. I had to sign an oath to have him altered—an oath! I was putting it off, the way I do things, and then one night, I dreamed this society to protect the racial purity of Russian Blues was after me."

"Were they going to alter you?" Fay asked archly.

"That was the idea. So I got up and made the appointment with the vet."

"Wouldn't you like a coat made of this?" Fay played with the cat's tail.

"A bed," Daria said without thinking and felt herself blush.

"His name is Marcus and he doesn't want to be your coat or your bed, although he looks like he'd probably sleep with you. . . . Did you take her to the row where Sandra María lives?"

"Not yet—" Fay began.

Daria interrupted. "I've got to get going." She stood with Marcus still holding on. The light seemed to gather on the tips of his fur. She noticed a carrying case near the door. "Do you take him to work?" She determined to make her escape before Fay made her hike through another twenty basements.

"That's in case of fire. You learn that a lot around here is in case of fire."

"Will you tell us the truth about whether your husband is home next weekend?" Fay scowled with indecision.

"Call me Friday evening. I'll know by then. If he's home, picket to your heart's content. Maybe he'll finally talk to me about what all these buildings mean. Call in on my number, though. I'll give it to you. Here."

"Separate phones? That's weird." Fay preceded her down the stairs.

"I get a lot of business calls. He didn't like answering the phone and having it be for me."

"Just like a man. My ex, he pulled the phone out of the wall one day just because he got mad at my mother. She used to call around dinnertime—that's when we both got off work. One night I burned a pie talking to her, and that did it. Pow, right out of the wall."

She had an urge to tell Fay about the morning's scene, still raw in her. She had never been really involved with any other man. Maybe all husbands acted in irrational rage sometimes. "Did he often lose his temper?"

"Only when he'd been drinking. Then after the electronics plant shut down, he didn't have to drink to get mean."

142

She wanted to ask what happened then, but she did not dare—not because it was not polite to ask personal questions, but because she did not want to hear tales about broken marriages. Broken like a leg, but a leg could be set and healed; it was only horses who were shot then. Failed marriage, like a failed exam. A twenty-two-year course of study and at the end you didn't pass.

She realized she had waved good-bye to Fay and started off in a random direction, for she had no idea where Tom lived relative to where she had parked. She had to turn and run after Fay, who was waddling briskly downhill. "Fay! Fay! I don't know where we are."

Fay looked her over again, shaking her head. "You're spaced. Do you take downers?"

"Nothing. No."

Fay patted her shoulder as if she had just come to a decision. "I guess this is all new to you. It took guts for you to come here and let us push you around. Listen, I'll talk to the guys about holding off till you tell us if your old man is going to be around next weekend. Nobody likes to picket anyhow except Mac. He gets off on it. Thinks he's a general. But the rest of us feel like horses' asses. Now where did you park near?" Fay led her off.

Secure in her Rabbit again, Daria leaned out. "Just call on my phone, remember. I'll tell you the truth, I promise. Till Friday." She headed for home.

11

"So I have no idea at all what's going to happen to us. To me," she said to Tracy, trying to make her voice sound calm. "It just seems to get worse between your father and me."

"I'll be home in just ten days for Christmas vacation, Mama. Just hold on. We can all try to talk to him."

"Your sister is on his side." She told Tracy the story.

"Robin is a suck and a wimp," Tracy said in disgust.

"Don't turn this into a battle between you and Robin. Please. Maybe you can help. I'm feeling very alone. I'm not doing too well, Tracy, I'm not."

"Of course you're miserable. I'm devastated when some guy I only went out with for two weeks drops me. I completely understand, Mama, really. You have a right to be unhappy!" Tracy sounded brave.

Turning to her eighteen-year-old for comfort felt wicked, but she could not resist seeking support, for her need to feel loved by at least one daughter was too great. When she got off the phone to let Tracy attend her nine o'clock class, she was sobbing. When Peggy arrived, she had not got control of herself. Therefore she gave Peggy an account of her troubles too.

"I thought something fishy was going on, Daria." Peggy nodded her sleek black cap of hair. "I thought that ever since I walked in and saw that big pile of dog-do and nobody seemed to know where Mr. Walker was hanging out." Peggy was a tall big-framed woman who looked stunning dressed up, but who moved much of the time like someone who was afraid she might break china with her elbows.

In the day's mail, her agent Laura returned the pictures with a brief note:

I know you like to use your hubby's photos, but these are simply dreadful and will not do. Call me Monday and we'll let your editor set up an appointment with whoever they're using.

She called Laura at once. "But what's wrong with them?" she asked cautiously.

"Daria, I know you adore your husband, et cetera, et cetera, and you've always made us use his less than professional quality shots. But these look like the mug shots of a bag lady. I showed them to your editor and she was rather sarcastic."

"I don't look like that?"

"Daria, are you kidding?" Laura's rich laugh broke out.

"I thought the camera never lied."

"Oh, come on, sometimes you like to play naive. With a camera you can make Attila the Hun look like Albert Schweitzer and vice versa. You put those shots on the back of a cookbook and everybody will think your food will make them sick. I saw some of the video while you were on tour, and you looked just fine. What's the problem?"

The problem was that she now feared the camera. It would catch her misery in its box. She put off Laura by promising to find a clear date and call her back.

They did little work that day. Mostly Peggy and Daria drank coffee and fiddled around with the manuscript, talking about relationships. Peggy had been married but she was back at home with her mother because her ex had skipped the state and run out on his child support. Peggy's family lived in East Lexington near the Arlington line in a rambling grey house. Plenty of room for Peggy and her son Eric, but she found it difficult to return from independence, marriage, her own apartment to an enforced adolescence.

"Why not confront this bitch?" Peggy asked. "What's to lose?"

"I couldn't!" Daria thought about it. "Maybe I could. But I don't even know her name. Just Gail."

"You know where she lives."

"It's a huge building."

"You followed him once. You even know where he eats lunch every Thursday from the American Express tabs—Frankie's." Peggy sat up, her blue eyes glittering with mischief. "We'll both go. We'll do it this Thursday. We'll put on some getup and be on the spot before he arrives. We'll scout out the restaurant and find some dark corner."

"Would you, Peggy?"

"It beats typing. Sure, you buy me lunch. I want to see who's the bitch he's cheating on you with."

"We'll do it."

Daria had been the calm one, the one who held her friends' hands, who saw them through their troubles, who listened, who nodded, who made tea and gave sage advice. In the last couple of months she had withdrawn from almost everyone, but now she could not survive alone. She found herself confiding in Gretta, in Tracy, in Peggy and now in Annette finally, sitting in her sunny maple paneled blue and white tile kitchen. She noticed as she talked that she was most forthcoming, most truthful with Gretta and Peggy. Tracy and Annette she fed a censored version which did not feature her steaming open of the letters, her inventory of their charge accounts, her morning of surveillance. She told Peggy and Gretta the more sordid details, because they were divorced. They had endured the splitting of their world, the sundering of the whole that had composed their lives.

Annette clucked and comforted. "Pierre had an affair. I never told you. . . . Do you remember the Archibalds?"

"The Archibalds? Her? But she's six feet tall."

"Pierre is six four. What I'm trying to say is that it isn't the end of the world. Affairs are transitory things. Men like to prove themselves, but they get bored. You can make a small thing into a large one by fighting too hard. My advice to you is, keep your mouth shut. Don't let him provoke you into fights. When it's all over, you'll still be there."

She wanted to take Annette's advice, but found it hard to follow. Since the fight when Gail's name had been mentioned, Ross had taken to spending many evenings out. Although he would scrupulously have Lorraine inform Daria by four o'clock if he planned to miss supper, she never knew whether he would walk in at nine, eleven or not at all till the next day. She started at every sound, sitting up well past midnight in case he did appear.

The house felt huge around her. Torte hated Ross staying out as much as she did. He would not give up and come to her bed but waited in Ross's room. If the door was shut, he would whimper till she opened it for him. In the middle of the night she could hear him making disconsolate noises across the stairwell, dragging himself up- and downstairs looking for his master.

Perhaps Ross was right and the house was too big. She had never felt that before. The house had always been overflowing with the children, their friends, Ross and his business associates, her friends, Cesaro's family, Tony's family, Gussie's kids. She lay in her bed wrapped in the birthday shawl to keep her shoulders warm with the kittens curled with her. They welcomed her into their litter, purring against her thighs, stalking her fingers drumming on the counterpane. She felt vulnerable in the house. She could feel all the doors, the windows as potential dangers. If she dozed off, she imagined heavy footsteps approaching. It seemed to her anyone could break into the house at will. Its vast emptiness frightened and reproached her.

Wednesday night Ross had invited the couple of the endless cocktails and rubberized scallops; she could not imagine why. He surely did not intend to initiate an endless series of dinners, so why return their invitation? He had also asked his partner Roger Kingsley and wife Barbara. Perhaps spending so much time with his girlfriend was wearing that affair too hard; perhaps Annette was right and it would end soon. Yet she felt as if Barbara knew something and was avoiding her gaze, as if Barbara felt embarrassed by her, bad omen of married women, scarecrow in the marital fields hanging on display in her somewhat loose finery of past years.

The evening ran very late. Without explanation, without preamble Ross followed her upstairs and into the room that had been theirs and was now hers alone. He climbed into bed with her as if this were any old night the previous spring. He did not initiate sex, but he gave her a brief kiss as he turned out the lights. "That spinach pasta you started with, that was excellent," he said ruminatively. "When they call next time, make an excuse."

She could not sleep. Tomorrow she was going to see the woman he had been preferring to her. In magazines, on television, across restaurants where she lunched with Gretta in Harvard Square, she kept seeing women who became the Gail of the day. Usually she saw Gail as tall, blond, impeccably dressed with the sculptured cheekbones of a model. Sometimes her hair was artfully curled; sometimes it was a brief Sassoon cap; sometimes it was long and flaxen, straight and fine as shot silk to the slender shoulders. Once Gail was a voluptuous brunette in a silver taffeta dress and mink stole Ross ogled, who inhabited a Ford commercial. Once Gail was a redhead hailing a cab in Harvard Square, wearing a mauve suit and carrying a lizard skin attaché case.

In the morning Daria avoided the mirror. She brushed her hair without looking. She felt ashamed. Something was wrong with her: middle age, and that meant she was ready to be traded in, a discard. He preferred to hers a body that had no stretch marks, no belly too rounded, no breasts that sagged in their fullness. Everything would be hard and firm as a mannequin, seamless with no hint of use or time or will of its own.

Peggy made her wear a peculiar black hat that concealed her hair and Peggy's mother's old sealskin coat. Peggy herself wore a blond wig. Frankie's was a dim oak-paneled high-ceilinged room that was a restaurant at mealtimes and a bar in between. They arrived just after it had opened at eleven forty-five and asked for a booth far at the back. "I'm allergic to cigarette smoke," she explained to the waiter, thinking of Tom Silver. Unfortunately American Express bills did not include information on time of day, so they might be in for a very leisurely lunch. "Eat slowly," she admonished Peggy. "They could come in at two."

She had no trouble taking her own time on the food. She had to chew and chew each mouthful before swallowing it. She did not think they were likely to be conspicuous in their booth. The main thing was to keep an eye on the door.

A little after twelve-thirty, she caught sight of him as he was crossing the room in the direction of several occupied tables. She scanned them fast. Couple, two men, three women, couple, a woman alone. Not that one, she felt instinctively. Her eyes travelled the range of tables before him, the booths against the wall. But when she glanced back, he had already seated himself with the woman she had dismissed as a possibility.

After that she did not try to eat. She stared at them, looked away, stared at them, looked away. She was afraid they must feel the pressure of her gaze. Even sitting, the woman looked gaunt. She was brown-haired, angled awkwardly forward as she tugged nervously at her cardigan and then chain-lit a cigarette off the butt in the ashtray. Her hair was nondescript, falling down straight all the way around just below her chin line, a lighter brown than Daria's. She looked about thirty. Thin she certainly was but did not in any other way resemble the radiant model of Daria's fantasies. She was very, very plain.

Peggy watched too, turning to crane over her shoulder. "I'm going to the john the long way. They'll never notice me. I'm going to get a closer look."

"She could be a client."

Just as Daria spoke, Ross leaned forward and took the woman's hand. They were strained forward over the table, talking fast and earnestly. That had to be Gail. She stared at them both in profile, angled over the tabletop making a bridge that almost met. Martinis arrived. Ross was doing most of the talking, trying to argue Gail into or out of something. She recognized the pose, the occasional flat hand gesture, the expression of intense concentration as if moving a mountain with a teaspoon.

"Well!" Peggy bounced onto her seat in the booth. "Maybe she's a great lay."

"I like sex perfectly well," Daria said defensively.

"Maybe she sucks him off all the time. If you don't like sex, sometimes it's easier to please a man. I mean, she's not exactly a raging beauty."

"Look at them, Peggy. They're lovers, check?"

Peggy glanced over her shoulder again. "Check. I'll tell you one thing. Her clothes may not look glamorous, but they're bucks. Tweedy, country, but heavy bucks. Thick cashmere. Harris Tweed, designer silk blouse. She's wearing about fourteen layers, so she must have blood of ice water."

Ross left first. The woman sat finishing her last cigarette. Ross and Gail seemed to observe some strange propriety about not arriving or leaving together. Then Daria, who had already paid the bill—in cash—walked out slowly, detouring past the table where Gail was just picking up her shoulder bag and a package bound in twine. Daria thought her gaze rested on the woman's face only for a moment but when she walked out into the air and let Peggy lead her away, she could see every feature etched vividly as if outlined in white light.

The face was long, ending in a chin that came almost to a point. The mouth was wide but the lips were thin, as if drawn with pencil. The eyes were wide in the narrow face, but Daria had not been able to tell their color. The hair was thin and fine, flyaway, of a light undefinable brown. The skin was a little leathery for her probable age, the skin of someone who was outdoors a great deal and whose naturally fair complexion was toughened by the sun as by the cold and the wind. Her hands were those of an overgrown child, with nails bitten, with stains of tobacco and something red. On the table among the cups and cutlery they crept over each other like albino grasshoppers. She had looked nervous sitting at the table alone, as if suddenly exposed. Her shoulders hunched, her head bowed, she did not look up as Daria drifted slowly past.

Daria clutched Peggy's arm and drew her toward a building as if looking into a gallery window full of gaudy sharp-edge paintings. She could not leave. She had to know more. "What are you going to do now?" Peggy asked.

"Follow her. I still know nothing about her. Nothing."

"Here she comes," Peggy hissed.

Daria kept her eyes fixed on the window. Superimposed on the jagged planes of the painting before her, Gail appeared stalking with a bobbing stride like a heron across the glass. Mechanically Daria turned, dragging Peggy after her. "She's just going back home," Peggy said. "You said she lives on Beacon."

Daria still followed, hungry for any information, staring at the narrow back in a camel's hair coat worn loose and long over a tweed jacket and a straight skirt. Gail had forgotten to tie the belt. One end dangled. Daria had an absurd urge to run up and catch hold of it, tripping the woman.

But Gail did not go home. Instead she turned on Marlborough and walked with her loose half-loping stride up the block and then glancing at her watch ducked into the doorway of a brick row house. As Peggy and Daria walked by, Gail was pressing a buzzer and the door was being buzzed back for her. A row of doctor's signs identified her goal as they watched her disappear into a door just off the front foyer.

"Let's hope it's not an obstetrician," Peggy said. Daria seemed rooted to the sidewalk, so Peggy strolled over to read the signs. "Either she's got eye trouble or she's seeing a shrink. You've got two shrinks in there and only one eye doctor, so the odds are on the shrink." Peggy steered Daria back toward her car.

Peggy drove the Rabbit back to Lexington while Daria sat hunched over—as Gail had in the restaurant at the end—unable to keep from asking repeatedly, "But why her? Who is she? She must be brilliant. She's probably an incredibly brilliant lawyer."

"I don't know." Peggy shrugged. "Looks more like the type that maybe would hang out in the library. Like some academic?"

"No. She spends too much time outside. . . . Maybe she's an athlete?"

"Chain smoking? Naw. She didn't look that healthy."

What famous Gails were there? The woman could be a writer. She did not have the presence of an actress or a singer, but she could be a composer. A painter. She could be a landscape painter. Or a sculptor, that would explain the battered hands.

She had seen her rival, her nemesis, and felt more confused than before. The affair must be serious. Gail did not appear someone capable of a brief happy fling. Rather she had looked mortally serious. What had Ross been trying to talk Gail into or out of? Daria supposed she would, unfortunately, find out. She would find out by having it land on her.

Remembering the peignoir set in Small, Daria realized that it would probably go on Gail without any trouble, for Gail was certainly thin enough, but Daria could not help feeling the result would be more comical than sensual. Certainly that gown would be short on her; but what Daria realized was that Ross certainly perceived Gail as small: in need of protection, perhaps, helpless, perhaps. As once he had perceived Daria.

Wait and see what happens, Annette said: wait and see what supposedly sound structural beam cracks next, what wall collapses inward. That made her think of the expectant tenants in Allston. I can't begin to help them, she thought, clutching herself tight as if freezing. I can't even save myself.

She could not take Annette's soothing advice. Her surveillance was crude, bizarre, undignified, unethical and must continue. She felt too helpless in her ignorance, too close to going mad. Her life was torn open and her marriage woven of lies. She doubted how well she knew the man she called her husband. The truth of her life, the truth of her marriage, that was the only medicine that could help her. She could not bow her head and wait for this misery to pass. She had to understand it. To survive it, she must understand.

12

FRIDAY Lorraine called to say Ross would not be home for supper; in fact he was called away on business for the weekend. Lorraine had become quite accustomed to delivering these messages in a perky upbeat tone, one that reminded Darla of the false cheer nurses often display among the sick and dying. It was a cheer designed not so much for the benefit of those in pain as for the benefit of those who did not wish to share that pain by contagion.

At seven Tom Silver called. "Did I interrupt your supper?"

By the mock solicitude in his voice, she recognized he hoped that he had. Her life, she thought, had become too complicated. She had forgotten Monday's promise to the tenants. "I'm not eating supper tonight. Ross won't be home this weekend."

"Oh? Are you sure?"

"That's what I was told."

"That's an odd way to put it."

"I've given you exactly as much as I know. I'm telling the truth."

"Where is he? Hamilton?"

"Your guess is worth as much as mine."

"You won't admit it's a little peculiar? It's seven P.M. Do you know where your husband is?"

"I won't admit it's any of your business." She slammed down the phone.

He had stirred up a roil of emotions. She paced hugging herself and muttering, "Damn nosy beast bastard." Daria seldom swore. At the moment she could not figure out if she was angrier with Ross or Tom Silver. Ross of course hurt her far more, but Tom Silver was a convenient lightning rod. These SON people were proving to be a damned nuisance, not at all appreciative of how she had tried to come halfway to meet them. Now they were going to make all kinds of impossible demands, another case of the powerless persecuting the powerless. She should have just let them shuffle around in the street.

She was still pacing the hall muttering while the cats watched from the stairs and Torte whined nervously when her phone rang again.

"Uh, it's me," Tom Silver said, rumbling and sheepish. "I want to apologize."

"Why pretend you aren't hostile, when you are?"

"Look, you're in an ambiguous position, Daria."

She felt a pang of annoyance at his using her first name; but then she thought of Fay Souza as Fay. She could hardly object. "Ambiguous, is it?"

"You're somehow caught in the cross fire. Most wives in your position would be in the confidence of their piggy landlord husbands. Either you're the best amateur actress I've ever met, or you really don't know what's going on."

"Be generous. Just assume I'm an idiot."

"Shit, Daria, you're acting like one. You've made a big decision to be innocent. Totally innocent. What kind of luxury is that? No adult is as innocent as you make yourself out to be."

"And nobody's as morally superior as you make yourself out to be!"

"Um." A longish pause hung there.

Why was she talking to him? Because she was miserable. Because she was lonely. Because sparring with him was better than staring at the walls while asking herself again and again what had gone wrong, what had changed Ross. All the spiky questions that made her bleed. Where was Ross? What was he doing right now? What was he saying to that nervous angular woman, seizing her hand avidly?

"If I'm coming down on you hard, it's because we had another fire, just two doors down from Fay on Wednesday night. . . . Let me ask you a question. What on earth did you think when the dead rat arrived? Did you think it was a gift from an admirer? Something to cook?"

"What dead rat? Have you done something disgusting like putting a dead rat on my doorstep?"

"Back in October, Fay mailed Walker a dead rat from her basement. To your home address. This happens so often it slipped your mind?"

"Nothing of that sort . . . Wait. He did get a package that smelled funny. I'm trying to remember. Before my mother died, I know . . ."

"When did your mother die?"

"The Sunday before Thanksgiving."

"Maybe that's why you seem not all there. It's so recent."

"Gee thanks. You're a warm and comforting man. Heart as big as a pinhead."

"Actually I do sympathize. I lost my mother a year ago August and I'm not used to it yet."

"How did she die?"

"Drowning."

"That's terrible. An accident?"

"She drowned in the lake she swam in every August for fifteen years. She used to swim across the lake every morning right after she got up. Every August since I was little they rented that place. A week later and I would have been there, with her. They said she must have had a heart attack." His voice thickened and he stopped.

"Were you close to her?" Partly she asked because she was curious. Tom did not readily remind her of any of Ross's friends. He was a new type to her. But partly she inveigled him into the personal to turn the conversation off her situation, the question of where Ross was and why she didn't know.

"When I was growing up. Then we fought a lot. Everything I did was wrong to them. Then after my girls were born, we made up."

"You were married?"

"Yeah. When this house was a commune, my wife Andrea and the kids lived here. Now it's just me and the Becks who are still downstairs."

"Do you ever see your daughters?" She felt as if she were questioning the ghost of Ross departed, Christmas Future. Do you ever see your daughters, do you care any longer, do you ever think of your ex-wife?

"When I can afford to. They live in California. I have them every August." He cleared his throat. "How did we get into all this? You don't remember a package arriving in October with a dead rat in it?"

"Actually on my birthday, a package came that smelled funny. Ross said it was a gift from a client, cheese that had gone bad."

"Why do you suppose he didn't tell you the truth, Daria?"

"Don't practice being a detective on me. What I suppose isn't worth much."

"What's going on with you and your husband?"

"A marriage. You had one of your own, right? Good night."

"That's a sore spot, isn't it? All alone on the weekend."

"Oh, shut up." She hung up on him again. He did not call back.

She forced herself to work, for she was falling seriously behind schedule on her book. The *Globe* had made her rewrite her Easter feast piece three times because it had not sounded festive enough, her editor said. It was the first piece in a year they had made her rewrite. The problem was that she had had no Thanksgiving and she was not at all sure she was going to have a Christmas. She had to make one for the girls, but she did not feel close to Robin. They had not talked alone since that phone call. Robin had stopped turning up every Saturday and Sunday to run with Ross, knowing that Ross was seldom to be found in Lexington. But Daria must still make a nice holiday for Tracy and for her family. Christmas was a time when her clan always got together, the siblings still around Boston.

Normally she shopped early and then near the holiday bought last-minute edibles and stocking stuffers. Daria loved holidays and feasts. Since childhood, she had thrown herself into buying presents for people she loved. Then she had had so little to spend that every individual dollar represented a tough choice to ponder, to stretch out for all her siblings, parents, grandma, Pops' parents, her aunts and uncles. She had kept a funny superstition as a child: she believed she must spend every cent she had saved during the year on presents or she would be unlucky in the New Year.

Sometimes Ross accused her of carrying that superstition into her adult

156

life. Certainly she believed in more gifts than he did, and besides she could lose herself in locating the perfect sweater to go with Peggy's black hair and blue eyes and then wrapping it so that it would be a surprise. If Daria dreaded going into department stores to clothe herself, she endured the crowds willingly when shopping for others. For one thing, she need not take off and put on her clothes eight times to buy a shirt for Ross.

She brooded about Ross, she brooded about Christmas, she brooded about the angular brown-haired woman she had seen in the restaurant. She must work: she must stop worrying and work, now above all. She did not let herself finish the thought about why now was especially important, but tried to force herself along. She recognized that the creation and modification of recipes and the figuring out of how to describe each process clearly as a cheerful little soprano aria had always had as a base drone love for her family. This is how I cook, I Daria who love my husband Ross, who love my girls Robin and Tracy; this is how I feed them and keep them strong and happy. This gives pleasure.

That foundation had been attacked. Now her work must stand alone. She was not convinced it could, but it must. She had no other way to earn a living. This was a poor time to try to return to the school system, with ten thousand teachers unemployed in the Greater Boston area.

Innocent, that hulking sadist had called her, innocent as if that were an insult. Maybe at her age it was an insult. Was innocent the opposite of guilty or the opposite of wise?

By four on Saturday she had been successfully working for several hours, without the speed of former times but with some pages and sketches to show for her time. She was firm enough in her concentration so that several minutes passed before she realized that someone was upstairs in the house.

Standing rigid behind the door of her office, she wondered if it was a burglar and if she should try to escape. But the person was making no attempt to be quiet, talking to himself. It was just growing dark. She crossed the hall and yanked open her bedroom door. "Ross! I wasn't expecting you. I mean, I'm glad . . ."

"What do we use for antiseptic?"

"What happened to your hand?"

"A dog bit me. Stupid beast almost took my hand off!"

"We should take you to Dr. Valentin. Oh, it's Saturday. The emergency room at Symmes."

"I don't need stitches. It just hurts like hell. Where is the damned antiseptic?" His hand had stopped bleeding, but blood was smeared over his blue shirt and a suede jacket that she did not think she had ever seen before.

"Let's wash it out with alcohol. I'll scrub it. Then I'll put Merthiolate on, if you like."

He had been bitten across the fleshy palm of his right hand. Two canines had penetrated the skin on the back of his hand and one on his palm side. He bellowed and writhed as she washed the puncture wounds with soapy water and then alcohol. All the wounds began bleeding again as she cleaned them out.

"What happened? Whose dog was it?"

"I was just minding my own business and the damned thing jumped me."

Gail must have a dog. Lately whenever Ross came in, Torte crawled laboriously over his jacket and pants to sniff them, making soft growly noises under his breath. Daria could not help being amused by Ross's plight but she also could not help worrying; for twenty-two years, that had been her habit. "Ross, I think we ought to go in and have it looked at. A dog bite is potentially dangerous. Could the dog have had rabies?"

"Rabies! Just a damned spoiled brat."

"You do know the dog, then. You should have it tested."

"Lay off the rabies. There's nothing wrong with that mutt a good swift kick across the street wouldn't cure."

"What kind of dog was it?"

"German short-haired pointer. What difference does that make?"

"This may sting." She intentionally used the word her dentist favored when he was about to light up her nervous system like a neon sign.

"Yow!" Ross jerked away.

"Darling, I have to get Merthiolate into the wounds. You don't want them infected. That's your right hand."

"Okay, get it over with." He held out his hand and yelped again as she worked on each wound.

She did her nurse's job carefully, with a pleasant tinge of sadism. When she had finished, she wrapped the hand in a loose gauze bandage. "I'd still feel a lot better if a doctor looked at it. You might need antibiotics. Why don't I drive you to Symmes?"

"Thanks." He patted her behind with his left hand. "Let's see what it's like tomorrow. If it's not better, you can drive me over to the hospital. How's that?"

Apparently he was now spending the weekend with her. She could not help wondering exactly what had happened with Gail and her dog; she could not resist hoping this turn of events signalled a change. After creeping up on the idea with great stealth, she ascertained he was staying for supper. She drove off at once to see Leo, her butcher.

His shop was uncrowded, for it was late on Saturday afternoon. Leo was cool with her. No big hello, no warm greeting, no flirtatious sallies. She had not been buying her usual quota, although she hastened to tell Leo she had been travelling a great deal. She wasn't going to feed Ross leftovers and she had defrosted nothing. This should be special.

"Come on, Leo," she coaxed him. "I want something first-rate. Let me look at the noisette of lamb. . . . Or what have you in the way of veal? That's the stuff, Leo. Right. I knew you could come through for me. . . . You know, I may be doing a television spot regularly soon. We have to talk about that. . . ."

He was beaming like a lottery winner. Now she was Ducky again. The veal was fine and pale.

Ross went downstairs to bring up a bottle of the Montrose. For once he seemed the man she loved, ready to eat a good supper and relish it, instead of behaving as if all food had become a plot to fatten him. Ready to share with her pleasure and conversation, ready to offer companionship. This night was a reprieve and as she went dashing about making ready, making pretty, she was determined to exploit the opportunity. She did not want to spend two hours in the kitchen that could be spent with him, so the meal she was putting together required skill and precision rather than extended labor.

Veal marsala, the lemon rice with a chicken base and Parmesan added right at the end, the spinach just wilted with olive oil and touched with garlic: the whole meal took exactly twenty-three extremely busy minutes. Her choreography was exacting but satisfying. Twenty-five minutes later the meal was all on the table and the only flurry was in setting that table in the last minute available.

She sat down and smiled at him, pleased by her own art. In a way seeing him across the table from her in their dining room was a measure of how much had deteriorated between them, that this little ceremony of food and wine should be of a fragile extraordinary character, when formerly this face-to-face leisurely duet over food eaten slowly and savored had been their norm.

She squirmed mentally, trying to stroke the moment with neutral and amiable subjects. She could not discuss anything pressing on her brain, which felt coagulated. She chatted about her cookbook; she questioned him about his work, but he was no more forthcoming on that than usual. She mentioned Torte's increasing stiffness. She recounted anecdotes from her last several phone calls with Tracy. She described the titmouse that had visited the birdfeeder. She made fun of Annette's new layered hairdo.

It was disorienting. Was she making conversation with some unsuitable stranger Ross had brought home to impress with a fancy supper? The man across the table was the man around whom her life had revolved since late adolescence. Once there had never been enough hours in the day to communicate all the observations they had to share.

After supper he watched the remainder of the seven o'clock news on NBC, which he had taken to watching after Walter Cronkite retired. When she was home alone, she watched Dan Rather. "Would you like dessert?" She knew what she wanted badly; she wanted him to turn and smile at her, seeing her.

His eyes on the screen he mused, "How about that apple thing?"

"Apple pie? An apple tart?"

"Not exactly a tart. It had slices of fruit on top. With Calvados."

She noticed that he was pronouncing that word differently than he had used to, as if it was Spanish, Calvádos—a habit picked up from Gail Dogbite? "Clafouti, do you mean?"

"Sounds likely. You used to make that in the big orange skillet?"

She did not point out that it was silly to make a clafouti for two, as she would have baked a wedding cake for two tonight, to prolong the charmed moments. Were they recommencing? Was Annette right? While he watched the news, she made dessert, put it in the oven and rushed back just as he shut off the set. In the hall mirror she saw herself, face flushed, a far more vibrant woman.

It was ridiculous to be surprised that conversation went a little bumpily: the important thing was they were together and trying. She was determined to make more real contact now. "Ross, those tenants in that group—SON?—have they been bothering you for a long time?"

He snorted. "You could say so. Indeedy! The little bastards."

"When I met with them that time, they said something about a dead rat?"

"Who? Who mentioned it?"

"I don't remember. I don't know their names." She was not sure why she covered for Fay. It was instinct: not to snitch.

"Try to remember. One of the guys, right? That Black queer?"

"I don't think so. I'm sorry, Ross, I don't remember."

"I'd like to take those losers and wring their necks." His face was animated, as if she had pushed a button and brought him fully to life. He sat upright in his chair, his foot tapping as if to march music. His eyes glowed fiercely blue. His cheeks were full of color.

"They really did that? Mailed a rat?"

"They're bloody pests, believe me. I'm sorry you had to see them." He sounded more sympathetic with her than he had in weeks.

This was the wrong time to tell him about visiting Fay. "They weren't so bad, honey, really. I do think they can be talked to, face-to-face."

"They got into my office once. Lorraine has orders to keep them out. Don't you see them again, I mean it. It's a mistake to talk to troublemakers unless you have your lawyer present."

"Are you my lawyer?" She laughed, trying to keep everything light. "I wonder if it was the same group who came to your office? What do you know about these people anyway?"

"There's a bunch of them. Some are welfare freeloaders, like that fat whore Fay Souza."

She noticed the coarseness of his language, both the political and the sexual insult. That he would use such terms startled her. She stared but he was past noticing.

"Then the real force behind them. Sixties-type commies. Ogilvie, with his Harvard connections."

"Harvard?"

"He's writing his thesis on the damned neighborhood. Nowadays education is a joke. They write theses on feces." He spoke as if it were an old and favorite joke. She had the feeling he had said that about Mac Ogilvie before.

"There was one . . . Tom Silver?"

"That aging hippie. He doesn't even have the excuse of being a tenant. Just a professional agitator. He goes around giving interviews to the local rags about fires, as if it isn't tenants' carelessness that causes us all a lot of trouble."

"He did talk about fires. He seemed terrified."

"What did he say? *Exactly*." Ross turned a hard gaze on her.

"Nothing specific I remember. . . . Oh, about a little boy who had been killed in a building they said we owned."

"Their parents don't take care of them anyhow. They breed like the rats their dirt attracts."

"Ross, how did we ever happen to get stuck with those buildings anyhow?"

"Stuck? Not on your life. I'll get those losers out, don't fret. I'm working on it."

"Working on what?"

"You don't understand development. Gentrification is in the cards. That land is golden. It's just that the economy has been sluggish. It's taken longer to turn than it should. But we're right on the verge there. We're merely weathering a temporary setback."

"But if you're waiting for the neighborhood to improve, wouldn't it pay to keep up the buildings?" See, she addressed Fay, I'm trying. She was pleased by their communication, even though she was startled to find how conservative he was growing. But a husband and wife could disagree politically and still love each other. Nina's father the anarchist had

162

dearly loved his pious Catholic wife. At least they were talking about something real together.

"You don't understand real estate, Daria, and there's no reason for you to bother yourself about it now—"

"But I want to learn. I want to share decisions and worries with you. You've been carrying too big a burden. I mean to understand your work now."

"It's never concerned you before." He waved his hand. "No reason for you to be troubled now. In fact, Daria, I'm going to move those buildings out of your name. You can stop fretting about them." He opened the attaché case leaning against his chair and brought out a pile of deeds. "Sign where Lorraine has indicated a penciled X in the margins and you can stop fussing about buildings altogether."

Slowly she fanned through. "I'll check the clafouti and be right back. And I'll turn on the espresso machine." Why was she reluctant to sign? She was not sure.

She drifted back to the living room. "Maybe fifteen minutes. . . . Ross, Christmas is coming very soon."

"Every year," he said with mock cheer. "Comes around every damn year just about this time. You can count on it."

"I'd like to count on it. It means a lot to the girls—a real family Christmas."

"Oh. You too," he muttered and did not elucidate. Gingerly he touched his bandage.

"I want to know whether you're going to be here at Christmas. If you're not, I want to know now. I want a firm commitment from you. Or if you won't, I want to know in time to make other plans."

"What other plans? Go to Florida?"

He'd like that and probably sell the house while she was gone. "I thought I'd have some of my family up here, for a white Christmas." She was bluffing; Christmas was a busy season at the Blue Lobster.

He stared at the fireplace. There had not been a fire in it for weeks. During previous winters they had had a fire every night they were home. "All right. I'll spend Christmas here. All right. You win that one. But I don't want your father hanging around trying to put the bite on me."

"If you're here, that's all I ask." She went to stand by the fireplace. "Wouldn't you like a fire tonight?" Vaguely she remembered Tom Silver saying something was wrong with the fireplace, a leak. She tried to think how to bring it up with Ross.

The phone rang in his study. As he rose to answer it, she had a sudden guilty conviction it was Fay or Tom calling to check on her veracity. Now they would think she had lied. She followed him to the door of his study, afraid they might say something in anger that would incidate she had seen them again.

"Well, well," she heard him say. "It's you, is it? . . . I'll say I am. . . . Did you expect that I'd find it a big joke? . . . Hold on, just a sec." He shut the door in her face as she stood there. She felt mortified. Now, now, she said to herself, no rabid indignation. You have spied on him with her, and if you could get away with picking up the receiver quietly enough, you would surely listen now.

She riffled through the deeds he had pulled from his attaché case. On impulse she copied the addresses on the flyleaf of a cookbook she was reviewing for the *Washington Post,* for an article on what was being billed as the new regionalism in cooking.

Four of the buildings were in the Allston neighborhood and indeed, one of them had Fay's address. But the fifth and sixth deeds were to buildings in North Cambridge. How many buildings did Ross own? In every case she was supposed to have bought the buildings under her maiden name from one of the trusts she recognized from the cancelled checks: Red Robin, Robert, Walton. He was selling buildings from himself to her, and now he was buying them back. All very peculiar. Lawyers adored generating paper, but this seemed especially perverse. Maybe he no longer trusted her. Maybe he was preparing to divorce her and did not want anything in her name.

According to the attached paperwork, he was applying for mortgages on all but one: that building being renovated where the boy had died. She blinked at the amounts and counted the decimal places, sure she was making some mistake, sure she was reading the numbers incorrectly. Three hundred fifty thousand? For those simple dilapidated buildings? She must have been in every one of them and they simply could not be worth that much, they simply could not. The mortgages were astronomical. Their own house would go on the market for somewhere in the vicinity of a hundred sixty thousand, but these were being mortgaged for amounts two and three times that. Why was he taking out enormous mortgages on ordinary and even on substandard dwellings? The banks must be mad. She wouldn't lend him money on those old brick apartment houses and those frame two-family or triple-deckers.

He was still on the phone. The buzzer called her into the kitchen. She took the clafouti from the oven, an open-faced confection like a pie crossed with a dessert omelette, drenched with apple brandy. The scent would even have tempted Robin, she thought complacently. She put the clafouti on a rack to cool slightly and then set the coffee table in the living room. Little elegant gilt-rimmed cups for espresso. The machine was ready but she hesitated to make the coffee. He'd been talking for twenty-five minutes. "Dessert's ready," she called just outside his study door.

He went on talking. Wandering back into the kitchen she loaded supper plates into the dishwasher, wiped the counters, tidied. Took off her apron and wandered back. Now he had been on the phone for forty minutes and the clafouti was rapidly cooling and sinking on itself.

She marched up to his closed study door and rapped smartly. "Ross! Dessert's getting cold. It won't be nice, shortly."

He bellowed. "I'm on the phone."

"Can't you call back some other time? You've been on the phone for forty-five minutes!"

"I'm busy. I can't speak to you now. Leave me be!"

She straightened the living room. Made herself espresso. Cut herself a slice of the room temperature clafouti and ate it in the kitchen, hearing the murmur of his voice through the wall. Although she could make out few words, the tone was not that of a business conversation. He lilted, he murmured, he coaxed. Outside the study Torte whined and pawed at the door, but Ross ignored him.

An hour after the conversation that had to be with Gail had begun, Daria ran upstairs and locked herself in her bedroom. There was nothing to be recovered from the evening, nothing. She felt like a complete fool. His rudeness hurt, his overpowering arrogant selfish rudeness. She was someone he did not bother to be polite to. He did not give a damn what she did with herself. He ignored her feelings. He commanded a dessert, had her rush about preparing it in vain hopes of pleasing him and then let it grow cold while he cooed to his poopsie. No more, she thought, no more.

In a little while, just a little while longer, Ross, she addressed him through the floorboards, I won't care. You're forcing me to cease loving you. You were my life, you damned fool. Now what are you? Someone who lies to me. Someone who lies a lot to a lot of people, I suspect. Someone capable of being vicious and cruel and casually rude. A stranger who invades me and then departs.

The love could still come back, the intimacy, the sense of family, it could be saved, she addressed him through the wide floorboards of this beautiful sturdy house where they had lived for more than a decade, but you must stop at once what you are doing to me. You must stop.

Around ten he knocked on her door. "What do you want?" she called. Did he imagine he could sweet-talk on the phone for two hours and then enter her bed as if it were an old slipper he was shoving his foot in?

"Sorry to bother you. Were you asleep? You forgot to sign those deeds."

That was all he cared about. She ground her teeth. "You're behaving like a monster to me and I won't endure it. Take your deeds and shove them."

She could hear him shifting from foot to foot outside the door. "But it's for your own good. To protect you from harassment."

"I won't talk to you. Go away! Go talk to your Gail some more."

"What are you complaining about now? I have a lot of business to conduct. Fine, you can sign the deeds in the morning." His footsteps crossed the hall, paused. "Hello there, Torte, old boy," he said in his warmest voice. "What a good old dog, come on, come on. . . ." He went on fussing over the dog loudly, as if demonstrating what a good man he was with the dog as prop.

13

NEVER had Christmas arrived in their house with less preparation and less fanfare. In November Daria had forgotten to bake fruitcakes. She did not think of a tree until the twenty-third when Tracy borrowed her car and went out to buy a Scotch pine. Tracy and Daria trimmed it that night. It was the sort of evening Daria had grown used to: Lorraine called at four to say Ross was held up by business. He came home after both of them had gone to bed.

Ross did however appear in midafternoon on Christmas Eve, to admire the tree and carry in his presents. Daria watched astonished as he placed load after load under the tree. He had never bought so many presents. Now he was heaping up several years' worth. Once again hopes that he might be reconciling began to tease her, but this time she suppressed them roughly. She would see, but she would not allow herself to dangle in his attention. She would reject no honest approach but she would not plead for civility.

In the afternoon Tracy had helped her make a grand Christmas pudding, now steaming in its bright mold. The hard sauce was in the refrigerator, firming. The goose for tomorrow's dinner they had picked up at Leo's, together. "That has to be your daughter," Leo said, and Daria felt proud, showing Tracy off. Tracy's brown eyes seemed luminous, liquid, her skin rosy with the cold. She not only seemed prettier, but firmer, more resolved.

"No, I can't," she heard Tracy say on the kitchen extension. "Nick, I'd love to. How about the day after Christmas? I'll explain later, but my mother needs me."

Daria had to lock herself in the bathroom and scrub her face hard to stop snivelling. Tonight, for the eve, she had planned a traditional English dinner of roast beef, Yorkshire pudding, of course the plum pudding for dessert. Too much consistency in English food would make anyone dull, so she steamed the brussels sprouts lightly to crunch between the teeth and served them with her own ginger sauce; the potatoes were lyonnaise and the dressing for the salad a light chive vinaigrette.

Robin arrived half an hour late, but Daria had permitted leeway and sailed calmly on through the diminishing tempest of her kitchen. Dinner was a success. Even Robin ate reasonably for once and Tracy and Ross ate steadily and long. She kept a mild conversation going, resorting to music. She put on Telemann, which she hoped would provide the right clarity and mellow briskness she sought. She gathered all of them were prepared to pull their oars for the family, to make the holidays glide on in domestic tranquility.

We are a family, she thought, in spite of our differences and momentary quarrels, still a family. We make a community together. But she glanced from face to face, seeking confirmation.

After the leisurely meal, Robin and Tracy volunteered (with some nudging to Robin) to clean up. Daria took her coffee into the living room, where Ross was starting a fire. She sank in a rocking chair and stared at the small leaping flames, letting her mind clear. So far, so good. In a moment she would rise and switch on the tree lights. Tracy had strung them this year; always that had been Ross's pleasure. She did not know why she felt so weary: perhaps because she was permitting herself to relax. Relaxation was something she had used to do well. She had tried over the years to teach Ross how to let go and enjoy, unclench.

Her eyes fixed on the darting tongues of the fire—orange with flashes of green—she half drowsed like a cat before the hearth. This was the first Christmas without Nina to talk to, at least on the phone. Nina had never liked Christmas in Florida; always she wanted to come north then. Daria yawned, her eyes closing. If she could pass through that scrim of memory that seemed so flimsy back into another year, how could she resist? To have Nina alive; to have Ross passionate and idealistic and sharing his work with her, to have the love between them alive and infused through every day like the air she breathed. The images of how it had been were so powerful she was tempted to believe all she had to do was force a little harder, try a little more intensely with him to break through, and suddenly all would be well again.

Suddenly she became aware of raised voices in the kitchen. Turning on the tree lights to excuse her rising, she waded slowly down the central hall, yawning.

"—a traitor, a Judas," Tracy was saying melodramatically.

"Bug off, Teresa. You can lay that on me and then take off for Amherst where you're out of it. All he's trying to do is get his priorities straight. You just want him to be nothing for the rest of his life but our daddy."

"Girls, could you forbear chewing each other out tonight?" Daria came into the kitchen shutting the swinging door. "If you want things decent, don't start an open battle. And don't involve him. Not tonight."

"You're the one who's been poking into everything," Robin said, her blue eyes slits of scorn. "Harassing him. Calling me up and accusing me."

"I do accuse you of siding with his girlfriend instead of your mother, and I wonder how in touch with your situation you are. Are you so eager for him to leave me for her? He'd be leaving all of us."

"He's not leaving you for anybody. He's trying to find himself." Robin shook her head furiously, Torte trying to throw off water. "You made him marry you, and he stuck by it all these years."

"I made him?" Daria asked quietly. She noticed Ali and Sheba on top of the refrigerator staring from one to the other, their ears flattened. "Where did that hogwash come from?"

"I know the facts, so don't try to pass off any fairy tales on me. You were pregnant."

"With you. How thoughtless of me. As a matter of record, it was your father's idea to marry, not mine, and he had to talk me into it."

"He felt obligated. How long does anybody have to feel obligated?"

"Getting married was his idea and he was stubborn about it. He wanted a wife, he wanted a family. And he wanted me. More than you are likely to imagine or he is likely at the moment to remember," Daria said crisply. "Now keep your voices down and fight if you must about something other than the sex lives of your parents." She marched out, shutting the door silently behind her in case she had not dampened their ardor.

She was furious as she plumped down in the rocking chair. How dare Robin insinuate she had leaned on Ross? She had intended to get an abortion. She had confessed her condition to Nina, and after some tears, Nina had come down firmly on her side. Ross was the one who longed for a child, whom he insisted on referring to as his son. Also he was madly in love with her, far more besotted than she was with him. Oh, she was fond of him, but she was not yet passionately in love. That had come slowly after marriage, which seemed to her a far more sensible and indeed traditional way to work out a good life. She darkly mistrusted infatuation, having had a ringside seat at the consequences of her mother's infatuation.

She had slept with Ross, not out of passionate desire, not because she felt swept away, but because she was annoyed with herself for being twenty-one, graduated from college and still a virgin. She considered Ross a good choice for her first lover. He seemed considerate. She did not think he was soiled by the virgin/whore dichotomy cherished by the young men of her neighborhood. She would not become less to him by giving way. She had left home and moved into an apartment with two other girls. She was celebrating her independence of body, of life, of judgment.

Some thermostat on her sexuality had been turned far, far down in childhood so that she could protect herself from Nina's fate, from the danger she sensed in adolescence from uncles, neighbors, from the boys who pounced and the boys who leered and the boys who begged. Years of marriage and three childbirths had slowly freed her sexuality.

Ross had really loved her and she had flourished, whatever nonsense he was telling Robin now, whatever mythology he was cooking up. He had praised her body, he had followed her about the house touching her, watching her dress and undress, admiring her breasts, her buttocks, her hips, her hair, her thighs, admiring her elbows, the small of her back, her nose, her earlobes. She had felt opulent, regal, rich in favors. Then he had been easy to delight.

170

Yet always there had been times he would rear back, when he would withdraw to gaze at her with a cold calculating scan as if deciding freshly if she were worth her price; moments when he would stare at her as if suddenly wondering if she was fully human. These were not usually times of argument or open anger. Often those moments of cold appraisal came when she was expansive, blatantly sexual, loudly happy, or sometimes with her family. At Tony's first wedding when she had twirled around with Nina, insisting Nina get up and dance with her, she had seen him appraising them with that cold, cold eye.

Those had been moments of doubt, of withdrawal, when his childhood and the racial contempt of the blond for the dark, the Wasp arrogance and vicious training of his parents and class would surface, but moments only encountered to be defeated and dismissed. She had been his first choice. He had pursued her and launched a campaign to persuade her to marry him. Robin was too attached to her father to want to know. Where had that attraction gone? What had killed it? Because, she knew, it was dead.

Cesaro called first. It was traditional on Christmas Eve to call each other. "No," he said firmly, "this year you come to our house. Come for dinner."

"Cesaro, I already started with the goose. How about dessert together?"

"A goose, mmmm? That beats our ham. Are you having Gussie?"

"Yes. But I haven't been able to reach Tony at all."

"That high flyer took his wife and baby south to Jamaica. Some way to celebrate Christmas. It would depress me, but Tony gets a buzz out of spending."

"I didn't know he was going. He never called me."

"Don't fret, Daria. Probably didn't have the time. You know how overheated Tony gets, all revved up. All right, bring Gussie and family along and we'll see you about seven, for dessert."

When she got off the phone she sat frowning. It was a clear break of their family pattern for Tony to go out of the country for several days without telling her. They could have exchanged presents before he left. "Ross . . . did you know Tony is in Jamaica?"

"Sure." He rose from his armchair, luxuriously stretching, putting Torte down. "Left last Thursday. Ten days of fun in the sun. Some little resort where you come into Montego Bay, then fly over by small plane."

"Didn't he want to get together before they left? I have presents for them all."

"They're not milk, they won't curdle. Besides, you don't like Monica."

"I don't dislike her. I simply liked Gloria a great deal."

"He didn't kill Gloria. He just divorced her."

"How convenient. Let's have them all to a party together."

The girls came straggling out of the kitchen. "Let's sing some carols," Ross offered. "Tracy, will you play?"

"God, Dad, I haven't touched a piano since August."

"Just the melodies. Look in the piano bench."

Tracy sat slumped and pouting at the upright piano in the darker end of the dining room. "It's out of tune."

"I'm sorry," Daria said. "I forgot to have it tuned this fall. But play anyhow." Your father's trying, she wanted to say, please help him try. Ross had a good trained voice. He had grown up singing in the choir of the Methodist Church. He had gone on singing in chorale groups, in Gilbert and Sullivan societies, in musicals until law school.

"It's not that bad. Soldier on." Ross clapped Tracy on the shoulder. "Come on, Robin."

Tracy visibly flinched at his hand, but Ross was looking around for Robin. Tracy pushed her curly brown hair out of her eyes and looked with hard curiosity at her father before turning back to the keys.

"Dad, I can't carry a tune," Robin pleaded.

"Anybody can sing carols. Even your mother."

They started with the easy ones. Daria did not sing on key and the first year she had lived with Ross, she had learned to keep quiet unless requested to sing as part of a group. Robin had inherited Daria's lack of musical ability. They were working on carols Tracy and Ross had to carry while Robin and Daria hummed, squawked and faked it, when at nine-thirty his phone rang. He took it in his study. After grinding through "Angels we have heard on high," the singing stopped. At first they sat around the piano, waiting for Ross to return. Tracy noodled around with her left hand making bluesy chords and progressions. After twenty minutes, they dispersed.

"I'm going to wrap presents," Robin announced, as usual the last. "Where's the paper? I'm doing it in my old room, so don't anybody peek."

"She ought to have them wrapped at the store, like Father does," Tracy said with a little sneer after Robin went upstairs. She arranged herself in a graceful coil on the couch, contemplating the tree they had trimmed.

The rebuff formed but she would have felt hypocritical voicing it. She had a vague sense of Tony conspiring with Ross against her. That was absurd; her own brother would not side with her husband against his sister. Yet she felt a malaise she could not dismiss. They were tight around work, although she did not understand the nature of their connection. Tony had left his older wife for a younger wife. Perhaps he identified with Ross's affair. She felt a tattered sort of monster, Frankenstein's patchwork thrown into the fiery pit, that her own brother and her own daughter discarded her.

Robin stayed over, so Ross of necessity shared Daria's bed, a situation she found she resented. By now she felt invaded when he entered the room that had become a sanctuary. When he took over the downstairs with his long phone calls to Gail or his loud hockey or football games, she could withdraw behind her locked door. All night Sheba and Ali kept trying to pry open the door. They also felt entitled. Torte ended up sleeping in Robin's room, where he had become accustomed to finding Ross, when Ross was home at all.

Ross lay way over in the queen-sized bed, sleeping on his side in quasi-fetal position. She lay on her back at her edge, staring at the ceiling. She was a complete fool not to rub against him, not to try to seduce him. Didn't she want him back? Shouldn't she do anything at all to keep him?

She couldn't. It was not exactly timidity that inhibited her, although rejection had abraded her confidence. She realized that she was no longer sure that she wanted him. That doubt paralyzed her with fear. Without Ross, what did she have to show for her life? Who was she? What would happen to her, dumped at forty-three? Surely survival dictated she should try to keep her husband. But who was he? Who was the man Fay, Sherry

Sheehan and Tom Silver hated? Who was the man to whom they mailed dead rats? Who was this man who held her in contempt?

Yet he must feel ambivalent about what he was doing. Saturday he had come home to her with his bitten hand. He had invited the new neighbors over that Wednesday. He felt at least some conflict. In a way she could not yet comprehend, all his choices cohered, representing a pattern that had slowly come to exclude her, a pattern she could not trace. Nonetheless he must not be entirely committed to his new path. He wavered back to her. She and what she represented drew him swerving back. Yet Gail had only to call for him to forget Daria. What passionate hold had Gail upon him? Unexceptional exteriors could hide passionate responses; she was no beauty herself. Yet the woman she had watched him with was so alien to her fantasies, she had trouble focussing on the actual source of danger. She kept expecting the Lou she had imagined for weeks to spring from somewhere, as svelte, as flashy, as glamorous as Daria had anticipated.

It was a lopsided Christmas. Always she had bought the bulk of presents for everyone. Ross usually had Lorraine purchase a couple of pieces of clothing; then he would pick up an edible or drinkable treat. Sometimes he would take Daria to buy some major gift, a coat or an important dress. When he bought jewelry, he selected it himself, viewing jewels as investments. Daria had always bought their presents for the girls, letting herself go in shopping for them and for him. This year, her spirits had been too thwarted, her energy too marginal to create her usual abundance.

Ross, on the contrary, had turned extravagant. Skis for Robin; a parka, running shoes. For Tracy, a fine blue merino wool robe, *La Bohème* and *La Tosca* on records, a pair of ice skates, which Tracy might even use.

Traditionally, the way they opened presents was that after a sumptuous breakfast, they gathered in the living room and each opened one in turn. Usually Daria ran out fast, so she also opened what they called House Presents—things she bought not for anyone in particular but for the good or pleasure of the family, delicacies to eat, perhaps small appliances, vases, pillows or bedspreads.

This time she had bought no House Presents and her personal pile was enormous. She opened and opened two presents for every one of the others. An Italian leather purse, a lavender cashmere muffler, Opium perfume, lambskin slippers from England with fleece inside, a wallet that matched the purse, a key ring that matched the wallet, a beige silk shawl, a rather large striped kaftan, another kaftan in purple velvet with gold trim. He seemed to have fixed on kaftans as something that did not require too exact a fit, although she had not worn one since her last pregnancy.

She sat surrounded by gifts and empty boxes, store wrapped in shiny bright boxes in primary colors, with wavy ribbons and pretied bows, and she was stunned, glutted. She stared at the heap without comprehending it. Was he reconciling with her? Was he apologizing? She must have piled around her a thousand dollars worth of shopping.

"Ross, I'm bowled over. I don't know what to say. Everything's absolutely beautiful, but there's so much. . . ."

"Didn't I promise a nice Christmas? Didn't I keep my promise?"

"Completely." She stared, trying to read his eyes, his expression. He looked quite proud of himself.

Gussie, Don and their four children came for Christmas dinner. Before, they exchanged the presents Gussie had knitted for those Daria had bought. "No fruitcake this year?" Gussie lamented. "I love your fruitcake. It's the richest."

"I didn't get a chance. I make them around Thanksgiving." Daria felt low, using Nina's death as an excuse. She had a strong urge to confide in Gussie, but the afternoon did not give her an opportunity. Ross insisted on showing Gussie all the presents he had given Daria, and Gussie was overwhelmed with jealousy. Gussie was hard put to find the money to get each of the kids one fancy toy they had been seeing on television for two months. Daria felt again the guilt that she was not doing enough for Gussie, but that was an old subject of debate between Ross and herself. If they had been close, she could have advised him not to show off; he simply did not think how that glittering display would affect Gussie and Don.

Daria did not take the time to do more than pile up the pots and scrape the dishes, loading them into the dishwasher. The girls were entertaining their younger cousins, playing Monopoly at the dining-room table. Gussie had followed her into the kitchen. "Daria, you know Bobbie enters high school next year. I'm thinking about enrolling him in Dominic Savio."

"How come? We both went to Eastie. Parochial school's awfully narrow."

"Oh, with the bussing," Gussie said. "They're bringing them in there now, and he could be shipped off to Roxbury."

Daria sighed. She burst out, "Oh, Gussie, can't you remember how the Irish used to talk about us? White people don't go there, they'd say about Lauro's Funeral Parlor or the Rialto Theater. They didn't think we were even white."

Gussie's face was closed like a plump fist against her argument. "If it was money for your kids, you'd spend it readily enough. You and Cesaro."

They drove in two cars to Cesaro's house, Don getting into his car first and leading the way. It was dark and traffic was heavy. A fine snow dusted down, giving headlights a flickering quality. Cesaro lived a short distance off Route 2 in Lincoln, where he had a rambling old house, a low-ceilinged, small-roomed colonial section, an imposing Greek Revival part and various modern additions, all connected to the horse barn. Cesaro's house lacked the unity Daria's had, but it offered more romantic eccentricity, odd-shaped rooms, rooms that opened off other rooms. Both her girls had always loved to wander in it. Gussie's kids had started about the house and the horse before dessert was half over. Even though it was dark, she knew Trish would take them out to the barn.

Vinnie served a dry chocolate cake. When Cesaro drew Ross off with the fine port afterward, she smiled, thinking that her brother was becoming more British than ever. Would he make it a regular feature for the men to withdraw over port and cigars? Then she realized he had not pulled Don along with them. Ross went off with Cesaro a little reluctantly, casting back upon her a look she could not read.

The two men stayed in Cesaro's study for an hour. Passing close to the door, she heard their voices raised once. What were they arguing about?

Business? Had Cesaro found out Ross was having an affair? How many people knew by now?

At ten they left, Gussie and Don taking the cranky overtired kids back to East Boston and dropping Robin in Back Bay. Only Tracy returned with Ross and Daria. Ross retired across the hall. Daria slept easily, for the day had seemed to heal them all a little toward each other. Perhaps Cesaro had put in a good word for her.

In the morning when she came down to start breakfast, he was already up, drinking a cup of espresso from the machine. "Daria, it's time for us to come to an understanding," he began. His voice was rich and resonant. He was fully dressed.

"I agree. Do you mind if I make myself coffee first?" Were they going to have a genuine conversation about their predicament? She wished she had dressed too, instead of coming down in her bathrobe. "I want us to start over, but we can't do that with you spending every night with Gail."

"And let's leave Gail out of this. I want to talk about us."

"We can't leave Gail out. For starters, what's her name?"

"What does that matter?"

"Ross, I can find out." She was pumping coffee from the machine, her back to him. "I imagine Tony will tell me that much."

"Don't think he's going to take your part."

"I don't. What's her name, Ross?"

"Damn it, you're trying to take over the conversation. I have things I want to talk about."

"So do I. We'll both have our opportunity. What's her full name?"

"Her name is Gail Abbot-Wisby. For all the good that will do you. I'm not leaving you for her. I'm leaving you to find myself."

"Oh." She swung around to stare at him.

"Damn you, Daria, I had things I wanted to say to lead up to this. You've forced me to dump the news on you without preparation. That makes me sound hard."

"Oh, I don't know." She forced herself away from the counter she had fallen back against; forced herself to stand straight. "The last few months have been some preparation."

"I'm moving into an apartment in the North End—"

"The North End?" The old immigrant Italian neighborhood where her grandfather had lived? That made no sense at all: old tenements, narrow streets, espresso and bakery shops, pasta factories, marble cutters.

"Just on the harbor. It's a condo we haven't sold yet. I'll write down the address for you." He pulled out a business card and wrote on the back, leaning on the dishwasher.

She remembered it was still loaded with Christmas dinner dishes, as yet unwashed. She had a brief bleak desire to break them all. "You want me to believe you're moving in there alone?"

He laughed dryly, a scratchy sound. "If you saw the size of the place, you wouldn't ask. I have to get my act together, Daria. I have to find out who I am. Too many years I have permitted our life to unroll, one compromise after another, from the first—"

"I gather from Robin you've been rewriting history. Getting married was your idea and you were keen on it. I didn't make you marry me. You had to argue me into it. . . . Remember?"

"The point is, the relationship is dead. We don't share a common world view. You're trapped in the liberal platitudes of a decade ago. You haven't grown—except more demanding."

"While you've been expanding your soul by becoming a slum landlord?"

"Don't ape slogans you don't understand. I'm involved in shaping the future of this city. There isn't one parcel I own that won't be excellent housing within five years. I'm building. I'm raising up."

"You just mean you're getting rid of people with less money and moving in people with more. I don't know that I think Tony is a better person than Gussie, for example."

"You love losers, you really do. Cesaro has a streak of that, but I doubt it will sway him in the long run. He knows where his interests lie. . . . Daria, can't you see, you're strangling me?"

"No. I do not see that I am quote strangling you unquote. I see that I was loving you. I see I was making a home for you and our children. I

178

see I was honestly trying to communicate with you while you were deceiving me."

"Daria, you've only kept me this long through guilt. It's a death of the spirit to remain in a loveless marriage."

"I agree your spirit's in trouble. By all means give it oxygen in your condo with Gail Whistler."

"Abbot-Wisby," he corrected automatically. "I told you six times I'm moving in by myself. I'm going it alone. I'm not about to hurt you, Daria, any more than I must to survive. There's no excitement between us. No lightning. No surprises."

"Don't say that, Ross. You've given me a number of surprises lately. You've surprised me half to death. And if I don't have any novelty for you, maybe that's because you haven't paid enough attention to notice anything."

"It's gotten stale. It's routine. It's duty. It's paying the bills. It's just grinding along. I'm entitled to more. I want to start over again, I want a new life, a fresh chance. I want to do it right this time."

"I don't think there's any right in what you're doing."

"Because you won't see!" He drew himself up, his eyes almost popping. "You could see it if you wanted to. I am right! If you could be objective for two seconds, you'd see that. You just won't admit it."

"You want me to say you're making a good choice?" she asked slowly. "I don't think you are. It's a cliché come to life."

"Damn it, Daria . . ." He broke off, drawing his breath. "I'll give you a more than decent settlement. You'll have to unload this house fast. You'll find you can't afford it, and we need the cash."

"I'm not moving. This is my home, even if it's no longer yours. I will not leave this house until Tracy is done with college."

For a moment he glared openly at her as if his anger had been struck with a loud clang. "I think you will. We'll discuss it when I work out your settlement."

"When are you leaving?"

"Today. I'll pack now—take what I'll be needing. Later we can make arrangements about the rest. . . . Why don't you rout Teresa out of her bed and go shopping? By the time you're back, I'll be gone."

"I don't feel like being put out to pasture this morning, thank you. I have a lot of cleaning to do from our family Christmas, and Peggy's coming in just for the afternoon."

"As you please. Do it the most painful way, of course." He stomped out and she heard him climbing the steps as if he were five fat men. Only then did she cry for a while, leaning against the still loaded dishwasher.

14

As soon as Tracy returned to college on January second, Daria felt the house swell around her, echoing like a church. As she tried to sleep, the house seethed with rustling, banging, muffled thuds. If she dozed, often she wakened in terror, sure an intruder stood over her bed.

Now for the first time, she was living alone. From the morning Ross had packed the set of matched leather luggage that had been a wedding present, she had given him up. She could not guess how he was changing and how he would further change, but she did not hope he would return. She grieved; she bled. Being deserted, discarded tore at her. She felt ugly, she felt used and used up. She did not, however, dream that Ross would return.

He had hurt her too deeply. He was no longer the man she loved. She had to understand him now not to love him better, to serve him better, but to be free at last of him. Their relationship was over, but not done with.

Because going to bed made her vulnerable to her fancies and fears, she retired late, to erode the long hours of darkness. Usually she was exhausted and managed to sleep. Then she woke between four and five every morning. Anxieties seemed suspended over her in a net that lowered instantly when she stirred. Finally she rose, ate a hasty breakfast and worked. The cookbook raced forward. She had no trouble concentrating. After the catastrophe, she had little to distract her and considerable desperation to goad her on.

Then she came downstairs to the house empty except for the ailing, heartbroken Torte and the kittens. Desolation settled over her like fine choking dust. How alone she was; how empty her life. She saw the years grey and dusty stretching ahead in which she was always isolated, in which she shrivelled slowly in her flesh and at last blew away on the wind, the fine ash she had imagined a cremation to produce before she had handled her mother's weighty and coarse ashes.

Finally she called Gretta and invited her to supper. It was something to look forward to, the first human face besides Peggy she had seen since Tracy returned to school.

"You haven't seen a lawyer yet?" Gretta flung down her napkin dramatically, thrusting aside the poached salmon in hollandaise, although she dragged it back at once. "You're mad! Ross is a lawyer and you're vulnerable. It's entering a tournament with a knight in armor and you're birthday naked."

"The only lawyers I know are all friends of Ross."

"Well, avoid them. Go to the guy who got me my settlement. He's a fighter. He'll take on old Ross with zest. Otherwise, darling, Ross'll pick you to the bone. . . . Are you sure you want to hold on to this big old house?"

"I'm not sure of anything. . . . You wouldn't like to move in?"

"That's sweet, Daria. If the timing had been different . . . But my apartment's just a bus ride from Harvard Square, and I'm having an intense thing with a young man I met booking a tour. It won't last long, but it's fun. . . . Daria: have you *ever* had an affair?"

Two large tears rolled suddenly down Daria's cheeks. She blotted them hurriedly in her napkin. She was a large secondhand rag doll whose stuffing was leaking from a detached arm. "Of course not."

"That's one of the pleasures of being left. You get to indulge yourself."

"I'm not the type."

"Everybody is somebody's type," Gretta said sententiously. "It would perk your spirits up. But getting a housemate isn't a half bad idea, if you do plan to stay. . . . What was his lady's name again?"

"Gail Wisby. He said, Gail Abbot Wisby—one of those triple names. I suppose that means she's divorced?"

"I suppose," Gretta said. "You call my lawyer tomorrow morning first thing, you hear?"

The most humiliating moment of the interview occurred as she was telling the chronicle of events and came to the day after Christmas. She started to cry, right there in his carpeted office overlooking Milk Street, with the portly balding man in his three-piece grey suit surveying her.

He gave her a seven-page form to fill out. Immediately it became apparent she knew the answer to almost none of the questions about expenses and assets and liabilities. "But, Mrs. Walker, you must know what you earn. You pay income tax every year, right?" He waited for her agreement, watching her as if suspecting she did not even pay taxes. "Then even though you file a joint return with your husband, you're a small business. Your earnings, your expenses are listed separately, inside the return. . . . You don't have copies? . . . Take a Kleenex, Mrs. Walker, you can ask your accountant for copies. You do have an accountant?"

"My husband does. His accountant does both our taxes." She felt as if he surveyed her, an aerial reconnaissance plane circling over and photographing a ravaged city. The destruction was apparent but his job was survey, not pity. He was not convinced anything could be salvaged. Probably he would recommend razing her life. She left his offices completely demoralized. The divorce would obviously be excruciating and she would end up homeless and impoverished. He refused to estimate costs.

She did not know if she could force herself to see him again. He made her profoundly uncomfortable. He made her feel an absolute fool. Perhaps she was.

That night she built herself a fire in the fireplace. Then she remembered, as the room filled with smoke and Torte cowered barking in the hall and the kittens dashed about, to reach up and open the flue. She found an open bottle of decent cognac in the back of the liquor cabinet. Pouring herself a snifter, she settled down with the lawyer's endless questionnaire. Peggy had brought together some facts for her. Daria had pried open the locked door to Ross's study. Obviously he had emptied two of his drawers, but that was all. As he had said, he would be getting the bulk of his materials later. Would he just walk in, the way he had done when he was spending the evening but not the night with Gail? That possibility unsettled her. She hoped he would call first. That would be civilized. Surely he would want to be civilized. He had left December 26. This was January 7, and she had not heard from him yet.

Among the items he had taken appeared to be their income tax returns. However, Peggy had made an estimate of her income for the past couple of years and had also estimated house expenses, since one-sixth were deductible as Daria's place of business, so they had some idea between them what figures they had given Ross each year. At the end of her first set of figures, her expenditures exceeded income by four thousand dollars.

She could not survive! She could not. Ross was right. She was useless and helpless. Then she thought, no, I will not go down. I will get a housemate. I will find a woman to share this house with me. I'll write an ad this very instant.

On her lined pad she wrote, "Woman in 40's, grown-up daughter." No. "Woman in 40's, college-age daughter home sometimes, wishes woman to share lovely house and garden, good schools nearby." That was important only if the woman had children. She considered and decided she would not mind sharing her house with children again. She would send the ad in tomorrow. But was there actually enough room if the woman had a child? She could move Tracy down to Ross's study. She must clear his things out. Then the woman and her child could have two adjacent rooms upstairs with the shared bath, the room that was Tracy's and the room that had been Robin's.

Besides, she did not eat that much and neither did Torte or the kittens. She had her garden. She would put in more vegetables in the spring. In a small East Boston yard, Nina had grown almost all the vegetables they ate summer and fall, and then would can and freeze for the rest of the year. She would not be entertaining lavishly, carrying the liquor bills or the fancy wine tabs. She would use recipes from her own working mother book, the kind of economical dishes she had made in her early marriage. She would do more Italian cooking and less French. Her new housemate might share food costs.

"Garage available," she tacked on. "Quiet pretty street." She added her phone number. She could cancel Ross's phone at once; that would save a little. She had the thermostat turned down to 60 and sat near the fireplace with both cats in her chair like living hot-water bottles. Torte came and went, dragging himself about querulously searching for Ross, demanding doors be opened to continue his search. He finally settled chin on the hearth staring morosely into the fire. The last few days she had not been able to get him to eat. He was in mourning.

Tomorrow she would cancel the phone. She would caulk the windows, a job she had begun in November and abandoned. She had bought six boxes of caulking, sitting in the basement. . . . What would happen if she had to fix the plumbing? If the furnace suddenly quit? If something went wrong with the toilet? If her car would not start?

What did other women do? They learned to fix things. They learned to call plumbers. They called friends. Gretta's son knew something about cars, for he worked on his mother's. The library would instruct her. Daria was a great believer in going to the library and finding a book when she needed to investigate any subject. On impulse, displacing both cats, she marched down to the basement and stared purposefully at the furnace. It was squat, menacing. It hummed meaningfully. She retreated, sure if she approached too closely, it might suddenly explode.

She would start with something easier: her finances. Yet however she tried, she ended up with projected expenses surpassing projected income. Take more lectures, do more cooking classes and demonstrations, close the deal with Channel 7, write more. Talk to her agent.

Make more; spend less; buy nothing; find the lost income: that was her program for survival. Her phone rang. "Uh, hi," Ross said. She almost dropped the phone. She managed to squeeze a greeting from her collapsed throat.

"I need more clothes. I forgot my slippers and my boots. I thought I'd come by."

"Not now!" she said in panic. "I'm busy."

"You don't have to be there."

"I mean I have company. It would be awkward." Why had she lied? Just from dread at seeing him suddenly.

"Oh. Anyone I know?"

"Ross, how about tomorrow around five?"

"Around five? That's a little awkward."

"Not for me. For me it would be the most convenient time."

"Umph. All right. Five. Really, I don't need you to be there."

"This is my home. I'd prefer to be here."

"Legally it belongs to both of us. Equally. You should remember that. You made me go through that damned fool business of changing the deed and reregistering it three years ago." He hung up.

Still mad that she had made him change the deed to joint, as she had thought it was all along. Interesting, she thought, but could wring little pleasure from his continued pique. Now she would have to see him tomorrow. Why hadn't she simply let him come ahead? But why allow him to see she did nothing but huddle by the fire in a big cold drafty house, alone except for her animals, her familiars. She must find a housemate and soon. Now how could she concentrate on anything for the next twenty hours except that she must see him?

The next morning the first job she had for Peggy was typing the ad. "You're really serious?" Peggy asked, smoothing down the shiny black bowl of her hair. "About getting somebody in here with you? You've never done anything like that."

"Yes, I have. Before I was married, I had roommates." She stared at Peggy. "What about you? Want to get away from your parents?"

"It's hard living with them. Every time I meet a guy I might be interested in, it's awkward. But my mother baby-sits for me. And living with your boss, I don't know, Daria."

"Well, think about it."

Peggy surveyed the two rooms carefully. Then Daria sent Peggy to the supermarket for boxes. When Peggy left at three to do some photocopying, Daria ventured into the room that had been Robin's and then Ross's and began packing the rest of his clothing. She cleaned out the closet, the dresser and then the toiletries and medicine he had not removed. She felt a pang when she noticed he had not taken his hemorrhoid medicine, for he was prone to that under stress. Then she was angry at herself for worrying. Let him suffer hemorrhoids till he couldn't sit; that would be Gail's little problem.

Here she was for the second time in a few months packing up the clothes of someone she had loved. Ross's things were much finer than Nina's, of course; she had chosen most of them. That Irish wool cardigan she had bought at Filene's the first year she had felt flush at Christmas. That holiday season, Robin was fourteen and busy with track and basketball; Tracy was eleven, pudgy, in love with all animals. Torte was a wriggling puppy. Ross had arranged for Cesaro to take the girls for New Year's, and they had gone off to an old inn in the Berkshires for a snowy icicle glittering weekend, a minihoneymoon far more luxurious than their original. She sighed, not even sure if she was grieving for herself or for Nina, both her losses blending.

Caring was a habit that died slowly. He had not taken enough warm socks. He had packed his raincoat but forgotten the zip-out lining. Everything went into boxes. Her back ached, but she was glad to have the clothing on its way. Every item of his left around was a little booby trap of memories.

At four-thirty she caught sight of herself in the long mirror, disheveled, wearing old wool slacks and a sweater that had been new when Tracy was a baby. She raced for a quick shower. She decided to dress as if she were going out to dinner; she would wear the red jersey he had never seen. Tracy had made her return the two tent-sized kaftans and had picked out three dresses for the same money from the designer shop, in the after-Christmas sales. She could not imagine where Tracy could have developed clothes sense. Daria had little, tending to want to replace a worn dress with one as much like it as possible, an open-ended series of sensible little black dresses with jewel necklines. Ross had always preferred his wardrobe in blue. Robin dressed like a preppie. But Tracy was demonstrating a sense of fabric and style that bemused her mother.

She sat at her vanity for once and actually combed her hair and put on makeup. Then she remembered the jimmied door of his study and flew down to lock it properly. She hovered in the living room, realized she did not want to be caught waiting for him and scuttled to the kitchen to empty the dishwasher. Lately she could go days at a time before it was full enough to turn on.

The doorbell rang. She had been afraid he would simply barge in, after his reminder on the phone that the house was still half his. She opened the door, stepping aside. As Ross came in, Torte raised his head and then flung himself through the air with astounding speed, colliding with Ross in midhall. Torte was hysterical as a puppy, leaping and licking, barking and snuffling, an explosion of joy.

"I packed up everything from Robin's room. I even found a few things in my bedroom, in that bureau."

"You didn't have to do that," he said in gruff embarrassment.

"It's easier for me, to have the things out."

"I wasn't planning to take all this stuff tonight. . . ." He came to a halt in front of the wall of boxes.

"I'm sure you can store the boxes someplace. You have a great deal more to pack, anyhow."

"I don't have room for all my books and files in my little condo. . . . That stuff can wait. . . ."

"Your darkroom stuff," she prompted. He did not look any different than he had when he left; she had expected some signs of change.

"Oh, I won't take the darkroom equipment away from you. You may well want to use it."

"Ross, you took the camera. And I've never done darkroom work."

"You might want to run off some of those publicity shots I took for you. Let's see, my summer clothes can stay for now. I haven't any storage to speak of. I'll get movers at some point. . . ."

"Ross, it's important that you do take Torte."

"Torte?" Ross caressed his head. "He's glad to see me, isn't he, old boy? The North End is no place for a dog."

"He misses you terribly. He's grieving—"

"Don't project, Daria—"

"I'm not projecting. I assure you he's grieving much more than I am. You were nicer to him than to me in recent months. He hasn't been eating. He's an old dog. He can't adjust to your disappearing."

"He's your dog too. Really, you can get him to eat if you remember to take the time to exercise him daily. Maybe the cats bother him."

"He's pining away for you. You have to feel some sense of responsibility for him."

He turned, glaring, his upper incisors resting on his lower incisors in a fierce grimace. "I've had enough of your assigning responsibility, Daria.

Lay off me. I'm not taking Torte to the North End. It's simply impossible."

"Because of Gail's German short-haired pointer?"

"You like to pretend you know so much. One dog? She raises them. Dozens of dogs, dozens and dozens! Torte would be miserable, I'm telling you. Now stop trying to make me feel guilty, because it won't work. I'm free of that."

He began carrying boxes out to his Mercedes, puffing and hauling. She did not offer to help but sat in the living room ostensibly reading an essay by M. F. K. Fisher. Finally he had the car loaded. He came to stand over her. She went on moving her eyes back and forth across the wriggling type until he spoke. "Daria, it's time to talk turkey. You must put the house on the market. I can do it tomorrow. I talked to Bud—"

"No. I'm staying." She put down her book, ostentatiously marking her place with her finger. "I will not be uprooted."

"We're going to sell the house, because I'm not going to leave my capital tied up in it. We'll split what we get, that's more than fair. You can keep your Rabbit. I'll pay Tracy's school expenses till graduation. How's that for fair?"

"I don't think it sounds fair, actually."

"Ferguson will explain it to you. He's doing the divorce for us."

"He may be doing it for you. He's not doing it for me."

Ross sighed, giving her a look of suffering patience, a man dealing with an idiot child. "Fine, Daria, hire that two-bit asshole who represented your hysterical friend Gretta. If that makes you feel better, dandy. Even that shyster can explain the facts of life to you. Just remember, the more money we spend on lawyers, the less there'll be left to settle up with. Just keep that in mind." He stomped out. Torte followed him to the door and tried to leave with him. Ross had to push the terrier back as he shut the door. Then Torte sat and howled. Putting her hands over her ears, Daria fled upstairs and threw herself on the bed. She hated Ross. She hated him.

Friday at four, her phone rang. It was Fay. "We're giving you another chance. We took the holidays off. Is Walker home yet?"

"Fay, he's moved out."

"Aw, come on. Are you convinced we're mental cases?"

"He left me. He has a girlfriend and he left me. He moved into a condominium in Boston on the harbor."

There was a short silence. "For real?"

"The day after Christmas."

"So that's what was happening?"

"Yes."

Another silence. Fay said, "I don't know if I should commiserate with you or what. I can't say I think zits of the man. But when my old man left me, I hated people who told me it was for my own good."

"It's just, I've been married to him my whole adult life."

"Figure you got a lot of it left. Myself, I discovered I like living alone with the kids. I'm closer to them, I don't fuss so much—you'd think I'd worry more, but I don't."

"Fay, I saw the deed to your building, and my name really is on it. He asked me to sign it over to some trust. He said it'd been put in my name just for convenience, whatever that means."

"Did you sign?"

"No, I put him off."

"So what happens now? You admit you're our landlady, so do we have to fight you now for decent conditions? I showed you the stairs and the boiler—"

"What happens is that I see a lawyer and find out if I really own it. In the meantime, yes, I'm going to act as if I do. I'll collect the rents. We'll meet and figure out what needs work first. Maybe we can make a gradual start on repairs—"

"Not so gradual, hey? We're living with that shit."

"But let me explain what's the problem. There's an enormous mortgage on your building, and I have to find out what the monthly payments are."

"A mortgage? What do you mean, enormous?"

"I don't remember exactly, but like two hundred thousand."

"Two hundred thou? That's impossible. You're making this up!"

"I had the same reaction, but I counted the zeros."

"Jesus. That's a new one. Maybe there's oil under the basement. I have to tell Mac and Sandra María and Tom about that one. . . . Thanks for the info."

"Do you finally believe me? That Ross left and that I don't know what he's planning and what he's doing in your neighborhood?"

"I guess so." Fay sounded reluctant to let her off the hook. Daria waited out a longish silence. Finally Fay said gruffly, "Yeah, I believe you. So now we're back to square one."

"Not if I do own the building. Then at least I have a right to find out about that mortgage."

"Maybe he's planning to evict us and renovate?"

"I suppose he could do a lot of renovating for that money. He could have it gold-plated."

"Listen, I'm going to get hold of the guys and tell them. You got his new address?"

"Be my guest, I'd love for you to picket him. Plus his girlfriend has an apartment on Beacon." She gave Fay both addresses. "Her name is Gail Wisby."

"I'll get back to you," Fay said. "Look, the first part after your old man leaves, that's the worst. Soon it gets easier."

Almost immediately afterward, her phone rang again. She assumed Fay was calling back, but it was Annette. "Daria, did you have your number changed? I've been trying to call to invite you over Saturday with the Gordons, but they say your old number is disconnected."

Nobody in the neighborhood ever used her business number; it seemed to shock them mildly that she had one. "I have one phone now. I need only one because there's only one of me. Ross left."

"Daria, that's awful. But he'll be back. It's a fling."

"I don't think so. He's already proceeding with the divorce. He's even worked out what pittance he's offering. It's all over but the paperwork."

"That's heartbreaking. I'm so sorry. Whatever are you going to do?"

"I don't know yet. Everything's up in the air." Or flat on the ground, she thought, as after a violent windstorm.

"If there's anything I can do, Daria, let me know."

"I'd love to see you. If you still want me to come Saturday . . ."

"I know how awkward that would be for you. We'll get together, the two of us, some morning." Annette and Pierre, like every other couple on the block where everybody came in couples, were not about to invite a separated woman to supper unless they had an extra man. "Er, Daria, what are you going to ask for the house? I've always adored your house."

"I don't think I'll sell it," she said quickly. "I *adore* it too."

She built a fire laboriously but this time remembered to open the flue first. She had fed the cats and walked Torte, and now she tried to talk herself into rising and cooking herself supper. She felt too listless. Her loneliness appeared to her visible, a wilderness spread around her trackless and howling. A Lake Superior in the winter of the spirit. She would be alone forever. The rest of her life would be like this evening, a treeless plain of solitude with a cold wind cutting her to the bone.

She wanted to call Annette back and berate her. What would it cost them to have one unattached woman to supper? A beggar at the banquet? Did they think she would crawl into the laps of her neighbors' husbands? They were always afraid of the damaged marriages. Avoiding the plague.

The doorbell rang. Instead of being glad, she felt like snarling. Who indeed did she want to see? Torte was already barking. She felt like ignoring the summons. Good old Ross dropping back to pick up some papers he had forgotten to remove from her scrutiny? Annette bringing over a covered dish as alms? The newsboy demanding to be paid? She feared it was Bud, the local real estate agent, and that Ross had put the house on the market without her consent. The bell rang again. She would not let the people in. Invaders!

She stood just inside, afraid. Torte was yapping fiercely. "Who is it?"

"Tom Silver."

She opened the door, blinking at him with surprise. As usual he seemed enormous, bearlike. He asked, "Did I startle you?"

"I gather Fay didn't reach you, and you came here expecting to picket."

"So I rang the bell? Fay reached me." He took off his pea coat, walking past her and unwinding his red wool mummy-wrapping of a muffler, and dumped those with his oversized fur-lined gloves on a chair. "A fire. Perfect." He waved her toward the other chair in front of the fire.

"I thank you for inviting me to sit in my own living room. Have you come to gloat? Or to check that Ross isn't hiding in a closet?"

"No. I called the number you gave Fay."

"Oh. Did you have a nice chat?"

"I got his answering machine."

"That's new. Probably so he won't miss his calls while he's at his girl-friend's."

"Fay will try to find that number. Her pleasure." He gave the fire a poke. "Have you found a lawyer? Or are you just waiting to see if he comes back, wagging his tail behind him?" He squatted easily, staring into the fire.

"I went to one." She winced. "Divorce is disgusting. Plus I felt like an idiot." As he turned, she waved at the forms still spread out on the coffee table. "Just the way you like to make me feel."

"It's your bloody burbling innocent act." He sauntered to the table, contemplating the forms. "I remember that, long as a book. All the law-yers who do divorce in Massachusetts hand them out to you."

"That's right, you went through it. . . . Did you leave her?"

"I'm still in the same house. Obviously not."

"She left you?"

He glared. Then perhaps deciding that after all she had a right to ask him questions back he fitted himself into the rocking chair. "I wasn't am-bitious enough. I understand it. I'm a carpenter. She's a professor in political science. Teaches at Santa Cruz now. Fancy school, fancy town. I make as much money as she does, but it's not as respectable. Not much to say at faculty parties. What department are you in, Mr. Silver? Oh, er, I built a fence myself last summer."

Surprising herself, she laughed. "Why did you come here?"

"Impulse." His eyes seemed to close as he sank way back in his chair, but she could feel him watching her. "Nosiness. Call it a long shot."

"What kind of a long shot?"

"It explains a lot, him leaving."

"To you, maybe. It's a thing I don't understand. But I will."

"Think you ever really understand why somebody else acts? Why peo-ple decide they love you or decide suddenly they don't?"

"I can come to understand how he's changed. How I was wrong about him and who he is now." And who this woman is he loves, she added mentally, what she has that I lack.

"Only if you take the trouble to learn the facts." He could not main-tain that sleepy facade he liked to hide behind. He was sitting forward, intent, almost passionate in his argument. "Listen, Daria, you can sit around from now to next Christmas making up theories. That isn't understanding. It's just creative storytelling."

"Facts." She stared into the fire. "Are you so sure they're what's real? I should put another log on."

"What are we going to do about supper? If you haven't started anything, want to go out for a pizza?"

She laughed again. "Sure."

"Then let's go. I'll put out the fire. I'm hungry. I eat on the early side because most days I'm at work already by eight A.M."

"Can we use my car instead of your van? Mine's more comfortable."

"Shu-wah." He imitated her pronunciation. "Get your stuff."

As she backed the car out of the drive, she asked, "Where shall we go? There's a place not far from here that's okay."

"We're going to what I consider one of the best pizza places in all of Boston—Santarpio's. I'll give you directions."

"I know how to get to East Boston, pal. I grew up there."

"You know Santarpio's?" He sounded deflated.

"Of course. My steady boyfriend in high school used to take me there Saturday night after the movies."

"That's a whole other side of you." He stared at her speculatively. "Born in East Boston."

"I lived on Havre Street right near Central Square till I was twenty-one. My sister Gussie still lives on Wordsworth."

"I thought you grew up in one of the genteel suburbs."

"You like to label people. You put people in little boxes and nail the lids shut."

"Hey, I'm a carpenter, not an undertaker. Do you think marriage is a kind of box?"

"If it is, mine lost its bottom and I'm spilled out, right?"

"You married security, huh?"

"I married an idealistic law student who was going into the government and make the system work for the disadvantaged."

He whistled. "What happened?"

"That's my question of the year." Driving against the fading stream of rush hour traffic, she knew the fastest routes between Lexington and East Boston from the years she had driven it twice a week. It made her feel less terminated to be out of the house, even with this man with whom she had little in common and more friction than good communication. He believed that she could provide him with information. That was not a bad basis for their evening, because information was what she too needed. Even going out for pizza was a rare treat these days.

Santarpio's was a ramshackle brown shingled building right by the expressway, where it emerged from the tunnel and toll booths. A bar ran along the right side and tables stood along the left. It was smoky. Tom's nose began immediately to run. They took the table nearest the door, where he could hope for occasional relief. Pizza and red wine, it felt familiar here, almost cozy. Dominic Fabrizzi had been as dark and as strongly built as Tom, although not as filled out. That had been their senior year. She had imagined herself in love, yet she had been afraid of him, that he might force her. Her physical attraction to him had scared her, so that she had always been cold with him, sure if she relaxed her guard, she would be lost. "Why not tell me right off what you want? What am I being softened up for?"

"You say you need to understand your husband. We have to understand him too, among others, because he's a major landlord in our neighborhood. There's a lot going on we can't figure out yet."

"He's trying to force me to sell my house. I might do it eventually, but my daughter's still coming home vacations, summers, some weekends—"

"How many children do you have?"

She told him about Tracy and Robin, even volunteering the brief facts about Freddy, which she seldom did. She was surprised, but put her frankness down to being so near base. Politely she asked him in return. He had two daughters, several years younger than hers. Then she dragged the conversation back. "I love my house—irrationally, powerfully. It's all I have left besides Tracy. Robin is siding with her father and his girlfriend."

"Why don't you get somebody to share the house?"

"I already put ads in several papers."

"You did?" He looked up from his plate, his eyes losing their sleepy look.

"You like to peg people neatly, don't you?"

He gave her a brief flash of grin. "You've been doing that to yourself for years, haven't you? Toning yourself down. Filing the rough edges. Planing everything smooth."

"All married people do. Especially wives and mothers."

"Wait till you meet Sandra María. She's got more elbows than Kali."

"I want to know if what he says about our financial situation is true. He wants to force me to sell the house. We'd split the money and he'd pay for Tracy's education. That's it. I think we must have mutual investments, savings, something."

From his wallet he extracted a dog-eared card. "See her."

"Another divorce lawyer?"

"She did mine. The kids were our bone of contention. She does some criminal law, discrimination cases, whatever appeals to her. She won't make you feel like an idiot."

"A very young woman?" She imagined Robin across a desk.

"My age. She started law school when she was twenty-eight. I've known her from way back when." He smiled nostalgically. "One time Dorothy and I were on an underground paper together, *The Old Mole*. A million years ago in another country. She has red hair too."

"My hair isn't red."

"It's reddish. Like mahogany or cherry, with red deep inside it."

"Maybe I'll try her. I called yesterday and cancelled my appointment with the lawyer I saw. I couldn't get that questionnaire filled out and I couldn't face him with it botched."

"Try her. She has good women's politics—"

"What is that supposed to mean?"

"Aw, come on, it means she understands what you're up against. Besides, any lawyer who does some criminal cases for ordinary people has to exercise patience. She has kids come in, she asks them, 'Why did you try to hold up the dry cleaners?' and they say, 'I dunno, I just thought of it. It was like that guy on *Magnum*.' If you do want to unravel Walker's affairs, we can help each other."

"Oh?" She sat back, regarding him from under her lashes. "Sure. The real purpose of your group is to give legal aid to the dumped wives of landlords."

"Shu-wah. You give it two syllables. Can't get the neighborhood out of the kid. Did Walker think that was cute?"

"I'm getting back all my old bad habits."

"You need to investigate Walker. We need to investigate Walker." He was talking fast now in his deep voice, leaning forward across the table, heat and energy coming off him like light. "You have some resources we don't, access to his papers, income tax returns. We have resources you don't. . . ."

Deliberately she sipped her wine, fighting being overwhelmed. "Look, Tom, it just doesn't make sense. You want to know about business. Frankly, if I could have just one question answered, I'd know who this Gail Wisby is and what's so special about her she could take my husband."

"Maybe she's just a pretext. An affair can help when you want to leave anyhow. Then you got somebody else saying, Do it."

"Can you really imagine I'm going to join your group and picket my husband? I can't just turn on him and go over to the other side."

He smiled sardonically. "Is he on your side?"

She shook her head no.

"But probably you just hope he'll come back real soon."

She shook her head, remaining silent an embarrassingly long time until she could establish control over herself. She must not cry in front of him.

"Go on, you can't even talk about him without breaking up."

"It hurts, damn it. I'm angry. I'm humiliated. . . . But the man I married isn't the man I'm married to. He won't come back. The man I want doesn't exist any longer."

"The question is, do you want to sit around and weep over it, or do you really want information you can act on?"

"It dragged on so long, his leaving. For months I thought I was crazy, was imagining everything. It tore me up. I have a life to make now, my own life. I know it won't include him."

"So give up. Let him take everything and drop what crumbs he wants."

"I can't afford to. I'm trying to survive. I'm telling you, for my own good I have to understand. But what I need to know, it's not buildings and real estate. It's the man."

"Daria, do you think somebody is more than the sum of their acts good and bad? You know somebody's real ideas by what they do and who they do it to."

"You just want to use me and my divorce and my troubles."

"So use us back, Daria. We have some knowledge and research techniques to get more. If you need help, and I think you do, make an alliance with us." He took her hand in both of his. "We're your natural allies, can't you see?"

His hands were large and hot, startling. She sat stunned and then with her free hand she salted his with the big shaker. "With a little of that! Don't try to be seductive with me. I'm impervious."

"Seductive!" He yanked his hands away. "I was being sympathetic."

She felt herself blushing. "You were just trying one more argument."

He scowled, his hands folded ostentatiously against his chest. "You don't know who's on your side and who's out to get you, do you?"

She almost apologized. Then she thought, I don't have to! She imagined Fay barreling along, dressing as she pleased and eating as she pleased and sounding off as she pleased. She did not think Fay was always scurrying around apologizing. For years she had been saying incessantly to Ross that she was sorry: when the sauce wasn't perfect, when supper was ten minutes late, when Torte peed on the new carpeting, when Robin left her ten speed in the drive and the oil truck backed over it, when Tracy was caught making love with Nick. Tom Silver was simply interested in trying to use her, and she owed him no apology. He thought her a simple middle-aged woman who would be a pushover for a little manly charm.

Smiling inwardly, she sipped her wine. She had handled that well, putting him smartly in his place. "I'm simply not convinced we do have the same interests. Fay and I can work together on conditions in her building, but otherwise, really, we have nothing to offer each other." She wished she could stop and see Gussie, but she didn't want to drag Tom along. "We don't want or need the same kind of information. I own Fay's building, it seems. But my responsibility stops there."

15

W E can't make people not fall in love with other people, but we'll see he does right by you," Cesaro intoned.

She could imagine him tapping out his pipe as he spoke, his forehead screwing into that judicious frown. However, Cesaro not only returned her calls but called on his own to check her situation; whereas Tony had returned none of her calls. "You've met *her*, haven't you?"

"Not with him. I have no intention of having them over before arrangements are made to your satisfaction."

"My satisfaction?" She felt like thumping the receiver on the desk.

"Justly, I mean. I must confess I had somehow assumed it was the younger sister Flip. Trish knows her from horse shows. I supposed it was Flip, because she's stunning, the racy type."

"And you don't think Gail is?"

"Oh, come on." Cesaro cleared his throat. "The middle sister. The oldest is Rowena Robson, the designer. Of course, both the other sisters are married and have a couple of offspring apiece."

"And Gail isn't married?"

"No, no. Daria, don't dwell on it. You can delay their marrying, but you can't prevent it. Remember how I helped you when you found your house was held in tenant in the entirety?"

"I appreciated that, Cesaro. Without your pressure he'd never have changed it, and I'd be sunk now."

"You see the lawyer whose name I am about to give you. He'll do the best for you that can be done." He sounded as if he were suggesting a second opinion on a hopeless cancer. Daria took down the name obediently. She was learning that everyone was going to press upon her the name of some lawyer.

She was satisfied with Dorothy Keough. Tom had picked well for Daria, whether by chance or insight or simply the association of Dorothy too having grown up in East Boston, although seven years later than Daria. "We grow them tough," Dorothy said. "If planes flying through your bedroom don't wear you down, and you can breathe pure carbon monoxide in the Callahan Tunnel for hours each day, then you can take anything else the system may throw at you." Dorothy told her she had three options. "You can accept your husband's figures as to what you're both worth. You can make up your own and try to bluff. Not recommended. Or you can put in some labor yourself. It's a question, really, of how much trouble you're willing to take. It'll cost you too much if I do it. Now I can make some phone calls for you. Right off I'll call this accountant who's sitting on the tax returns and have copies of the last seven years sent over. That'll be a start."

Dorothy had lighter brown hair than Daria with more carrot in it, a scattering of freckles makeup could not hide and light sandy eyes. She was short, plump and low-voiced, with ears double-pierced in which she wore tiny diamond studs.

"I'm easy with her," Daria explained to Tracy on the phone. The telephone had always been Daria's enemy, cutting into her work time, disrupting her tight scheduling of blocks of time for work, preparation for Ross's social evenings, the daily tasks of running a complicated household. Now the telephone offered companionship; it cuddled against her shoulder bringing instant intimacy, the buzz of friendship, news, comfort. She talked with Gretta every other night and could scarcely recall how she used to wince when the phone rang and Gretta was on the line. She often broke at one on weekdays when Alice was in her office in the botany department at MIT eating a brown bag lunch. Although Daria had been friendly with Alice for seven years, previously they had seldom spoken unless she had a question for Alice about plants.

Now she talked to Gussie three times a week. Many people like somebody in worse trouble than they are, she learned, especially when the trouble is new. Everybody told her their infidelity stories, their divorce tales. If she was rarely invited out socially, then at least she was sought out by other women to swap stories of broken marriages. Alice told her about her first husband. Alice also referred her to an accountant.

She felt incredibly adult, having her own accountant. For all the years she had worked, never had the money been real to her. She liked making money. She met her deadlines sedulously and tried to do a good job with demonstrations, classes, contests. But the money she earned had melted away into their life, so that it was seldom she could point to something and say, I bought that, I invested in that.

Her accountant—what a self-important ring that possessive had—was a tall lucid man with pale hair and pale grey eyes a few years younger than Daria, about the same age as Dorothy. He made bad jokes and had his office decorated with Kliban cats, but he gently explained and explained to her. On the phone to Ross's accountant, he was hectoring. His cold authoritative demands pleased her. Accountant to accountant, lawyer to lawyer, the joust got under way. The phone gave her a web of arteries that pumped in the blood of connection. The only time it betrayed her was when she answered it, hoping for a shot of warmth, and got Ross instead.

"Daria, old bean, how are you doing?" He used that caramel voice she used to hear through the door when he was on the phone to Gail.

"What do you want, Ross?"

"Just to know how you are. You know I still care about you, sweetie, still have your interests close to my heart."

How could he say that? She was so angry she could not think in words but in a fiery red light that would not translate into words. Besides Dorothy had told her to avoid giving Ross any information about her own plans.

"Daria? Are you still there?"

"Here is where I am, yes." She tried to invest her tone with some of the bitter irony she felt.

"Thought I'd come by and get a few papers I need, how about it? Have a drink, talk things over."

"If there's something you need, how about Thursday at five?"

"What is this five o'clock bit? That's very inconvenient." His voice rose in pitch and decibels.

"It's very convenient for me. Doesn't interfere with my evening."

In truth she was putting him off till Thursday because she had begun going through the papers in his study on her lawyer's advice, looking for clues to their financial situation. Her real fantasy was finding a big manila envelope labelled Gail Wisby that would contain everything she wanted to know about the woman who had taken Ross from her; emotional history, vital statistics, sexual habits, secret lore. She figured ruefully that she spent at least an hour daily inventing Gail Wisby—invention out of despair because she had so little to build on. One small item of interest she had learned from photocopied tax returns—learned when the accountant pointed it out to her—was that Ross had opened an account the year before in a bank near his office, an account he had never mentioned to her, presumably before he had ever met Gail.

This time she made a list of those trusts that seemed to siphon off a large part of their income. She did not know how to pursue further exactly what they were, but she was a firm believer in libraries and was convinced all information was somewhere accessible. Ross had also paid over eight thousand dollars directly to Tony over the past three months. There were three IOUs signed by Ross to Tony, dated the last year, marked paid.

The next night the phone rang at eleven, when she was in bed reading. A little warily she picked it up. It was her brother Joe. "Yeah, but it's not late to me," he said. "We don't close till now and besides the rates go down. How come we had to find out the news from Cesaro?"

"I didn't see any reason to worry Pops about it. After all, nothing's settled yet."

"Cesaro seemed to think Ross was for sure divorcing you. Is he full of hot air as usual?"

"Ross left me the day after Christmas." She got so weary of saying that. "He has a girlfriend. I'm sure Cesaro told you all that."

"I figure you're going to sell the house, right? So you ought to come down here. You can keep house for Pops."

She was so astonished she could not speak for a moment. "Come down there? I couldn't possibly."

"What it is, you have a boyfriend too? I don't believe it."

"Of course not. But I have contracts, commitments, my book to get in on schedule—"

"You come on down and live with Pops. Plenty of room in the garden apartment. Pops likes the idea, we had a family council tonight and we worked it out."

"Is there room for my secretary too? Joe, I work. *Here.* Tracy's in college here—"

"She can transfer."

"She doesn't want to transfer and I have no intention of leaving my home." When the conversation was finally over, when she ended it out of fatigue, she realized how completely invisible she was to her father and her oldest brother. After that phone call, she almost believed she was mistaken about her profession: that she really had none, that her writing, her lecturing, her cooking-school work were all childish pretense, on a level with decoupage and collecting salt and pepper shakers, as Nina's friend Liz used to do. They saw her as a middle-aged child. My lawyer, my accountant, my agent, she said over to herself, my secretary, my editor. What I do is real, it is!

When Ross arrived Thursday, she felt jittery, afraid he would notice something amiss in his study, but he seemed on edge himself. "Did any mail come here for me?"

"I assume you're having it forwarded. There's a pile of junk mail and some catalogues on the table in the hall."

He riffled through the pile. "You can throw all that out. . . . Have you had any more threats from that tenant group? Any harassment?"

"They haven't bothered me. Why?"

"Just wondered. We have to protect you by moving those buildings out of your name." He started to open his briefcase.

"I'm afraid my lawyer won't allow me to sign anything prior to the divorce agreement."

"These buildings have nothing whatsoever to do with divorce. They were merely placed under your name for convenience."

"Talk to Dorothy, please. I don't know anything about it." She was slightly ashamed to play dumb, but she was not about to sign his deeds.

He paced around the living room, frowning. "If they do bother you, call my office and let me know."

"Why would they?" She did not sit but stood in the doorway to the hall. She tried to understand what she was afraid of: that he would question her, that they would have a dreadful fight, that he would figure out her strategy? She feared more pain from him.

"It could be dangerous, you know. You can't tell what they might do, with you here alone."

She felt ashamed for him. "Ross, forget it. They have no reason to be angry with me."

"Once you sign those papers, of course not. In the meantime, you're vulnerable to them." He was trying to sound friendly. "I don't like to think of you here alone dealing with them."

She could not even summon up the irony to congratulate him on his concern. She found herself embarrassed by what she saw as his willingness to lie not only to her but most overwhelmingly to himself.

He was sitting in his old chair, so that she almost expected him to turn on the television and start watching a game, but for once he was looking directly at her. "It's sad that it came to this," he murmured. "We had a lot between us, old darling."

"Do you think you could manage just once to address me with some phrase that did not include old in it? I'm younger than you are, old boy."

He tsk-tsked, as if her folly depressed him. They both seemed to feel the other had lost a grip on reality. He said then, as if suddenly struck, "You remember my fortieth birthday? When you gave me that absurd party?"

"Nobody but you thought it was." She started to sink in her rocker, then rose as if stung. She would not encourage a long conversation. She remained standing, her arms folded across her breasts. "It was a lovely party."

"For you! Everybody fussing about you. Look what Daria has done!" He mimicked falsetto voices. "What cakes, what cookies, what hors d'oeuvres. Daria! Daria! Daria!"

She had rented (at a special price to her) a restaurant where she had several times run cooking classes. There she had staged a surprise party.

Ross had been feeling depressed about turning forty, and she had sought to buoy him up. It had been a great success for everybody but him.

"Ross, I really don't want to have a long conversation now."

"You're avoiding me."

"You've gone to some lengths to avoid me. You moved out."

"That was for the best, can't you see?" He glared. "I'm not made of money, if that's what you told that fat little shyster who's working for you. Things are tight. Very tight. I need my capital out of this house, I'm warning you."

"I need this house to live in. So does Tracy when she's home. This is my office as well as my house, and I like it just fine."

"If you drag me down, you'll go down too," he said darkly and retreated to his study, slamming the door.

Ten minutes later, she banged on it. "Would you please take what you want and clear out? I have company coming."

"Who?" He opened the door a crack.

"No one you know." She crossed her arms, facing him. "I'd like your stuff out of that room completely by next week. I need the room."

The door flew open. "You need the room! For what? The cat box?"

"I live here. You don't. You live in a condo and with your girlfriend. I don't want your office effects in my house any longer."

"It isn't your house."

"It isn't all my house *yet*. It will be."

"Damn you, you're coming out a complete bitch." He pushed past. As he dragged on his overcoat he turned with a scowl. "Remember when I had heatstroke, how you made fun of me in front of my mother?"

"Ross! I didn't make fun of you. I just knew you weren't dying."

"Mother was right about you. If you want war, you'll have war, but it'll ruin both of us." He ran down to his car.

Dorothy called the next day. "We have his financial statement. I'd appreciate your coming by to take a look at it. Ross appears to be a pauper."

"How can that be?"

"Oh, planning for divorce is as tricky as planning for taxes. I expect he's hidden his assets away in some of those trusts you mentioned. He doesn't list that bank account your accountant uncovered. I'm going to send a copy of Ross's statement to him and have him compare it with the tax returns. I think we'll turn up a lot of goodies that have disappeared."

"But what can we do?"

"Hit him with some facts, give him another chance to make a correct statement. We can require him to make a legal deposition. Lying on that is perjury. We have a lot of moves, Daria."

That evening she had supper with Gretta at Mario's. The relationship remained cordial, and she could count on a reduced-price meal with wine on the house. She had not been there, she realized, in a year. Ross claimed to think the restaurant had gone downhill, although she suspected what he disliked was the fuss around her when she walked in. Usually she went with Gussie and Don, to give them a treat on birthdays or anniversaries.

Gretta loved the fuss and the free wine. They worked through two carafes in the course of a relaxed and bountiful meal—hot antipasto, including the zucchini with anchovy-flavored stuffing she had invented a decade before, seafood cannelloni, a crisp salad of endive. Over espresso Gretta dipped into her huge leather purse and began to spread out brochures. "Now what you need, darling, is to busy yourself. Join things. Meet people."

As Daria hefted the catalogue from the Cambridge Adult Education Center, a harsh sigh rose from her. "I taught a course there. I don't think—"

"Surely there are dozens of things you always wanted to learn. French? Plant identification. Then you won't always be having to ask Alice."

Envisioning herself taking earnest notes in a classroom, she felt more depressed. "I didn't love school. I prefer learning on my own."

"But the point is to meet people."

"I do meet people."

"Men, silly. Pick out a sport. Did you ever play tennis? Ski? Ice-skate? There are always lots of men at political events. Work for a candidate. Join something environmental."

"Gretta, it sounds like being in college again. All that's lacking are freshman mixers. No, really, I don't crave male company."

"But you will. You must! You can't just rattle around in that house talking to your cats and making yourself elaborate soufflés. He's retired you to the shelf, but I want some fighting spirit before rot sets in."

It was nine when they finished and rose wavering. On the sidewalk, Gretta clutched her arm. "Ross lives around here, doesn't he?"

"Actually, I have the address. On Commercial."

Gretta poked her. "Let's go look his scene over."

"Suppose he sees us?"

"Darling, he'd be nonplussed if he did."

"I'd be mortally embarrassed."

"Besides, you don't imagine he sits at the window all evening looking at his view? It's Friday night—he's out with *her*. As I would be with my dear young man, if he wasn't in Vermont skiing. Frankly, escape is nice now and then. He's dear in the obvious respects, but he has a sweet tooth you could drive six sugar horses through, and he watches far too much telly."

Daria found herself giggling as they picked their way over the ice-rutted narrow sidewalks of the North End, rivulets of ice between the tall old brick tenements, past bakeshops and noodle factories, past butcher shops where furry rabbits hung.

Commercial Street bounded one of the harbor edges, a broad heavily potholed thoroughfare where the small winding streets came out suddenly to windswept space, old brick and granite wharf buildings, the grey water beyond. In her childhood those massive wharf buildings had still been warehouses, but now they were luxury condominiums with expensive restaurants, decorators, architects and lawyers on the ground floors.

"I bet it's that one." Gretta pointed over to Union Wharf. The granite slab was refurbished and the double row of brick town houses had been erected farther out on the old wharf.

"Wrong address. It's got to be on the land side."

They clambered over hills compounded of dirt, ice and solidified exhaust fumes. Some of the narrow brick buildings on their side had already been renovated into dim and woody restaurants called Chez this and Aux that, realty offices, Scandinavian design shops, homemade ice-cream parlors with long lines even on a freezing night. On the corner stood a six-story functioning cold storage warehouse that doubtless would blossom out soon as a luxury condominium.

Ross's building stood farther along, facing a still active warehouse that blocked the water view. Some buildings on his block had already under-gone their transformation; others were untouched; some had dumpsters in front receiving the rubble from surgery in progress. Ross's was in the final stages of renovation, although most of the apartments looked in-habited.

"Reklaw Reality." Gretta chuckled, reading the sign. "What a name."

"He owns it," Daria breathed in amazement.

"This? It's a little pricy, isn't it?"

"But look, that name is Walker spelled backward. And the phone num-ber is his office."

"You're kidding." Gretta squinted at the sign. "You're not kidding."

Which would number five be? She stood out in the street but could not guess the interior layout. A man crossing the street stopped beside her, following her gaze to the building. "Are you one of the other poor suck-ers who bought into this mess?" The man asked.

"Not yet. I was considering it," Daria said. "Is something wrong with the building?"

"Is everything wrong?" He pointed to the unfinished floor. "It was supposed to be all done last September. I've moved in but they're still building around us. Think of the suckers who thought they were mov-ing in six months ago. I'll tell you, for the last three months, nothing's happened. The workmen haven't been back. No wonder people are sell-ing out already."

"What reason do they give for not finishing?"

"They don't give any reasons. You just try and get them on the phone."

"But the man who owns the building lives in number five, didn't you know?"

Gretta giggled audibly.

"Are you sure?" The man stared. "Number five?"

"Mr. Ross Walker. Don't you know him?"

208

"The one with the dogs? He's never there. But I'm going to lie in wait for him. Number five. Thanks, I mean it."

Daria felt chilled by the blast of the wind off the cold waters of the harbor, but quite pleased with herself. "You want to stop and have a cannoli on Hanover?" she asked Gretta. "We deserve it."

Saturday Daria interviewed women she had not screened out on the phone. She knew she could not live with a twenty-year-old. She wanted somebody her own age, give or take ten years.

Her first visitor would have been fine, without child. The boy in question within twenty minutes broke a cup and saucer, pulled the books from the bookcase in the corner of the living room and peed on the braided rug while his mother sat beaming. She didn't believe in breaking a child's spirit, she told Daria.

Number two chain-smoked. Daria thought perhaps she could try to get used to that. After all, the woman's son seemed housebroken. However, the woman turned out to be a strict and proselytizing vegetarian who, while smoking furiously, lectured Daria on the carcinogens in meat. Seeing anyone cook it sickened her and Daria must be careful to leave no meat scraps visible; they would use the kitchen at different times on a fixed schedule. Daria did not point out that the cats and the dog were carnivores.

Number three was sweet but obviously distraught. She kept glancing out the window as if watching for someone. Daria could not decide if she were paranoid—perhaps just released from a mental institution—or if she had a husband she was escaping, whom she expected to drive up with a tommy gun. Daria did not want to find out which possibility was the bad news in question.

Number four had three children and needed more room. She wanted Daria to move into the downstairs study and give her the whole upstairs.

Number five was a darling, an older woman who worked as a bank teller, loved gardening, seemed literate with no striking oddities. However, she was allergic to cats. They parted in mutual regret.

* * *

"Yeah, I was in the old neighborhood last week eating with a friend, at Santarpio's," Daria said. She was chatting with Gussie cradling the phone between ear and shoulder while doling out catfood. Ali had climbed on the counter to eat from the can. Then Sheba leaped up behind him and batted him in the rear. As he swung to retaliate, Sheba lunged and they tangled among the dishes and opened can.

"Susie said she thought it was you, but she wasn't sure. Susie Croto, used to be Calacitto when you were in school together?"

"Susie Calacitto! I didn't even see her. Where was she hiding?"

"You wouldn't know her. There's twice what there used to be, you know how it is. Shut up, Bobbie! She said she's seen you on TV a couple of times, so she knew it was you for sure."

"I wish she'd said hello."

"You know how people are. So who was the guy?"

"Him? He's a carpenter."

"Doing some work for you?"

"No, he's a representative of this tenants group who are mad at Ross." She carried the phone on its long cord to the trestle table in the dining room.

"Is Ross really trying to screw you over, or what? Tony won't talk about it. Our sweet brother. You know he's siding with Ross. Tony and Ross are tighter than ever. Proving money is thicker than blood."

"Ross and I are fighting about a settlement. . . . Gussie, you know how when we got back from Florida I took some of Mama's things to her old friends, Liz and Patsy?"

"I would've done it. But you were the one who went through everything. . . . The kids love having that afghan Grandma knit."

"When I went to see Patsy, she wasn't friendly. She had a grudge against me, something about what happened next door."

"Jesus, sissie, what do you expect? She's still living there. Why wouldn't she be pee-oed?"

"Gussie, why? It wasn't our fault the house burned down. Was it?"

"That's a matter of opinion, isn't it?"

"How come?"

"Daria, why rake over these old issues? Patsy remembers because she lives right next door, but nobody else cares anymore."

"But, Gussie, what did people get angry about? What do they think happened?"

"You guys let the house run down. You didn't put one cent into it. It made me feel lousy when I went by. You know how nice Mama kept it. With her garden out back and his arbor and all."

"The tenants beat it into the ground. It's not fair to blame us."

"You picked the tenants. You didn't keep it up. Every year it looked crummier. You just milked it for what you could get out, subdividing it, letting it rot. Okay so maybe it was the boiler, who will ever know?"

"I thought it was supposed to be a tenant smoking in bed. What do you think it was?"

"Aw come on, Daria. You know what everybody says."

"I don't know what everybody says, or I wouldn't be asking. I'm begging now. What are you talking about?"

"Like they say, go sell it to the insurance company. You know. Instant Parking Lot."

"That's the same phrase Patsy used."

"So what did you think she meant? Honestly, Daria, sometimes you like to play dumb! It's been that way since you were a kid. You pretend you don't catch on to things you don't want to notice."

"That's not fair, Gussie!"

"Oh, yeah? You must have known, really known for months that Ross had a girlfriend."

"Gussie, do you believe what you're saying? That Ross and I burned Mama's old house?"

"Ross and you and Tony and Cesaro. You all had money tied up in it. You know how parking is near the Square. That lot does a good business for local parking and for the airport."

"I can't believe my own sister is saying this about me!" Daria's eyes began to water.

"Daria, come off it! What do I care? You're still my sister. But don't be so innocent about why Patsy isn't your friend no more."

"Gussie, you're wrong. I know how close together the houses are. In a strong wind they could all go up. I'd never do anything like that, and neither would Ross or Cesaro. . . . On Tony, I wouldn't care to place any bets."

"We're used to it here. You look around some time and see what's happening. But honestly, Daria, you've been the same way all your life. I remember when Pops left us for two months and he was living with that Panzini woman, you pretended to believe he was off working in New York. When your girlfriend Maureen was knocked up, you were the only one around who went through the motions of believing she got a job in summer camp, ha-ha. You're the only person I ever met, who if I told you I ran into a doorknob and that's how I got a black eye, you'd believe me. Or you'd pretend to. I think you just like to avoid trouble."

After the phone call, Daria felt roughly shaken, as if Gussie had picked her up like a kitten and rattled her bones. She was still feeling confused through and through when Ross called. "Daria," he crooned, "I wanted to talk to you. How are you?" he asked unctuously. "How are you doing? Are you really all right?"

"Fine," she said shortly. "What do you want, Ross?"

"I don't want anything, except to know how you're doing. I don't want us to be enemies. We were married for twenty-two years. I want you to know, Daria, I mean the best for you. All this business of lawyer calling up lawyer and accountant screaming at accountant, it has nothing personal to do with us."

"Of course not," she said sweetly.

"Trust me, Daria. I want what's best for you. That's the only reason I worry so much about your failure to act on signing those deeds. I wouldn't hurt you for the world."

"Thank you, Ross. And how's Gail?"

"This is hard on her. It's a very uncomfortable time for her."

"If I dropped dead, I'm sure everybody on your end would be a lot more comfortable." She hung up.

She paced the downstairs. What was she to do with herself, with her life? What was she to do with every evening for the next thirty years? Passing the stack of brochures Gretta had pressed on her, she dropped into her rocker to riffle through them. She did not want to take a course; it felt an enormous step backward. She gave courses, she did not attend them. That was arrant snobbishness, but she did not want to run about with no more purpose than to "meet people." Gretta had filled her void with romance. Daria did not want a romance. She wanted connection. She wanted purpose.

Tossing the brochures into the grate, she thought over the women she had interviewed the day before and tried to persuade herself that one of them might work out. She could not persuade herself. Peggy had not brought up the idea of moving in. She could not press her secretary further.

How could Gussie believe she had burned their family home? How could anyone think that of her? Why would she burn a building that belonged to her? The idea was absurd, yet Gussie obviously believed it, and Patsy had held it against her. She longed to disprove them.

She had to understand what Ross had involved her in, what he was doing. Things I Must Find Out, she wrote on a pad used for grocery lists. (1) What are our finances exactly, what do we own and how? (2) What changed Ross and who is he now? (3) What went wrong in our marriage? At that point her gaze fell on Torte who looked at her reproachfully as she wrote on, (4) Gail Wisby: who is she and why does Ross prefer her and her army of German short-haired pointers?

The pad told her she had a purpose if she would give in to it. She had a whole research project mapped out. But how she could ally herself with Ross's enemies and investigate her own husband? Well, how could he leave her? How could he lie to her? How could he blame her for everything wrong in his life? How could he try to force her out of her home?

She did not have to ally herself with those tenants to talk with them occasionally. At least she could learn what they knew about Ross. Her goals were different from theirs, but who else could possibly help her at all? Tom had indicated they could teach her how to find what Ross owned, and that would be a start. She had no idea how to go about it on her own. Before she could waver with Ross's voice echoing in her ears urging her to trust him, that trust Gussie had derided as willful blindness, she dialed Fay's number.

She got one of Fay's sons. "She's at Tom's. They're having a meeting. You got the number there?" The way he talked, numbah, he could have been one of her own brothers back in high school.

It made her smile. But at Tom's it was Mac who answered. She recognized his clipped tones. "And who is this? Oh, Mrs. Walker. One moment. I'll see if Mrs. Souza can come to the phone."

Fay was warmer. "I'll tell the others and call you right back. Glad you decided."

Half an hour, an hour passed and the phone did not ring. Several times she checked that it was firmly on its stand. She straightened the downstairs, regretting that she had put herself forward. With only her at home, it hardly got dirty. Surfaces collected dust and her bathroom needed cleaning now and again as did the kitchen, but the house required little. She could not even find busy work tonight. Outside snow was lightly falling. Sheba kept following her, throwing herself belly up in front of Daria so that she almost stepped on the lithe black kitten. Sheba was insistent on affection, as if sensing Daria's disturbance. Daria felt lost. Which way led forward?

Finally the phone rang. It was Tom. "The meeting's just broken up. Can Sandra María and I come over?"

"Now?" She glanced at her watch. It was nine-thirty. "Oh, all right."

16

SANDRA María came as a skeptical interrogator. Sandra María was thin, quick, nervous. Her skin was a pale olive. She spoke a clear unaccented precise and very fast English. She had been born in Puerto Rico and emigrated with her parents to Boston when she was five. Her buzz of nervous energy, foot tapping, fingers drumming, a loop of dark brown curl twisting between her fingers as she talked, reminded Daria of Ross and made her feel by contrast slow as a hippopotamus on land.

"But if I teach you to do the research, you have to go on with it. Try to understand, it's boring. It takes hours to find out anything in the Registry of Deeds. I'm in graduate school, I have a child, I work. I can't put in the time to train you for a whim."

Gradually Daria understood there had been an argument in SON about her working with them. She felt insulted. Did they imagine it was an easy decision for her? Perhaps she should seize on their doubts as a convenient exit. But Tom was persistent. He had succeeded in persuading Mac and Sherry, the most strongly opposed, that if Sandra María thought Daria could help, they would try her out.

"What does Mac have against me?" Daria burst out.

"He says your class interests are opposed to ours," Tom boomed. For once he was out of his work clothes, his flannel shirts and overalls, dressed nicely in maroon wool sweater and navy wool pants. He had doffed his red kerchief, but the little stud still winked in his ear. She did not know why she always found herself staring at it. It seemed rakish.

"His class interests! He's at Harvard."

Tom gave that big grin that opened his face, his teeth bright against his ruddy skin and dark hair. "You noticed that. We're his material."

Sandra María said, "Ah, but Tom wanted you to do it more than Mac wanted you not to. Tom doesn't take on Mac often, but when he does, I notice he wins. Eh, Tom? Throwing your weight around."

Tom was scratching Sheba's belly as she writhed on the floor, insistent on attention. "I can always threaten to sit on him," Tom said morosely. "He's just a welterweight."

"You're not fat," Sandra María said. "It's just how you usually dress, like a slob. You're strong as an ox. But when you changed out of your overalls tonight, I almost fainted with surprise."

Daria decided that Sandra María was not his girlfriend, as she had thought at first. She flirted with Tom, as Daria noticed all the women in SON seemed to, but pro forma as a kind of teasing that had become ritualized.

"Has anybody alive ever seen an ox?" Tom tried to push Sheba away a little. "I've spent my whole life being compared to one. What the hell kind of beast is an ox, anyhow? I bet neither of you have any idea."

He wasn't fat; he was big-boned and muscular, actually. "It's a castrated bull," Daria said sweetly. "I looked it up once, when I was reading a Paul Bunyan tale to my daughter."

Sandra María burst into a short sharp peal of laughter. "Oye, Tomás, I didn't mean that!"

He glared at both of them, his face glowing dark with anger. "With a public image like that, I should retire to eat grass in the park."

Sandra María was trying to repress her amusement. "Don't you think Daria demonstrates an ability to retain researched materials? She might be good at this paper chase."

Daria was becoming embarrassed by Sheba, rolling around the floor howling for attention. Maybe she was spoiling the cats, now that she lived alone. Tom was sitting in a heap, steaming and broody. Something in the epithet had pierced his defenses. Finally the women ignored him, speaking to each other. Sandra María said, "My building is owned by

216

Revco, a trust set up by Charles Petris. So is the building next door. But the one on my other side is owned by Anthony Porfirio—your brother? Now, is he a straw for your husband?"

"A straw?"

"Sometimes they put a building in somebody else's name to conceal ownership or hide assets. Like putting Fay's building in your name. Often it's somebody with no resources and lots of loyalty to the real owners—"

"Tony has resources. He's a public adjuster who lives—very well—in Belmont."

"A public adjuster . . . fascinating." Sandra María beamed at her.

"Not really. It's something dull to do with insurance," Daria explained.

"Public adjusters help people who've had fires collect from insurance companies. Especially if there's any question about the legitimacy of the fire. They take a percentage of what their client wins."

"But why is that interesting?" Daria stared at Sandra María.

"How close are you to this Anthony brother?"

"At the moment we're not speaking. He's taking my husband's side in the divorce."

Daria found she could not successfully ignore Tom, brooding on the far side of the room. Perhaps because of his size, he had a strong physical presence that forced itself on her awareness, as if chafing her.

"Tomás, compañero, listen to me for a moment and stop making like a volcano about to erupt."

"Oxen don't erupt, according to Mrs. Walker."

She had trouble keeping herself from smirking. She could not have said why she knew what would get to him, but she had known. They were such opposite types, they set each other on edge simply being in the same room. He was always staring at her as if she puzzled or annoyed him too. She was sure each of them loved to figure out how to needle the other.

"Anthony Porfirio is a public adjuster," Sandra María said with the air Ross had when he discovered a ruby kinglet at the feeder.

"Porfirio . . . her brother." Tom looked up, coming into sharp focus. "I bet his knowledge of fire is proving useful to all."

"Tom's our resident conspiracy buff." Sandra María was trying to make him smile.

"What conspiracy?" Daria asked. Sheba was making a nuisance of herself. Even Ali seemed alienated and had taken refuge on a bookcase, from which he peered down at her.

Tom turned, his dark eyes gleaming with anger. "You tell us."

"Tom just means that your search among deeds and mortgages may sort out the situation of who owns what with whom."

Sandra María, Daria realized, was talking as if their cooperation was settled, and somehow it seemed to be. There was something quick and light in Sandra María that Daria liked. Sandra María was a small orange flame at which she could warm her hands and her mind. Although the woman was only five or six years older than Robin, she seemed a full generation more mature.

Sandra María bounced to her feet. "Mariela's sleeping at my mamá's tonight, but I still have to truck on home. Up early tomorrow. But Thursday A.M. I can meet you at the Government Center T Station. There's only one entrance. Nine o'clock on the nose. I'll show you the ropes. If you can get into it, it absorbs you."

Tom rose to follow Sandra María out without saying good night. What a moody vein he had in him. She smiled. As he was going out he swung back suddenly, putting an arm out and catching the door as it was about to shut. "I wouldn't tell you except she's too small to be allowed to have kittens, but your cat's in heat."

"Sheba? She's too young."

"They all say that. Too young or too old. Or maybe you think she's castrated too." He slammed the door.

Tom was right. Poor Ali tried. Although they were litter mates, he was not quite sexually mature. He tried and she tried and they hissed and screamed and spat and chased each other through the house. They drove Daria crazy. Such insistent sexuality, the little wriggling body, as Sheba pursued her from chair to bath to bed, offering herself. Annette's big orange cat took up residence on the stone terrace off the living room in spite of the cold and the snow. Sheba rubbed shamefully against the glass and they sang duets through the intervening French doors.

* * *

City Hall was a massive new building of poured concrete nine stories tall standing in a windy plaza downtown. Sandra María came up the escalator just behind Daria wearing a maroon wool coat with a pom-pom hat on, against the near zero cold of the morning. They hastened together out of the wind into the tall glassy lobby. Sandra María led her directly to the tax assessor's office, where she fended off the query that greeted them and made directly for the books spread out on a wide shelf.

Sandra María spoke softly in her ear. "Always seem as if you know exactly what you're doing or they'll tell you you can't do it. You look up the street in this book first. This is assuming you're starting with a building and you want to find out who owns it. Let's look up the building next to me. First we find what ward and precinct it's in—that's how they file things here. There, you see, that's Ward Twenty-one, Precinct Seven. So now we pull out that book and we look up my address and we find out who pays the taxes—where the tax bills are sent. Revco Realty Trust."

"But that doesn't put you much further ahead, does it?"

They were crossing the lobby to the elevators. "Sure it does. When we finish up here, I'll take you across the street to the Registry of Deeds." Sandra María pushed the button for the eighth floor. "Now in this place, you have to know exactly what you're looking for, because they won't help you much."

Daria thought, she really is mistrustful. Perhaps that was what being Puerto Rican in Boston did to someone, even a woman as young and pretty and bright as Sandra María. Certainly Sandra María seemed a little paranoid. Daria had always found that if you spoke nicely to people in bureaucracies, you could generally get them to help you. It was a matter of not being defensive or unpleasantly aggressive.

"This is the office of building inspectors. That is, the one for complaints about the inside. They have a different office catty-corner in the building for outside things, structural things. You'll see." They walked into a long and drab office with a counter around the entrance.

Leisurely a young woman came toward them. "What do you want?"

"We'd like to see the file on Seventeen Granville," Sandra María said in dulcet tones, with a friendly smile.

"Who are you?"

"You have a file on Seventeen, don't you?"

"What do you want to see it for?"

"We'd like to check out the recent violations."

"What for? Who are you?"

Daria could not believe that rudeness. She stared at the young woman. Sandra María did not appear to find anything extraordinary. She simply persisted, never raising her voice, "We're with a tenants group. We'd like to see the file on that building. We're legally entitled, according to the decision of—"

"Do you live in the building?"

"I live next door."

The woman stalked away and at first Daria thought she had simply deserted them. Finally she came back. Seeing they were still waiting she asked, "What was that number?"

Finally she brought them a folder and slapped it down on the counter. "There's nothing current." She did not let go of the folder.

Sandra María had to pry it gently from her. Daria got a brief look at reports that listed complaints by tenants and reports by building inspectors. Then the woman snatched the file away, repeating "Nothing current! Nothing current!"

"What does that mean?" Daria asked in the hall.

"There's nothing on the court docket now, on that building. Either the tenants gave up or the complaints were settled in court."

"That woman was crazy. She won't last long at that job."

"Sure she will. That's how they all act in City Hall here."

Indeed as Sandra María led her from department to department they were challenged, they signed in and had to leave their phone numbers before seeing the file in the other, structural office of building inspection, they were called stupid, their conversations were butted into, they were refused, harassed and yelled at. With a great sense of relief Daria followed Sandra María across the street.

"Now most of what you'll be doing is in the Court Building, the Registry of Deeds, but I wanted to show you the whole process before we settled down. I hope you're not dressed too warmly?"

"But it's freezing!" They crossed Cambridge Street and went through to the second building. Just inside the door they had to pass through a metal detector and have their purses searched, as if they were boarding a plane. The guard took Daria's little cassette recorder. She was to get it back when they left. Then she followed Sandra María through a low tunnel into the old part of the court, through a high marble nineteenth-century lobby and up a rickety elevator that was operated by a chatty balding old man.

The building was hot: she understood Sandra María's question. The Registry of Deeds was a vast room with many tables and few chairs with walls painted in marine and pale blue, full of men and women bustling about pulling out the heavy books and shoving them back. She felt far more comfortable there. The information was accessible although obscure, and the atmosphere was purposeful, intent.

The room was divided into grantor and grantee sections, sellers and buyers, and in those sections, by blocks of years and then alphabetically, every heavy book numbered. Daria looked up herself and there she was as Daria Porfirio, having bought ten buildings over the past four years from Ross Walker, from Anthony Porfirio, from Revco Realty Trust (Fay's building, she recognized at once), from Red Robin Trust. She had sold four buildings, she found in the other index, basically to the same set of characters. One building of hers in Dorchester, recently sold to Tony, had been in a lot of trouble with the city for back taxes. She had been a lively real estate operator, buying and selling, getting mortgages on mortgages, scrapping with the city, wheeling and dealing mostly in the SON neighborhood, but also as far away as North Cambridge and Dorchester.

Ross ran for a solid page. The little entries told her cryptically what was in each of the massive books scattered around the room. Some were statements of trusts. Red Robin was a trust set up by Ross two years before. Revco was indeed the Petrises, but Ross appeared as attorney. Walton was Ross and Tony in business together. She was astonished to see that Robin too was down as owner of a couple of buildings, one on Fay's street. Reklaw was, as she had supposed, Ross again but this time with his law partner Roger Kingsley, who was King Cole Realty and seemed also to enjoy an ongoing relationship with the Petrises.

Sandra María stood at her elbow, by the chair she had captured. "Daria, I think you've got the hang of it. I'm off to Northeastern for my class. Will you be all right?"

Daria glanced at her watch. She was astonished to discover it was twelve-thirty. Now she would be late for her appointment with the people at Channel 7, unless she had luck with her taxi and traffic.

Her lawyer Dorothy encouraged the search. "Find out whatever you can. We need a list of all properties acquired in the course of the marriage. This isn't a community property state, but it recognizes your interest."

"It takes me half a day just to follow one set of transactions."

"That's part of the idea—to discourage you." Dorothy smiled stiffly. "There's something as your lawyer I ought to know. Did Tom send you to me as a friend? Or are you one of his ladies?"

"His *ladies*? Me?"

"He walked the straight and narrow with Andrea, but I knew him before they got together. As your lawyer I should know if you have any involvements your husband may use against you."

"Absolutely not," Daria said as for some reason the image of her wriggling cat came into her mind. "Tom? We're barely civil."

"With him, you never know." Dorothy gave a slight sigh and Daria realized with a pang of mild dismay that Dorothy had once been involved with Tom, perhaps more involved with him than he had been with her, to judge from the difference in the tone of their remarks about each other.

"Dorothy, I'm older than he is. Besides, if I had ten boyfriends, Ross left me for another woman. What difference would it make now?"

"Haven't you heard of the double standard? It's alive and kicking in divorce court. It doesn't matter if he was keeping a mistress for twenty years, if you're a bad girl the judge will punish you. Judges live in a world of judges, Daria, and they do their best to ignore what life is really like for most people."

"I'm clean. My life is dull and lonely. Down to the Registry of Deeds and back. They think I'm a professional title searcher."

"Incidentally." Dorothy looked at her over the top of her glasses. "We have to keep in mind those buildings you wouldn't sign over to Ross. How are you going to pay off those mortgages?"

"Oh!" Daria felt a start of pure fear. "I never thought of that!"

"If you don't meet the payments, they foreclose. . . . I'm hopeful we can work things out with Ross long, long before that stage. Besides, there's all that money somewhere. He lists those as liabilities but he acquired a lot of cash and it's tucked away someplace. Listen, Daria, he's hot to trot, his lawyer is huffing and puffing in my ear every day. Just get me the facts."

"So that was Ross's first fire." Tom's eyes glowed with excitement as he took more Hunan beef from the dish nearest him.

"Watch the peppers," Fay cautioned. They were all eating take-out in her kitchen, Fay, Daria, Tom, and Fay's two sons. Tom had insisted this was the best Chinese take-out around, and indeed it was pretty good.

"I like things hot." Tom picked another pepper out with his chopsticks. "I just can't help it, I'm hot-blooded."

"It isn't really hot," Daria demurred, taking one too. She wasn't going to let him get away with acting macho about a few peppers. "I see no reason to assume it was intentional, just because Gussie believes that. A house had to be worth a lot more than a parking lot."

"Not in terms of cash coming in. You say it's a busy lot." He was sweating a little from the spices. He unbuttoned his shirt halfway and rolled up his sleeves, his forearms massive and muscled as a boxer's propped on the table beside her. She felt a little crowded although she wasn't.

"I don't say that," Daria said sulkily. "Gussie says that. Central Square lacks parking. People park all over the damned place."

"And a great way to launder money, being a cash business." Idly Tom's enormous hand was exploring a wooden bowl filled with fruit, as if on an errand of its own. Fay had told her he had made the bowl as a present. His fingers sought and chased its grain. "He collected the insurance, which I bet was more than the building was worth, and now he has a tidy cash business."

"You're making up stories," Daria said. "That trust is Cesaro, Tony and Ross together. The rents were chicken scratch and the neighborhood was red-lined so we couldn't get any money to rehab it."

"Your own sister thinks they burned it," Fay put in.

223

"Gussie has a grudge against the boys. She feels they could help her more than they do. She's just repeating gossip."

Fay rapped her fingers on Daria's outstretched hand of protest. "It upset you enough. You believed it."

"I did not! I was just upset that Gussie believed it. And my own neighbor when I was growing up, Patsy. She used to take care of me."

Johnny yelled, "That last egg roll is mine, you pig!"

"Fire isn't real to you," Fay said. "Shut up, Johnny, and give Mikey the last egg roll. You know he doesn't eat shrimp. It's real to me, I'll tell you. I come awake at three A.M. with my heart thumping from nightmares the house is going up. We've had too many fires around here lately."

"You're exaggerating," Daria said. "You walk around East Boston and you see burned buildings everyplace, vacant lots where houses used to be. But here, I've seen only two, three burned out buildings in the whole neighborhood."

"Most fires aren't so big the whole building goes," Tom said, putting down the bowl he had made. "Just enough to get a tenant out. Or move them all out. They don't destroy the brick structure."

"You talk as if anybody could decide what kind of fire is going to happen," Daria said scornfully. "This is a city that's always had fires— miles of frame dwellings, aging, not up to code." She was learning rapidly about codes.

"I agree with Daria," Fay said. "If the buildings were up to code, we wouldn't have those fires. All the claptrap wiring from the Year Zero. They said those last two fires were electrical. It scares me."

Mikey began imitating a fire engine siren. Johnny said, "Ma, you never get enough egg rolls. Never! If you'd send me, I'd come back with the right amount, but you never do!"

"You'd come back with the whole restaurant. You're going to be the size of Tom, you know that? Lift refrigerators in one hand. Jack up a car with your fingers. Eat your mother out of house and home."

A little shyly, Johnny asked Tom, "Did you work out when you were my age? Some of the guys, they use weights."

"Just what they made us do for football," Tom said. "In spring, are we going to have a softball team this year?"

"Are we?" Johnny's voice rose, breaking. "Are you going to coach us?"

"Coach you hell, I'm going to play," Tom said. "SON can lick anybody this year."

"Except the landlords," Fay said. "We ain't doing so good fighting them."

Faintly, faintly she was beginning to trace Ross's activities. Tony, Cesaro and Ross owned the parking lot together through a trust whose last activities centered on a building farther out along Commonwealth near the Chestnut Hill Reservoir, which they had turned into condominiums. It was in the last three years that Ross had begun buying heavily into the SON neighborhood. Cesaro had apparently refused to follow Tony and Ross into that venture, because his name was on none of those buildings or the trusts under which they were held. Roger Kingsley or his wife Barbara appeared frequently. Carl Johansen, Ross's other law partner, turned up only once. Most of their mortgages were with the Allston Savings and Loan. She began to understand that mortgages were means of generating the money to buy other buildings and that was how Ross had expanded so far so fast. But the mortgages, although they were set up to require the heaviest payments late in the life of the loan, still had to be paid off, as Dorothy had warned her. Was that why Ross wanted to turn their Lexington home into cash? She was still formulating more questions than answers.

"What are you dragging your heels about? Your lawyer isn't returning my lawyer's calls," Ross said on his end of the phone.

"We only began this painful process the day after Christmas—"

"We began this painful process twenty-two years ago."

"If you were so miserable, why did it take you twenty-two years to clear out?"

"Obligation. Guilt. Commitment," he said sonorously. "I'm cursed with a sense of responsibility. You've often pointed that out."

"How about comfort. Affection. The knowledge you had a pretty good deal. Lots of love and good food and good company and a lovely home and good sex and friends always welcome."

"I want matters cleaned up, Daria. I want the situation straightened out fast."

"But aren't you happy living in your condo? I thought you wanted to live on the harbor?"

"It's a tiny hole and the other people in the building are driving me crazy. I need to be settled."

"Oh, dear. I thought you wanted a bachelor life. Desertion takes a couple of years, you know." She lay on her bed surrounded by real estate notes and black cats.

"I'm prepared to fly down to the Dominican Republic. We can get a divorce overnight and be free of this nightmare."

"How self-sacrificing of you, Ross."

"I told you, I'm willing to do it. To spare us both the degradation of a nasty day in court."

"But I, as yet, am not," she said sweetly. "It's all moving so fast, Ross. It's going to take me a while to recover from my shock." She had no intention of letting him know about the research. "It's just too painful for me to deal with yet. I'm still getting used to it."

Ross did not speak for perhaps two minutes, while she remained silent, waiting him out. She was finding in herself various useful although disagreeable entities, alternate personalities. Sometimes when she was handling Ross in one of these bitchy chats, she felt as if she had taken on Gretta's persona, tall, lean and silvery. She was being forced to change into someone she liked less, in order to survive, someone who cared less, someone less accessible, less warm. She was not being allowed to remain the woman she had been.

"But, Daria, it'll be less painful to get it over with. Reach an agreement and get the situation cleaned up."

Like an oil spill. Now she became tremulous and fluttery. Ruffles and chiffon scarves formed around her. "Ross, we were married for twenty-two years! Can't we go on being married a little longer, even on paper, just till I'm used to the situation? Until I have time to recover, a small bit, from the traumatic shock of your departure? It's hard to do without you, however you may feel."

"Daria . . . Daria!" His voice thickened. Probably he too was acting in a little movie of sensibility. "Of course I understand. I miss you too, of course, but—"

"Thank you, Ross, thank you for understanding. Now I must say good night. I can't endure speaking to you any longer just now." Her voice sounded thick with tears. She hung up and giggled. What charades. It was disgusting. She could scarcely believe she could play these games with him, yet somehow they helped. She needed time to do her research, and the roleplaying put emotional distance between them.

Sandra María's building, a small apartment house in a row of similar brick apartment buildings, had belonged to Ross at one time, but he had sold it the year before in a transaction in which it appeared a fair amount of real money had been paid to him and in which the purchaser was Revco Realty, the Petrises. The Petrises were larger developers than Ross. They owned heavily in North Cambridge, where the Red Line was extending, had a piece of a plaza along Alewife Brook Parkway, had been active in condo conversion in Brookline across the near border. Ross or Roger Kingsley frequently turned up as their attorney on deeds and in court proceedings.

What Daria learned was that Revco had sold Ross a building at the same time. It had been almost a trade-off, although Ross appeared to have cleared perhaps ten thousand in cash. That was how and when Ross had acquired Fay's building. Dorothy was not quite sure that Ross had not been doing a little divorce planning, letting the Petrises take over a much better building for the time being with perhaps an arrangement to buy it back after the divorce. Sandra María was dubious because Revco owned the building next to hers and the one beyond that. They were putting together a parcel, as she put it, for some kind of development. Sandra María's row of old brick apartment houses backed onto large buildings on Commonwealth that had already been remodelled and sold as condominiums.

Daria's days were divided between work on her cookbook and research downtown. After every research session she reported to Sandra María, explaining what she had found out and what still stumped her, odds and ends they were sometimes able to resolve together. Sandra María was the friendliest of the SON members, perhaps because they had not met until after Ross had left and Daria decided to work with them, on however limited a basis. Perhaps they had good rapport because Sandra María also came from a large family she remained close to, although her brains and upward mobility had led her into a life quite distinct from theirs. They understood each other more easily than she could reach Fay, who was born working class too, but remained there. Perhaps Sandra María's having a daughter, Mariela, helped. Sandra María's boyfriend Ángel, a photographer, was not Mariela's father. About that man Sandra María never said a word. She said she had been seeing Ángel for two years, that he wanted her to move in with him, but that she didn't want to. She didn't think she could handle living with him and going to graduate school at the same time. She and Sandra María had struck a personal note early and easily. As mothers of daughters, they shared their experiences.

Daria found it strange to turn from the Registry of Deeds, where a building was a listing with various notations about its status, to the neighborhood, where the documents became real homes scarred with time, inhabited by women and men and cats and dogs and children and goldfish, mice, cockroaches and rats. In that window geraniums bloomed; there, a woman in a sari hung out clothes on her porch.

As she walked through the straight and winding streets, the short hills of the Allston neighborhood, she was learning to see the neighborhood many ways simultaneously. Sociologically it was mixed. The large condominiums along Commonwealth were inhabited by professional and business people, affluent, almost all white. The streets behind were more polyglot and parti-colored. Some houses had been bought and individually improved like Tom's, like the two-family houses Chinese moving out of Chinatown had bought. Some apartment houses catered to Third World people, some Black, some Asian, some Hispanic, a few Indians. The neighborhood was home for poor and middle-class whites, lots of singles, gay men, elderly people, mothers alone with children. Up on the hill were a smattering of refurbished houses, islands of the affluent. Actually this was a pleasant and viable neighborhood. It had crime problems, insufficient parking and too much traffic. It also had a pleasant local park, good shopping, a healthy variety of neighbors to befriend or ignore.

She could also see the buildings as investments, an area developers planned to change. She could see tax shelters, in which income earned elsewhere was written off, depreciated, protected. She could see the buildings as bank enterprises, paper written on many of them far beyond the property's worth as the banks too decided how and whether the neighborhood would change. It was political turf, tenants and property owners fighting an unequal battle. How would those puffed-up mortgages be paid for? That introduced a hidden factor of volatility under the busy but tranquil enough streets.

Ross had been renovating one of the buildings still in her name, the one where Bobbie Rosario had died, but the work appeared to have halted. Another listed under Red Robin had been emptied, gutted, rebuilt and was now on the market, with a model condominium available for viewing. He had done no violence to the lines and style of the old building, Moorish in inspiration. A tasteful rehab.

In a way, she thought, hastening toward her car parked in front of Sandra María's building, she could now say that she was taking that interest in Ross's work he had complained she lacked. In educating herself to fight him, she was also educating herself to understand him. He might not be one of the worst landlords, she thought, admiring his completed building. Perhaps he was doing the right thing ultimately, in spite of the SON people.

17

I took Daria a moment to realize her room was dark, she had been soundly asleep and the phone was ringing. As she snapped on the bedside lamp, she saw it was two thirty-five. She hesitated, her hand over the phone. Something had happened to Tracy? To Pops? "Hello? Who is this?"

"Sandra María's building is burning," Tom burst out. "Come over."

"Sandra María? Is she all right? What about Mariela?"

"They're safe, but badly shaken. Come over now, Daria. Come and help," he barked and hung up.

What could she possibly do to help? She ought to go anyhow. Presumably they had been awakened as suddenly as she had, but not by the phone. Hastily she dressed and rushed out. The night was bitter cold with a harsh wind blowing from the northwest across a clear icy black sky pricked with tiny sharp-edged stars. Driving fast, she got to the neighborhood in twenty minutes. A fire truck and a hook and ladder blocked Sandra María's street, so she parked way up the hill in Tom's driveway and trotted down the icy curve. She was suddenly aware of herself, a woman alone in the middle of the night on a city street, and looked around warily. Above the engines, could the people on the next block hear her if she screamed?

She hastened as much as she dared, sliding on the ice, around to the row of brick apartments. Enormous black hoses ran into the front door, and the firemen were trying to haul another up the steps. Other firemen were on the roof, chipping away with their axes. Occasionally a hunk of burning roofing fell over the side into the street. The radios spat words and static; the engines and the pumps made the sidewalk thrum under her feet. In spite of the hour and the intense cold, a crowd stood in clumps on the other side of the street watching the firemen. Many nearby apartments had lights turned on. At the windows worried faces showed, peering out.

An old woman sat on the curb, shaking. A young man in a bathrobe who was awkwardly grasping a little dog was trying to comfort her. The dog yapped incessantly. A woman with a coat over pajamas brought out blankets. "I've lost everything," the old woman was sobbing. "Everything! All my things, gone."

Daria could not find Sandra María or her daughter. Frightened she turned back to the building. She could see flames shooting up from the top floor, where their apartment was. Had they really gotten out? She worked her way through the crowd, looking for anyone she knew. What seemed to be a large family group was talking excitedly in Spanish. Maybe they would know Sandra María. Still she felt shy about asking. She had studied Spanish in college, but she had never used it. Finally she picked out the teenage daughter of the family, whose hair was hacked off in a punk cut just beginning to grow out. Timidly she said, "I'm looking for my friend Sandra María. Sandra María Roa Vargas. That's her apartment burning. Did she get out, do you know?"

Tall and chunky, the girl squinted at her. Yet when she spoke, in spite of her brusque manner, her voice was low and melodious. "Over there. In the doorway." The girl jerked her shoulder.

She caught a glimpse then of Tom carrying a child in his arms and talking excitedly with Elroy. Suddenly they were all illuminated in a ruddy burst as the flames leaped through the roof and towered over them. She stared, involuntarily flinching. It was as if a giant rose suddenly over the street of low brick apartments. With a sharp rap and tinkle of falling glass, a fireman pushed a smoldering object through a window into the street below. It landed with a thud and scattering of sparks and lay there spewing smoke until it was well drenched. An overstuffed chair, had it been? Where was Sandra María?

She wriggled through the sidewalk crowd to Tom. At last she saw

Sandra María, huddled in the doorway behind him. She was wearing a parka of Tom's about three times too big for her, with a long pink nightgown underneath and bedroom slippers. Mariela had been bundled into her own maroon winter coat with mittens pinned to the sleeve, but her feet were bare. Tom had wrapped her legs in his muffler, but obviously he could not put her down, or her poor naked feet would quickly freeze. Mariela should not be outside dressed so lightly on such a frigid night. It was good after all that Daria had come. As she stepped closer, she saw Mariela's face swollen with crying. "Give her to me, I can hold her," she said to Tom. With a thud and splash, another piece of smoldering furniture fell to the street, flooded with water from the hoses and melted snow.

"She's a lot to hold," Tom said dubiously. "Hi."

Mariela was six but small for her age, thin and light-boned. "I can hold her," Daria insisted, holding out her arms. "What's wrong, Mariela?"

"Bring her here," Sandra María called.

"We left Mr. Rogers," Mariela sobbed. "We left him inside."

"You mean the TV set?"

"Her hamster," Sandra María said wearily. In the harsh light of the streetlamps, she looked stricken. She stared at the burning building with a look of exhausted despair.

Daria tried to decide if she should say something encouraging, but the sight of the flames soaring from the top floor dissuaded her. "Are you cold?"

Mariela nodded. Sandra María stirred herself. Obviously she was finding it hard to do more than stare at her home being destroyed. "Oh, your thesis," Daria said suddenly.

"My notes, my papers, my books. Everything except what was in my briefcase. I grabbed Mariela, my purse, my briefcase, and that was it. Then we just ran! The hall was already full of smoke."

"You can't stay here in the street. Do you want to come home with me? I have plenty of room."

"I shouldn't just stand here, I know it. We're both frozen to the bone."

"My car's in Tom's driveway."

"Take us to my mamá's, okay? I want Mariela in bed." Sandra María visibly roused herself, stood, thrust her body into motion. "We both have some clothes at my mother's and she can take Mariela tomorrow while I check things out here. That would be the best choice, I think."

"Maybe everything isn't lost," she said, sounding falsely cheerful. "And you're alive and unhurt."

"There's that!" Sandra María stumbled along after her, her slippers sliding on the ice.

"Take my arm."

"You've got Mariela."

"Mamá, hold on," Mariela said. "You always make me put on my boots."

"Hijita mía, there was no time for your boots tonight. Just be good and hold on to Daria and we'll go to your abuela's."

"What about Mr. Rogers?"

"Mariela, we can't do anything about him now. Your poor little cold feet!"

Daria drove them to Dorcester and saw them safely inside. Then she sat a moment in her car uncertain what to do next. Obviously she could go home. She couldn't understand why Tom hadn't simply loaded them in the van and taken them at once to Sandra María's mother, but she had not minded helping. Finally, without being sure why, she returned to Allston. The burning building seemed to summon her, as if to witness what fire really meant. Perhaps that was why Tom had called her, to involve her, to show her, to cause her to bear witness.

As she drove back slowly, she realized that Sandra María would be homeless now. She liked Mariela, thin as her mother, darker of skin and very fast in reaction. Mariela was a skinny bright little girl who would be fun to share. Yes, she thought, I will invite Sandra María to move in. She's a student and hardworking, she's serious, and Mariela will fill the house so that there's no more room for loneliness and silence and the house will be only the proper size again. But Sandra María doesn't have a car. That will be a little difficult. Maybe we can share the car too: we'll figure it out.

As if under orders she parked again in Tom's driveway. The fire trucks were still down at the foot of the hill but the urgency was gone from the firemen's movements. No more flames showed at the broken windows, although smoke still drifted up and out through the damaged roof. The fire itself seemed from the outside to have been mostly confined to the upper floor, but Daria supposed it was a bigger mess inside, with water damage as well as what the flames and the smoke had done. Glass lay all over the street and the sidewalk.

Tom was talking with one of the firemen, arguing it appeared. When he saw her he gave it up and came toward her. "Are they okay?"

"I took them to her mother's. Mariela's still crying about her hamster. Sandra María seemed stunned."

"They can't help but smell the damn gasoline, I swear it!" He shook his head in fury. "Those people, the captain said, those people live like animals: they drop their garbage in the hall and they drop their butts everyplace when they've been drinking wine. That's what that damned racist creep said." He linked his arm in hers and bore them away uphill. "Watch the ice."

"Then slow down. What happened? How did the fire start?"

"That old woman, Mrs. Richter, she smelled it. She doesn't sleep soundly and something woke her. She thought she heard somebody on the roof—she has the top back, next door to Sandra María. After that she was too terrified that a burglar was going to break in to go back to sleep. Then she smelled gasoline. She was still thinking about that when she smelled smoke. She put on her robe and went out in the hall and found the upper stairway to the roof on fire. So she grabbed her little dog and ran downstairs shouting and banging on doors."

"Did everybody get out?"

"They did, and for that I'm glad. It was a professional job. I bet the damage is confined to the stairwell, the roof and the upper apartments. And the smoke detector Sandra María put so much pressure on Revco to install, never functioned. It was a dud or turned off."

She turned to look back at the firemen still working on the building. One of the trucks was leaving. She felt suddenly weary through and through. She did not accept his paranoid assumptions for a moment, but she was too stunned by the power of the fire to argue. She thought she could understand why he had to believe such a disaster could be blamed on some individual.

234

"Be glad it's Friday," he rumbled. "Local fires are usually in midweek. Tomorrow we can all sleep late."

"Not too late," she said. "My daughter's coming home for her break."

"I thought you weren't on good terms now."

"This is my younger daughter, Tracy. She's on my side." Strange what they knew about each other, an intimacy of convenience. Sometimes she thought he had already learned too much about her life. "You saw your own daughters at Christmas, didn't you?"

He sighed for answer. Then he said, "It's hard like that. August is better because there's time for it to be ordinary and natural again."

She slipped on the ice, he steadied her and she yawned. Oh, she was tired. It amused her to note that she was not at all nervous about being out in the middle of the night, walking up the deserted hill with Tom. She had her private bodyguard. "Do you think Sandra María might move in with me?"

"Move in with you?" he repeated, openly surprised. "Did you ask her?"

"I only thought of it after I dropped her off. Do you think she'll consider it?"

He plodded uphill, frowning. "I think so, Daria. She's lost that place, so much is clear. She doesn't want to move in with Ángel. And she doesn't like Mariela's first grade teacher."

It surprised her what he knew about the people around him. Ross would never have known that Gretta disliked her son's teacher, or that Fay had just given walking papers to her boyfriend because he drank too much in front of her boys. For a man, Tom had an uncommon interest in the details of people's lives. Gossip, Ross would call it, but she thought it was just being interested in people. She stumbled on the ice and he righted her.

"I'll admit to being surprised how you two get on, the way you've become friends." He was still mulling over the possibility. "It might work out. Ask her tomorrow, before she makes other plans. . . . Sandra María, by the way, can't boil an egg."

"I can cook for her and Mariela as easily as for myself. In fact, I'd prefer it. I miss the company." She yawned again, hugely. Oddly enough, it felt almost cozy stumbling up the hill together. Maybe she and Tom were also becoming friends, as unlikely as that sounded. Surprisingly, they talked easily to each other, and there was little nonsense between them.

He steered her firmly past her car. "I'll make coffee. You shouldn't drive home half asleep."

"You needn't bother." She yawned again. The excitement of the fire had brought her to full alert, but that verve had ebbed and left her limp. She decided not to argue further and added lamely, "If you want to?"

His apartment was warm and smelled of bread and cinnamon and faintly of marijuana, which he must have been smoking earlier; or someone had. He owned no ashtrays but in a saucer a thin butt reclined. He noticed her gaze as he hung their coats. "Waiting for the kettle. Oh, do you want some dope?"

"I don't have the habit." In spite of her fatigue, she looked around curiously. He must have made the coffee table with its curves and strong grain. All the wood of the archway and sleeping loft had been shaped and rubbed to bring out its warmth and texture.

"I used to. One period of my life I was stoned for a year. You could have smoked my body fat to get high. But I've lost interest." He had tucked an ivory pajama top into jeans to go out for the fire; its full sleeves made it resemble a pirate shirt, his earring glinting.

"You divide your life into sharp neat phases when you talk. As if you were a different animal in each: that was when I was a little green caterpillar."

He laughed, letting himself down with surprising lightness beside her on the couch. "Men like to make their lives out to be more rational than they were. We don't like to admit how much energy we spend just chasing some scent through the grass."

"I see that in Ross. He's rewriting our common history and all—"

"No Ross tonight. Leave him outside. Enough. Besides, I'm not rewriting my history. Just trying to organize it so it makes sense to me."

"In a way that's what I'm doing too."

"I know that. And in my underhanded overheated way I'm trying to help."

"I guess I do know underneath it all you mean well. . . ."

"But what?" He extended his arm along the back of the couch.

She felt almost afraid to notice the gesture. "Oh . . ." The words came out of her oversized, balloons bouncing in space. "I guess it's just how we rub each other the wrong way."

"*Rub* each other?" His hand slithered down from the back of the couch to close over her neck.

Her body responded by becoming very still and going into a state of warm shock. It took her several moments to remember how to form words. "I hope you aren't going to do anything silly right now. That you aren't thinking of anything silly."

"What I'm thinking about is exactly what you think I'm thinking about. Which is what I'm usually thinking when I'm around you. Except that I'm tired of thinking about it." He did not lunge at her then because he moved very slowly toward her on the couch so that she could leap up, could move away, could rise, could say something in protest, in anger, in rebuff, at least say something; in fact what felt like a glacier of time passed over in which she could have done many small abrupt actions that would have prevented his closer approach, and in which time she did nothing but stare at him with the skin on the back of her neck burning and her body in a state of anxiety and intense seething curiosity and apprehension. Repeatedly she ordered herself to get up off the couch, but she did not move, except suddenly to remember to inhale when she realized she was holding her breath.

With infinite slowness and patience as if she were a bird that might fly off or a strange cat that might bolt, he eased his body toward her until his thigh was pressing hers and then he put his other arm around her and bent to kiss her. At the last moment she gave a great shudder and attempted to avert her face as his mouth moved over hers that opened as if to speak but let in his tongue instead.

Kissing him was very different from her experience of twenty years. His lips were full, sensual, active. Ross had narrow lips and the tendency to hold them rigid when he was kissing. This was something far more sensual, more enveloping, more overwhelming. Way, way back, yes, kissing Dominic had been that way, almost frightening, as if she might lose herself, as if she might escape through her parted lips, that her essence, her soul would pass out of her in kissing, or maybe only that her control would melt. She did not want to let herself dissolve into passion.

It was her sense as Tom kissed her that he was holding her with extreme care, that he was controlling himself as if in pincers. He was afraid to frighten her, to push her. That sense of a difficult control over what?—passion? Appetite? His desire?—moved her until she realized with a knowledge of capitulating to unexpected disaster that she should never have permitted him to touch her if she expected to extricate herself. She experienced him suddenly as vulnerable and that undid her. Even as he constricted and constrained his desire, what he had to control made her feel him as extraordinarily open to harm.

The kettle was shrieking. She finally took her mouth away. "The water's boiling."

"Damn it. I should never have put it on."

"Turn it off, then."

He drew back slightly to fix his gaze on her. Dark eyes, large, wanting, fierce black eyes of specific and singular hunger. Something slipped in her, worked loose, a slide of warm mud deep inside, a thawing downward from the head slowly through the chest and into the groin. He said, "I don't know if I care to let go."

"I'm not about to disappear." She sighed.

He bounded to the kitchen in three strides, silenced the kettle and came galloping back.

Staring at him she babbled, "This is not the best idea. We have to work together. I'm in the middle of a divorce and Dorothy says it's a time to be careful. Discovering an attraction doesn't mean one should act on it. I'm ten years older than you are—"

"Seven. Daria, shut up, please. Come on. We won't get there by talking first." He drew her to her feet, his hands, low, enclosing her buttocks. Then he had a sudden idea and picked her up, carrying her across the room to set her up on the sleeping platform. "See, there's some use to being built like an ox."

"You're still mad about that."

"Daria, if you don't know you were goading me sexually, it's because you don't want to admit it yet." He scrambled up beside her.

She had a sudden sharp sense of being out of place, sitting up on a sleeping platform, an object as exotic to her as an igloo, about to permit this large hairy stranger to penetrate her body. But only her mind was wary. Her body was sensuous and clamorous as Sheba's had been. "I guess we should get undressed," she said calmly. She was a little shocked at herself; she had taken five months to reach this point with Ross, the only other man she had ever slept with.

For the first moment their nakedness collided, her teeth chattered briefly, an instant of shock, of fear. Then she relaxed. She imagined a great pile of clothes, of words, of masks, of postures and poses and cherished notions all fallen on the floor under them. Of course each of them would resume their clothing and their opposing notions. Probably they would also resume their sparring. But this too was real.

He was the more active and she the more acted upon, as it had been in the early years with Ross, but Tom did not otherwise remind her of her husband. His body felt different. His bones were bigger, his musculature far more pronounced, his body hair more plentiful and more irregular. In places his body was smooth and sleek, in places covered with a pelt. He was more attentive to her reactions than she was used to. Over the years women must have instructed him about their bodies until he knew many different caresses and zones of arousal. He did not fall into her and flail there but felt his way by trial and response, tuning himself to her breathing, her little movements, her hands and flesh responding against him. Again she had the sense of an exhausting control in charge, a restraint that totally directed him. At last he slowly urged his penis into her, sliding himself gradually forward until she lunged to complete the coupling. He moved carefully in her for perhaps a minute and then the control blew.

With a deep moan suddenly he changed and instead of carefully levering himself he writhed and bucked and heaved and seemed to spread out through her. She stopped judging him as a lover. She stopped thinking. For a period of suspension she simply moved with him and felt him in and around her, felt him like a storm or like her own flesh in strange high breaking waves.

When he had come at last and lay inert and winded on her and then slid slowly out and off, she kept her arm around him. There they were landed back in reality, all covers flung off, his body runneled in sweat

239

that had drenched her too. She was rather stunned, rather pleased and if anything more fascinated than she had been on the couch, when she had recognized her sexual curiosity about him.

"You didn't come," he said in a minute.

"I haven't done this in months. I don't think I could ever come the first time with anyone, although I'm not generalizing from much of a sample. . . ."

He was not done with her. He slipped his hand between her thighs and began to work on her with a finger inside and a finger on her clitoris. She felt embarrassed at first. She was used to being excited before entry, but in her limited experience, if Ross was not able to make her come by intercourse, that was the end of it until next time. It felt oddly naked and selfish to lie with a man working on her and her reactions exposed and apparent and singular. "You don't have to do that."

"But I want to."

She decided to believe him. She relaxed and floated on the sensations. The orgasm that finally released her was neither deep nor prolonged, but that she felt it at all surprised her. She was beset by questions she could not or did not dare formulate. She was also exhausted. Between them they pulled the covers roughly over them. As she lay in his arms trying to decide how to begin talking over what had happened, she realized from his breathing that he was asleep, and then she was.

She woke early, having to pee, and almost fell off the platform before she realized where she was. He lay on his side curled toward her in deep sleep. In the light from the kitchen they had never turned off, she stared at him and for the first time thought him handsome with his dark brows, black curly hair, his strong nose and chin, his sensual mouth. He lay like a fallen tower in the bed, and she had to resist an impulse to wake him as if accidentally to investigate further the sexual energy and concentration she had not guessed in him, at least not consciously. The powerful curve of his shoulder and back was exposed above the quilt. His eyelids closed and flushed with sleep, he looked utterly vulnerable, a vast child-man, a creature in whom sensuality and sensitivity and that loud morality warred.

She shook herself abruptly and let herself off the edge, creeping with her scattered clothes to the bathroom to dress. Seven-thirty. She must go.

Tracy would be coming. Tracy! Panic hit her. She felt plastered over with sex, reeking. She must rush home at once, bathe and make herself presentable. It was crazy of her to have done this. She stood in her coat, pondering a note and finally left one on the dining-room table next to a vase full of the vermillion berries and stark black twigs of deciduous holly, "Gone to pick up my daughter, D."

Then she fled to her car. She drove home, feeling as if she had been raised high in the air and all her joints and muscles shaken hard, and then given a good long hot sauna. Her body was loose, liquid, formed of warm honey and chocolate. She must pull herself together before facing Tracy. She would hurry on home and clean herself, the house, straighten, bake, plan, offering a silent apology to Tracy.

18

ONCE she got home, bathed, dressed and had breakfast, instead of feeling exhausted she found herself bouncy with energy. She took Torte for as long a walk as he would tolerate. Then she decided it was late enough to call Sandra María.

It took Sandra María five minutes to make up her mind to move in. The rest of the conversation was working out details. Sandra María said she would ask her boyfriend Ángel to locate a decent used car. She was prepared to move as soon as Ángel arrived and drove her to Allston to pick through what remained of her belongings. She did not know if she still had any usable furniture.

"I want to get out of there! I'm a marked woman. I don't feel safe, I don't feel it's safe for Mariela. That fire was set, Daria, I know it, and it was aimed at me. Because I'm a troublemaker. I organized the tenants in our row. Mr. Petris knows I've been researching him."

She imagined the bland egg-shaped head of Sandra María's landlord and felt, privately, that Sandra María was being hysterical. "A fire's so frightening. I hope you can salvage something."

"Whatever, let's see if we can get everything straightened out this weekend. I can't just camp on Mamá. And, you know, I told you about what I don't want to do, and pressure from him will just grow if I don't make another move fast. I want Mariela settled. This has been a real trauma for her."

After Daria got off the phone, she ran upstairs to look at the two rooms across the hall. Robin's old room was thoroughly cleaned out, but Tracy's was full of her things. On the phone she had warned Tracy she would probably have to rent that room and give her another instead. Tracy had been agreeable, but any minute she would be arriving to find changes that would be all too real. As the day went on, they could only become more evident. Tracy might feel martyred indeed.

As she turned away, she felt the sensation of his mouth on hers, that full sensual kiss. It welled up, rising as if her body and not her mind remembered being in bed with Tom only hours before. She had a twinge of acute embarrassment, a hot flush burning her skin, and cringed before the imminence of Tracy's arrival. What she had done seemed inappropriate.

Slowly she felt her way downstairs, gaze blind with memory of how he had looked asleep beside her, his eyelids flushed, his mouth relaxed, heat shimmering off him. She could not honestly find in herself regret for the night. At least someone had wanted her, if Ross didn't. She was still a functioning woman, miraculously. That had been an odd breakthrough for both of them, but she expected little change in their antagonism. From the lateness of the hour, the excitement of the fire, they had fallen into bed. Nonetheless she found herself smiling as she floated down to plan supper.

Sun spilled into the dining room, winter sun yellow as cheese catching the row of cobalt bottles. A pair of cardinals, red male, green female with their strong flesh-colored beaks, picked at her offering of seeds. When had she last made a meal she wanted to make for people who would sit down and enjoy? People she wanted to talk to, not boring clients of Ross with whom she had nothing in common. For whom she was his pet chef. Yes, I own this famous writer of cookbooks, this unlikely personality from your TV, so my table is justly famous and reflects prestige on my business dealings. She found herself humming and stopped, astonished. She was humming a silly song by some group whose name she did not even know, a so-called New Wave group Fay's son admired, something that had been blaring from Johnny's ghetto box the last time she was in Fay's busy kitchen. What surprised her was not that she should be humming a rock song but that she should be humming at all. Ross had trained her to keep quiet, unless requested otherwise, her and Robin, who could not carry a tune either.

She stopped humming and leaned against the refrigerator. In the long run the rejection by Robin hurt more than the desertion by Ross. Would they ever be reconciled? She was not yet ready to forgive Robin, and Robin showed no sign of missing her or seeking her company.

Tracy arrived at ten-thirty in a red Fiat sports car that sat in front of the house for fifteen minutes while she had an intense discussion with the boy driving it. However he did not come in and as the top was up, Daria peering out invisible she hoped behind the draperies, could not get a good look at him.

Tracy finally came dragging a suitcase and duffel bag, with a bookbag over her shoulder, luggage a little excessive for a weekend, Daria thought, until she discovered almost everything not in the bookbag was dirty laundry.

"Mama, how are you doing? Have you been keeping up your spirits?" Tracy hugged her before running off to say hello to Torte. The cats were out on the ledge, but when they heard Tracy calling, they came running in great awkward stiff-legged bounds through the snowdrifts. Torte growled, wanting the greeting to himself and pressing his nose into Tracy's palm. Maybe he would cheer up for the weekend.

As Daria had been calling Tracy at least once a week, she did not have a great deal of news, aside from recent events she was clearly not going to report. The other news she must break carefully. "You know, ducks, I've been looking for someone to share the house—"

"Did you decide you really have to? I thought maybe when things settled down, you'd find you didn't need to bother."

"I'm afraid I can't manage the house just by myself—"

"By the way, Daddy's behind on my tuition."

"Damn it!" Daria struck her palm in weak anger. "He said he'd pay that. All right, I'll try to get hold of him. Or maybe you better ask him directly."

"I don't want to!"

"I don't want to talk to him either. And he's not mad at you."

"He's always mad at me."

"Tracy, I think you will have to call him. What I'm trying to say is, if

244

he doesn't come through, I'll pay it. But that means I definitely need a housemate. I have a good prospect anyhow. Her name is Sandra María Roa Vargas. And she has a little girl Mariela."

"Sandra María Vargas . . . she's not Puerto Rican?"

"Yes, she is."

"Did she answer an ad or what?"

"No, I've known her for a while. She's a graduate student in public health at Northeastern. I like her, Tracy, and I think I can get along with her. She just got burned out of her apartment last night—"

"Burned out?" Tracy's eyes were wide. "Where on earth did you meet her?"

"She's involved in a neighborhood organization with a lot of people I know."

"Around here?"

"No, in Allston. Anyhow, her daughter is six and I want to try sharing the house with them."

"With a Puerto Rican woman and a little girl?"

Daria nodded, meeting Tracy's gaze steadily. "Fifty years ago when your grandparents came over to the United States, people used to talk about Italians the way they talk about Puerto Ricans now, even the same jokes. I didn't ask her to move in as a minority representative or to achieve racial balance, Tracy. I asked her because I like her. I thought we might have a chance at getting along. You ought to have met the crazy ladies who came to answer my ad."

"I wonder what the neighbors are going to say?"

Daria blinked. "Oh my. To tell you the truth, I hadn't thought about them." She had had little contact with her neighbors after explaining to the first few about her separation. She suspected they all viewed her as already moved out and were waiting impatiently for the couple who would surely buy the house and assume a social role in the ongoing web of couples.

Tracy visibly thrust back her shoulders and stuck out her chin. "I think it's wonderful, Mama, how you're coping. If we don't have money any longer, and we have to share our house with all sorts of people, I think it's very strong of you. We'll just have to get along with them as best we can until things get better!"

Daria suppressed an urge to giggle. "That's the spirit. Now the hard part. Obviously Sandra María is going to need two adjacent rooms for herself and her daughter. I'm afraid that's going to have to be Robin's old room, which is cleared out, and your old room. We talked about that on the phone. . . . I'm sorry, Tracy, but we're going to have to manage that way. I was thinking you could take your father's study downstairs for a bedroom. It's as big as your old room and it has that handsome oak panelling . . ."

"No, Mama. I don't want to be downstairs. Why don't you take that for your office?"

"But I have my office . . ."

"But that would make such a darling bedroom, I've always thought so. It's such a cute little room. It has its own back stairway. I can run down to the john under the stairs or I can use yours."

"But, Tracy, it's cold in there."

"So we can get a space heater. I'm hardly here in the winter and in the summer it's the pleasantest room in the house. That private stairway doesn't help you. I mean, you don't come in late and not want to wake people. . . ."

Daria wanted to refuse. She was attached to her little office; she had written all her books there. She was used to its limitations and its virtues. She liked being able to run down to the kitchen or cross the hall to her bedroom. On the other hand, Tracy was being asked to sacrifice her old room; Daria should also sacrifice her accustomed arrangements. "All right. . . ."

"You'll have more room to work downstairs, Mama, and that room is set up like a real office. And I know *exactly* how I'm going to fix up my new bedroom. I'm going to paint it pale peach—"

"Love, why don't you wait till you come home for spring break to paint? If we're moving everybody around today, it's going to be hectic enough."

"Okay, but let's get your stuff out now."

By lunchtime they had moved Daria's office downstairs and then put some of Tracy's clothes into the small closet. Daria also gave Tracy the closet in the master bedroom that Ross had used, and then they filled that. They were chattering over French toast and coffee when Tom's van arrived outside and Mariela came running up to bang on the door. Daria had a brief intense desire to run and hide under the bed. With Tom's van, she was sure, had come Tom.

"We're here! We're moving in, Daria." Mariela shouted up at her. "I'm coming to live with your kitty cats. Because Mr. Rogers died. He died in the fire but Mamá says he went to sleep first from the smoke so it didn't hurt like it does if you touch the stove. Where are the kitty cats?"

"What's your name?" Tracy knelt. "Oh, you're so cute," she gurgled, fussing over Mariela exactly the same way she did over the kittens. "I'll show you where my cats are. Do you know how to pet cats? You don't pull their tails or whiskers."

"I know all about cats, because Tom has a cat. Who are you? Tom's cat is named Marcus. He's a boy and he's Russian and he's grey. Do you live here?"

Tracy would be all right with her. Daria felt weak with relief. She turned then to immediate problems. Tom, a wiry young man she assumed was Ángel, Sandra María and Elroy were carrying armloads of random objects up to the house: piles of dresses, a few open boxes from which she could see protruding a toaster and a lampshade, a vase and a pair of boots. Torte began barking hysterically. Closing him in the study that was now hers, which still held Ross's papers and old lawbooks with her furniture huddling in the middle, she ran out to help. She had the sense of her life as having suddenly doubled in speed. She had been plodding along considering, mulling, brooding, grieving, and now everything had begun rushing in a blur of jerky motion like an old two-reeler comedy, Keystone cops doing pratfalls and wild horses galloping.

"They haven't even sealed the building properly. They're not going to investigate. They say since proposition two and a half they don't have the money to investigate every fire people claim is arson." Sandra María was panting as she dragged along an orange crate of books. "Oh! I have to spread these out to dry. Is there a basement, maybe?"

"Right down the kitchen stairs, I'll show you. What happened to your thesis?"

"Some of it's readable, some of it isn't. What I had in my briefcase is safe. I'll have to do the first chapter over again, I don't even want to think about it yet."

Daria carried up an armful of coats from the van, passing Ángel and Tom wrestling along a four-drawer filing cabinet between them. Then she found Tracy, who was playing with Mariela who was playing with the cats. "Tracy, we've got to move everything out of your old room—that's for Mariela. We must hurry."

"Oh, she can have my old twin bed. I don't want it. I know what I want, Mama. I'll sleep with you tonight, but then when I come back next time, we can go buy it—a four-poster bed. And I don't want a little bed. That's fine for a child. I want a full adult bed."

Daria raised her eyebrows. What Tracy was saying, translated, was that she wanted a double bed in her new room, which combined with the desire for the use of the back stairway spelled out to Daria that Tracy was sleeping with the red Fiat's owner and had got very involved with him and expected to go on being so. Tracy was making plans that included spending nights with him here. Now that Ross was gone, Tracy must be convinced she could persuade her mother. Her mother suspected she might be right.

She had another moment of wanting to lock herself into her own bedroom, crawl into bed and pull the quilt over her head. Wait for them all to go away. Wait for them to settle among themselves the new and exotic shape of her world.

Actually a lot was taking shape without her. Tom and Elroy were doing most of the hard hauling. Ángel and Sandra María carried in the lighter objects and bickered about where things should go. Ángel had a strong aesthetic sense and Sandra María had strong practical ideas. The van was quickly unloaded so that most of its contents reeking of smoke and soot stood like a sale of damaged goods in the middle of the living-room floor. The fire had come down through the ceiling and through the stairwell and destroyed everything in the living room beyond use. The kitchen too had been badly damaged. Mariela's room and Sandra María's bedroom had suffered mostly water and smoke damage, and most of the salvage came from there.

Off went the van for another trip. She had managed in the crowd and bustle to avoid meeting Tom's gaze, to avoid face-to-face confrontation. Perhaps it would be all right. They would go along as if nothing had happened. What had would remain their small secret concerning no one else and in no way altering their patterns: a small explosion in the middle of the night, not unlike a fire but one that burned and left entire. No ash, no regret, no smoke damage. It might not have happened, although she knew it had. She felt quite safe. Sandra María and Mariela would protect her now from loneliness and temptation. She would have an instant family.

Daria had to drag Tracy away from Mariela. "Mama, she's so smart. She's wonderful with the kittens. She loves animals. Then we were watching the birds at the feeder and you could just see her taking all that in—she'd never seen a feeder before." And on. Frantically they both worked to move Tracy's things across the hall, through Daria's bedroom to the room over the garage that had always been hers. She had no time to waste regretting the loss of what had been for eleven years her sanctuary. "Nobody appreciates how smart kids can be, Mama, how much they take in. I think I was like that, like Mariela, don't you think so? I think I always noticed all kinds of things that Robin would ignore."

If only Tracy would slow down her reactions: first fear of the Puerto Rican invasion menace; now total infatuation with Mariela. Well, better that way than the other.

The van returned. This time as they were unloading, Annette came out with a snow shovel and picked away at the edge of her front walk, watching, as if Daria had ever seen Annette move one shovelful of snow in all the years they had lived next door to each other. A service came and plowed Annette's walk the same as they did Daria's. She smiled and waved at Annette.

Annette came over at once. "What's happening, Daria? Have you sold your house or rented it? What is this . . . van?"

"Sandra María is moving in," Daria said boldly. "You've heard me talk about Sandra María." She blessed Tracy for having alerted her that the neighbors would not be overjoyed.

"Bud Buchanan told Pierre you had an ad in the paper. . . . You're not renting, are you?"

Because that was illegal. Their neighborhood was zoned against what they would call a rooming house. "Of course not. I ran the ad and then I changed my mind. Too much trouble."

"Then what's this?" Annette waved at the van.

"Why, it's Sandra María. You know. My brother's ex-wife and my niece. I've always been very close to them. She knows I'm lonely and the schools are good here. I think it'll work out for both of us." Relatives were permitted under the zoning.

"Oh. Your niece. I didn't see her. How old is she?"

"Six. Very bright," Daria said loftily, making gestures to escape toward the house with the box of books.

"Does . . . Sandra María have a lot of things?"

"Oh, she'll leave most of it in storage," Daria said, backing away. "We simply don't have room for it here. . . ."

Annette called after her, "Don't you think you'll find it difficult to live with a little child again?"

"I think it'll be rather fun," Daria called back. When she turned at her own door, she saw that Annette had gone back inside, making no more pretense at shoveling.

It was five-thirty, the house an obstacle course with contents of rooms half moved into other rooms, smoke- and water-damaged goods everywhere and all of them exhausted. Elroy went off in a taxi for his Saturday night date, but the rest collapsed in the dining room, the only usable room in the house besides her own bedroom. Daria made linguine with a red sauce based on her frozen tomato sauce from the summer's garden, two pounds of hastily defrosted chopped meat and some dried mushrooms from the cupboard. She used to cook a lot of pasta, but not since Ross had become too conscious of his waistline and too interested in serving dishes with more pretentious credentials to dinner guests. Tracy was on the phone in Ross's old study, still not quite Daria's office. Daria had the kitchen to herself.

The sweet smell of heating olive oil filled her head, a golden late summer smell along with the tomato, the basil. September came to life, ripe, full, warm. The onions lay in the oil growing translucent, the color of old silk. Daria felt rather than saw Tom enter the kitchen, as she tasted the sauce critically. A dash of cinnamon, yes. She did not turn, pretending she did not sense his presence. In a panic she simply could not think how to greet him. She could find nothing whatsoever to say, while silence swelled up in her. At the stove she stood frozen, mindlessly stirring the sauce round and round.

His arms enveloping her, he kissed her neck gently. Barely touching her, asking permission. A huge warm animal nudging her back. The spoon jumped from her hand. Her body temperature rose to feverish, the kitchen hot as an oven with the cool house surrounding like snow. Very slowly he turned her to him. By the time her face was angled up to his so close she could smell his scent compounded of wood always, the smell of fresh-cut wood that clung to his hair and sweater, woodsmoke from his Danish stove, a leathery tang and something of lemon, it was Daria who kissed him. Free fall, she thought, it's all still there between us.

It was also Daria who disentangled. "The sauce will burn!"

"I wasn't trying to make love to you over the stove." He grinned broadly, a stove door opening. "I just wanted some acknowledgment that last night wasn't my wet dream."

She laughed. "You want to keep your hand in. Never mind. If you want to do something useful, set the big table for six."

He started opening cabinets. "Where are your dishes?"

"Use the good dishes in the dining room. The house is a big enough mess. And this is a celebration. Plus if you go down to the foot of the cellar steps and look against the north wall, you'll find a rack with some wine still in it. Get a couple of bottles of Zinfandel. The late luxuries of my late marriage."

As they sat at the table, everyone was so hungry that eating consumed all attention for the first twenty minutes. When conversation began, it felt awkward. She realized no one at the table knew all the others. The men were on one side, the children on the other, and she and Sandra María at the ends. There was almost as much size discrepancy between the frail tousle-headed Ángel and massive Tom as between Mariela and Tracy. "I never introduced you all," she said timidly. "This is my daughter Tracy . . ."

She could see Tracy was mad to ask questions, trying to figure out the relationships, staring especially at Tom and Ángel. Finally Tracy asked Angel, "Are you related to Sandra María?"

Daria was embarrassed, because she felt the question so patently was, Are you related to Mariela? Are you her father? Ángel threw Sandra

María a look as if of appeal. He was slow speaking and was still making little noises in his throat, about to force out some answer when Mariela answered at once, "Ángel is my mamá's boyfriend, Tracy. And Tom is your mamá's new boyfriend."

Sandra María burst into laughter. Daria sat stark still not believing what Mariela had said. Even Tom looked flustered, lowering his chin onto his chest. Sandra María said rapidly, "I told you she understands everything! She listens to everything! Even when she's asleep, she's listening!"

Daria wanted to pretend nothing had happened, but Tracy was staring from Tom to her, speechless. She must say something. "Well, Mariela," she began in her best lecturing tone, "it's not exactly the same. Angel is your mamá's regular boyfriend, for two years. Tom is only a little bit my boyfriend. We've only just, we've just begun seeing each other. Mostly we work together."

"Work together?" Tracy repeated.

Damn it all. She wanted to question Tracy about the boy with the red Fiat, and here was Tracy looking like a mother about to question *her* daughter about a presumed indiscretion. I'm forty-three, she thought in sudden rebellion. I can see a man if I want to.

"Your mother has a lot of admirers." Tom smiled at Tracy. He was not at all nonplussed. "You're a good-looking family, but your mother's other admirers make her cook for them. I cook for her. That's the secret of my success, such as it is."

"What are you studying at Amherst?" Sandra María asked, who knew from Daria the answer to that and a great deal more. "Oh, do you have any idea what you're going to major in? . . . Art history sounds wonderful. Imagine getting paid to go around to museums and do what you'd want to do on your vacation anyhow. . . . Do you know Angel's a photographer? He's photographer in residence for the State Council on the Arts in a school in Lynn this year. . . ." Sandra María was moving the conversation steadily up to high dry ground and safety. Across the flow of talk Tom gave Daria an apologetic glance and then shrugged. "Sooner or later," he said very softly.

"It was awfully sooner," she mouthed back. Then she remembered to explain to Sandra María and company Sandra María's official new identity in the neighborhood.

When they went to move more boxes after supper, Sandra María exclaimed in exasperation when she saw that the smoke stained water had leaked onto the wall-to-wall carpeting in the living room. "Daria, I'm furious at myself! I should have been more careful. What are you going to think about us if we start out spoiling your carpeting?"

Daria stood over the ruined carpet smiling faintly. "To tell you the truth, I've always hated this beige carpeting. It was Ross's idea. I think it's ludicrous in a house with flooring this beautiful. Let's tear it up and just put down a couple of small rugs."

"Daria, you're being saintly about this—"

"No. It's not to my taste and it reminds me of Ross."

By ten they were all exhausted. Almost immediately after the men left, Daria and Tracy went to bed. But Tracy was not too tired to ask questions. "Is he really your boyfriend?"

"That's an unfortunate term." Daria sat on the bed's edge brushing her hair hard. "He's a man I'm interested in." He was, she realized. She felt a stab of panic as if she were suddenly jumping into a river she had not committed herself to crossing. She had simply enjoyed sex with him too much to resist wanting it again. She had either to flee the whole involvement with SON or to proceed with Tom. They would not remain around each other without exploring what sexual connection bound them. And it was too late to rethink her commitment to SON, when she had just moved one of its primary organizers into her house. She felt unglued, but she was not about to confess that to her daughter. She must sound strong and sure.

A long silence followed. Nervously Daria climbed into bed beside her daughter. Then Tracy said, "He's not at all like Daddy."

"No," said Daria firmly to the dark ceiling over them. "He certainly isn't."

"That's not necessarily bad," Tracy said, being reasonable to her wild mother. "I guess if I'd ever thought about it—I mean, I didn't—I would have thought you'd be interested in a lawyer. A doctor. Some professional."

"No," Daria said firmly, again. "I'm tired of being a professional's wife. I'm bored with duty entertaining. I'm sick of spending evenings with old farts and pallid wives who have nothing to say. Men who talk about nothing but real estate and money."

"What does Tom talk about?"

"Politics," Daria said. Real estate too, but from a different point of view. "Food. People. Relationships." Now she really had to talk with him. By lying that she knew him well, she was forced to get to know him better.

"I thought you liked Wasp types. Like Daddy. Fair and skinny."

"I want someone more like me." Daria sounded so convincing that she stopped and realized she agreed with herself.

"But why does he wear that earring?"

"I suppose he likes it. It never occurred to me to ask." She was seized by the realization how very little she knew about this man she had admitted to her life. "I'm not saying I'm sold on Tom. I may not go on seeing him."

"I understand," Tracy said bravely. "I'm just surprised how fast things happened. But of course you want to figure out if you're really interested. I went out with four different guys last semester and at various times I thought with each of them, something might develop. But nothing exciting happened. I even went out once with Scott, but we didn't click then—"

"Who's Scott?" Daria asked quickly, pouncing on what she wanted to know. "Is he the boy with the red Fiat?"

Tracy began to tell her about the last intense two weeks, including at least half of what Scott had said. His opinions were unexceptional. Daria realized she would have to inspect Scott and form her own estimate. Tracy was obviously at least mildly infatuated. They fell asleep in the middle of talking.

19

s Tom had promised Tracy, he cooked for Daria at least once a week all through February and into March. Tonight he made a Mexican meal, as the stores were full of ripe black avocados. They had an agreement: whoever cooked, the other cleaned up. She felt that was not entirely fair, as at her house, he had simply to wash pans and load the dishwasher, whereas at his house she had to wash dishes by hand. Nonetheless she enjoyed having him cook for her. It was a small but marked luxury.

Afterward as they sat down to coffee at his long satiny maple table, Tom took from an old satchel a pile of cards written in his small huddled handwriting. His writing always surprised her whenever she encountered it on notes or lists, for his huge hands produced a cramped careful script as if paper were precious and he was concerned to waste none of it, but to rather crowd the smallest piece available with the most information.

He cleared his throat. His dark eyes brooded on her from under drooping lids. She had a moment of foreboding. "Is something wrong? Are you annoyed with me?" She tried to think what she had done or failed to do.

"I am not Walker. Whenever anything in my life goes wrong, I do not automatically assume it's your fault. When I'm worried, it doesn't mean I'm blaming you."

"Great. Because nothing is ever my fault. I'm glad we agree."

He frowned at his notes, spreading them and closing them together like a hand of cards he was hesitant to bet on.

"You might as well read those to me. Ten more buildings I don't know I own, all mortgaged to the hilt? What is the hilt of a house, anyhow?"

The buzzer sounded. She cursed softly. As soon as she came into a room with Tom, her thoughts began a subtext under whatever was going on, would they make love that night? Although they saw a lot of each other, they managed little time alone, and that little was precious: precious and constantly broken into by just about everyone.

People were always coming by, members of SON, others in the neighborhood. They came by to tell him something disturbing they had noticed. "And there's two vacant apartments in there now and they're not even trying to rent them, because my cousin asked." They came by to talk politics, international, domestic and very, very local. They came by to ask him to look at their leaking roof or figure out how they could have more cupboard space in their kitchens. They came by to tell their troubles and just hang out.

Here was Fay puffing up the stairs with a kid in tow, slight in build, dark-skinned, all elbows and teeth, about Tracy's age. "Come on, Orlando, tell Tom what you seen."

"It wasn't nothing. It was dark."

"Have a piece of double chocolate cake," Tom said. "You want milk with it? Or coffee."

"Coffee, man." Orlando began spooning sugar in.

"Are you offering that cake around in general?" Fay asked, helping herself to a piece. "Well, I had a set-to with the fire marshal's office. They are understaffed, overworked, they say it was accidental and would we please get lost. . . . Okay, Orlando, you been bribed. Tell Tom what you saw, already."

"Nothing much." Orlando finished the slice and cut another. "I was up on the roof with my girlfriend. When we can, we sneak up there at night. The roof don't belong to nobody. The old lady next door, she yells at us sometimes, but it ain't her roof, man."

Tom slumped back in his chair as if he were bored. "So what else is new? Do I care if you screw Sylvia on the roof? You'll get frostbite, but that's your problem."

"A couple times lately we seen this guy on the next roof. He don't live in that building. He don't belong in our whole row. But Sylvie says she seen him around before."

"Up on the roof?" Tom's voice rang out. He was no longer pretending boredom. "Doing what? Counting pigeons by starlight?"

"Just looking around. Looking at the chimney, looking at the roofing. Always after dark. Real quiet."

"Ever get a good look at him?"

"I told you, Sylvie recognized him. But she don't know his name. She says she seen him going in and out of that bar, Footsie's. Only that time, she says, he was wearing a suit."

"Describe him." Tom was openly making notes now.

"He's kind of nothing looking . . . medium height. A skinny guy. Near as you can tell in a biker's leather jacket. Only thing I noticed special is he sports this straggly moustache."

"A straggly moustache. . . . What color?"

"He's white, man, if that's what you mean."

"I'm still working on the moustache. What color hair?"

"Sort of nothing color. Ashy."

"Orlando, take another piece of cake. Take two." Tom grinned. His face changed so abruptly when he smiled that she still found herself charmed, while other people responded as if he had given them a gift.

Fay put her arm around Tom. "You think we've found the guy who lit Sandra María's?"

"We haven't found him yet. So, Fay, you bring me evidence for a crime you don't believe in?"

"Just in case you're right for once. Go on, kids, have fun. I'm leaving now. I promised Mikey a hot game of Scrabble." Orlando was already out the door with the last two pieces of cake, but Fay leaned on the doorframe, winking at Daria. "We all don't know how you did it. That the dead should walk again. This guy's been sitting around sucking his thumb since Andrea ran off. Sour? Nasty? Sorry for himself? Don't mention it."

"Oh?" Tom lowered. "If your ex-husband had taken your kids to California, you'd be out dancing the next night?"

"Anyhow, when you get tired putting up with him, I got a waiting list from the neighborhood." Fay eased herself down the stairs.

"Enough," Daria said. "Before I'm ambushed by somebody who wants your body, read me whatever is on those cards."

He fanned out the cards again. "I shouldn't have done this. I thought of it as sort of a present."

"Get on with it! You're making me nervous."

"Well, you have this obsession with the woman Walker's with."

"I wouldn't call it an obsession," Daria said dryly. "It isn't irrational to want to know. If I represent a set of values he's rejecting, then she represents what he wants now."

"So you really want to know?"

"You think I'm some dreamy adolescent who prefers bad fantasies?"

"Okay, so I ran her to ground for you." Closing the cards into a neat pack again, he fixed his gaze on the top card. "Gail Abbott-Wisby. That's a hyphenated name. You screwed me up thinking her last name was Wisby. It's Abbot-Wisby. When the Wisbys married into the Abbots, they were taking no chances on anyone forgetting that feat."

"What does she do? Is she a writer? Or an artist?"

"What does she do indeed? Not much." Tom traced the empty plate with his index finger, licking it delicately. She remembered that she had had a dream about him the night before in which he had merged with Ali as one large pantheresque tomcat. "She came out, of course, at the appropriate time—"

"Came out?"

"As a debutante, not as a lesbian." Tom grinned. "I wish I hadn't given away all the cake. She went to Wellesley with some appropriately vague major. She married right after college. He was the one who came out in our current lingo. Messy divorce, rumors of nervous breakdowns. She seems to have been institutionalized in a fancy nut farm for a while, but who can prove it?"

She realized she was holding her breath and made herself inhale. "How old is she?" Her voice emerged tiny, high.

He riffled his cards. "Thirty this past May. She's the ugly duckling between two swan sisters—"

"Cesaro said something like that. At first he thought Ross must be involved with her younger sister."

"But older and younger sisters married men richer than they are and spawned oodles of toothy and I'm sure nasty children. The Abbot-Wisbys seemed to have broods of three to five, never less. Overpopulation, a family custom. Rowena, the oldest: society designer with a couple of boutiques where you can buy a snappy eight-hundred-dollar shift off the racks. Philippa, the youngest, was a deb beauty and modeled briefly and not all that successfully. But it entitled her to be referred to as Mrs. Charles Rutherford III, the former fashion model Flip Abbot-Wisby. Gail is the ugly duckling, the middle sister who pretty much fucked up."

Daria brooded. "Is he saving her? I can almost see that. Ross thought he was saving me—I was pregnant, not that I needed salvage, thank you. But I think he was saving me from being pregnant and unmarried, from being Italian and from being lower middle class."

"That means working class, doesn't it? With pretensions."

"I suppose it means you expect to move up a bit. We all did, then."

"Did you, now?" Tom turned over a card and skimmed it. "That was your peers. Mine expected to start a revolution. So the expectations of your lot were the more accurate . . ."

"Read me more about Gail."

"Gail may or may not have married again three years ago. She breeds dogs—"

"That I know. German short-haired pointers."

"She got involved with one of the help. The rumors are they were married and then her family trucked her off to Happyville Sanatorium for an encore and had the marriage annulled. Anyhow he disappeared— he seems to have been Australian—with his pockets bulging and Gail was once again her family's problem. In danger of becoming an old maid, in danger of marrying the gardener or the gamekeeper, or going off her rocker altogether."

"Tom, how sure are you? You're trying to make me feel better. Handing me a line of propaganda."

"I'm surely trying to persuade you that imagining yourself less glamorous and less attractive than Gail Abbot-Wisby is a waste of time. But I haven't told you right out what Gail has that you lack."

"What?"

"Connections, kid. Money, honey."

"Money?"

"You haven't asked the right questions. Who are the Abbot-Wisbys, that they hyphenate their silly name?"

"So tell me. You're squirming in your chair."

"Bad little boys squirm. Adult men like me simply move suggestively. It's daddy who's interesting. Roland Abbot-Wisby is the president and believed to be one of the principal stockholders in the Allston Savings and Loan—as well as two other banks on whose boards he sits as director."

"The Allston Savings and Loan," she repeated. Then she saw a page. *Know all men by these presents that Robert Realty being a trust duly established under the laws of the Commonwealth of Massachusetts via its trustee Ross V. Walker, for consideration paid hereby unto the Allston Savings and Loan Association, a corporation duly established under the laws of the Commonwealth of Massachusetts with Mortgage Covenants to secure payments of Two hundred fifty thousand dollars, with interest thereon and principal payable as provided.* She shook her head slowly as if to clear it. "But Ross has mortgages with them."

"Have you any more questions, my child?"

"What do you think it means?"

"A business deal. He's so far into that bank by now he's way overextended. They believe the neighborhood will gentrify, which is why they let him get so overextended. But it's not happening fast enough. He's buying in on a different level. Taking the troublesome daughter off their hands and promising to settle her down steady."

"I don't believe it. I can't accept that Ross would sell himself that cold-bloodedly."

"All evidence suggests Walker is a pretty cold fish when it comes to money decisions. Besides, with the right dowry, she could look attractive."

"But that's not the only bank he's into."

"It's the primary one. It's a wonder he hasn't put out a contract on you.

The Abbot-Wisbys are not going to pay for an affair. It's marriage or nothing."

"No wonder he keeps pestering me." She shook herself, rising in her seat. "We could be making all this up. Where did you get your suppositions? I won't call them facts."

"I've done power structure research in my day—part of my lurid but sometimes useful past. Besides, you have to understand people have many strange hobbies. On all the local rags and local media, there're people whose pleasure it is to watch the moneyed. To watch the real estate operators. To observe the politicians at work and play gobbling up the till. There are people who keep an eye on big machers and finaglers. All passions like any other. I ran down the essentials in the BPL. Then I got the gossip from my old buddy Stan at the *Globe*. Instead of bird-watching, he watches Brahmins."

She let her head down on her propped hands. "It's sad. If it's true, it's so depressing!"

"Why? Because you still care for Walker?"

"I hate him. At times. But I can't stand to see someone I cared for so much and so long turn into someone who can be bought."

"You couldn't be bought?"

"Could you?"

"I used to worry about that a lot. Haven't thought of it in years. Nobody's bidding any longer."

"What's power structure research, exactly?"

"Oh, it was a thing we did a lot during the antiwar years—"

"We? I don't remember doing any myself."

"The political *we,* the movement." Tom shrugged. "It involved the attempt to demystify who owns and runs corporations. Who makes decisions, in whose interests? Who controls banks, insurance companies, how they interlock. How decisions get made—like invading a country or backing some sleazy dictator or breaking a particular strike."

"It sounds like the same thing you do with local fires—blaming people for things that happen. Finding villains. Don't you think it's a little like tribal people who think a god is behind every storm? The gods are angry. The rich are plotting."

"And you want to go on believing neighborhoods change like the weather. My, it's getting white around here, isn't it?"

From under lowered lashes she regarded him. She had blundered into caring for him and she stayed because he was such a completely vulnerable passionate man in bed, tender, open, wholly physical, that she dropped her inhibitions with her clothes. She could give vent to her sexuality with him as she had been able to do only during the very best of times with Ross, if ever, but at moments like these, with his theories of universal conspiracy, she wondered what she was letting herself in for.

"You want to be blind." He was scowling. "That's the thing I resent most about you. You think there's virtue in pretending not to notice, like a lady who just stepped in dog shit."

"And you! You think somebody bought a dog just to make it shit," she snapped back. "Rich people have dogs just so they can bring them to shit on your lawn!"

On the drive back to Lexington, she could not figure out if she was more annoyed with him or with herself. She lost her temper with him easily, too easily perhaps. After years of being mild and even-tempered with Ross, after years of living with the volume control turned way down, she began to remember the adolescent who had made scenes in the kitchen, the girl who shouted back at her brothers, a stormier more passionate Daria who had sunk into the wife as into a stagnant pool but now emerged, apparently intact. She and Tom fought often without ending their relationship or even threatening it.

Torte was not waiting at the door. He would be upstairs in Mariela's room, where he seemed to have moved. Mariela took him walking every day around and around the block, for she was not allowed to cross the street. Torte waddled gravely in front of her and she pattered behind holding tight to his leash, as if anything could have persuaded him to take a step without her. As Daria watched them together, she felt a great relief. Perhaps Torte would never stop missing Ross, but he was no longer grieving.

The light was still on in Sandra María's room. As Daria climbed, she paused to listen. When she heard the uneven rattle of the typewriter keys, she went on to her own room without knocking at Sandra María's closed door. The cats followed her, chasing each other over the furniture as she undressed and climbed into bed.

She did not feel drowsy and could summon no desire to read the manuscript of a Rumanian cookbook her publisher had asked her to review. She had a large knot in her belly that could easily have been loosened. She had jumped at him, ready to defend Ross. How casually she had overlooked the hours Tom had put into trying to dissolve her obsession. She had not even thanked him.

Finally she reached for the phone. "Tom, I'm sorry. I took it out on you, what you found out."

"I shouldn't have bothered. You don't want to know facts. I give you credit for too much genuine curiosity."

"I'm glad you found out. I just didn't like what you learned. It hurt."

"That's ridiculous. What I proved is that you have no reason whatsoever to envy Gail Abbot-Wisby."

"Tom, when I feel bad about Ross, it doesn't mean I'd rather be back with him than with you."

He grunted. Still sore. She tried another approach. "When Andrea left, did you ever feel she was choosing a different set of values?"

"She didn't leave me for another man. It was for a job."

She could sense him fending her off, but she doubted she would make progress probing on the phone. She made up her mind, however, to ask more questions, a great many more. Her life was supposed to be a subject for study and controversy, while his past remained off limits. She smiled at the dumpy plastic phone standing in for his presence. "When you loved someone a long time and that person makes a choice you find mean, it calls into question your whole previous life."

"Was Walker your whole life?" he asked sullenly.

"Of course not. I had the children. My work. But the bulk of my life was him, Tom."

"It sounds to me as if the bulk of your life was things you liked to do, your books, the garden and cooking and futzing around the house, all of which had nothing whatsoever to do with one Ross Walker. I don't garden here, but I cook and futz around the house. You thought it was being married to him that made you enjoy those things. But what I discovered is that they have nothing to do with being married. You had a classic low input, low output relationship. He dealt with money and occupied space. When I ask for more than that, you push me back."

After the conversation, she lay under the covers fuming. That was what she got for trying to apologize. "Low input, low output"—what a creepy mechanical way to describe a love relationship.

That phrase reminded her of Ross's accusation that her life was only adjacent to his. For the first time, except in a mood of self-hatred when she felt fat, middle-aged and frumpy, she wondered if Ross might not have had good reasons for leaving her. Certainly she possessed severe drawbacks as the wife of a landlord hip deep in manipulating his tenants, shutting off services, trying to evict illegally, pyramiding mortgage on mortgage for the acquisition of ever more properties for speculation in the hopes of expelling present populations for more affluent ones. She must have been a nuisance to him when she had acted as rent collector at her parents' old home, constantly fussing about what the tenants wanted and how the neighbors were reacting.

She no longer felt fat or frumpy and she had forgotten about dieting. No doubt she had lost fifteen pounds during the late wars with Ross, but she had stopped fretting about her weight. Low input, low output. Tom was accusing her of a kind of wifely opportunism, not intruding on Ross's choices and failing even to notice her husband had become someone who operated on the margin morally and financially. Sort of Mrs. Albert Speer.

Still she was convinced, whatever Tom might think, that Ross had talked himself into believing he was saving Gail. She could see them at the restaurant table, Gail huddled as if a cold wind blew on her rangy hunched back. Daria herself had obviously not seemed in need of more salvation. In their early years when he had been the liberal government lawyer righting wrongs and she had been the dull comfortable substitute teacher, housewife, mama, he had been the center of attention always in family, among friends, out among strangers—as he had been with his parents, the only child, the son they adored and expected to do great things.

Maybe she should just get on with the divorce and forget grappling for position. No. She could not give up the house, especially when she had just populated it to her satisfaction. She liked living with Sandra María and Mariela. In spite of being furious with him at the moment, she liked Tom. It was all satisfying and interesting, she realized, sitting up abruptly in the dark. I like my new life, she thought with astonishment, as Sheba purred beside her.

20

Daria would have liked to question Dorothy about Tom, but she did not dare. How had she got into a position where she had to withhold information about an affair from her lawyer, lest she arouse her jealousy? she asked herself. Ross, after falling silent for a week, was pressuring Dorothy: "The bank is going to foreclose if she doesn't start paying off that mortgage, or turn it over to me. It's my building."

Daria along with her research downtown was compiling a dossier in her head on Tom. She questioned Sandra María openly and tried to pry information from Fay with seemingly casual chatter. Tom had been born in 1947 in the old whaling port and textile town of New Bedford in a working-class Portuguese neighborhood, mixed white and Cape Verdian Black, although his father's parents had been Russian Jews who had both worked in the Wamsutta mill. Tom's father had been apprenticed to an electrician. His mother was a librarian, still unmarried at twenty-eight, four years older than his father. She had a college education acquired with difficulty during the Depression. She had grown up in Chelsea and moved around the state from job to job, liking the adventure of independence and exploring new places, until she met Tom's father at a 4th of July picnic. They were married within six months and over the next decade had four children, of whom Tom was the youngest.

His parents had been strongly in love. Tom had grown up with the same admiration for his mother that his father felt. She was smart, adventurous and then dead too young in that freak swimming accident. During the Vietnam War, Tom had quarreled with his parents and still felt distant from his brother, who was in the Army Corps of Engineers. At Rosh Hashanah and Yom Kippur he went to see his father; on Passover his married sister in New Bedford made a seder, but the only sibling he was close to was his next older sister Sharon. She had also bounced around the landscape and now lived on a farm near Woodstock, Vermont, raising apples and goats with her female lover and the children of two broken marriages. Tom spent part of every summer there with his girls.

He had been called up to serve but had not gone; Fay said she heard he had had himself tattooed with a heart saying HARRY AND TOM AND BUTCH, but Daria knew that Tom was not tattooed. Whatever he had done, he had not gone into the Army, but his life had suffered total disruption. He had become involved in something called Vietnam Summer that involved door-to-door political work in Dorchester. In the fall he had simply not returned to college for his senior year. Dorothy said that when she met Tom, he had been confused and angry. He had cast himself into whatever the enthusiasts around him proclaimed was important at the moment (We must organize in the factories! No, we must take to the streets! Now we must create our own media!). He lived out the slogans and emerged dazed and without center, guilty still, guilty for whatever he did with his life. The war went on. Friends of his childhood, guys he had played football with, guys he had fished with, guys he had drunk beer with down by the water and smoked dope with in old cars, came home in boxes or came home junkies or came home with an arm missing or simply disappeared as if they had never been. He could not talk to the survivors. They could talk to each other, but they too could not understand the language of his friends. His life had been torn loose. He spoke the language of his army and they of theirs.

But Tom had not dropped out of Harvard; he had dropped out of Southeastern Massachusetts University. Tom received no allowance from home. His parents possessed the accouterments of working-class comfort: an aging two-story wooden house with an apartment upstairs where his oldest sister lived with her husband and kids; a rented cottage every August; a dinghy with a motor; a new car every four years; a huge color

TV and for his mother, a subscription to three different book clubs. However, they never got much ahead.

The movement had talked much about class in its later years, but only as the full furor of political ferment abated did Tom begin to brood about what class meant. His friends resumed at Harvard or Boston University. They emerged doctors, lawyers, professors of history, political science, economics or Far Eastern studies. His friends moved up from the casual journalism of the underground papers to the *Phoenix* and then to the *Globe,* Channel 4, CBS, UP, forever up. The little details that had once demonstrated his solid proletarian credentials now told against him. In the tight world of Boston, it would have been better to emerge wordless from the jungle like Tarzan than to have put in three years at Southeastern Massachusetts University.

Tom was twenty-six when he married Andrea, in 1973; she was twenty-two, a year out of Vassar, passionately in love with him and soon pregnant. Daria remembered what it was like to get used to being married and used to being a mother all so quickly, a note that sang to her of her own experience out of much that was strange. That baby was the first daughter, Rosa; the second came two years later and was named Georgia (for Georgia O'Keeffe and George Jackson simultaneously, Tom told her). Andrea's father was a developer and her mother an assistant principal in a small town near Schenectady. They gave some help till Tom, unable to wangle a real job in journalism, joined a carpentry collective and learned on the crew.

The next year when Andrea decided to go to graduate school, her parents came through with the tuition, astronomical since she got into Radcliffe. Feminism having influenced their marriage by 1977, Tom took over a large share of parenting. Moreover they lived in a commune where everybody shared child care. Andrea had pursued her degree in political science, finished everything but her thesis within two years and landed a teaching job in U. Mass Boston. By the time her thesis had been successfully defended, one chapter had already been accepted by the *American Political Science Review* and another by *Foreign Policy*. When a job offer came from Santa Cruz, it was clear that Andrea would take it and increasingly clear she would just as soon not take Tom.

Exactly what had happened between them neither Fay nor Sandra

María nor Dorothy could tell Daria. Afterward Tom had crawled into himself. Except when his girls were with him in August, he had spent his time working with his carpentry collective, puttering around his kitchen, playing with his cat and reading a great deal in pursuit of the education he felt he had fudged. Only the organization of SON and the rash of fires had dragged him reluctantly from his routine. "He was turning into an old maid," Fay said. "At least you been good for him." Grudging praise. Perhaps Fay felt Daria had stolen Tom; that one of his own from the neighborhood was entitled when the giant finally woke from his sorrow.

They made love powerfully and warmly. They worked together politically. They talked. They argued. He loved finding unlikely restaurants to spring on her: Armenian, Vietnamese, Portuguese. They vied with each other in cooking. But he did not open up verbally. She felt that thick shell inside his skin, protecting tissues and organs. She resented it. She poked, she prodded. He denied he had anything to say about himself. He described himself as simple, physical. He was far more communicative in all other respects than Ross had been, but he persisted in referring to himself as one who dealt in grunts and moans. The only road in was sexual, when his protection fell away.

If he doesn't open to me soon, I'll give up, she would tell herself. Who wants to deal only with a surface? But the surface was pleasant, sensual, at times joyful. She was beguiled, she was busy. Then she would experience an ashy despair and ask, Will he ever trust me? Will he ever open? Is he capable of giving himself in love?

Tom had hired Sylvia and Orlando to hang around with him while he searched for the man they had seen on the roof. A week, two weeks passed. Tom was also asking questions widely but discreetly in the neighborhood. Orlando's father owned a Spanish-American grocery where Orlando himself worked, more to have a job than because they really needed him, as his older brother worked there too; still it was a social node of the neighborhood, and someone there should have recognized that man's description. Every night Tom was glum. "That guy's vanished. Sometimes people know who I mean, but nobody knows who he is."

Finally a hint. Orlando said, "I keep asking around too, you know. Boz told me he used to see that guy all the time over on Brainerd. Going in

269

and out of that crappy building my bro Roberto lived in last year with that blond bitch."

"Did moustache live there?"

"Naw. I asked Roberto and he says he used to collect the rents."

"Mmmmm. That side of Commonwealth. . . . You know the number?"

"Man, you can see it for a block. It's standing there empty. They had a fire."

"A fire. A fire!" Tom clapped Orlando on the back. "When?"

Orlando shrugged. Sylvia, who was leaning on the kitchen counter petting Marcus, cleared her throat. Sylvia was the girl Daria had met in the street the night of Sandra María's fire. Her punk cut had grown out considerably. She was a big-boned girl who tried to look tough but who seemed to Daria on closer inspection rather sad, disconsolate. She stuck close to Orlando. "Just after I was out on school vacation. So the end of February."

"Great!" Tom exulted. "You kids have done just great!"

"But we don't know who he is," Daria objected.

"Maybe he's the rent collector. Maybe he's the owner," Tom said. "If we know the address we can find out who owned it. Daria, go down to the tax assessor's office and get the info tomorrow, okay? After supper we'll cruise past the shell and get the exact number."

"I'll find out what address the tax bill was sent to," Daria said, making herself a note.

"I guess you're done with us, huh?" Orlando said. "I mean, we found out what you wanted to know."

Tom looked hard at him, probably reading the disappointment. "Not yet. We still have to keep an eye out for him in the neighborhood. See what he's into, what he's up to."

"I didn't mind it at all," Sylvia said in her low melodious voice. Her voice always surprised Daria, as if a tough little game bird should suddenly warble. "I ask about my brother too when we go around."

"Your brother?"

"Eduardo. He disappeared last summer."

Orlando shrugged. "So he ran off. Big deal. Your mother leaned all over him."

"He wouldn't go without saying good-bye except he's in some kind of trouble." Sylvia trailed off.

Mariela had just learned to fold and cut pieces of paper into snowflakes, experimenting with different materials including the day's *Globe* as she lay on the living-room floor. The floor was bare now, the boards sanded, refinished and studded with small Oriental rugs. Sandra María and Daria had done the floor the previous weekend. Daria thought the room looked warmer and certainly less pretentious than it had. Mariela's toys lay here and there, and on the arm of the smaller rocker, a Beatrix Potter book about a mouse that Gretta had given Mariela the week before.

They were still working out a division of tasks, a way of living mutually pleasing. Daria had discovered that, frankly, she did not like Sandra María in the kitchen. Sandra María if she set out to heat water in a kettle would let it boil dry. She would put the garlic press in among the forks, where it would be lost for two weeks. Daria claimed the kitchen as her turf. She cooked, she cleaned up, she planned meals. Sandra María cleaned the downstairs and took care of the laundry, which always seemed sixty percent Mariela's clothes. They both shopped together or separately and cleaned their areas of the house. As the earth thawed they began putting in the hardy garden, planting sugar snaps, Lincoln peas, spinach and rocket, fennel and lettuce. All the south-facing windows were lined with flats of tomatoes, sweet and hot peppers, eggplants, broccoli, red cabbage. Ross had never let her take over the public parts of the house with seedlings, so she had had to buy most of her tomatoes and marigolds in previous years. Starting them was more fun. She almost wished Ross could see how different the house looked. It even smelled different. It was less to be contemplated and admired and more to be used. She felt the spirit of the house approved.

"You really like living with her . . ." Sandra María said softly as they both watched Mariela, dark curls obscuring her face as she cut away clumsily at the folded paper. When she finished a design, carefully she shook it out and then looked up at them, holding high the symmetrical pattern proudly and demanding great praise. "I worried beforehand. It's been a long time since you lived with young kids."

271

"Not so long. Maybe that was the happiest part of my life. It makes me feel better to remember, as if there's some continuity and everything isn't destroyed."

"Daria, he can't destroy your life." Sandra María jerked her chin in the direction of her busy daughter. "Her father was a disaster with fireworks. But out of him, look, my pearl." Sandra María settled back, putting her bare feet on the hassock. She wore a kimona and her hair was up in rubber curlers. On her lap was a tangle of Mariela's clothing she was mending. "My own mamá tried to make me marry him. But I knew I'd got in something sticky. I put my back up and kept saying no and he took off, which I never for one minute regretted. I think he would have abused her, because he'd started on me."

"That's one thing Ross never was, abusive. I don't think he ever hit the kids. I did sometimes, I admit it. Sometimes I think I lost my temper more with them because I couldn't lose it with him."

"See!" Mariela was demanding their attention. "See how I did? I made hearts. You know how you do that? You fold up the paper . . ." Mariela insisted on demonstrating.

When Mariela finally returned to her experiments with scissors and paper, Daria said, "One pleasure I've discovered with Tom is the simple one of losing my temper with an equal. Not with the kids, where I really shouldn't have—"

"I don't know about that," Sandra María said. "It's rotten to hurt them, but it's no good never to get mad. You bring them up to think nobody will ever scream at them. Then when somebody raises their voice, they wilt or fall right over." Sandra María held up a pair of denim overalls. "Damn, I sewed it through. Got to take it out and do it over, ai yi yi yiii!" she yelled and then subsided. "Mariela, give your mamá the scissors for just a minute. I goofed. I sewed your overalls shut."

"Sometimes I think Andrea sewed Tom's mouth shut before she left. He has such a strong sense of his own vulnerability and he's got in the habit of protecting it so well, he's on the point of losing it altogether."

"Well, you go on working on him. I get can't over how he bounds around these days. You know, you aren't the only one to have a go at him. He had lots of visitors, Daria. Women I think he'd been involved

272

with back before Andrea. They came and they tried. You'd see them with him a couple of times, and then no more."

"I know what defeated them. That protective cocoon."

Sandra María sewed doggedly for a while. Suddenly she smiled. "I can't tell you how good it is to sleep again."

"You mean because it's quieter here."

"Because I'm not afraid. When a landlord is after you, you live in fear. Will they burn you out, the way it finally happened? Or arrange a little accident? Or hire muscle? Or just harass you and your child? This February the bulb kept being missing at the last turn. I'd put a new bulb in and again the next day it would be gone. I can't tell you how that scared me. Every time I had to come home at night, I'd start thinking how that bulb kept being taken out by someone and what for? Why did they want the stairway dark?"

She did not want to encourage Sandra María's paranoia about the Petrises, Mr. and Mrs. Egg, bland and grey with their aviator glasses. "We have our own problems without a landlord. Who do we call if the furnace goes out?"

"Oh, Daria, you already solved that problem. We call Tom."

It was her turn to present Tom with a card from her research on who owned the burned building where Orlando had seen the moustache. "Golden Realty," she announced. "Belongs to one Louis Henry Ledoux. His home address is in Belmont. He works alone, apparently, but he owns several buildings."

Tom reached for another drumstick. "Our next step is to visit lovely Belmont. How would you like to keep me company at dawn outside Louis Henry's?"

"A stakeout, like in the movies," Sandra María said. "Be glad, Daria, that spring has come."

"Glad? It'll be cold enough." But she began to get excited. "I'll pack us a breakfast tonight. Thermos of hot coffee. What else can we have for breakfast in a parked car?"

"You aren't going to have steak? Like a cookout? I thought Mamá said you were cooking steak? I don't like steak. It's too red and dripping. I like chicken. Why can't we have a chicken out?"

"Mariela, don't feed the cats under the table! The food gets into the rug," Sandra María said, doing something with her foot.

"But they like it!"

"But I don't."

"We could feed them *at* the table," Tom said. "They'd like that."

"We could feed them on the table and we could eat on the floor," Daria said. "I'm going to make some kind of fruit bread. Cranberry? Apricot? Cranberry-apricot? Cranberry-apricot-orange?"

"Can we do that, Mamá? Can we do what Daria says?"

Sandra María glared at them both. "For two people who claim to have raised kids yourself, the two of you have both forgot what's a joke and what's not funny to a little kid. No, Mariela, we can't eat on the floor and let the cats have the table. Not unless the cats wear clothes and eat with knives and forks. If you teach them to eat with knives and forks and spoons, they can sit at the table with us."

"Okay! It's a deal!"

That night for the first time Tom slept over at her house, instead of her going home with him. Mariela was long asleep. Sandra María did not believe in lying to her daughter about her own involvement or about Daria's, but Daria was not used to such openness and felt easier if Mariela did not know.

It was strange to lie with Tom in what had been her matrimonial bed. It made her wonder if he had ever felt peculiar about being with her in his apartment. She asked him.

"I built the sleeping loft two years ago. Andy never saw it."

"When I can get you to say anything about her at all, it's like a door slamming in my face."

"Your skin is the world's softest." He was stroking her. "The silkiest fur made into flesh. It feels edible. As if I could bite into you and you'd be sweet and juicy like a fully ripe plum."

He was changing the subject, but the flattery made her feel gorgeous to him. She could not escape the awkwardness of being there with Tom while the ghost of Ross watched. But Ross was miles away with Gail Abbot-Wisby and her two-hundred-marching-dog band, and never thought of her except with fury that she stood in the way of his immediate marriage and his getting his hands on the money he saw as frozen in the house. She could not keep her room as a shrine to a dead marriage. Still this night was another step into an intimacy still partial that she was not sure could ever fully develop.

The Belmont house was a sixty-year-old Cape that had had strange things done to it. It had picture windows prized into its facade. It had a cupola stuck on top, modern and raw looking in its shingling. It had a long addition strung out behind it with sliding glass doors and awning windows. It had a garage added and then some kind of room over the garage, in the form of an imitation barn with hayloft doors, a breezeway intervening. It was a corner house. Its neighbor had thrown up a wall of shrubbery and cardinal autumn olive, a fast growing screen. Here lived the owner of the building on Brainerd, burned when it had taxes owing for five years and the city had begun moves to take it over to sell at auction.

She had never been in this neighborhood in Belmont before, although Tony lived only ten blocks away, just off Common Street in a big brick Tudor on a fancy street. Belmont was a changeable town. They were across Common, in an area of many multiple family dwellings, some triple-deckers and many two-story buildings with one or two or three apartments, a neighborhood of aluminum siding and do-it-yourself home improvements. Most of these buildings were owner-occupied with at least one rental unit carved out of them. Nobody paid attention to the van.

They huddled low in the seat of the van, drinking café au lait from the quart vacuum bottle and eating prebuttered slices of cranberry-apricot-orange bread and nibbling temple oranges. They cuddled and nibbled and the waiting was not unpleasant. Daffodils were blooming beside the walk, made of reddish cement slabs in an S design from curbside to the front porch, past bright plastic duck and ducklings and a recently planted sapling with a label still affixed from the nursery. Inside the wire fence they could see a half grown Doberman pacing, a tricycle tipped on its side and a plastic baseball bat, left out in the light morning rain.

"I always had two images of myself," Tom was saying. "One image I was big and strong. The other, I was big and fat. In grade school I was the fat boy. Then I shot up in middle school and suddenly I was towering over the class and everybody wanted me on their team. When I feel good about my life, I feel good about my body. When I hate my life, I hate my body."

"I grew up with a fashionable body for my time. Now it isn't the right kind any longer, but somehow I'm still happily back in the aesthetic I started with. I know I'm supposed to be skinny and flat now, but I don't want to be skinny and flat. I like flesh."

"So do I. Yours in particular."

"What did your wife look like?"

She could feel him tighten. Then he answered her, his voice thick and low. "She was fairly tall, with honey blond hair. The last three years we lived together, she was always on a diet. After a while, whatever came up, was it going to the movies, was it fucking, was it making friends, her only interest was in how many calories it had. The first thing she'd say when she was describing somebody was whether they were overweight or not—according to her. I felt like an elephant."

"I guess that's a thing people do now when they're dissatisfied—with their lives, with their lovers, with themselves."

"If you come to represent the flesh and the flesh is bad, then you must be punished." He groaned. "Aren't I being talkative about myself? Sandra María gave me a lecture. She says if I don't open up with you more, you'll give up on me."

"Tom! Somebody's coming out! Through the breezeway."

Huddled far down and resting a pair of binoculars on the dash, Tom stared through them at their quarry. "All right! He's got a moustache. Could be our man."

The silliest thing was that she had a funny feeling that she recognized the man. "Let me look too." Where would she ever have seen Louis Henry?

"Sorry." He handed her the binoculars, but she could not get a good view until the man had backed out his pickup truck, loaded with his gear. As the truck backed and then turned past them, she got an excel-

lent view of his profile, bent forward to light a cigarette from his dash-
board lighter.

Something troubled her. Grey blond hair on his bare head and a droopy
moustache. Leather jacket that looked too big. She had seen him before
and not only in her mind's eye, she knew she had.

"That's our boy," Tom was exulting. "There's our torch. We got him!"
After the pickup truck had vanished, he started his own engine.

Snow on the ground then, yes, and her hands had been shaking. She
had been following Ross in the rented car, yes, but he had not gone
toward his office in the Little Pru office building. He had walked briskly
toward Mass Avenue where he had paused outside a coffee shop. Yes.
That was the man who came out to him. "Now I know where I've seen
him." Her head whipped around to stare back at the house as if she
could watch him walk out again, to be sure.

"Where? In Allston?"

"No. When I was jealous of Ross, I followed him one morning. He
went to Gail's apartment. Of course at the time I didn't know it was
Gail he was seeing, I thought her name . . ." She stopped abruptly, the
breath kicked out of her.

"Yeah, well, go on, where does our Louis come into it?"

She almost could not speak. Louis Henry Ledoux was Lou. The glamorous lady of her nightmares. She spoke slowly, as if by rote. "I waited
outside. When Ross came out, he didn't go straight to work. He walked
down to Mass Avenue and there he met that guy. Lou was in a coffee
shop. Ross stopped outside and Lou came out to meet him. They talked
for a moment and then Ross went off to work."

"You know what? You've just tied a little knot for us."

"No!" She was horrified. "That doesn't mean there's any real connection between them. They both own buildings in the same neighborhood."

"Did Walker hand him anything?"

She was frightened, because it was almost as if Tom could read the
memory, could snatch it from her. Here was Tom assuming Ross's guilt
just because she had seen him stop and say hello to some man he knew.
Ross might care more about money than he used to, but Tom simply did
not know Ross as a person. Landlord was a category that made Ross a
complete cartoon villain. She was sorry she had mentioned seeing Ross with

Lou. "I'm not even sure of the identification. I was way across the street."

"But did Walker hand over anything at all to him?"

"I don't remember! I didn't see!" She did not want to think about it. She would not expose Ross further. Why had Lou been writing to Ross anyway, the mysterious Lou she had believed was Ross's love interest? Did she really want to know?

"Did they talk long?"

"I don't remember! No. They just said hello or something and then Ross went on to work." Daria glared at Tom. "Don't push me so hard! It was something trivial, that happened months ago."

"Daria, you aren't betraying him. If Lou is working for Walker as well as for Petris, we may be dealing with deliberate arson. If Walker is involved, you can't protect him."

She shook her head mutely. "I hate the way I was then—shameful, prowling through his papers. Following him in the street. Steaming open his letters. Can you believe I did all that? It embarrasses me dreadfully to remember. How can you trust me, when I acted that way with my own husband?"

"Look, if one person lies, the other tries to find out the truth. If one person in a couple hides something, the other tries to uncover it. I don't think you'd act that way with somebody who was levelling with you."

She had a moment of guilt remembering how she had been questioning Fay and Sandra María. Was that investigation the same obsessed pursuit? Perhaps digging to know had become habit and she was turning into a monster of persistent curiosity.

He tapped her arm. "Want to go home?"

"Please. Peggy's coming in today and I'm feeling unravelled."

"Why would seeing that guy Louis unravel you?"

"It's just remembering that bad time. I was half crazy."

"Why did you call him Lou?"

"I don't know! Maybe I heard Ross say the name to someone. Don't you think it's an obvious nickname for Louis?"

He glanced at her sideways and she felt sure he was suspicious of her suddenly poor memory. She felt guilty for covering up for Ross and suspecting him herself. Tom was silent for a while, frowning. "Lou is the weak point. We can get at him, I know it. Wait and see!"

21

WHEN Cesaro invited her to dinner, she had a hard decision. She wanted to bring Tom, so that he would
begin to know her family. However, she was not quite
sure she could trust any of her brothers. Only Gussie
knew about Tom. She decided she would be cautious and wait longer.

Cesaro tried to question her like a corporate father about her finances.
Then he told her that Ross was genuinely worried about Gail. "He's
afraid it's too much of a strain on her, waiting and waiting. He thinks
you're dragging your feet to be punitive."

"Cesaro, you can tell him that as soon as he produces an honest financial statement, I'm sure we can work out an agreement. It's only his lies
that are holding us up."

"Don't you trust me at all? What's happened to you?" Ross whined
into her ear. "You always used to be so accepting and easygoing."

"But that's what we have lawyers for. So they can do our fighting for
us and we can be easygoing."

"Daria . . ." His voice was coaxing, warm taffy, the way he used to
sound when he wanted her to cook something particularly complicated
for eight boors. "We can work it out together, we can!"

Did he suddenly want to come back? She was interested to note that
her first reaction was fear. She really did not want him back. "We can
work out what?" she asked cautiously.

"The settlement! You didn't think I meant . . . ? Daria!"

"I didn't know what you meant," she said sweetly. "I thought we were doing just that—working on a settlement with the aid of our lawyers."

"Do you have any idea how much it's costing?"

"Not as much as if we fight it out in court, right?"

"Daria, if you'd just sign the agreement we drafted, I could fly down to the Dominican Republic next week and it would all be over the next day."

"But, Ross, I'm in no hurry. I have no wedding plans." She waited, curious, to see if he would say anything indicating he knew about Tom.

But he only snarled, "That's your problem. I do."

"Then it's your problem, isn't it?" Oh, she was enjoying herself. Those months of being reduced to tears and then treated as an imbecile for crying; preceded by years of creeping around him pleasing, trying to please, failing to please, the standards of what would please him always raised higher like the bar at high jump until at last she missed and sprawled ignominiously on her back.

"Daria, when are you going to sign that agreement?"

"That one, never. My lawyer says it won't do. You should have our response in today's mail."

"All the grasping, demanding side of you I've always hated is boiling out. You can't get me back this way, no matter how you try to ruin my life all over again!"

"Ross, you're going to have to split more property with me than you want to. You're going to have to share more of what we own."

"And what the hell would you do with it? Fritter it away. It's throwing property down a rathole. You don't know the first thing about what you're asking, just because you hired some out-of-work title searcher your lawyer put you onto. It's throwing away property to turn it over to you."

"Good night, Ross."

Dorothy looked pleased with herself, the first time she had projected anything but a wary combativeness in Daria's presence. "We've got him where we want him. He's hungry for it."

"What did he say when you showed him a copy of his holdings?"

"He was furious. He also tried to say those buildings have nothing to do with you. In other words, the family has been living on your earnings, and his have gone into real estate. I told him that wouldn't fly. But it's fascinating. He really does seem to believe that all that is his and your money was used up in living expenses, as if you earned red money and he earned blue money and they were different."

"He said something about flying to the Dominican Republic."

"That's a quickie divorce. But we must have the financial agreement completely worked out here. I hate to be optimistic before the fact, but he's under pressure from his girlfriend. How much are you prepared to give away?"

"I want the house I live in. I want the building Fay lives in, but with that huge mortgage paid off. I want the cash in the savings certificates when they come due. We had some stocks we should split fifty-fifty. You can bargain with everything else. Oh, and Tracy's tuition paid through college."

"We're talking about whole or part interest in another eleven buildings."

"I'm not going into the real estate business. It's all pyramided on those huge mortgages. Do as well for me as you can. But you know what I really need."

Coffee was one of their new rituals. Sandra María had learned to drink cappuccino, although if she came down first, she would simply make café con leche, using the same dark roast. Morning coffee, blinking, sleepy, each of them mumbling about plans and schedules. Chatty coffee when both came home or stopped work. Coffee after supper when Mariela demanded their attention, soaking up love and praise like a bit of good bread taking up gravy. Coffee Sunday morning with Tom and Ángel in the dining room in view of the tulips making a brave display against the ledge, as she had imagined in the fall.

Mariela now ran to her and crawled into her lap. Mariela now stormed at her, stomping her foot. When Sheba came into heat again and was locked into purdah, Mariela spent much of those days shut in with her, consoling her, she said. She also let Sheba out on the third day, "to see what would happen and what they would do." This time Ali figured it out.

Sandra María and Daria must decide: kittens or no kittens. Sheba had to be altered at once or allowed to carry her litter. The children of incest. Cats seemed to find such matters irrelevant. Mariela wanted kittens. "We can't have five or six cats," Daria said. Then she raised her head sharply as if hearing a voice behind her. "But why not? If we want to." There was no sensible father to say no. They could have fifteen cats, birds, goldfish, poodles and iguanas. Or simply the kittens.

"It would be good for Mariela to see kittens born," one or the other would say, and then they would think but not if brother-sister incest produced little monsters.

They had evenings of popcorn and fires, evenings of a return to adolescence and fiddling with each other's hair and wardrobes. Daria had not laughed as much since the girls were little. Permission to be silly. Permission to get down on the floor with Mariela and the cats and play with a piece of string or a pile of lego blocks. Permission to talk about problems with her book, a conversation with her agent, the final negotiations with Channel 7, and never to feel that she was being tactless to admit that she was concerned about her work.

They were dyeing eggs for Mariela's basket when Sandra María said, "I don't want to hurt your feelings about this, Daria. But it's kind of weird living with all those old photographs on every wall."

Daria did feel slighted. After all, those were her daughters, her husband, herself. But of course they were merely Ross's recordings.

"I'm sorry I said anything. It's not a big thing."

"You could put up your photographs too."

"I guess so. Ángel has taken enough in the past year. . . ."

Daria could imagine what was going through Sandra María's mind. Ángel favored bleak urban landscapes, the shape of an ironwork drawbridge at sunset, gulls on the ice of the Charles, the stiff body of a dead cat on a South End street. She would not find it easy to live with Ángel's city images.

As she moved about the house that day she became aware of the eyes of those dead selves watching. Therefore Thursday night when Tom was working overtime finishing up a job that had been driving his crew crazy, while Sandra María was at school and Mariela had been bathed, read a story and tucked in, Daria found herself slowly taking down all the old photographs.

Hers she discarded cheerfully. Only in some early photos where she was holding up an infant did she look natural. None of the others resembled her inner image of herself, for they were too tentative, too conscious of pleasing or displeasing. The message of those faces to the camera was, *Please don't.*

The infant wrapped in blankets she cuddled on the grass was Freddy. Tom could not understand Ross, because he saw him as all landlord. Tom could not imagine how Ross had suffered when Freddy was dying slowly, never having lived. How Ross had lain in her arms weeping for his damaged son. No, Tom could not understand that Ross had a heart.

He had left her because he wanted to be young again, he wanted to force his way back into the world of those pictures when they were newly married, when he was madly in love, when the children were young and she was almost entirely wife and mother—a little boring but desirable in her soft way. If she let herself think his desertion meant he was an evil person, she was crazy. Sometimes when Gretta talked about her ex-husband, Daria felt there was no limit to Gretta's malice. She did not want to pass from love to hatred. Once those nasty but crucial details about money and property had been worked out lawyer to lawyer, surely they might sometime face each other as friends.

Gently she laid the photographs in albums she had bought earlier that day. A tenderness radiated between her hands and the paper. Oh, she could look back now and read the fretted ambition in Ross's face. That snapshot had been taken when he was running for the school committee in Newton. After he had lost, he took a dislike to Newton and their home there, discarding it along with his short-lived incursion into electoral politics.

She had loved Ross, and she had gone on loving him and enjoying their life together long after he had gradually ceased being the man she loved. If the past no longer felt to her just beyond reach, the potent and beautiful past so much sunnier and riper than the stark present—for her present was succulent in its own way now—nonetheless she did not remember with less gratitude or pleasure. Tom had cut away his past. He displayed it labelled in his heart's museum. Ross wanted to revise his past so that it could be written off like a bad investment. She refused both gambits. The good in her past she would try to embody in some new form, and the bad she would try to understand. That was her strategy for survival.

What Tom refused to see also was that while she would fight through Dorothy for a decent settlement, she had no intention of forcing a gap between them so great they could not bridge it to come together occasionally for the girls, to provide what the girls needed, to do for them in trouble. In the long run, Ross would come to feel grateful to her for holding on to this home for Tracy as well as herself. Perhaps in time Robin would return, although when she thought of Robin she felt a stab of pain that never seemed to soften, her daughter who seemed to have divorced her far more swiftly and cleanly than her husband. But the girls were the hostages held against her, the reason she could not afford to remember any more about Lou than she had let slip to Tom.

"Lou was about to lose that building on Brainerd for taxes when he burned it," Tom said. "So, interesting point: two weeks ago he sold it for more than he paid for it. Sold it burned. And already today Orlando tells me there's a demolition crew taking it down and a sign about what's going up there."

"He's rehabbing a place around the corner up the hill a little. Near the boys' club," Fay said.

Tom's face twisted in scorn. "Did you see it? Did you just see what he's doing to that house? Aluminum siding over that fine old clapboard. Aluminum awnings. The man is crazed for aluminum. Then a stupid picture window smack onto the building across."

"Are we down on him for bad taste, or because we think he's a torch?" Daria asked. It took her a moment to figure out why she was taking mild offense. Because what Lou was doing to that building reminded her of how Joe had fixed up his house in Medford before he moved his family south after her parents. "And we should give high points to Ross then. His rehab where that fire happened is staunchly bourgeois and very tasteful. His condo in the North End is an architect's dream."

"Lou's a small operator who's in too deep." Sandra María spoke from the dining area of Tom's apartment. She had covered the table with a big chart she was working on. Daria had provided much of the data, along with Sandra María and Tom's older research on local landlords, the detective work down at the Registry of Deeds that had originally brought them to picketing Ross. Now Sandra María was turning all of their findings into a neat graphic display. It was Tom and Sandra María's theory that when they finished the chart, they would be able to predict who was going to have a fire next and perhaps even which buildings were likely. "Lou does almost all his work himself. He doesn't care whether he rehabs or burns, almost a roll of the dice. If he's flush he rehabs. If he's broke, he burns."

"That fire on Brainerd totalled his building," Tom said. "We have more careful fires over here: just to empty a building and provide capital for the rehab. Obviously if he is the local torch, he has the know-how to do a controlled burn. He's a tidy workman, I'll give him that."

"Careful, huh?" Fay snorted over the pile of envelopes she was addressing. "Jesus, what short memories. Nobody remembers little Bobbie Rosario anymore? And whoever the hell that other body was, a bum or something."

"We don't know he was the torch for every fire," Tom said. "Although we do have that tentative link between Walker and Lou."

Daria said, "I hope you haven't convinced each other that every fire that happens around here is arson."

There was a long silence. Sandra María continued filling in the chart on a window shade that covered most of the dining-room table, and the other three went on putting out their mailing to call a meeting.

"I'll be so damned glad when this Waltham job is done, I'm going to throw a party," Tom was saying. "We have another job under way I really like, but they're driving me crazy out there."

"Yeah? What's wrong?" Fay asked, licking stamps and making a sour face.

"We're almost done, and suddenly they decide a window's in the wrong place and let's move it."

"Well, don't they have to pay?" Fay asked.

"It's not that." Tom shrugged. "We did it once and we did it right. It won't be right done over. I hate undoing what we did. I have to rip out the bookshelves I put in for them. It's the waste of it."

"You mean you won't do as good a job the second time?" Daria asked.

"Of course not. Because we did it once. It doesn't feel right."

Sandra María stepped back from her chart and cleared her throat. "Daria, I'm afraid I have to say I think your estranged husband is due for a fire. Too much outflow and not enough coming in. He's stuck. He's used the mortgage money for buying more buildings and I doubt he has the capital to rehab. Now money is looser again, he's got to get moving while the market's opening up. He can't get his money out if he doesn't rehab soon and start going condo. The only way he can finance it is from a convenient little fire. It's his turn, I'm telling you."

Saturday afternoon, Tom insisted they go for a drive, alone, the two of them. Where they drove was an old town house in Cambridge near Inman Square. "This is where we're working."

"Where the people made you keep taking out windows and putting in windows?"

"No, I wouldn't show you that. It makes me ashamed. You want to bet they'll take a year to pay us? We're just starting another job in Watertown, but this one you can see what we do. . . . I wanted you to know."

Basically the first two floors had most of the interior walls removed and the outer walls stripped down to plaster and original fireplace brick. "We opened up the downstairs to one large room with interruptions, and then a bath added and what's a sort of exercise room-*cum*-guest room-*cum*-study. That's what those rings are for. The wife hangs from them."

Even with the walls incomplete, she could recognize that Aaron Aardvark did handsome work.

"Oh, sure, we're good," he said. "We turn down more jobs than we take on. And what we do is good clean work. We give value. We save buildings and turn old buildings into homes that will stand a long time."

"Why are you saying this so apologetically? You think I'm Andrea, I want you to be a professional man and go to an office?"

"I worry about that sometimes. Sure. But my work, it's gentrification too. We're not working for developers like Walker or his partners or Petris. We're hired by young professionals who are buying run-down houses and improving them. But it's the same thing in the long run. People without money can't afford us."

"But it isn't quite the same. You aren't forcing people out."

"Boston has one of the lowest vacancy rates in the country. Sometimes when they buy buildings, there are tenants they get rid of. Then there's less housing for the folks who need it the most and have the least choice. I know all that. We make a living by providing a service for the affluent."

"But I don't feel you're ashamed of what you do."

"I like it. I can't help liking it. But I want you to know, I do see it in context."

Daria walked through from room to room, imagining them growing day by day into a home. "I'm glad you brought me here. I don't know why it should matter to me, but it does—to know exactly what you do."

"Because with your husband, you didn't."

"Check. Because I didn't. Because I don't want to live without knowing how I'm living ever again."

"You're tired of being innocent?"

"You shouldn't be so surprised, that I listen to what you say." She turned toward him. He was standing on a patch of recently redone flooring, not yet stained to match the rest of the floor. A pattern of red and gold lay on one arm from a stained-glass window the sun glimmered through. Her flesh gave a kind of invisible lurch toward him that made her smile. She had a sense of physical kinship with him, standing there in the midst of his work. His hands were workman's hands like her father's had been and her grandfather—a stonemason. She imagined them meeting back a hundred years when both their families had been peasants. They would have met, been attracted and married with the dumb surety of routine. No, for he was seven years younger than she was, although she scarcely thought about that any longer. And they were not dumb. They made love in words and they tried to communicate, increasingly. She could not say why she felt so moved for him, standing there with his hand splayed on the wood as if communing with it.

"Surprised? I'm flattered. No, that sounds stupid. I mean, that's what

I want—for us to listen to each other." He turned away as if embarrassed, caressing the wood of the stairway. "I'm putting in a closet here, part linen closet, part bookcase. I like the proportions. I finished it with this curve, very gentle, see?"

They went for an early supper to the North End, parking under the expressway. Over his manicotti he started talking about Lou again. "He grew up in Brockton. Got in trouble in high school for dealing pills. Picked up once in connection with a stolen car ring, but not prosecuted. No trouble with the law since, probably 'cause he got out of Brockton, away from whoever he was hanging with in those days. Put in a year or two at Bridgewater—the college not the prison."

"What do you care about his background? You're as obsessed with him as I was with Gail Abbot-Wisby. You've been researching him!"

Mario wasn't in, but Aldo, his second-in-command, hovered near them as if to try to guess from their expressions if they were enjoying the food sufficiently.

"He married in his twenties. Still with the same woman. They have three boys and a girl. The oldest boy helps him sometimes—he's thirteen."

"You're around the same age," Daria said slowly, "background similar—"

"Yeah, yeah," Tom said roughly, signalling for more wine. "Don't think I haven't figured out why he bugs me. We both come from stone working-class families who got a little comfort. Neither of us made it up and out. I became a carpenter finally and he became an electrician. He does crappy rehabs. If I was him, I'd do a better job. He's more competent at burning than building."

"Tom, you're very different people, with different tastes, different politics. He's not your doppelgänger or alter ego."

"What goes through his mind when he burns people out? I don't understand. I can't see into him."

"Maybe he thinks he's just doing the job he's paid for. Maybe he says to himself, great, I made a clear two hundred tonight or whatever they pay him. Maybe he thinks well, there's the kid's dental bill, and let's hope another job shows up real soon."

"He knows people live in the buildings. I just don't understand how he thinks about it, what he feels when he lights a place where people are sleeping upstairs."

288

Had she sounded that irrational in her fixation on Gail? "What he thinks makes little difference, right? They say that pyromaniacs experience . . . pleasure. I mean, they say they have an orgasm."

"He's no pyromaniac. He only burns what he's paid to. It's a job. But how does he justify it? What does he tell his wife?"

"What came of the meeting last night?"

"Patrols. We're patrolling the couple of buildings Sandra María decided Walker's likeliest to have torched. They never burn in the daytime, so we figure we need a night watch. If Walker's planning to burn either Number Twenty-seven or the house where Bobbie died, he's not going to find it easy."

The conversation had become unreal to her. They would all see nothing was going to happen. She need not argue on Ross's behalf, because time would prove Tom wrong. In the meantime, their patrol might frustrate burglars anyhow. "People liked the chart?"

"They were pretty impressed. Now if we can only get the authorities to look at it. . . . Mac and Fay have been batting back and forth between the police and the fire department. They say with the layoffs, they have no one to cover arson and besides it's somebody else's business and besides we have no proof."

"But Sandra María said there'd been legislation passed setting up a special arson force."

"On paper. Lost in the budget cuts. You know what politicians do when you finally persuade the media there's a problem. They set up a task force to study it and issue a report a year later. They hold a big conference and put out some more paper and then they go back to business as usual." He mopped up the last of his sauce. "This was good food. I wish you could come to meetings, Daria. I miss you there."

"After my divorce," she temporized. Meetings were not for her. "That's my recipe. Years ago I worked here."

Early Tuesday morning a phone call came to her in Lexington from an excited Fay. "Someone tried to burn Number Twenty-seven last night. Old man Schulman was on patrol. He don't have the keenest ears in the world and they pried open the basement door before he came on them."

"Did he catch them?" Daria asked.

"How in hell could he do that? Use your noodle. We're not trying to get ourselves killed, right, but the opposite."

"Did he see who it was?"

"Not to give any kind of description. One guy wearing a leather jacket was on the steps inside. He thought he saw another guy with him when he ran, but Mr. Schulman wasn't sure. After all he was pretty excited and it was two A.M."

"But don't you think they were probably looking to rip off a television set or something?"

"Around here we get that kind of shit in the afternoon mostly. But they weren't into no carry and cash operation. They left their calling card behind. Right outside the basement door, deary: a big drum full of gasoline and nice well-soaked papers, ready to go up."

"Oh." Daria was silent. She was becoming so defensive that she recognized if she hadn't spent the night with Tom, she would have almost been ready to accuse him of playacting to prove his point. But not Mr. Schulman, an Orthodox Jew living on a disability pension with a sick wife and a prize dahlia garden out back: he wasn't engaging in charades. Someone had actually tried to burn Number 27.

Early Saturday morning she had a call from Ross. "I want to come by this morning and get the last of my stuff out. What I still really want. The papers in my study, the darkroom equipment, my summer clothes. I've got two men coming by with a truck and I'll be there by the time they show up."

"You should have given me more warning—"

"Don't bother being there. I have a key."

"All your papers are in boxes in the basement, against the north wall. They're labelled."

"What did you do? Go through all my stuff?"

"I needed the room."

"What for? Your bowling league? You've got a barn of a house ten times bigger than you need anyhow. You didn't have to mess up my files."

"You'll find them in order, inside the boxes. And I do need the space—" She was about to mention Sandra María and Mariela, when he hung up on her.

He did not seem to know she had taken in roommates, interesting because Dorothy had indicated Ross might resort to a private detective to discover if she were seeing anyone. Apparently not. She had been convinced the possibility would not occur to him. Her family's line on Daria was that she represented the nice dull mommy model, unsuited for romance or adventure. She realized that never in her life had she caused Ross to be jealous of her.

She had been sorry he had not allowed her to mention Sandra María and Mariela, because she wanted to demonstrate to him how much her life had changed, but as she dressed hurriedly and made herself presentable, she decided silence was for the best. Why give him any leads on what she had been doing? He might deduce her connection with SON. She attended none of their public meetings, so that only the inner core knew of her involvement.

Sandra María drove off to the library in the old Dodge Ángel had found for her. Mariela was home, but Daria gave her a little speech about saying nothing to Ross about living there or who her mother was.

Mariela was very interested in Ross when he arrived at ten, his Mercedes pulling into the garage into the old spot beside her Rabbit he had always used to occupy. A small van arrived at the curb right after him. As Daria opened the door, without giving him a chance to use the key, Mariela was right behind her, peering out to see the famous monster.

Ross stared at Mariela. "Who's that?"

"I'm Mariela, but I don't remember my last name," Mariela said smugly.

"The daughter of a friend," Daria said. "I'll show you where your boxes are piled."

"I don't see what call you had to rifle my files," Ross barked, heading for the basement stairs. "You have plenty of room here."

"I don't see what business it is of yours how I use my space," she said. "I threw nothing out. I simply boxed it. It's been over four months since you moved out. That's a long time to store your things for you."

When Ross disappeared downstairs, Daria whispered to Mariela, "Go hang around the movers and ask them anything that comes into your head. But be sure to ask them where they're moving all this stuff. Put on your jacket first."

Mariela had the answer in five minutes. "Hamilton," she said proudly. "That's a place, not a name like it sounds. Did I find out right?"

"Perfect." They watched the two men and Ross carry up his files and darkroom equipment. Then Ross came back into the kitchen and motioned Daria to follow him through the rest of the downstairs. "I want the Sandwich glass and the two camphor Victorian hens-on-the-nest dishes. That Spode candlestick. The Seth Thomas rosewood clock. The Haviland tea set. Let's see." He consulted a list in his pocket. "Definitely that Hadley chest in the hall."

"Don't you think we should divide things formally? I've submitted a list to the lawyer of all our antiques and semiantiques."

His face took on that frozen look she had grown to fear over the years, that meant she had thwarted or crossed him. It used to precede not an explosion but rather a massive withdrawal.

"I want my things now. I'm not asking for much." His voice took on a quavery timbre of self-pity. "I'm not asking for half, even. Just the few things that I really care about."

"You don't have room for Torte but you have room for Sandwich glass and a Hadley chest. . . . Oh, never mind. Sure, take what you want, so long as I keep a list."

"What happened to the living room?" He demanded, as if caught off guard.

"I got rid of that carpeting I could never stand."

"Where's that cutdown ladder-back chair we had dated to 1790?"

It was in Mariela's room. "I have to look for it," Daria said. "I'm not sure."

"How can you not be sure?" He directed the men to the Hadley chest. Daria had to run quickly and unpack it, full of tablecloths and napkins. She had Mariela carry them into the dining room.

"Ross, this is rather an imposition, marching in here without warning and trying to carry off half the house. I'm going to try to reach my lawyer for advice." She had Dorothy's home number, if she wasn't in her office.

292

"All right, all right. Where's that marble-topped bureau?"

"That's in Tracy's room. It's *hers,* Ross. It was given to her. By us. You can't take it back now."

"You are being a complete and utter bitch, Daria. Complete! You're doing this to frustrate me, but you can't stop me. I'm free of you now!"

"Anything else?" one of the men asked dryly. They were lounging in the hall waiting.

Ross consulted his list. "That little table with rope-turned legs . . . where is it?"

"In my office. . . . No, not upstairs. Right here."

"My study?"

"It's mine now. Far more convenient. Peggy and I were always crowded upstairs. Ross, isn't it time to give me the keys? You have what you want out of here now. I could use an extra set."

He slapped his pockets. "Forgot them! Another time."

She was not sure she believed him. Surely he had brought his keys along in case she was not home. Perhaps this was a final expression of his ambivalence about leaving her, retaining a last option represented by the keys. But the option no longer really existed for either of them. He would come to realize that, too. "Ross, I really would like them back. Could you drop them in the mail?"

"I can pass them along to your lawyer along with our new statement," he said. "How's that?"

He followed the movers with the table, fussing about its progress. Then he got into his Mercedes and drove off with a small burning of rubber. The movers disappeared for a while, leaving the van on the street. About an hour later they reappeared, finished roping the furniture in and drove off, presumably to the home of the Abbot-Wisbys.

22

MARIELA invaded the kitchen. "Me, I'm going to learn to cook," she announced. "Then I can cook for my mamá. And Ali and Sheba. And Torte too. Everybody. We'll all sit at the biggest table and me, I'll be the cook."

Daria could remember first Robin and then Tracy making little pies while she made big pies, giving them golf balls of dough to roll out and sprinkle with sugar and cinnamon. She remembered Robin shaping round hamburgers like fat eggs, then being upset when they were raw in the middle. But Robin had wanted them round. She should have taught Robin to make Swedish meatballs instead, she realized. How silly of her. She could have saved Robin's pride. She had been too distracted by cooking and cleaning and taking care of the children, trying to fix up the new house; she had been ghostwriting her first book.

She shook herself free of that sweet-sour nostalgia, caramel in a sore tooth. "If you want to learn, I'll teach you. We'll start with spaghetti. First we boil salted water in a big pot and put a dab of oil in." She saw it then. Yes, as soon as she finished the calendar book: the mother-daughter cookbook. Or rather, mother-child. Ways to involve your kids so they don't grow up helpless; teaching them to help rather than to hinder you. Teaching them to know and love food and cooking instead of craving junk food. It was a winner, she knew it. The hour was just a shade too late to catch her agent in the office. She'd call Laura tomorrow. Daria liked to know exactly what book she was going to be working on next, so that when she finished the current project she would not feel lost and aimless. But her recent life had been too chaotic and until this moment she had no energy to spare generating ideas. What she would do is divide the tasks of making typical meals into ones that the mother would perform and ones the child would do, designed to educate about basic skills and basic foods.

Mariela stuck with her until Sandra María walked in. Then Daria could speed up the process. She was still humming with her idea. If Mariela really wanted to learn, she would teach her as a way of working out ideas for the book.

She managed to eke out the first real salad of spring, their own vivid greens from the thinnings in the rows poking up and the thinnings from the peat six-packs she had put out that afternoon. Little baby finocchio plants, little lettuces, Chinese cabbage, turnip leaves, garden cress, arugola, the young violet leaves, chives and mint thrusting into the spring sun. Spaghetti alla carbonara—bacon, eggs and cheese. Pie from grapes she had frozen in September. As she put their meal together she found herself singing, again some song she had assimilated through her pores at Fay's.

Sheba now ran for the food first and Ali stood a little aside, waiting. She was beginning to show and seemed to spend a great deal of time washing her own belly, but five minutes later, she would be chasing Ali upstairs and dashing over the furniture a foot above the wood like a kitten.

At supper Daria asked Sandra María, "Did you like being pregnant?"

Sandra María frowned, remembering. "Actually, no. It was all mixed up with getting free of that one. And I felt invaded." She grinned at her daughter. "Even though I wanted her, wanted her so bad, I kept thinking there had to be some easier way. At the end it was hot and I felt like a wounded whale on the streets. But the minute she was born, all shining and curly, she was worth it and more."

"I liked pregnancy myself." Daria smiled apologetically.

"How could you? Swollen up like that."

"I felt . . . powerful. I felt bigger than Ross. I felt immense and that seemed special. It felt as if I could expand and simply expect everybody else to accommodate, for once in my life. I felt very satisfied with myself."

"Then why didn't you have more than two?"

"I had three. The third was born with Down's syndrome, a valve problem in his heart and half a stomach. The doctor said it could happen again."

Sandra María shuddered. "I had nightmares like that."

"It was a nightmare. I couldn't go through it again, I couldn't!"

Meals were pleasant, the earthier cooking she preferred on a regular basis, the easy communication. In recent years she had made conversation with Ross, manufacturing it like ersatz butter out of the detritus of her day and what she fervently hoped might interest him. Inside as he had sat there spooning up coquilles St. Jacques, what had he been thinking as her voice flittered about him? Money? Always money? Empire building? Pyramiding mortgage upon mortgage, changing neighborhoods, emerging as a rich and thus well-respected large property owner? Some magic line he was hustling to cross between being a small insignificant landlord and being a man of real property, a prime customer of local banks, invited to sit on boards of directors, sharing big consortium deals with men who could buy him out now without blinking. Were those the dreams that had chased around inside his forehead as she sat across from him trying to make contact, trying to create conversation like plates of fancy but untasted hors d'oeuvres at a failed party?

After supper Ángel came over with rolls of film to develop and was disappointed to discover that the darkroom had been dismantled. However, the sink was still there. "Maybe I should get a safelight. I need my own equipment for printing, but it's been nice to be able to develop while I'm here."

"Great idea," Daria said. The more ways her house was used, the better she liked it. She was obliquely proving to Ross at least inside her head that she could use such a big house, that without him she could create a rich and satisfying life. It was easier to strike up friendships without him, not only because they were attracted to different people but because she could simply go ahead and invite someone without consulting an elaborate social calendar.

Daria drove over to Tom's, leaving Sandra María to study for an exam, Ángel to prowl the basement figuring out how he would set things up, Mariela to play with the cats. Fay and Elroy were both at Tom's, doing the supper dishes—Tom had obviously cooked for them—and hot in an argument about Lou, who had become a family member. They knew his taste in clothes: the leather jacket and jeans when he was rehabbing or burning; the three-piece off-the-rack suits from Robert Hall when he was being social or businesslike.

They knew his pickup truck with the gear in the back; they knew the yellow Camaro he drove when out with wife and family. They knew the local bars and the Combat Zone bar at which he drank, sometimes too much, never with the wife. The wife stayed home and raised the children. Once she sported a black eye behind dark glasses. They fought, about what? What Lou did? He never seemed to crawl free of debt. If Ross was overextended on a middling scale, Lou was stretched mighty thin on a piker's scale. The buildings he bought had sometimes already been seized for back taxes and auctioned off, or he bought them from somebody else who had failed to make them pay. They were marginal. Everybody in the SON core group speculated on what prompted Lou to set to work on one building with his son and a couple of hired carpenters or to milk another until it was a shell with scarcely a functional foot of plumbing, and then torch it. Maybe he chose by whether he liked the building. Maybe it was the time of month, the phase of the moon. How broke he was or how broke he felt.

"We can con him," Tom was saying, sitting over coffee while Elroy washed and Fay dried. "I know we can. He can't be sure Mr. Schulman didn't see him."

"Tom, I talked to the police and the fire marshal's office. They say we got nothing. It won't prove in court." Fay shrugged.

"But we don't want Lou in court—yet. We want Lou sweating. We want to turn Lou so he talks about who's hiring him," Tom insisted.

"Why in hell should he do that?" Elroy demanded. "I know. All we got to do is pay him twice what the landlords do. Easy, man." He pulled an imaginary roll from his back pocket and peeled off bill after bill. "We just buy him. I'll just sell off the Rolls or that spare Mercedes."

"Since we can't afford greed, we have to work with fear," Tom said.

"Wow, I got it!" Elroy snapped his fingers. "We threaten to burn him out."

"We have to make him feel he's the patsy. He's going to get the law down on him while the big guys get away free." Tom radiated excitement.

"The only thing makes me feel some hope is, we got ahead of those guys at least once." Fay was drying slowly, polishing a plate over and over. "I'm proud we stopped a burning. But this cops and robbers stuff, you should watch less TV. I think we're on to something with the neighborhood patrols."

"But, Fay," Daria objected. "It works in the short term, but how long will people give up sleep twice a week to patrol buildings?"

"She's not wrong," Elroy said. "We can keep it up, but how long?"

"As long as people don't want to wake up to a fire," Tom said.

"People got other things on their minds, you know. Right after a fire, they worry about fire. Then the bills come in, they worry about bills. Then their lover starts running around on them." Elroy shook his head.

On such a fine evening people kept dropping by. Daria was tired and had to get up early. She had a lot of work to do with Peggy tomorrow. She decided this was one of those evenings when she could not wait out everybody else.

"You're leaving." Tom walked her to the door, looking downcast. "Can I come by later?"

"Not tonight. I'm tired. Let's make it tomorrow for sure."

"Come over at seven, and I'll make supper."

"No, you come by my place. Then we're sure of having the evening."

In the hall he kissed her good night; then she hurried down to her car in his drive.

She did go to bed early and slept soundly, with Sheba curled under the covers against her side and Ali on top of the quilt at the foot of the bed. Very late she wakened once, the habit of long years of being sensitive to the children in the night, a habit established when she was breastfeeding and never entirely lost. Footsteps in the hall. Sandra María probably. Couldn't sleep? Ten to two by the clock. Or Ángel? No, she had not seen his car outside, so he must have gone home before she returned. She dozed again; it was as if she had never awakened, for the small noises of the house entered her ears, were registered and dismissed without quite drawing her from the warm cave of her sleep.

Ali's yowling woke her gradually. She had the feeling as she rose sluggishly, from sleep that he had been yowling ever more frantically for a while, that he had run back and forth across the bed to wake her before he crouched making his deep plaintive bellows from the floor. She felt a surge of annoyance. Damned cat! Sometimes in the early morning he demanded to go out, before she was ready to rise. He would howl and wake her until she threw him out of the bedroom. That early morning waking was a habit she was trying hard to break. She woke angry at him, a bar of headache pressing against her eyes. Damn. His piercing wail. "Ali, shut up! Damn you, shut up!" she yelled, sitting up, and began to cough as if choking.

Something wrong. Awkwardly, weakly she rose from bed and almost passed out. For a moment she thought she was having a stroke. A stroke as Nina had. She was dying of stroke. She could not breathe and her sight was failing even in the dark. But why was Ali upset, running frantically across the bed and around the room now with his fur on end?

She was coughing, choking. Without thinking she staggered across the room and pushed at the window feebly, pushed the window finally high. Her dizziness, her nausea receded. What she was smelling was smoke. Smoke? Her brain felt sore. She took deep, deep breaths of the clean pure air and gradually realized how full of smoke the room was, a layer in the middle of the air. Mariela! Sandra María. She rushed to the hall door, flinging it open, then shut it immediately as more acrid smoke surged in and she felt hot air push on her. Her house was on fire! She fumbled for the switch. The light still worked. She must wake Mariela and Sandra María, she must. Torte was sleeping in Mariela's room; maybe he had wakened them. But she heard nothing except the crackling now of the fire and a dull thud as something downstairs fell. Grabbing her shawl she ran into her bathroom and soaked it. Then she held it before her face as she opened the door to the hall, shut it behind her to protect the cats, and ran across the hall.

She could see flames in the hall. The entire floor seemed to be burning, below. She saw flames licking at the baseboard, flowing like bright water in reverse up the wall. For a moment she could not move, hypnotized by the flames below her.

She raced into Mariela's room first. But she could not wake Mariela, sprawled in her single bed, the bed that had been Tracy's. She thrust open the window. Torte woke from his doggy bed and wagged his tail. But she could not stir Mariela.

She rushed next door to Sandra María. The hall was filling with thick heavy black smoke rising from below. She felt the nausea seeping through her again. Her head throbbed, swollen, huge. Her skin hurt. She could scarcely see. Her eyes watered and felt raw. Her throat was sandpapered. Whatever was attacking her seemed to pass right through the shawl, although that kept her from convulsive coughing. She flung open the door, slammed it behind her and shook Sandra María, hauling her back and forth by her thin shoulder. Even at this moment she could not help noticing how young, how vulnerable, how lovely her friend looked tousled and flushed with sleep, her face rosy. Finally she began to slap Sandra María hard. Sandra María groaned and kicked, turning over. She pushed Sandra María to the floor where she landed with a thump, whimpering. Daria fell beside her where the air was better and slapped her again and again. Finally Sandra María tried to sit up. "The house is on fire! Listen to me, Sandra, the house is on fire! We have to get Mariela and clear out!"

"Mariela!" Sandra María rose in an adrenaline rush and flew next door. Daria followed, coughing. Sandra María was already shaking Mariela, shaking her violently, but her small head just snapped back and forth. She looked rosy with health, peacefully asleep, but she did not wake. The child must be unconscious, in some kind of faint. Daria yanked at Sandra María's arm. "Come!" she spat out. They were both coughing, choking. The flames were licking at the bannister, smoke pouring from under the carpet runners on the treads. Mariela was still breathing shallowly, rapidly, but could not be wakened. Daria again yanked hard on Sandra María's arm, doing a dance of panic. Finally Sandra María lifted her daughter and carried her over her shoulder, staggering. Then she paused in the doorway, choking and shuddering as she stared with horror down into the flames.

The air scorched Daria's nostrils, her throat, her lungs. She thought her forehead would burst. She could not speak for coughing but motioned Sandra María to follow her as she tried to drag Torte by the collar across the hall. But he would not go near the flames spreading up the stairwell. She tried to grab at him and her hand closed on something hot, burning. She screamed and started choking. She could not get her breath. Torte snapped at her, tearing loose, and ran back into Mariela's room.

Daria flung open the door to her bedroom and dragged the almost blinded Sandra María staggering under her daughter's body into the room. They were both coughing convulsively. Daria felt as if she would never be able to breathe again, to draw the air she needed into her aching and scalded lungs. "The little stairway," she gasped.

She ran past Sandra María to see if the back hall was still passable. Smoke hung there but not as black and oily as in the central hall. She saw no flames below. She motioned Sandra María past her and down. From the chair by her bed Daria seized her coat, thrusting into it, grabbed her purse and tore the sheet from the bed with Sheba wrapped in it. Then she called to Ali and Torte. She could not get her hands on Ali but at her heels he ran down the steps as she followed Sandra María. "Torte! Ali!" She coughed and choked and called, tears running down her face as she half fell down the steps behind Sandra María. "Torte! Ali!" She could hear Torte barking behind her. She croaked their names again and again, flinging herself down through the dark.

The door to the garage was still locked. She fumbled with it and then they poured through. No flames in this part of the house yet. She dumped the sheet containing Sheba in the backseat, grabbed Ali from the garage floor and thrust him in as Sandra María laid Mariela down in the backseat. Then Daria stuck her keys in the ignition. "Go! Take her to the hospital. Quick!" She raced across the garage and opening the fuse box threw the main switch to cut the power in the house.

Sandra María started to slide into the driver's seat. Then she stopped, still coughing brutally, and turned a panicked face to Daria. "But I can't drive stick shift." Sandra María hopped back out. "I'll take my car! Where's the hospital?"

"Do you have your keys?"

"No! They're upstairs!"

"I'll take her. You go next door, wake Annette. Please! Call the fire department." Daria slid in and started the car. "And call Torte again. If you keep calling him, he'll come." Daria started to back out.

"Wait! The garage doors." Sandra María ran to open them and Daria gunned the Rabbit backwards, turned with a screech in the road and floored it downhill. As she roared off, she had an afterimage of Sandra María standing just inside the garage staring after the car with tears rolling down her face, still coughing, and then turning to trot in her flannel nightdress across the lawn toward Annette's house.

The cats stayed crouched in the backseat. Ali was washing Sheba. But Mariela lay limp as a dummy. She could not tell in the rearview mirror if Mariela was still breathing. Oh, please, she begged, please, please don't let her die. Please. "We'll be there soon, I promise, soon!" She muttered in her raw scraped voice and ran a red light, gunning the car hard.

She carried Mariela into the emergency entrance at Symmes. The first thing they did, of course, was shove papers at her. She realized she had no idea what kind of health insurance Sandra María carried and standing there with the unconscious Mariela in her arms she made an instant decision. "Daria Walker, W, A, L, K, E, R. Blue Cross, Blue Shield. This is my daughter Teresa."

They wheeled Mariela away, leaving Daria to complete the forms. She did and waited, waited, waited. She had not heard anything, pacing in the anteroom in her nightgown and coat, when Sandra María ran in. She was wearing a dress of Annette's two sizes too big on her and surprisingly, her own maroon wool coat.

"She's in there." Daria pointed. As she did she felt the burn on her hand for the first time. She stared at her flesh and the pain began to register. "I wonder if there's ice around. A soft drink machine?"

"What did they say?"

"Smoke inhalation. Carbon monoxide poisoning."

Daria found a machine and put ice on her hand. Then they sat side by side in the waiting room. A man was asleep in a chair. A little boy was brought in with a bad asthma attack and a teenager was carried in unconscious. "Did the firemen come?" Daria asked. They held hands, her good right hand in Sandra María's cold left.

"About ten minutes . . . Annette and her husband ran over to the

302

house and unlocked the front door while we were waiting for the firemen to come. They took the small Oriental out of the front hall and that china umbrella stand and all the coats. So if we got nothing else, we have umbrellas and coats."

Daria laughed, sharply. "I can't believe it yet. I can't!" She looked at the wall clock. It was just short of three A.M. "Sandra María, did you happen to get out of bed, maybe half an hour before the fire? Maybe an hour at the most?"

"Me? No." Sandra María was still coughing. Her eyes were bloodshot and swollen, her face flushed. "Ángel left about ten. I studied maybe another forty-five minutes. Then I took a hot bath and went to bed. I'd heard you come in. I fell asleep right away and I slept straight through till you came in and woke me. . . . What woke you?"

"Ali! Bless him. He howled till I got up. I was going to hit him, Sandra María, I was so angry I was going to hit him. . . . Torte! Did you find Torte?"

Sandra María squeezed her hand. "We couldn't get to him and he wouldn't come. We told the firemen about him. Maybe they got him. Or maybe he even ran out the door and we didn't see. Let's hope so. Annette drove me over here as soon as the fire trucks came. Then she went back."

The nurse swished into the waiting room. "Mrs. Walker? Your daughter Teresa's conscious now. We're keeping her on the respirator a while longer. But as soon as she's off, you can come in and see her."

Sandra María raised her eyebrows at the name, but catching Daria's look, said nothing. The nurse stared hard at Sandra María till Daria thought her lie was blown, but what the nurse asked was, "Were you exposed to the smoke? I think you'd better come along. I want the doctor to see if he doesn't think with that high color you've had a dose of carbon monoxide too."

"But I didn't pass out—"

"I want the doctor to take a look."

"Sandra María, take this for cab fare. I'm going back, since she's awake. . . . Do you have medical insurance?"

"Through the university."

"Then you can disentangle my little fib. I thought it would expedite treatment."

Sandra María squeezed her hand. "Go! I'll straighten it out."

As she approached her Rabbit, the cats stared at her through the side window, two sets of yellow eyes round and wary. They must think she had gone crazy. She lured them to the far side of the car so that she could then sprint back around, unlock the driver's side and climb in. Fending them off, she drove slowly back, keeping them from sticking their little heads through the steering wheel or squeezing under her foot as she hit the brakes.

Her left hand was lit up now with pain. Her head ached. Her throat was scraped raw. Her eyes kept watering. She had a deep racking cough. Somewhere she had acquired a set of bruises along her right side. She had made it from the burning house to Symmes Hospital in less than ten minutes. Driving back took twenty-five minutes. She dreaded what she would find. The fire engines were still blocking her street. Great coils of hose fed from the fire hydrant up the block into the front door and through a broken living-room window. Lights were on in both her neighbors' houses and across the street, scattered lights on the rest of the block at . . . she glanced at her watch and found she wasn't wearing it. Of course. It was in the fire too. The clock in the Rabbit read ten to four.

She sat on in her car, staring at the wreckage of her home. She saw no flames, but in the glare from the streetlight she watched a fireman up on the roof hacking holes in it. She could still see smoke drifting out, casually, lazily. Obviously they had the fire under control. They sloshed about as if dog tired. However, she had little hope for her home. She had seen the flames in the stairwell, licking up the walls. Its heart must be gutted.

One hundred forty years it had stood, until tonight. Sandra María had not been walking around when Daria had heard someone in the hall. Ángel had long since gone home. Mariela was sound asleep. No, she had heard a substantial tread. Furthermore, Annette had had to unlock the front door. She herself had unlocked the door between kitchen and garage. Someone had entered the house without breaking in, and when they had left, they had tidily locked up.

She shut off the engine. The smoke in the hall had been pungent and black. Oily smoke. Whoever had set the fire had a key. It had not been

Annette's, certainly not Tracy's, unlikely to be Peggy's. The other keys to the house were in the hands of Robin and Ross. Ross had not mailed the keys to her or given them to Dorothy, as promised. She knew whose key had been used.

A few slow tears welled from her sore eyes, rolled down her cheeks and dried. She felt as if the core had been carved out of her, like the house. She felt light as ashes and as grey. Shaken. Broken perhaps. No. She could find by digging in the ashes of her fatigue some bone still of strength. That had certainly been one way of getting his money out of the house. Had he cared if she died? Had he hoped she would die? An added benefit? What the person—Lou?—had been doing in the upper hall when she had heard his tread was clear now: he had been disconnecting the smoke alarm there. Without Ali, she would never have wakened at all. She scooped him up to hold him against her face, his muscular springy warm flank. He purred for her loudly, nervously. *Three die in Lexington fire.* The animal lover had saved some of the best antiques but had not bothered to remove Torte.

It was not only that she felt betrayed. It was not only that she felt attacked in the heart of her new life. It was not only that he had taken from her the home she loved, not only that he wanted to annihilate her, to burn her alive like a witch. She felt all those pains, arrows stuck into the Saint Sebastian she remembered staring at as a child on holy days in church. But the pike lodged in her chest between her scalded lungs was that in the person of Ross whom she had loved she had encountered evil.

Often enough in her life she had been angry, although for years she had learned to dampen that anger. On occasion she thought she had even hated. She had hated one teacher of Tracy's who had picked on her daughter, held her up to ridicule for her naive enthusiasms. Daria had always been a better lover than a hater, but she was learning.

Evil had been something abstract; the threat of rape to Tracy when she came home alone in the evening, that long walk from the bus. The threat of total annihilation in nuclear war. That sense of outrage she could dimly recall against a war that had gone on and on, burning children and simple people in their own land; burning their livestock, their rice fields, their small homes, their sweet flesh and slim bodies honed by endless hard work and hunger. Evil was something that the powerful did someplace else—in Asia, in Central America—or acts that faceless rabid criminals rose from the depths to wreak randomly.

But to find evil in the man she had lived with half her life stunned her to a weariness she found paralyzing. She felt not so much numb as struck senseless, hunched, clenched around a hollow like a great cave of the winds inside that must be filled with a knowledge she could not yet endure.

23

Daria stood shivering in the dark street, waiting to speak to the fire captain. "Did you ever find my dog? A little terrier."

"We didn't see him. The other lady mentioned him too."

"I believe this fire was set."

He had a reaction she could not understand, till he took her firmly by the elbow and walked her a few steps away, out of earshot. "Lady, that kind of thing is hard to prove and you won't collect on your insurance."

"That has to be the least of my worries. It was aimed at me, and I'm scared. My estranged husband has a key to the house—"

"You have any family around here? You ought to go stay with them. When those old furnaces go in a frame house—"

"I heard someone in the hall upstairs about an hour before I woke to the fire. Could you look at the smoke detector there? I bet it's disconnected or tampered with."

"Lady, everything in that hall is long gone. . . . We got another call. If you really want, I'll put in a report for you."

"Who should I talk to?"

"Don't worry about it. They'll be in touch."

Crazy he thought her, shivering in the street in her nightgown and coat. She watched the fire apparatus leave. Annette came out to meet her as she walked toward her ruined house. "Daria, oh, Daria, what a disaster! The flames were shooting out twenty feet. Are you all right?"

She nodded dumbly. All right? All wrong.

"Your sister-in-law said her little girl was unconscious?"

"She's at the hospital, recovering. . . . Thanks for saving our coats." Her mouth twisted up in an inane grimace.

"I wish we could have done more, but we didn't dare go in. The fire was tremendous! You're lucky to escape." Annette trailed after her to the back of the house. "They said to stay out."

"I'll be careful." Stay out of her own house? She turned on the flashlight she had taken from the Rabbit. "Where's Torte? Is he with you?" She envied Annette being dressed, wearing shoes. She still had on her flimsy mules, soaked through from the water in the street.

"No . . ." Annette said. "I hope he's not lost."

The glass of the door that led from the terrace into the living room was broken, but she could see the lock was still on. Reaching carefully through the broken glass, she turned the catch. The beam of the flash played over smashed and overturned lamps, waterlogged and gutted upholstery, a charcoal ruin that must have been the draperies, all surrounding like spectators an immense hole chopped through to the basement. She retreated with a groan. Lost, all lost.

"He came and took most of the antiques. I can't believe it!" she said with sudden passion. "His papers, his photography equipment. And the antiques he thought worth the most! He had a list!"

"What are you talking about?" Annette hovered on the terrace, peering at her.

She could not speak, rage closing her throat till she thought she would choke. The kitchen door that led into the yard was locked too. She opened it with her key. "Wait here. It might be dangerous. I don't know how much of the floor's left."

She walked into her kitchen and before she thought about it, turned on the light switch. Nothing happened, of course. It was unnerving to creep around bearing a flashlight and playing its beam over the counters and cabinets, proceeding so cautiously into such a familiar room. As the fire had not reached the kitchen, it had a comforting semblance of order, although the floor was tracked with mud composed of charred material and water. The gas, she thought, I wonder if they disconnected the gas. Oddly enough they had not. The pilot lights were out but the stove functioned. She lit them with a match. It was ridiculous that the one intact object in her entire house should be the stove.

The air stank, almost unbreathable with the stench of charred wood, plaster, plastic, wool. The air itself seemed scorched. But perhaps only the living room was seriously damaged. She could picture the rooms as they had been in the light of day, could picture them so clearly that surely they must still exist. She turned back to the open door. "Annette, would you have any boxes? The food in the fridge. In the freezer. I might as well save it."

"Of course." Annette sounded oddly placating. "I must have some boxes in our garage. I'll be right back. But be careful. You really shouldn't be in there."

The hall was a gaping hole. She could not reach her office. So much for her hopes. She stood on the verge of the blackened pit that had been the central stairwell and wept with rage and sorrow. She did not know how long she stood there but finally she shook herself. "Torte!" she called half-heartedly. She could not believe any living creature could be hiding in the ruins of the house. She called him twice more. Then she walked to the entrance to the dining room.

Her favorite room. The firemen had broken through the floor and the far wall. The trestle table had survived and her things in the near corner cupboard. The chandelier was smashed. Fragments lay scattered about the floor, making walking treacherous, particularly in slippers. She retreated, too sad to press further. This was his revenge on her: revenge for what? Failing to say, don't bother sharing our accumulated property with me, I can live on rice crackers and water? The house had represented her: he had wanted to kill her and he had almost succeeded. He had killed the house.

Picking her way back across the kitchen, she began to climb the narrow steep back stairs down which she and Sandra María had fled. "Torte?" she called again. When she heard a sound she called his name again loudly, but it was only water dripping. Cautiously she climbed, testing each runner, playing the flash over the treads.

Tracy's room was intact. Too bad it wasn't still Daria's office. The door to her bedroom stood open. Calling her dog, she crossed to the hall, but it was a blackened shaft down to the basement, dark and dank as a mine and dripping. She could not cross from her room to the far bedrooms. She turned back. The floor was puddled and the firemen had broken through the wall against the burning hall, knocking over a bureau. Her bed lay as she had left it, the sheet pulled off, the covers askew. On her vanity all the little bottles stood in their places under a new dusting of ash. Her robe lay on the floor marked with a big footprint.

She was chilled in her nightgown. Quickly she pulled underwear from her dresser and clothes from her closet, putting them on mostly by feel with the flashlight perched on the edge of the vanity. Perhaps she could dare to hope about the contents of her office, directly underneath the bedroom, as was the kitchen. The fiercest blaze seemed to have attacked the center of the house and the side where the living room was located downstairs and Sandra María and Mariela's rooms lay above.

She wanted her everyday black shoes with the little heels. Kneeling with the flashlight she looked under her bed. They lay where she had kicked them. There too lay Torte, his head pushed into his paws. "Torte!" She grabbed at him. But he was dead.

She sat with her legs straight out, her back propped against the bed holding him across her lap and weeping again, quietly. His fur was matted with the water that had seeped under. He had deserved far better than to die alone, deserted, terrified. He must have been killed by the smoke. Why hadn't he followed her? She should have been able to save him, she should have. She couldn't grab all three animals. She had caught up the pregnant Sheba in a sheet—the easiest choice. Ali had followed her on his own. But somehow she should have been able to save Torte. She had betrayed him. Why hadn't the firemen found him? But they had had an out of control fire to contend with. And she had Mariela to rush to the hospital. If Mariela had been conscious, if Sandra María had been able to drive a stick shift, if Torte had followed her when she called him, if she had held on to his collar when he snapped at her, if she had not burned her hand grabbing for him. . . . But Mariela had been unconscious and she had to run ahead to find her purse with the car keys in it. . . .

She heard Annette calling. Wrapping Torte's body in the rug beside her bed, she carried him down, surprisingly heavy. She bore him out to Annette and laid him in a bundle on the grass. "My old dog," she said, her voice shaking. "I'll bury him when it's light. . . . You have the boxes. Fine. I just remembered, there's a cooler in the garage. Hold on."

She talked Annette into unpacking the freezer into the cooler and the refrigerator into the boxes. She set up a battery-powered lantern from their camping days for Annette to see by, and took two candles from the kitchen drawer for herself, to supplement the flashlight.

"Be careful!" Annette warned.

"With the candles? Yes, I wouldn't want to start a fire." She went back to her bedroom, dragging her suitcase from the closet, and packed by candlelight what she would need for the next few days. Tracy's off-season clothing stored in the closet that had been Ross's looked damaged, but except for what was in the dresser that had fallen over into the puddle, her things smelled of smoke but were salvageable. The cash she had in the house was still in the top drawer of her vanity so she took that too. Then she closed her jewelry box, tucked that under one arm with the suitcase under the other and felt her way down the steps one at a time.

Leaving Annette still unpacking the freezer, she went around the outside of the house to shine her flashlight through the window of her office. The venetian blinds were down. It was frustrating, but she could not figure out how to gain access to her office to find out what remained. A year's work. Her notes. Her files.

Sandra María got out of a cab, as Daria was still trying to peer through the window. "Daria! For a moment I thought you were a burglar already."

"How is she?"

"They're keeping her overnight. But they say she'll be fine—weak for a while. A day's bed rest. She had a lot of poison in her blood. They made me breathe a heavy oxygen mixture for a while."

"Is she frightened?"

"Very upset. She kept asking about the animals."

"Torte's dead. We'll bury him when it's light. But don't tell her yet." She found tears starting again and backhanded her eyes roughly.

"He was an old dog. He had a good life with you."

"But he didn't deserve to be dumped by his master and he didn't deserve to suffocate under a bed, alone . . ."

"What are we going to do?" Sandra María made a hopeless gesture, of palms up. "I guess I'll have to move in with my mamá. Or Ángel."

"No! We have to figure it out." Daria began walking toward the back.

"I don't know if we can camp here really. . . ."

"No! We can't. The house is gutted at the core. Maybe it can be rebuilt, but I wouldn't bet on it. And not by us."

"I was afraid you'd think we could get Tom to fix it up. . . . I think it's past that."

"I know it. What I loved here is gone."

"Daria, are you all right? Of course you aren't." Sandra María held her, rocked her.

"I liked living with you and Mariela, I really did. At first it was to save money, but I like it better than I did being married. Maybe someday you'll live with Ángel, but till then, I like us being together."

"So do I. Believe me, it's ten times better. Better for Mariela and better for me. . . . Maybe we can find a big old house to rent?"

Annette was waiting for them. "I took the food out for you. Don't you think you should come home with us and get some sleep? I'm exhausted."

"Oh, Annette, I'm sorry. I should have sent you home half an hour ago. Go to sleep, now. I'm not thinking straight."

"But don't you want to get some rest?"

"I will. Don't worry. I'll go with Sandra María."

Annette seemed relieved to escape. Daria felt grateful, although that overlay her resentment of Annette for dropping her entirely after Ross had left. She did not want to sleep at Annette's, but she recognized that both Sandra María and she were close to exhaustion. Her head and her stomach both ached, as if simultaneously too empty and too stuffed. Sandra María turned to her in the light of the lantern sitting on the drainboard. "What now?" Sandra María asked, leaning back on the refrigerator door.

"I should call Tom. . . . But we have no phone."

Sandra María sighed. "I felt so purposeful last time. How many times can you get burnt out? I feel as if I can't move."

"Burnt out physically. Burnt out emotionally . . ." Daria tried to stir herself. "Maybe we could just lie down and sleep on the kitchen floor."

"No! And wake up with no hot water and no bathroom? I need some taking care of. I think I want to go to Mamá's for the balance of the night. . . . How am I going to drive my car with no keys?"

"I'll drive you. Doesn't Ángel have a set? He can bring them to you when you get up today."

"So much work to do."

Wordlessly they hugged. Daria said, "I'll stop at a pay phone on the way to your mother's and call Tom. Then I'm just going to land on him. . . . I wonder how he'll take it."

"You could double up at my mamá's. Really."

"With two cats and a hundred phone calls to make in the morning? No, Tom has me for the moment. I want taking care of too. He might just do it."

It was well after five when she finished telling Tom what had happened and climbed into the loft to resume the sleep interrupted hours before. Worries, images chased round and round in her head. She found herself moaning and twisting in the covers. The man she used to lie beside for years and years had just tried to kill her. Had just tried to burn her at the stake. Had just paid someone to roast her in her beloved house. Had destroyed that house. For money or for revenge? Revenge against what crime, what betrayal? How did he justify himself? As she tried to sleep, she kept seeing little snapshots far more brightly lit in her memory than they had been in the dark house: her rocker upside down, its runners smashed to kindling; Torte lying under the bed with his head in his paws; the chandelier reduced to a pile of broken shards; the mullioned windows bashed out; the boards of the living room Sandra María and she had sanded and polished, nothing but a crater.

Finally Tom sat up. "I'm going to put you to sleep. And then just get up myself. Do you know, you smell like a burnt dinner? I'm going to draw you a bath . . ." He let himself down and she heard him moving about.

"With crayons," she muttered, remembering an old joke of Robin's, the little girl with pale gold hair. She began to weep. "I couldn't bury Torte. It was too dark to see in the yard."

"We'll take care of him later." He stroked her hair, standing by the loft, his head on a level with hers. "Your bath is running. I'm off to work early. I can get started ahead of everyone, because I'm doing finishing. I'm going to take off at twelve and come back here. Are you listening, Daria?"

Under his hand she nodded.

"Then we'll go over to your house and bury Torte and get whatever else you need and see what the scene is. I can tell if it's repairable—okay, peaches?"

She nodded again.

"Don't worry about what's going to happen. You can always stay here indefinitely."

"I don't think so," she mumbled into the pillow. "It wouldn't be a good idea for us," she almost said *yet*. "The divorce and all."

"Fuck him. He just tried to murder you." He sniffed at her as Marcus was doing from the other side. "You really do smell like a barbecue gone wrong."

"I'd have been a barbecue by now if it wasn't for Ali. . . . Where are my cats?"

"Under the couch."

"Give them something to eat, okay?"

"I did. A saucer pushed into the gloom. Four yellow eyes glaring at me." He rolled her over the edge of the loft, catching her. "Come on, peaches, your bath is set. Wash your hair too."

"What are you so cheerful about?"

"I've just decided to solve everybody's problems. I'm going to shoot your husband, and then I'm going after Lou."

"Oh, very funny." She let herself be pushed toward the tub. "That would solve all my problems? You'd be in Walpole prison and Sandra María, Mariela and I could move in here." She let her clothes drop.

"All those buildings and no place to live. Poor little rich girl." He started scrubbing her back. "Okay, now I'm going to get dressed, eat breakfast and go to work early. By twelve-thirty I'll be back."

She yawned hugely, the hot water loosening her. Then she nodded, words dissolving like sugar cubes in her head. While she was still soaking, she heard him leave. She could hardly manage to crawl from the tub, dry herself and creep toward bed. She almost decided to sleep on the floor instead of trying to climb the loft, but the sheets and pillows and quilt looked too inviting not to make that last fading effort. Even the pain from her hand could not keep her from sleep.

She slept through till eleven, when the snarling of the cats woke her. They were lined up, Ali slightly in advance of Sheba who posed with her fur standing up like quills, turned sideways in puffed up menace. Marcus at the other end of the living room with his fur on end was making operatic sounds back. She was terrified and slid out of bed to stop a cat-fight, but it seemed none of the parties intended to advance within ten feet of each other. It was a battle merely of bloodcurdling oaths and arias of homicidal intent, delivered from a safe and comfortable distance.

Images from the night began to flash through her mind again. Torte lying across her lap, heavy with death. The hall like a shaft in a coal mine, dripping, dripping. She shook herself like a dog, the way Torte used to do, she shook herself hard. She must move. She could not let Ross do her in, as he had tried. She must not cooperate. She would survive him. She would survive his attack and his malice.

She remembered too, standing in Tom's sunny apartment holding herself across her breasts and watching the bushed-up cats, how Sandra María had seemed devastated by despair. She must think not only of herself but of Sandra María and above all, of Mariela. To be uprooted again, again to wake terrified and choking, again to lose, again to move, again to start her life over: what price would Mariela pay? She must not let Ross's malice crush Mariela. She must create hope for all of them. Instead of focussing on Torte's dead body she would focus on the face of Mariela as she had last seen her, flushed she now knew from the carbon monoxide poisoning, but rosy, relaxed, flowerlike. She would keep Mariela in mind and she would move fast, she would speed ahead, she would do the five hundred things that needed immediate attention and she would salvage from the wreckage some kind of hope, flowerlike as Mariela's face.

She found her head clear and her purpose sharpened and herself hungry. She ate granola and found coffee he had left in the Chemex. She put a low flame under it and called the insurance company and then Dorothy. Dorothy was with a client but called back as she was finishing her second cup of coffee.

"Isn't this Tom's number?" Dorothy asked sharply.

"Dorothy, I told you the truth when you asked me. This has developed since. Maybe your idea started it off . . ."

"You should have told me."

"Ross doesn't suspect, by the way."

"I think you're right, but I also think you're lucky—so far. You can blow the whole thing. You shouldn't be staying there."

"The reason I'm here is quite simple."

After Daria had run down the story, Dorothy said, "This is a whole new ball game, although what we can prove is another matter."

"I'm going over shortly. . . . Dorothy, if I own those other buildings, what's to stop me from moving into one of them?"

"Are you going to start evicting tenants?"

"There's one he began renovating. He left a couple of apartments vacant in there. Only the second floor is occupied."

"Are you changing your minimal demands to include that building?"

"After last night, you bet I am. That and two others. I don't want him owning so many buildings in *my* neighborhood."

"Do you have a key?"

"SON does. They've been patrolling at night, to prevent fires. Fay has all the keys."

"Who's Fay? Never mind. Why not move in? It shows a healthy interest in the real estate and might argue in your favor—your name's on the deed and you're living in it. . . . Are you sure your home's totalled?"

"I think the insurance people are coming by today. . . . Do I want to tell the adjuster I think it's arson?"

"Not if you want to collect. . . . But if you want to introduce that in evidence in the divorce, you can't have it both ways. It can't be arson for the divorce judge and accidental fire for the insurance company. I'll get right on the horn to Walker and Company. How long are you going to be at Tom's?"

"Around twelve-thirty I'm going to Lexington. Then I plan to move directly into the ground floor apartment of that house."

"Good. I would strongly advise against taking up residence with Tom while we are in this critical negotiating moment. I have your husband's fifth revised statement of net worth before me and remember, we're proceeding to the depositions tomorrow."

"Of course I remember. I've been dreading it."

"You'll have your lawyer and your accountant and he'll have his. As long as you tell the truth under oath, you're in no trouble—unless they find out about Tom."

After hanging up, Daria rubbed her hands ruefully. How she would have preferred that Dorothy not find out; how she would have liked Dorothy's suspicions to remain just vapor. She had no need of Dorothy's legal reasons to dissuade her from moving in with Tom. A forced intimacy would crush any chance for a real one. No, what she wanted was to continue her new family with Sandra María and Mariela, whom she must check on. Next call, the hospital. Living with her new family, she operated from a position of strength with him. Intimacies she might have tried to force from him came from them, leaving her a grace with Tom to work out what they could without desperation. She must keep that.

The hospital said Mariela would be released that afternoon. The insurance company called back to say the adjuster would view the house soon; it had already been arranged, they said. Fay clucked with sympathy and ran over between customers having their hair done to drop off the keys. All this time Ali and Marcus sang challenges to each other from opposite ends of the living room. Sheba had climbed on the couch and was washing herself, bored. After a while she shuddered and stretched out like a long black bow. Ali and Marcus were still attempting to terrify each other vocally.

"I'll tear your paws off one at a time and eat them for breakfast," sang Marcus, tucking his own paws under him neatly and giving a small lick to his plush grey velvet.

"Listen, you ball-less freak, I'll tear out your ears by the roots and feed them to the mice," Ali sang back, tucking his black paws under and throwing a quick glance at Sheba to see if she was admiring him. Sheba was asleep. Neatly he arranged his tail along his sleek side.

By the time Tom appeared to collect her, Ali was curled up with Sheba on the couch, embracing belly to belly, while Marcus snoozed in the loft on Tom's pillow. She felt confident nothing violent would result from leaving them alone together.

They swung by Northeastern to catch Sandra María on her way to her one o'clock lecture. Tom double-parked and Daria ran in. Sandra María came plodding along still in Annette's old dress with her own coat over it, looking blear-eyed and sad. When she saw Daria she cried out, "What's wrong?"

"You know what's wrong—nothing new." Daria kissed her. "Don't be upset. So Mariela is getting out at four? When can you leave here?"

"I could cut everything but this one and borrow notes. What's up?"

Daria dangled the keys Fay had given her. "Our new apartment."

"Where?" Sandra María snapped to attention. "How big is it?"

"I've never seen it, to tell you the truth, but Fay says it has three bedrooms. It's that big yellow house Ross has near the park that he started renovating. We're moving into the ground floor apartment."

"The building where Bobbie died?"

"Come on, we almost died last night. And it's not that apartment—that was on the top floor." She did not remind Sandra María that a second and never identified body, too charred for identification, had been found on the stairs.

"Listen, I'll meet you at our old house in Lexington at two-thirty, three o'clock. Okay? But how do we know he won't burn us out of there next?"

"Because we're going to scare the hell out of him," Daria said with far more confidence than she felt.

24

Tom was inside with the adjuster. Daria had just helped Sandra María load her Dodge with salvage to carry to their new apartment. Daria collected her day's mail, dropped neatly through the slot in the front door to lie on what remained of the flooring just inside. When she heard a car pulling up out front, she thought Sandra María had forgotten something. It would take many trips to salvage what they could. She strolled around and met Ross trotting across the lawn. She stopped so abruptly she almost lost her balance. Seeing him was like hitting a wall. Her eyes fixed on his hair. Fiery, she might call it. What a weak chin he had, fishlike. She realized that she found him unpleasant looking; she no longer experienced him as attractive. She was no longer even slightly in love, as if the fire had burned up those emotions entirely. "Surprised to see me alive? Or had you heard the bad news already?"

"Sweetheart," he said with something of the old emphasis, "I was worried sick when I heard!" He made as if to embrace her but she ducked back.

"You had reason to be sick: here I am stubbornly alive."

"A terrible thing. I told you to get that furnace cleaned. If only we had sold the house . . ."

"How do you know it's supposed to be the furnace?"

"I spoke to the insurance agent, of course." He brushed past her to the front door, then hesitated.

"Didn't get your key back yet?" she cooed. "Never mind, there's no front hall anyhow."

"Where is he? I know I'm a little late. I took the Pike and there'd been an accident. . . . Is he here?"

"The torch with your key?" She stopped herself from saying "Lou" although she wanted so strongly to scare him that she had to call up Tom's angry face to control her tongue.

"You're crazy, Daria. Spite has unbalanced you. I came over here frantic with worry. And what's this business of some child going to the hospital?"

"There were three of us living here." She followed him around to the back of the house. How awkwardly he moved, like a wind-up toy. He lacked Tom's animal coordination. "Would you like to see Torte's body? I just buried him. I'd be glad to dig him up."

He rushed into the kitchen, looking around. "Ray," he called, "are you up there?"

Tom came down first, his eyes at their heavy lidded somberest. He looked enormous towering over Ross. For a moment Daria thought he might actually pick up Ross and throttle him. "Who are you?" Ross barked at him.

"Hi, Rusty, how're you doing? A sad business," said the brisk little man coming down behind, dusting off his hands. "This is Tom Silver, he's a contractor your wife has looking at the house to see if it can be repaired. But I think we've come to the unhappy conclusion it would take the full insurance money to make a start. . . . I understand you're separated and dividing it?"

Ross glanced at Daria with disbelief. "Repaired?"

"I'm abandoning the idea," she said sweetly. "You understand abandonment. Mr. . . . Ray? I want you to look into the possibility of arson. I believe this fire was intentionally set."

"Dear lady, that's a serious charge." The brisk little man dusted his hands again. "I understand from Rusty here you're in the midst of a somewhat acrimonious divorce. Sad business. Happens to everyone. We don't want to drag bitter domestic quarrels into business matters. I work with your brother often, dear lady, and I'm sure he can explain to you how unwise it is to try to use insurance companies to carry out battles better confined to your lawyer's jurisdiction. I'm quite satisfied the fire started in the furnace room and spread rapidly through the extremely dry wood of an old house." He and Ross walked out together, although not before Ross had peered for some minutes into the dining room. Computing an inventory of what remained?

Tom followed them to the door. "You won't mind, I'm sure, if we bring in someone else to examine the fire's spread?"

"Someone else?" Ross stopped, turning to frown at Tom. "What business is this of yours?"

"Houses are my business," Tom spoke slowly, his hands clasping each other behind his back. "I have a colleague who knows a bit about fires too. I'm sure you'd both be delighted if he looks things over."

Ross stood, obviously eager to be gone and obviously confused. "Look things over for what? Our claim is in. Ray assures me there's no problem."

"Mr. Silver," the adjuster said, "tell your client that if she causes trouble, she causes it mostly to herself. Certainly she can dispute her own claim. My company would be pleased not to pay. But is that really in her best interest? We can cut off our noses to spite our faces, in these matters."

Tom followed them out and watched them off. Then he told her, "I'm going to desert you for a while. I have to find my pal Donald. He's one of our experts. I want him to take a look. He's a private detective who does mostly security work these days, but he used to be an insurance adjuster himself. He knows one hell of a lot about fire. I want him and his camera here."

"Do it. I have hours of packing."

"Daria, be very careful walking on these floors. You're all right on this side of the house, but the rest is too dangerous." He paused again, at the door. "You won't be scared here?"

"In broad daylight? Ross won't be back. He couldn't wait to leave."

"I didn't hit him. You have to give me credit. Someday soon, I'm going to lay him out flat. But today I didn't."

"I also thank you for not coming on any stronger in front of Ross. I know that was harder than not hitting him."

"How could you stay with that creep so long?" he burst out.

"He didn't start out being that creep."

"I bet he always was," Tom said. "I'm off to look for Donald."

Donald was a middle-aged, middle-sized, carefully nondescript man balding in a semicircle and peering through bifocals. He hummed as he worked, taking little samples of char, of floorboard. He had a camera and lights that he set up. He had a sketchpad on which he drew arcane diagrams with arrows. He had a steel measuring tape and a pocket recorder like hers on which he made notes.

Tom drew her aside. "We're paying him two hundred plus lab expenses. I'll split it with you."

"Why should you?"

"Because it's all my idea and nothing may come of it. I want Donald in on it. He'll do some simple tests for an accelerant—probably gasoline."

"That's not the upscale accelerant of choice of your more polished torches," Donald interrupted his rendition of "Some Enchanted Evening." "But if this is the same bug we have in Allston, he uses kerosene usually, sometimes gasoline. He's skillful with it. Nothing fancy for him. No electric timing devices. Just a book of matches, a bit of soaked fusing and some well placed accelerant. A few oil soaked trailers from the original set—"

"Trailers?" Daria repeated.

"Kerosene or oil soaked papers or rags—something to lead the fire quickly where the torch wants it to go." Donald motioned them out of his next snapshot. "His art is in placing his set and his trailers well in the building structure."

"He knows his building," Tom said wryly. "We want this evidence for us, Donald, not for the police."

Daria paused, wrapping glassware in towels. "What do we want it for, then?"

"To scare the shit out of Walker, so he'll make a settlement and you can be rid of him."

"That's fine with me." She went back to her packing. "We're going to need a lot of trips in the van."

"This won't take me long." Donald was humming "Oklahoma" as he lowered a ladder into the hole in the dining room floor. *"Pump*-a-dumpah dumpah, Dah dee dah de dah de de dee! We had a guy a couple years ago leaned to fireplace logs, broken open. Very fine job. Combusted completely in the ensuing blaze. And one torch, remember, Tom, who liked a forty-watt bulb in a box of sawdust. What have we here? Hmmmmm?" Something was being scraped across the cement floor below as Donald sang "Tomorrow! Tomorrow!"

When he emerged from the hole in the floor, he was carrying more of his sample cases. "One thing these guys forget is, fluids flow downhill. And your basement floor is quite uneven, Mrs. Walker. Under where I gather some kind of rack stood on the north wall, I got a nice sample broken loose which I think even to the nose is kerosene, definitely kerosene."

"You might turn up some alcohol mixed in under there. We had some wine against that wall."

"Thanks for warning me. Although alcohol is so volatile. . . ."

"When I spoke about arson to the fire chief and to the insurance adjuster, they acted as if I'm crazy. Am I crazy? Don't try to please Tom. Tell me the truth, I beg you. Was this an accident?"

He fixed his mild gaze on her through his bifocals. "First of all, arson falls between the cracks. The fire department, they have enough trouble putting out fires. They rush from one to the next, understaffed, overworked. What do they want to know about arson? They don't have the funds. The insurance companies, they pass on the cost to you, the policyholder. Even in neighborhoods where they have fires every week, if you have enough money, there's always somebody who will insure you. If the reputable companies won't touch it, there's Fair Plan. If Fair Plan won't touch it, there's Lloyd's of London. There's the so-called unlicensed companies beyond them."

"You haven't answered my question." Daria planted herself firmly between Donald and the door. "Am I crazy to think this is arson?"

"I don't think you're crazy. You might be mistaken. I'll know when my lab results are in. But frankly, the spread, the rapidity of the spread, makes me highly suspicious. And even to the nose I'm convinced there was kerosene used. Unless you had some stored right against the furnace, how did it get there? And under where your wine rack stood? My opinion is that someone poured a nice puddle of kerosene smack in the middle of your basement floor and probably had trailers to lead the fire up the steps and into the first floor hall. I got some nice char samples there. But I won't be quoted on this till I have my lab results—understood?" When Donald left, humming "The Rain in Spain," he said over his shoulder, "Results in a couple of days. Be in touch."

The next morning as Daria was waking from what would be, she hoped, her last night homeless, she had a call from Dorothy. "They've cancelled on us. Monday same time."

Although Daria had dreaded the deposition proceedings, she had looked forward to being over that hurdle. Now she would go off once again to the house site, where Sandra María and Ángel would be coming by with a U-Haul.

That afternoon Tom pried out the window of Daria's study, and with Peggy's help they were able to recover her files. It was a gloomy task, picking through the shattered and baked debris. What was destroyed by the fire and what survived felt wholly arbitrary. She had her Robot Coupe and no washing machine; she had Ross's old law books and no living room furniture.

Daria was now an official member of SON, a legal resident of Tom and Fay's neighborhood. Sandra María and Daria had a phone installed, electricity connected and their mail forwarded. Nothing had come of Daria's attempt to talk to the insurance adjuster about arson, except that Donald had come through with what looked like solid evidence that the fire had been set. Sandra María and Daria were moved into their new flat in high discomfort. They were camping out with what furniture they had salvaged from two fires, plus what friends and SON members donated. Their couch was a mohair relic from Fay's basement with strong smell of old dog in the upholstery. Daria had her bedroom furniture, including her old bed with its permanent scorched aroma, and Mariela had what there was of Tracy's, who came home Saturday to help.

"Allston," Tracy said, appalled. "But why did you want to move here?" In one quick move Daria had rushed more than halfway back toward East Boston. Make do, that was Daria's new motto. What other course of action lay open to her? As Gretta had, she could move into a small apartment in a neighborhood considered better; but just as romance had not been her choice as a palliative for loneliness, moving into an exorbitantly expensive and tiny apartment was not her remedy for class slippage. Keeping her new family intact was her priority, and however minimal this flat might be, it fulfilled that need.

The fit was tight. They had three bedrooms, but that arrangement left no room for Tracy and no office for Daria, who had to set up Peggy in the living room. "We're going to persuade the second floor tenants to move up to the empty top floor apartment," she said with false cheer to Tracy. "The top floor's been completely renovated, so that deal ought to be attractive to the Wongs. Then we're going to turn the first and second floors into a duplex. You'll have a nice big room—I promise, ducks." She tried to sound confident, but she knew nothing could happen until the insurance money came through, or until her divorce settlement was worked out. Monday was to be deposition day, when all the actors—husband, wife, their respective lawyers and accountants—would collect in Dorothy's office with the court stenographer who would take the official record of their sworn testimony.

"But why couldn't Tom fix up our own house?" Tracy kept asking, until Sunday morning Daria took her by on the pretext of checking for more salvage. Tracy wept openly on the return to Allston, but dropped the subject of moving back.

Daria had said little about the fire, from queasiness at accusing her husband to her daughter, but now Tracy began to ask about how the fire had started and exactly what had happened. She could lie or she could tell the truth. "Mama, there's something you're not telling me. What is it?"

Daria sneaked off to consult Sandra María. "Of course you have to tell her," Sandra María said, squeezing Daria's shoulder. "You have to warn her about him. She has to know what you know."

Daria adopted what she herself considered a cowardly ploy: she gave Tracy Donald's report. It was highly technical, she knew, but its meaning was in the end clear. In Donald's opinion, the fire had been professionally set.

"But who would do it?" Tracy demanded. "You don't have enemies like that. I mean, the kerosene and all. I can't imagine why this guy would make that up—and I guess you suspected something, or I can't see you bringing in some detective. But who would do it? Do you have any idea at all?"

"I'm afraid I do. . . . Sometimes when people are getting a divorce, they start to hate each other. They don't remember they ever loved each other—"

"*Daddy?* He couldn't. He couldn't try to—I can't believe it."

"You don't have to believe it. I hate even to tell you what I suspect."

Tracy sat down on a box of books with her head fallen forward against her chest, Sheba on her lap, brooding. Daria left her alone. She felt guilty about telling Tracy and yet compelled to do so. She was freshly angry at Ross for presenting her with such a prickly dilemma.

Tracy's new boyfriend Scott was coming by to take her back to school with him at eight Sunday evening. At seven-thirty, Tracy knocked on Daria's door. "Mama, I just wanted to tell you. I reread that man's report and I thought about it. I don't want to believe it, I don't, but you've never lied to me. I've been considering it all, and I know you wouldn't say it if you didn't have good reasons to think it's true about Daddy. So I wanted you to know I believe you even if it hurts, and I'm on your side."

"Ducks, I don't want you to have to be choosing up sides."

"Mama, after that, there's no option, is there?"

After Tracy left, Daria and Sandra María were united in a conspiracy to pretend they liked the move, a conspiracy Mariela refused to join. Mariela woke screaming from nightmares, Mariela whined and wept and complained. She wanted Torte. She wanted to go to her Lexington school with her new friends, not to the old school she had disliked before. She couldn't stand to change schools again. It wasn't fair! She wanted her yellow dress with the red flowers, she wanted her fuzzy bear Jorge, she wanted her Christmas doll with yellow hair, she wanted her little chair they had just given her, her own size. Mariela was angry, sulky, disobedient. Getting her to bed at night was no longer a pleasure but an act of war.

They must make do, they kept saying to each other with feigned cheer. The living room was a fine ample room with a corner fireplace shallow but handsome and a big bay window on the street. They had no dining room, for what had originally been one had been converted into a bed-

326

room and bath. The other two bedrooms with a bath between them were on the other side of the central hall, long and dark and echoing, that led back to the big light kitchen with a pantry off it. The flat had been partially modernized: the bathrooms redone, air conditioner boxes installed, the floors stripped and refinished, the electricity rewired and brought up to code. But the kitchen had not been touched, furnished with twenty-year-old appliances—a refrigerator that shook when it ran, which was most of the time, a stove whose oven had to be lit with a match, whereupon it caught with a great dangerous whoosh of gas, ugly metal cabinets nailed up at a tilt, a sink whose faucets dripped reverberatingly at the resonance agreed most effective by professional interrogators. They were in the midst of ripping out the old kitchen and moving the Lexington kitchen into the flat entire.

Daria had moments of sharp angular depression, especially when she woke in the new room which she had not yet had time to decorate, whose windows had unsightly tan roller shades on them, and when she walked out into the flat with its makeshift arrangements. Then she felt overwhelmed by the work they must do simply to make the flat endurable. No amount of labor would turn this into her old and beautiful house, but she tried to persuade herself that this abode too held promise. The yard was unkempt and long neglected, partially paved over when the building had been cut into small apartments. She would break up the old paving and reclaim it for garden. Gradually she must transplant her favorites, making a new garden here. They had only a handkerchief square in front, but their lot was reasonably deep behind. They were up on a hill near a big park.

The cats mooned at the windows, but showed no signs of intending to trek back to Lexington. Nonetheless they must wait until she had the backyard in order before she could begin to let them out. What she missed most was a house she had turned into her own and loved, a garden she had created as a source of fresh vegetables and cut flowers but far more, as an aesthetic pleasure in every season. From childhood on, she had lacked ability to draw, never demonstrated the least grasp of light and shade and framing with a camera. She could scarcely sew on a button. She had never taken up knitting or crocheting. Aside from her work with food, her only talent appeared to be gardening. In the garden she sculpted. With flowers and their colors, with the shapes of tall stately lupine and delphinium, with the sharp steeples of veronica and anchusa, with the buttons of marigolds, with the enormous rosettes of dahlias, the bonnets of columbine, she made sculptures, placing light green against dark green, setting both off with the occasional grey of santolina and wormwood and the far more occasional yellow of sedum. There she had given her mother a setting that would have pleased her. She would not move Nina's ashes until she could make her a worthy garden.

Sandra María, burned out for the second time, had lost far more than her books and class notes. Every time she had begun to create a decent life for herself and her child, she was slammed back to the starting line. Although she had kept a complete copy of her rewritten thesis in her library carrel, she had lost most personal effects she retained from the first fire, clothing, jewelry, photographs, letters.

Daria missed most having her own place to write. Little of her manuscript material or files had been destroyed. The Selectric had to be replaced because of water damage, but it was insured. She felt as if Ross had tried too to deprive her of a means of making a living, attacking her workplace as well as herself. The book was not going forward, because all her energy and Peggy's went into reproducing what had been lost, while camped awkwardly in the middle of a living room.

She missed Torte and still felt guilty—guilty and angry, with a cold fury gathering under her brisk exterior. She felt an equal grief for the house, that had endured many generations and preserved something of all the women who had lived in it. Now it was slashed open and spoiled, violated, dead. She lacked the morning light slanting through the mullioned panes onto the trestle table, although she was glad she possessed at least that object from her previous life. She had her dishes and glassware, but nowhere to put them, so they stayed in their boxes. Tom would create cabinets for them, he had promised. Tom thought she was not angry enough with Ross, but he was wrong. Her anger had turned cold in her, but it had not weakened. Still married to Ross, she felt vulnerable. She wanted passionately, she wanted without cessation or interruption of focus, to be free.

When she woke, when she turned in a moment of solitude to herself, she felt like someone recovering from a serious illness, an operation, who stares in the mirror at the ravages and cost but who decides to live; who takes what pleasure she can in the small accomplishments and salvage (her own pans and appliances, her own garden tools and baskets) and who experiences daily as she attempts to reembark upon the activities of her life, the difficulties, the losses of her diminished situation.

But she had not been ill; she had been attacked. There was all the difference. Quietly she promised she would not forget, for Torte, buried in Lexington; for Mariela, who woke screaming, who cried every day before school, who never wanted to go to bed but put Sandra María and Daria through an hour of fierce bickering and tantrums every night, because she feared sleep. Daria would not forget; she would never forget. Someday soon she would have justice.

Uprooted, torn from her schedule and accustomed ways, she began putting more energy into SON. She joined the patrols. She went to meetings of the core group and the public meetings.

Monday morning laden with a briefcase stuffed with papers and notes, Daria travelled the subway to Dorothy's office, not wanting to bother finding a parking space downtown. She was prompt but nobody was there except Dorothy, who met her with a rueful shrug. "Sit down, Daria. Sorry. I called you as soon as his lawyer called me, but you'd already left Allston."

"What's wrong now?"

"Suddenly his accountant can't make it."

Daria accepted a cup of Dorothy's bitter coffee. "Maybe Ross didn't think he'd have to meet with me—that I would be quite dead, or at least hospitalized. The Shriner Burn Center?"

"I huffed and puffed at his lawyer. We're set up for a rematch Friday, same time, here."

Daria put her head in her hands. "Is this a war of nerves? It's getting to me."

"It may be a war of attrition. Have you anything new for me from that detective friend of Tom's?"

"Donald. Yes." Daria pawed through her briefcase. "I almost forgot."

"I may well need this." Dorothy scanned the report. "Ha! Definite residues of kerosene accelerant found in basement floor. . . . This may do the trick." She tucked the report away. "Maybe upping the ante annoyed him. After all, we're asking for far, far more than we were."

"We have now suffered far, far more damage than we had. I want those buildings."

"With this little report, we may have some leverage at last."

That night, the last of April, she was eating take-out at Fay's and helping write a press release about the local fires, when Orlando came by asking for Tom, the silent Sylvia in tow.

"He's in the bathroom," Fay said. "What's up? Maybe I can help."

Orlando would only wait until Tom came out. "Hey, Tomás, that guy with the dirty blond moustache, we seen him again. Not on our roof. Not where they had the fire. But the house past that. Number Seventy-one. We seen him up there poking around."

"We have to put a patrol on that building. Who owns it?"

"Petris," Daria answered. "He seems to be putting a parcel together to develop. He hasn't started working on Sandra María's old building yet, so he may be waiting till he has more empty and planning to do all of them at once."

"When was this incident?" Tom asked.

"Last night. Don't I tell you right away? We have another fire, my old lady's going to have a heart attack. She's scared all the time now. . . . Man, can I talk to you private for a minute?"

"Hey!" Sylvia snapped to life, putting down the *People* magazine she had been flipping. "What are you going to talk to him about? Orlando?"

"Cool it, girl. None of your business."

"None of your business, none of your business," she muttered stalking about the room as Tom and Orlando disappeared into the boys' bedroom.

"You ought to let me do your hair," Fay said. "It's still growing out funny."

"He made me grow it out. He said he was ashamed to be seen with me with my hair punk. Ha!"

"You ever hear from your brother?" Fay asked.

Sylvia shook her head, glowering. "Nothing. Like everything else."

Afterward, when Daria was returning to Tom's—much more comfortable these days than her setup—he said, "The wages of sex on the roof. Sylvia may be pregnant."

"Didn't they use anything?"

"Orlando thinks it's not macho to use condoms, and Sylvia, as he explained with real indignation, is a good girl. Good girls don't admit they know what they're going to do, so they can't take precautions. I gave him a sales pitch about condoms, but I doubt I got anyplace. . . . Kids!" Tom said with intense distress.

Two days later it was their shift, midnight to four, at Number 71. Daria had stood a shift Sunday night with Tom, and they had spent the night talking, mostly about their daughters. It had been a good warm experience, making her look forward to their next patrol, a block of four hours with little to do but chat quietly in between their rounds. Tonight however Tom seemed to take the patrolling far more seriously. He kept shushing her and repeatedly left her at one entrance while he paced through to the other.

"Tom, are you angry at me?" she asked finally.

"How could you think that?"

"I feel as if you're avoiding me tonight." Back to the beginning, she thought, when he would discuss nothing personal.

"It's a hunch, Daria. That *he's* coming tonight. I want to get him so bad my hands itch with it. I need to get him!"

It was a passion that excluded her, for Lou was far more real to Tom than to her. She did not hate Lou but rather Ross. Lou had had nothing personal against her. He was merely the tool. Her malice, her anger, her energy slipped past the shadowy figure of Lou to hurl fruitlessly against the walls of law and money and custom that protected her estranged husband. Night after night SON members waited in these buildings where their presence prevented arson, so long as they could keep it up, different batches doing without sleep on different nights. But for Tom to imagine he would ever get his hands on Lou was a useless and perhaps dangerous obsession. Fay was right: they should concentrate on prevention. The landlords would eventually give up and begin to heed the tenants' demands to make the buildings livable.

She had half dozed off—her watch when she raised her hand read two-thirty—when she heard a loud thump overhead and then voices and someone clattering down the back stairs. She rushed through the house in time to see a man running down the alley.

Yet as she climbed the stairs toward the roof, she heard voices from above. She climbed quietly, yawning to herself, half asleep still and embarrassed that she had dozed while on duty. Tom and one of the tenants, no doubt. They must have prevented another attempt. Next time she was on patrol, she would bring a thermos of hot coffee.

Emerging onto the flat roof of the brick apartment house, she stepped from the shelter on top of the back stairs. The roof was dark, but the moon was at the half and up, casting enough light for her to pick out Tom standing with his fists clenched about six feet from another man, much smaller and slighter than Tom. In the moonlight, the man's hair looked grey. Tom was facing her and the man—Lou, yes, it had to be—stood hunched forward with his back to her. "You meddling bastard," Lou was saying in a low but extremely angry voice, a compressed and flattened roar, "who the hell do you think you are, the fucking Lone Ranger? Now get the fuck out of my way and stay out of my way!"

"You're an alley rat, Lou. You're just a cheap hangman, Lou," Tom sang, taunting him with his name.

"Wha?" Lou stood off balance staring.

"Surprised I know who you are? We know all about you. Golden Realty. Louis Henry Ledoux. We've been watching you. Easy!" Tom feinted sideways to try to step past Lou, to block him from the exit.

Something flashed in Lou's hand, dimly in the moonlight. A knife. Tom backed away, but not before he caught sight of Daria, edging cautiously forward. She shook her head at him to be silent.

"Listen, you bloody big fool," Lou snarled. "Who cares who you think I am or what you think you know. You get back and stay back or I'm going to carve my initials in your face." Lou backed toward the stairs and Daria.

Slipping sideways she picked up the brick used to hold the upper door

332

open and let the door shut slowly, keeping it from hitting the jamb. Her heart beat in her throat as if it had blades as sharp as the knife her eyes fixed on, almost feeling it cutting into Tom's flesh.

"You're caught and caught good," Tom said, watching Daria with a puzzled frown. "Put down the knife. You have to talk to us."

"I don't have to talk to any of you losers." Lou started forward at Tom. Daria wound up and threw the brick as hard as she could. The brick caught Lou hard between the shoulder blades. Screaming, he pitched forward. Tom fell over him, bringing his boot down on the hand holding the knife. Daria picked up the brick again and pounded the captured hand until Lou's bruised fingers let go of the knife. Her anger astonished her. Then she seized it and jumped back, out of the way. Tom was wrestling Lou into a half nelson.

Tom said, "That was a damn fool thing to do."

"It wasn't!" She was shaking, partly from the aftermath of that astonishing galvanizing wave of anger.

"Well, it scared me." He grunted with the effort of holding on to Lou, who struggled violently. Lou, cursing mechanically, stared at her.

"Daria, give me the knife. Carefully. Go around wide. Then run and wake Elroy. Between us we'll walk him over to Fay's."

She made a wide detour around the struggling, cursing Lou, squatting with his arms behind him in Tom's grasp. Tom let go with one hand and took the knife, putting it against Lou's throat. "I'm on my way," she said. "Be careful. I'm going to send someone up on the roof with you."

"Wake up Charley, in number four."

Forty minutes later, they had Lou in a kitchen chair at Fay's. "Listen, you got no right to hold me," Lou snarled. "No right at all."

"If you'd done a better job Tuesday, we'd be turning you in on a murder charge." Tom loomed over him. "You've been very busy lately, Lou."

Louis Henry Ledoux was slender, of medium height, with the grey blond hair she recalled, short on his head but longer in his walrus moustache. His eyes were light brown and no orthodontist had ever worked on his teeth: sign of their common class background, Tom and Lou and Daria herself, whose teeth had always been a little apart in front. In her affluent adult life, dentists had often offered to fix that for a few thousand. Lou had the same fault, to a more marked degree. His face was thin, a little compressed to the sharp edge of his nose, the jut of his chin. His forehead was high and his hands long and shapely, one braced on his bony knee, the other cradled against his chest.

"You can't hold me. I'm suing that lady for busting my hand. I want a doctor. I'm suing you all for kidnapping, and you're the ones going to be in a shitload of trouble."

Tom said, "That lady has a gripe with you all right. You burned her out last Tuesday night. Remember that fire in Lexington?"

"My husband Ross Walker gave you the key. You came upstairs and turned off the smoke detector, so we wouldn't have a chance. Then you went down the basement and set the fire with kerosene."

Lou stared at her. His mouth opened, then closed and he said nothing. He was not to be broken so easily. She felt cold pricklings of dismay. She walked away to sit on the couch with Fay's two sons, Mikey and Johnny, who were watching bug-eyed and, on orders from Fay, in utter silence. There was a period of desultory questioning, mostly by Mac. He had taken the time to dress in his usual flannel shirt and jeans with a Harris Tweed sports coat, while Fay was still in her bathrobe. She felt they were all depressed at how resistant Lou was proving. Perhaps their common fantasy had been that all they needed to do was catch him in the act and confront him, and they would have all the evidence they needed to bring their landlords to justice. She kept thinking of her own violence on the roof. She had not felt that galvanizing anger since the girls were small, when Robin had been beaten up by an older boy, when Tracy had been attacked in the park by a Doberman. She felt half ashamed and half amazed at her response to Tom's danger.

"You really didn't have to wield that brick back on the roof," Tom said, still brooding. "I was handling things fine."

"Bullshit," Lou butted in, giggling weakly. "She saved your ass."

Mac planted himself in front of Lou, with his thumbs hooked in his belt loops. His high Brahmin voice rasped on her fatigue.

"Mr. Schulman saw you at Number Twenty-seven where you left the gas behind when he interrupted you. He can identify you."

"That old man?" Lou stared from one to the other. "He couldn't identify his mother in the dark. It's all hot air. And I'm suing you for everything you own. Kidnapping, that's what this is. If you had anything real on me, you'd have called the cops."

"We'll call the cops all right," Fay said, gathering her fuzzy pink bathrobe around her. Daria wished that Fay's hair were not up in pink rubber curlers. "Very, very soon we'll call them. You're the fall guy, Lou. You're caught dead to rights. We got you placed by two witnesses at the fire at Number Sixty-nine. We caught you with the goods at Number Seventy-one. And Mr. Schulman saw you, when you left your gasoline behind, at Number Twenty-seven. Plus you practically left your calling card out in Lexington, didn't you?"

"Why would I go around this neighborhood setting fires? You think I'm some kind of nut? Some kind of pervert? Listen, I'm a landlord myself. I own buildings here."

"Including the one you torched on Brainerd," Tom said. "We know you're paid by the landlords. I bet when the DA subpoenas your bank account, they'll figure out exactly what you were paid per fire. I hope it was a lot, considering what you're about to go through."

"He's a loser, what he called you up on the roof," Daria said, walking back over. "Whatever they paid him, he's going to do a long time in prison for it."

There were so many of them gathered around him now, Lou was forced to turn and turn again in his chair to face them. He leaned back, forcing a grin. "You're a team of hot air artists. You got nothing on me. No proof. And I'm going to take you for everything you got when I sue, if you own anything to begin with."

They had almost no hard evidence. Daria turned away again to prevent him from reading her aura of doubt and fear. She had attacked a man she didn't even know tonight, perhaps broken his hand. That would look great in the papers. Beating a man with a brick. Perhaps he really could sue her. What did they have on him besides suppositions? It was close to four in the morning. Mikey and Johnny had dozed off on the couch, leaning together. Fay was making another pot of coffee and even Mac was looking wilted. How long could they hold Lou? Why didn't he just walk out? He seemed afraid to try, perhaps because there were after all seven of them against him, if he counted the sleeping kids.

Elroy strutted up to Lou, putting on a swaying walk. "Poor honey pie, nothing much. Just witnesses up the ass. Witnesses linking you, in person, star billing, to four different fires, for starters. You don't know how we been following you since that fire at Number Sixty-nine when you were seen, honey, by two witnesses, live ones. We followed you home to Belmont. We know how you been fighting with your wife and gave her that shiner. We know what you been buying and we know what you been selling. Now your little store's closed down."

"We'll pick up the kid later," Mac said, reenergized, resuming center stage. "Come on, make it easy for yourself."

"You don't know who he is. What kid?" Lou tugged his moustache.

"I know how to find him," Tom said. "He hangs around that Spanish grocery. I know the kids in this neighborhood. Orlando will know his name. We should have him on deck inside twenty-four hours."

"We had a description of him from Mr. Schulman," Daria said, on a gamble. "And I got a look at him last night when he ran down. It didn't take us long to find you once we had a description, did it?"

"You haven't been following me." Lou looked from one to the other. "What kind of bullshit is that? You're lying. You couldn't follow a parade down the street."

"I even saw Walker meeting you outside that coffee shop on Mass Avenue and giving you money. In Back Bay," Daria said.

He was staring at her with eyes that widened rather than narrowed with suspicion, making him look oddly boyish with roof tar on his cheek, a bruise darkening the skin under one eye, his hand held before him crumpled. "My hand really hurts. I bet you broke my hand."

She had to push, she knew it. They had to break him tonight or they would never have another shot. "Is that the hand you write those nice neat elegant notes with? Linen weave paper you like. Yours, Lou."

His breath seemed to stop. He was staring hard. She met his gaze and held it. It was unpleasant, it was almost vile to hold his gaze and hold it on and on, a contact far too intimate. Something very cold was being exchanged.

She went on in a lighter voice. "Want to know something funny, Lou? Before we figured out who you were, for a while I thought you were Ross Walker's girlfriend. I was reading all those notes and thinking they were for little rendezvous. But then he'd set himself up a nice alibi—have

336

folks over for a big dinner party catered by yours truly. All those notes, Lou. You sure liked to write them."

Now he was sweating hard, still staring. She felt as if he was trying to stare her down or alternately, to read through her face to her brain. The sweat was standing out on his forehead, over the wide open light brown eyes. Finally he shook his head hard, breaking the stare. "He said he burned them," he muttered. "Some goddamn smart lawyer he turned out to be."

"Ross isn't big on cleaning up after himself," Daria said.

"I didn't like the job in Lexington. I don't know that neighborhood. It's awful quiet at night. And he didn't tell me there were so many people. He said you were living there alone."

"What would that have mattered to you?" Fay snapped. "You burned that woman and her daughter out once already, in Number Sixty-nine. You had two cracks at killing her. Like Bobbie, remember? Little Bobbie Rosario? And whoever that tramp was they said had taken refuge in the hall."

"This hand really hurts, you know that?" Lou turned from one to the other. He held up his hand. "You mean that little kid was in all the papers, I didn't have nothing to do with that one. They had somebody else burn that. That's before I started working for them."

"Who did it, then?" Tom asked.

"How do I know? Some punk, some kid don't know his ass. Look here, are you really calling the cops on me?"

"I think we may try the attorney general's office." Mac was standing braced, hands in belt loops again, smiling expansively. "I've been developing a contact there. Look, we know you're small fry—"

"I got four kids to support! I'm no millionaire—"

"We'll send you to Walpole with pleasure," Mac said. "But if you don't look forward to ten years hard time, understand we'd rather go after the guys who hired you."

"Yeah," Fay said. "We know we can put you away. We have you over the fire and toasty warm. But those guys have us. They're our real enemies."

"Maybe we should call our friend Eleni to look at your hand," Elroy said. "She's an RN."

"It hurts a lot. Get somebody to look at it! You mean work out a deal with the DA? How do you know they'd do it? They'd just take me and forget the guys who hired me. They don't want to mess with guys with money. These guys are loaded. Walker's like that with the bank." He held up his left hand, fingers crossed.

"My contact in the attorney general's office is interested," Mac said self-importantly. "It might work out to their advantage politically. Big crusading deal. The AG has ambitions. That is, if we can give them the case on a platter."

Elroy grinned at Lou. "Nice slight fair guy like you. It don't matter you're thirty-five, you're still in good shape. Pretty face, tight ass. They're gonna have a time with you, mmm. In Walpole, you're gonna be one popular gal."

Tom said, "Of course you can trust your wife all that time. Too bad you won't see your kids till they've grown up."

"Ah, shit, what do you guys really have on me? Nothing!"

"Nothing?" Mac roared. "Nothing but a whole pile of circumstantial evidence, a whole slew of witnesses and you just confessed to torching Mrs. Walker's house. In front of all of us."

"Are you ever going to call that nurse?" Lou whined.

"You still planning to sue us?" Fay asked.

"Listen, I just try to get along. Just try to make a living," he said. "My hand really hurts. They hired me and they tell me what they want and I do the job. At Sixty-nine the boss says—"

"Chuck Petris?" Daria butted in.

"Yeah, he says, just the roof and a bit of internal damage around the stairwell. Only the front apartment. Nothing major. Same for Seventy-one. Now your husband, he wants it totalled. I don't choose. I do what they pay me for. I give them just the kind of burn they want."

"Doesn't that take a lot of skill?" Mac asked innocently. Tom turned his back on all of them and went to stand at the window, scowling out.

"I'm calling Eleni," Elroy said. "Right now. She'll fix you up."

They were going to have to coddle him. They were going to have a relationship with him. He was going to be their creature. Daria felt at once light-headed with relief and disgusted. She moved back behind Lou. Mac was fussing over him now, questioning him more gently, in almost flattering terms. "How did you do that technically, just burn enough to clear a building? How do you contain a fire?"

Daria sat down beside Mikey and Johnny on the couch. They had been wakened when things got noisy to follow the interrogation. "Mom really gave it to him," Mikey whispered to her.

She stared at Lou's slight back, the man whose footsteps had briefly wakened her that night. She would like to cast Torte's death in his face, but of course what was an old dog to anybody whose dog he had not been? She understood why Tom was scowling into the yard outside Fay's kitchen window. He had half hoped Lou would continue to resist them. Just as he had wanted to confront Lou personally on the roof, his anger driving him into danger, so he wanted Lou to hold out now. The victory was too easy. He could not savor it, and neither could she. Although she had invested Lou with little energy of hostile fantasy, she found him disgusting, banal and disgusting. A worm who turned too easily. He had been bought by greed; now as Tom had predicted, he could be bought by fear. He was theirs and she shuddered at the proximity. Your enemy has a face. It was neither handsome (in spite of Elroy's flattery) nor ugly, simply a pinched nervous face, a sharp face, a hungry face, a thirty-five-year-old father of four who was still a gangling adolescent.

"I got to go home," Lou whined. "My wife gets crazy if I stay out too late. I always go home by three. Always! It's after five."

"If you think she's awake, we'll call her for you," Fay said.

"Yeah? A woman calls up, I'm dead. Let me call her. Don't worry, I'm not planning to give her some secret message in code. Tell her to burn the files. I got no files. It's all in my head." He tapped his narrow high forehead. Eleni arrived, a big woman with iron grey hair in a bun, to look at his hand. "I remember the floor plans, I remember the wiring in every building I ever worked on."

"Doesn't your wife know where you are?" Fay perched on the table.

"She thinks I tend bar sometimes, filling in for a friend. That's what I tell her. She knows I get paid. It's none of her business, just so I pay the bills, right?"

That's how Ross had felt. Two worlds. Two personae. But they became one. Perhaps what Ross sought with Gail was permission to be entire again, to slough off the dead skins of values he no longer held and emerge in his bright bold colors as entrepreneur, real estate developer, sculptor of neighborhoods, master of tax shelters and mortgage pyramiding schemes.

From the window Tom turned and stared at Lou, paced around him, then fled to the window again. The questions he wanted to ask: she could feel them seething in him, an angry confrontation he must contain. She experienced the physical connection between Tom and herself more sharply than she ever had, not this time in sexual attraction but in empathy. It was being arranged that Fay and Elroy were to sit up with Lou, for they did not dare let him out of their sight. In the morning Mac would talk to his contact in the attorney general's office and try to give Lou over to them. At the last moment as they were dispersing, Mac decided he too would sit up. In exhaustion Tom and she stumbled out into the dawn, heading for his apartment merely because it was closer than hers.

25

"Bᴜᴛ we were up all night. It's crazy to try to go to work as usual. You could hurt yourself."

"I'm a working man, Daria. I'm no professional—"

"You take time off more easily than Ross ever did—"

"More willingly. Not more easily. I took off to help you move. I took off to help you with the insurance adjuster. I'm going to start on your kitchen this weekend."

"Tom, I don't want you to do anything for me. I'm just worried because you're exhausted."

"I haven't been carrying my load in Aardvark. Everybody's pissed. I have to show up today. We're getting behind and it's my fault."

"Nobody else ever gets sick? Nobody takes a trip? You told me Jenny had a baby last year and was out for three months."

"Yeah, but we had nine months notice to plan around it. . . . I have to go and don't drive me crazy about it. I feel too mean this morning. Let's just stay out of each other's way."

As she walked the two blocks to her new flat, she wasn't sure what they had been quarreling about. She had not actually expected him to stay home from work; perhaps she was merely asserting her right to care. He was then asserting other commitments? She did not know, except that she retained a tingle of anger as she was sure he did.

Their new phone rang all day, as she was trying to work with Peggy under extremely minimal conditions. Mac was hogging negotiations with the attorney general's office; but Mac was the best person to talk to the state. He could speak bureaucrat's language. He was a Harvard man and assumed command even when he wasn't granted it. Their best argument with the attorney general was their inability to persuade city officials to listen to their complaints, and Fay was frantically putting together the documentation on their failed efforts to interest other authorities.

Tom was disqualified from the maneuvers because he could not remain in the same room with smokers. That kept him out of meetings with the attorney general, even if he had taken off work. Tom felt a little sorry for himself, being excluded. Fay was angry about Mac's domination of the new offensive. Lou followed Mac around like a puppy dog, she said. They had agreed to tell nothing to the SON membership at large yet, because the AG had talked of wiring Lou and sending him back to record his business dealings with the landlords he worked for.

Donald was being officially brought in. Tom had persuaded him to take char samples and photographs of the previous fires starting with the one that killed Bobbie and the presumed tramp in the house where Daria now lived, but SON and Donald had lacked the funds to do the lab work or print the pictures. Now he was to be paid as a consultant to work on the evidence he had collected and locked away but never analyzed.

In the back of her mind Daria was brooding over Tom as she was proofreading the manuscript being retyped. Peggy was coming in four days a week now, to redo what had been water damaged. Maybe Daria's moving into Tom's neighborhood worried him; perhaps he thought she would make many more demands, and wasn't he right? Here she was with a house screaming for renovation and she did need his help every day. If Dorothy could only pull her settlement out of Ross, she could hire someone to do the work. Sandra María, Mariela and she needed a functioning kitchen, needed it badly and soon. They must create together some new pleasant daily rituals. She did not know who felt guiltier toward Mariela, still cross and sulky, Sandra María or herself. Sandra María felt she had failed to make a decent life for her daughter. Daria felt she had persuaded them to move in, and exposed them to danger brought on by her acrimonious divorce.

The new sink had finally been plumbed; the gas company was to send someone to turn on her old six-burner stove today. Ángel, Elroy and Tom had wrestled in the refrigerator from Lexington. Sandra María and Ángel had laid a slate floor in a mosaic of greys and grey-greens. Daria had painted the kitchen a pale gold. But the old metal cabinets had been taken down and no new wooden cabinets put up. They were still eating from paper plates and drinking from sodden paper cups. She wanted her appliances standing in efficient rows on the counters ready to chop and whip and grind. She wanted the right tool in the right drawer. She wanted the order out of which she could create pleasure. She needed Tom's help, and perhaps that need itself was dangerous. Assuredly something had gone wrong between them over the last week. He was acting broody, sore.

She dreaded the evening. She had invited Tom to supper, assuming the stove would be connected. She intended to try to cook her first true and full meal in the new dwelling, even if it must be served on paper, a braised dish she called Sweet California Beef, because her recipe used California port.

Finally at three the gasman came. The last bottles of her wine cellar had been destroyed in the fire, but Ángel had promised to pick up something. For all the improvisation and difficulties as she cooked on her own six-burner stove, she decided this could be made a better kitchen than her old one. It was large and more rationally shaped, without a stairway and back hall cut out of it; it was much lighter and the ceiling considerably higher, giving the heat from cooking someplace to go. As she grated the zest of an orange, she worried about Tracy. As soon as Daria had cash in hand, she must start the alteration. Tracy had been given far more to deal with than was fair. At least she must have her own nice room. With two floors, they would go at once from being jammed in, to being spaciously and luxuriously spread out.

Supper was like a good picnic. Everybody ate well and even Tom seemed relaxed. The evening was mild, the door to the yard standing open. Daria imagined a deck just outside the kitchen but she said nothing, fearful that Tom would feel drafted. How varied were the sounds that drifted in: bird cries as in Lexington, yes, because the neighborhood had just as many trees, and in fact a more varied bird population because often the yards held fruit trees, but more human sounds, radios tuned to salsa, Chopin, punk rock, all news; the whack of a ball next door; hammering from the corner where Mr. Vernalli was working on his roof when he got home from work; the steady drone of conversation from the Schulmans' yard where they sat out on mild evenings, the invalid wife, Mr. Schulman, the old people upstairs, their friends next door, drinking endless pots of coffee and eating cake.

After supper, Sandra María and Ángel took Mariela off to see a movie while Daria sat on the doggy sofa beside Tom in an uneasy silence she was not accustomed to, with him. Did all men run out of words after an initial burst of passionate interest? His being so attracted to her had been in the nature of an irrational miracle. Had it worn itself out?

"Tom. Don't tell me you're not mad at me this time."

"Okay. I won't."

"What are you angry about?"

His profile seemed wrapped in the dark clouds of sullen anger. "I don't know, if you don't. What would I ever be sore about?"

"Because I hit Lou with the brick? That's macho silliness."

"I was pissed about that, but I admit it's stupid. I thought you could have trusted me to handle him. Then I thought I wouldn't have stood there watching like a spectator either. So I forgive you."

"Forgive me! For doing the right thing?"

"For doing the right thing." Briefly he grinned. He was still facing straight ahead, as if he were driving down a treacherous road. She had a strong desire to stand in front of him waving her arms and making faces. "Okay, I'm forgiven for keeping you from getting carved like a Christmas goose. What am I not forgiven for?"

"Lying."

"Lying?"

"Lying. To me!"

"Oh." She had a flash of Lou in the chair sweating. "Because I told Lou I'd seen Ross give him money."

"That's part of it. You said you hadn't seen anything."

"I saw Ross hand him something. I never saw what it was. I had no idea then who Lou was—I was looking for lovers, not business connections. I'd never heard of arson, except as a minor item in the morning papers."

344

"But you remembered. And you didn't tell me. You lied."

"Tom, I didn't remember right away. We never spoke of it again after that first time I recognized Lou. I did tell you where I'd seen him and that I'd seen Ross with him."

"You're telling me you remembered later about Walker handing Lou something? And about all those notes? Suddenly you remembered."

Daria was silent, her hands tightening on each other in her lap. "No. I remembered it all right away. Although I couldn't remember what the notes said till I'd concentrated for a long time. I was still protecting Ross—"

"Why? Why in hell?"

"I didn't think he could ever have burned people out. I just didn't believe it. I thought you had a grudge against him—that you were making him into a villain."

"Until he tried to kill you. Other people were just fine."

"Tom, please listen! Until you turned out to be right, when Schulman found Lou with the gasoline, I didn't believe it, but then I did!" Tom wanted total acceptance, but she was still coming to know him. He wanted from her a kind of belief and trust in him they had not earned between them, but she could think of no way to phrase that, that might not alienate him further. She was in no state to offer the trust he demanded, for her propensity to think the best had landed her in sorrow and trouble. "Only after that did I think about those notes and set out to try to remember what they said. Ross burned them all. But I didn't let Lou know that. I read one of them by chance—" She stopped abruptly, her mind flashing on that October Monday.

"I'll never believe you forgot you'd read them." He sat like a fortress, squared off, retracted.

"I may have forgotten something better than that." She jumped up. "I may have saved that first one. Wait a minute!" She ran into her bedroom, tripping over the bamboo blind she had been trying to install. Then she caught up her jewelry case and brought it back. Opening it on her lap she felt for the loose spot in the velvet lining. "Here it is." She unfolded the note carefully. "It's the very first I ever saw. After that I steamed them open as they came because I thought they were from Ross's girlfriend. After he read them, he burned them each time."

"You hold it. I don't want my fingerprints on it too." He leaned forward to read aloud:

"Dear Rusty,

You can expect our little visitor Tuesday night. I won't disappoint you.

Yours,
Lou

Now how in hell did you ever think that could be a note from his lover?"

"I was looking for another woman, not some man."

"We should turn this over to the AG. But you put Walker first all this time. You trusted him instead of me."

"I was married to him for twenty-two years, Tom, twenty-two years! I couldn't discard that chunk of my life. And yes, it was hard for me to believe in landlords burning their own buildings. I did think you were exaggerating. I thought you were being a little bit paranoid about fire."

"Just going along, humoring me. Thinking I'm some kind of nut."

"Can't you see my situation? I had three children with him. Do you tell your kids your ex-wife is ambitious, status mad, obsessed with control and being skinnier than anybody?"

"Andrea hasn't committed any crimes against people."

"Would you leap to believe it if someone told you she had? For all you know, she deals heroin or runs a string of call girls out of her garage."

"Ummm." He actually looked at her, sideways out of the corner of his eyes. He would not yet turn his head.

"I was committed to trying to hold on to the best feelings I could salvage. I fought hating him."

He finally turned his head and met her gaze for the first time. "How do you feel about Walker now?"

"You know the answer. You could tell when I was manipulating Lou last night. I hate him. And I find that excruciating. It's a defeat." She felt dangerously close to despair. Since the fire she had tried to keep busy, to keep moving, to proceed on every possible action that could improve her family's situation; always underneath she had felt despair like a fathomless dark sea under the floor washing away the foundations. "Do you

346

think I'm so stupid and easygoing, I'm not angry, murderously angry, at someone who tried to kill me?"

"I've been feeling a little used."

"Because of putting in the cabinets? I know. You work all week and then we try to get you to do it for us free. Listen, Tom, as soon as some money comes through, I'll hire someone to do the work. I don't want to go on imposing on you."

"That's not it." Abruptly he rose and started pacing.

From the couch she watched him lurch to and fro across the room. "Have I seemed . . . too demanding lately? Perhaps moving here . . ."

"Why didn't you move in with me?" He glared at her.

She was silenced by surprise. "Move in?" she repeated clumsily, her mind momentarily blank.

"Why wouldn't you? Why go through all this rebuilding?"

"But . . . I thought it was a bad idea just to move in to save myself trouble. That would have to be something we talked out . . ."

"Why didn't we talk about it? Why didn't you ask me what I wanted?"

"But . . ." Realizing she had never seriously considered moving in, she pictured his apartment and understood why. "It was never a possibility. We could never live together in that space."

"Why not?" He stopped in front of her, glowering.

"Tom, your apartment is beautiful—for one person. You've made a gorgeous big space, with one small bedroom for guests and when your daughters come. But I have two daughters and Tracy lives with me part time. I have a secretary. I work at home. There's no room for my office there."

He cocked his head, his face relaxing. Then he let himself down lightly beside her. "How often does this secretary come?"

"Three to four days a week, nine to four."

"I forgot about that."

She realized that she was not in despair, after all; she had been distracted. Was it a remnant of her Catholic girlhood that made her view despair as one of the ultimate sins, or just a matter of her disposition? Tom was opening up, as so often requested on her part. She must be a little more honest too, it was coming close to home on that. "Tom, it's more than I've said. I like living with Sandra María. Plus I've taken on a relationship with Mariela. Where were they going to move? What was going to happen to them? They've been burned out *twice*. Mariela's taken this hard, very hard."

"Then it wasn't because you don't ever want to live with me?"

She was about to say she hadn't ever really considered it, when that struck her as cruel, since obviously he *had* been thinking about the possibility. She felt a little pushed, but then she had been pushing him to open up to her. What did she want? Intimacy Tuesdays, Thursdays and Saturdays? "Tom, I couldn't live in your place," she temporized.

"I'm sort of bored with my apartment anyhow. I haven't done anything new to it in more than a year." He frowned again. "But it's more than living space that's at issue," he said with a return to sullenness. "I'm sick of hiding out and lurking around. I'm sick of acting scared of that turd you were married to."

"Am married to. Still."

"I do wonder if that's the reason?" His voice was thick with sarcasm. "I've introduced you to my friends. I think the real reason is that—just like Andrea—you're ashamed of me."

She jumped up. "That's nonsense!" Of all the silly fears for him to come up with. She felt a loosening of tension. Everything else had been on the mark or close to it, but this was so ridiculous she felt more like pulling his hair than arguing seriously with him. "How can you say that with a straight face? You've met Tracy. You haven't met Robin because she and I are not speaking."

"You have to do something about that soon," he said in his normal voice, an aside in his anger that made her smile. "I haven't met your friends. I only met your secretary after the fire."

"You never even told me you'd been involved with Dorothy when you sent me to her."

He raised a puzzled eyebrow. "That was a century ago."

"Not to her."

"Oh." His anger was lifting slowly, like fog. "I guess I thought if anything she might do me a favor for old times' sake."

"That strikes me as ill-conceived, but never mind. Tom . . . is that when you had your ear pierced? With Dorothy?"

He looked puzzled, his hand touching his lobe as if expecting from the contact some illumination. "Yeah . . . it was. One of those stupid things. We were intense for a while, and it was what we did instead of rings or something like that. I'd forgotten."

"Anyhow, I'd like you to meet my family. Besides, I haven't met yours."

"I wanted to ask you to my sister's seder, but I didn't know how you'd feel about it."

"I've never been to one. Of course I would have gone." She put her arms around him. "Stop sulking. Your wrongs are imaginary."

"I'm not sulking."

"You can meet Gretta tomorrow. Want to meet my sister Gussie? She won't tell the boys."

He pulled her toward him. "Peaches, my family is dull as a day down in the Registry of Deeds. All they talk about is people I knew in the fifth grade and what the kids said yesterday."

"What will they say about me not being Jewish?"

"Probably they'll figure Italian is closer than Wasp. At least it's the same sea." He drew his finger along her cheek. "I do want to meet Gretta. But look, you backed into this thing with me. You didn't really choose it. Don't you see that's a problem for us?"

"I'm not convinced. I have a long record of choosing not to know things I really know. Gussie said that to me. I'd like to change." She knew from the strength of her relief that he wasn't just bored with her, how much she wanted to continue.

"I guess I'd like it if we were more of a couple. Working together's been good and what we've been doing, important. But I need more than that."

"I thought you were mad because I was asking too much." All day she had felt pressing upon her the fear that it was over, as if she expected it to go quickly bad the way things with Ross had gone slowly bad. Maybe she suspected that all love relationships were doomed. But when she tried to imagine her life without Tom, it seemed to her not so much lonely as drab.

"Daria, nobody minds putting work into what's *theirs*. But we haven't made ourselves into an *us* yet."

Her head was flying apart. For a moment she couldn't formulate any reply. Seven, eight voices were screaming in her head, everything from grab him, love me, to run, run, run. "You're talking about . . . emotional commitment?"

"It's called love," he said dryly.

She had been worrying whether he was capable of it, but was she? She knew she could love him, but she was afraid. "Is that what you want from me?"

"When I realized you'd lied to me, I was furious. It really hurt. You take him far more seriously than you take me."

"That's history. You and I have just begun, tentatively."

"I feel like you're more tentative than I am."

"But your marriage broke up three years ago. Mine is still fracturing!"

"Do you think if you wait three years, you'll meet anybody who'll appreciate you more as you are inside and outside than me?"

"Don't you think I appreciate you?"

"Not as much."

"Tom! You're comparing me with young girls who chased you, years ago. But a lot of times young women want a man, a boyfriend, and you'll stand in for the ideal till you're clearly not ideal or until someone better comes along. I'm a knock-down drag-out realist. My appreciation may not sing and dance and do doggy tricks, but it's based on you and not on some fantasy."

"I guess I do want to be adored a little more." He was grinning.

She smiled back. "I will try."

"Saturday morning early I'll get started on the cabinets." He rose and strolled out to the kitchen, his walk looser, rangier. When he wasn't angry, he was always graceful, she thought, following him. "The Wongs agreed to move to the top floor?"

Daria nodded. "It's a good deal for them. We're giving them a break on the rent for an apartment that's renovated. Theirs wasn't."

"You ought to put a fire escape on. Leave the front stairway open for all floors. Close off the back stairs at the second floor and open it up inside the duplex. That's your internal stairs."

"That's a great idea. . . . You've been thinking about this house."

350

"I can hardly help it. I'm always sitting in people's living rooms redesigning the whole place. We could make something really fine out of this structure."

"I want the dining room back, the way it was originally. We can leave that bathroom in, but I want a dining room instead of a bedroom there."

"I assume the second floor has the same layout?"

"Identical, but it wasn't renovated." It was fun to talk about the plans with him. It reminded her of the best years with Ross, when they planned their antiquing jaunts, when they used to talk about the girls seriously, caring and worrying and figuring things out together. "I'm going to take the living room upstairs for my bedroom. Sandra María's going to move upstairs, over where she is now."

"Would you like me to draw up tentative plans?"

"We seem to have had too much that's tentative. How about some definite plans?"

He ran his hand along a joist exposed by the removed cabinets. "I'd enjoy that."

She had a moment of feeling that in some way they had merged, an almost tactile sensation of connection. In some recipes before cooking is commenced, the disparate ingredients must sit together for a time: it is called the marrying of the herbs, the spices. At a certain point the flavor is different than the sum of its parts. That is happening, she thought, we are changing each other, we are making a new whole.

Friday morning, once again Daria took the subway to Dorothy's office, this time not bothering to be prompt. Once again when she walked in no one was present except Dorothy and her secretary. "Again?" she shouted. "I can't take this. Dorothy, I can't! Can't we compel them somehow? Somehow?"

Dorothy grinned, putting her hands on Daria's shoulders and pressing her into a chair. "You can stand this. In fact you can stand it just fine. Prepare for good news."

"Ross dropped dead of a heart attack last night. I'm a widow."

"They caved in. We have a settlement. We couldn't get all the additional buildings we were asking for, but we did better than I ever expected. It's a good settlement. Frankly, I'm proud of myself. Phyllis is just typing it up—I'll have it for you in five minutes. Want some coffee?"

Daria paced, declining the coffee for she felt too wired to need caffeine. "It was Donald's report?"

Dorothy nodded. "His lawyer convinced him you'd proceed with relinquishing your half of the insurance settlement to have his hide if we didn't get a total agreement fast. He may have that adjuster in his pocket, but he doesn't have the insurance company."

"I can't tell you how happy I am. Let's ram it through quick, before he gets tired waiting and tries to do me in again."

"He's in a bigger hurry than you are. Once this is signed at his lawyer's this afternoon—by messenger no less they're picking it up—he flies down to the Dominican Republic Monday and you're divorced as of Tuesday."

"Divorced by Tuesday? Is that legal?"

"Perfectly, so long as the property settlement is worked out under Massachusetts law, and we finally accomplished that feat. I forgot to ask, do you want your maiden name back?"

"I'd love it, but all my books are under his name. Too bad." She ran through the agreement, as the secretary handed it to her. She had got what she asked for during the first round (suffering the loss of the Lexington property and splitting that insurance money instead); and three of the buildings she had requested the second time, Fay's, the Schulmans' and her own. She had also got Ross to agree to pay off the mortgages on those within two years. As Dorothy had insisted, the property had been used to raise money for other purposes far beyond its value and that money had to figure in the settlement, or the buildings were doomed to abandonment. The building Daria was living in had a modest mortgage she was prepared to assume; his renovations had been financed from the fire insurance. She would use the money from the Lexington fire.

"Daria, I know it's not everything you wanted, but it's all we're ever going to get. If you delay longer, you may end up with far less. He claims to be in such a precarious position he could choose bankruptcy. I'm not convinced a judge would give you as much. Your adultery, if discovered, weighs ten times as much as his. And if you have to use the

352

arson evidence in court, you can't get that money, obviously, to renovate your Allston house."

"Okay. Just add a note that I can remove my plants from the yard at Lexington until, say, November fifteenth of this year."

"I'll draw up a memo to that effect right now and you can sign it, but I believe we should go ahead with or without your rosebushes. No delays, Daria, take it from me. He was furious about Donald. He went on at great length how it had never occurred to him to stoop so low as to hire detectives."

"It never occurred to him I might do anything interesting." Daria signed. This was considered a good settlement, she thought as she returned on the subway: she was receiving twenty to twenty-five percent of their married property.

That night at her new flat they drank champagne, California but satisfying to all. Orlando came by with Sylvia to have a private conversation with Tom. Then he said to them all, "Hey, you know, there's some guy sitting outside in a green Subaru. I seen him around yesterday too."

Sandra María sat straight up in her chair. "I saw the same car."

Tom went to look. "I think old Walker hired a detective belatedly."

Daria walked over. "After all, we have Donald. But let's play it close to the vest. We'll all live a chaste life till Tuesday, okay?"

The surveillance continued through the weekend, although the detective could have learned little except that Mariela's girlfriend Suzi dropped by, that they were visited by Fay, Ángel, Tom, Orlando, Sylvia, Elroy, Eleni, Gretta, the oil truck making a delivery, and that a great deal of building activity went on. Work on the kitchen began at eight o'clock sharp on Saturday morning, as Tom had warned. By four Sunday they had a beautiful kitchen. Then Daria in an access of joyful energy unpacked her dishes, glassware, utensils while Ángel, Sandra María and Mariela had a picnic in the park in the mild May afternoon and Tom lay on the couch drinking beer and watching the Red Sox play the Yankees on the grainy-pictured set Mr. Schulman had dug out of his basement for them, while Fay kept them company as chaperone. They were taking no chances, with the divorce so close at hand.

When she finished they decided to go out to eat. Daria was beginning to feel curious about her new neighborhood, and Tom was eager to share what he enjoyed. Fay took off to prepare supper for her sons. As they all left, Tom crossed the street and rapped on the rolled-up window of the green Subaru. "Pardon me, but I thought I'd just tell you, Mrs. Walker and I are going out to eat. We'll be back in two hours, if you want to catch some supper yourself. When we get back we can tell you where we ate, if you want to put it in your report."

The man, about Donald's age, but thinner, balder, stared at Tom and then laughed silently. "Tell me where you're eating and I'll meet you there."

"I have a yen for Rubin's Deli, but if it's crowded in there, it might be Grecian Yearning or the Allston Depot."

"Then I'll have to follow you. Too bad." The man rolled up his window and started his engine.

Monday morning the green Subaru was gone and a phone call to Dorothy confirmed that Ross had flown to the Dominican Republic. By Tuesday she was a divorcée. Her decree would arrive in the mail. It felt strange. She had been pushing on a massive oak door that she could scarcely budge, leaning her weight on it and thrusting with all her strength until her muscles ached. Suddenly it had folded back like a paper fan, leaving her still poised to push, unbalanced with surprise. She was free to move forward now, it seemed, at her own speed.

26

S HE had not noticed they had lilacs in the yard until she woke
one warm May morning to their heavy sexual fragrance. She
discovered them in bloom near their common fence with the
Schulmans. Cutting an armful, she brought them to mingle
their perfumes with the smells of new wood and sawdust. Overhead an
electric saw was already whining. With a dragging thump something
heavy was being toted through the empty rooms up there. Monday Aaron
Aardvark had begun. Tom had talked another renovation into waiting
till fall with an inventive patter about how hot weather adversely affected
high quality cabinetwork. Her insurance money had come through. The
money that was to flow from Ross to the bank to pay off the mortgages
on the other two buildings was reputed to be "in process," whatever that
meant.

Sheba lay on the kitchen table, washing her swollen belly where the
glossy hair was thinning. She was a little cross and snapped at Ali when
he tried to snuggle. Her belly was definitely in the way and her nipples,
swollen. Daria had a birthing box all prepared in the darkest closet.

She was working out the minimal amounts of sugar or honey that
made a rhubarb compote palatable, with and without orange juice, so she
had four different combinations simmering. Her mind was partly engaged with variations (nutmeg; ginger; candied ginger; orange peel;
cinnamon) and partly engaged with how to prove to Tracy, who had

only been home once since the fire, that life in the new house could be tolerable.

The phone rang, forcing Daria to turn down the fire under her four variations. "Cesaro! It's been a long time."

"Yes. . . . Well, how are you doing, Daria?"

"I'm surprisingly fine. Ross had me burned out in Lexington, you know."

"Now, Daria, he said you'd made wild accusations—"

"Did he also tell you I finally got most of the settlement I wanted because I hired a private investigator who found kerosene residues in the cement floor of the basement?"

"Why didn't you call me when you had the fire? I was shocked to hear about it."

"I called Gussie—"

"That's who told me. Why didn't you call me?"

"Cesaro, I haven't had support from anyone in the family but Gussie. In many ways you're closer to Ross than to me. Tony and I no longer even speak."

"Please don't be bitter. I've tried very hard to put pressure on Rusty to make a decent and just settlement. I truly have. . . . I have a few things to tell you. . . ." His voice deepened, trailed off.

"So what's new?"

"Daria, Rusty was married last Saturday, to Gail."

"My, my, he sure was in some kind of hurry." She was annoyed, but not as hurt as Cesaro expected. The news brought back her anger with a grating rush. A door opened and a hot dry wind laden with grit and smoke blew in. "Big wedding?"

"Small, by their standards. In the rose garden at Hamilton. Only immediate friends and family. Perhaps eighty people. Ninety at the outside. They have a big old house—a white elephant in Greek Revival style. Then there are a couple of smaller houses. Gail and Ross are going to be living in one of them, near her kennels."

"How many dogs attended the wedding?" She understood that Cesaro had gone.

He chuckled. "About twenty. I'm glad you're taking this well."

356

"I wish them each other."

"Just before he flew down to the Dominican Republic, Daria, Rusty told me he still loves you. That the marriage had just become impossible. Your life-styles were incompatible."

"He sure loves with a fiery passion. He tried to kill me, Cesaro, and if you don't believe me, I'd be pleased to show you the detective's report."

Cesaro cleared his throat. "You're not aware Rusty set detectives on you just before the divorce."

"I am aware of it."

"Oh? Anyhow, he dug up little to your detriment, I want you to know, except that you seem to be involved with a radical group of troublemakers who are trying to prey off property holders in Allston."

"Having moved into the neighborhood and having experienced first-hand Ross's use of fire as a personal and financial tool, I have a lot in common with that group—SON. Which I do not find a radical group, anyhow."

"Daria, Rusty told me that the Boston Red Squad has a dossier on one of them, a common laborer Rusty said he'd seen with you—apparently you approached him about rebuilding the Lexington house after the fire?"

"He's a very good carpenter," Daria said smiling.

"He's a dangerous person—"

"As for the common laborer, he's skilled, and just how would you have described Pops? And do you remember the Boston Red Squad pestering Grandpa because he was such a dangerous anarchist and played bocce at the old anarchist picnics?"

"Daria, I know you're not involved with this man, but you ought to be careful about your associations."

"Cesaro, I would say the same to you, in spades. How involved are you with Ross's machinations? Cut free of him. I won't warn you again."

Cesaro was silent for a moment. "What do you mean?"

"We both know what I mean."

"Rusty has insurance with me, of course."

"Cesaro, I know you're not cut in in any obvious way, as opposed to Tony who's in over his head. I don't think you've owned anything with them since that perfectly legitimate condo near Chestnut Hill Reservoir. But clean up your act. I'm serious. I care about you. Don't repeat this to Ross."

"I won't. I'm not sure exactly what you're hinting at?"

"Just put distance between you and Ross in your business dealings. Marriage or no, Ross is going down. Don't let him pull you with him."

There was another silence. "You never used to take much interest in Rusty's business."

"That all changed with the divorce, didn't it? I let myself remain ignorant. I was wrong. That was close to immoral."

"I don't see what morality has to do with it."

"If you don't like immorality, try illegality. Cesaro, listen to me."

"What could happen?"

It was her turn to remain silent. She shifted awkwardly in the kitchen chair looking longingly at her simmering rhubarb.

"I shall consider what you have said to me very carefully, Daria. And I would like to see that detective's report. Send it on to me, please."

The assistant attorney general, Bloomberg, assigned to work with SON on the arson case had authorized wiring Lou. The next afternoon Lou had a meeting scheduled with Chuck Petris to explain why he had not managed to set fire to Number 71 and when he would make his next attempt. He was to explain about the patrols and suggest a daytime fire.

Mac was running Lou, as he put it, borrowing his jargon from spy novels. Indeed, both Mac and Lou were acting in a thriller of their own devising. They met in prearranged public places. Lou insisted on seeing Mac daily, for he pinned his faith for a good deal on Mac: the Harvard man would save him. He confided his worries, his troubles, his feelings about his family to Mac.

A deep mutual contempt between Lou and Tom ruled their few interactions. Out loud at SON core meetings, Tom commiserated with Mac for having to deal in such a daily and intimate way with scum; but Daria observed that Mac was enjoying himself. He was putting together a history of what Lou knew about the real estate manipulations of the men he had worked for, prime material for Mac's thesis. It was a symbiotic relationship that seemed equally fascinating to both men. Lou had his own college professor, as he called Mac (ignoring his status as graduate student and instructor) who was interested in his life, his ideas, his struggles. Lou was flattered. What did Mac want? Perhaps he was touching what he thought of as reality, brute reality, proving himself tougher and more streetwise than the working-class people in SON. Lou was Mac's own first-rate informant.

Mac gave them all reports on Lou, daily weather reports, as he stood before them pushing his glasses back on his snub nose, playing with a lock of his own moderately short, moderately curly brown hair, fingers wandering to the bowl of the pipe he was forbidden to smoke at SON meetings. Mac purported to admire what he called the technical brilliance of Lou's arson. In his high-pitched nasal voice he declaimed, "Lou has on call inside his head plans of every building he's ever worked on or burned—"

"What's special about that?" Tom demanded. "Of course you remember your own work."

"When I discuss with him any particular set, he has the uncanny ability to describe precisely how the rooms were laid out, the floor plan, the wall construction, the roofing material. He has total recall on how he arranged that fire. It's a highly developed skill with a methodology he has mastered. He has the brains to apply himself to something better." He looked straight at Tom. "The man doesn't have to be a common electrician or carpenter. He could be an architect, an engineer, not something completely mindless."

"Sure," said Fay. "The way things are going he'll end up a college professor, and we'll have you running around the streets setting fires, you're so gaga about him. So tomorrow's the big day when he's going to tape Petris?"

The next evening in a bar in farthest Brighton where they had arrived separately for a rendezvous in a dark booth, Lou boasted to Mac that he had managed to have an explicit conversation with Chuck Petris. "I got him to dot the i's and cross the t's. He was in a good mood for once. A shitload of money just came through for that North Cambridge development. Listen, man, he mentioned sums for the burning. He chattered about old jobs I did for him. He was talking my head off."

Daria's phone rang within half an hour of Mac's getting home. Mac was in an unusually expansive mood to call her, for she was on the bottom of his private hierarchy of the SON core group. But tonight Mac was a proud papa excited by what his Lou had done.

The following morning Mac rushed to the attorney general's office to listen to the tape. The assistant attorney general, Bloomberg, played what turned out to be strange burbling sounds, static and occasionally Lou sounding like a foghorn or the bellowing plaint of an ocean liner in distress. The other voices consisted of underwater moaning, the subaquean calls of whales.

"The FBI has expertise in taping from witnesses," Mac announced that evening with a bitter grimace. "I don't think those state bozos know how to do it right. Lou and I were keenly disappointed."

Fay made her eyes big. "Unless he screwed up on purpose."

Mac pulled his lower lip between his even white teeth and glared. "You think he's two-timing us?"

"Spy versus spy," Tom said with mock sympathy. "It's dreadful how you can't trust your own double agents these days."

Lou balked at returning to have the same conversation with Petris a second time. "I got to tick off that Number Seventy-one soon," he complained. "They won't trust me anymore if I don't get it done."

The attorney general's office claimed that Lou had used the recorder incorrectly; Lou claimed he had used it just the way they had set it up. Daria wondered if the case would peter out in a fizzle of ineffective technology.

In the cat care book Daria had purchased, it said that cats preferred privacy and darkness for giving birth, a closet, a drawer. Sheba commenced her labor on the kitchen counter between the Robot Coupe and the convection oven, in a large mixing bowl which she had prepared herself on the sly by tearing the morning's *Globe* to shreds along with a couple of pages of Daria's neatly typed manuscript. Sheba lay purring and occasionally giving guttural cries but the first kitten did not begin to appear till after forty minutes of second stage labor, while the three of them were trying to eat supper. That ended any formal meal. Daria ran for the birth box and set it up in the center of the kitchen. Sheba wanted attendants, clearly.

Mariela proudly called Tom, saying his number aloud, as Daria squatted over the birth box making sure the kitten was emerging properly, in this case with the paws extended, just fine. Black. Sheba sniffed with some puzzlement at the slimy wet thing and Daria was afraid she would not know what to do. Then Sheba began licking the membrane, nuzzling and licking to stimulate breathing. The second kitten came quickly, also black. As Sheba leaned to deal with the second, after eating the first placenta, Daria examined the first. Female. Daria remembered from childhood that if you did not sex them when the fur was still wet, it was harder later. The kitten seemed normal, intact, ready to nurse, with ears folded down and eyes closed but the small mouth parting to suck. The first two in their emergent state looked more like little hamsters than cats.

Number two was female, out head first. Sheba was behaving purposefully, severing the cord, eating the afterbirth, cleaning the kitten and herself. "Could that be all?" Daria asked aloud. Sheba lay down with the kittens and stared at everybody, crying out in what Daria could only think of as crowing, but she was still panting. Daria grew nervous, wondering if something was wrong. She feared a stillbirth blocking the canal, or an improper presentation. She was glad when Tom came and went running to hug him; but he had never seen kittens born and was more fascinated than helpful. Daria had her cat care book in the cookbook holder, had gathered the recommended cotton balls, sterilized squares of towel, surgical scissors et cet., but she was nervous. She finished her dinner standing over the box.

"Mariela, don't," Sandra María warned. "They're too frail. You'll upset Sheba. They'll grow fast—be patient. Now you just look at them."

The phone rang. Daria did not think to move and neither did Sandra María, both deep in empathy with the laboring cat. Tom picked it up. "It's Robin."

"Robin?" Daria swung around. "My daughter?" When she took the phone from Tom and spoke, "Robin? Hello. Are you all right?" she heard her voice issuing differently, as if she had a special mother's voice. Perhaps she was merely nervous.

"You didn't even call me about that fire."

"Robin, after the way we parted last, I wasn't about to call you for anything. I was very hurt."

"Well, you can laugh at me now, because it's my turn to be hurt!"

Melodrama was unlike Robin. To Daria's alarm, her stoical daughter began to sob into the phone. "Robin, what is it? What's happened?" When Robin didn't answer she continued, "Do you want to come over here?"

"I don't even know where *here* is. I called home and I got a recording with this number. Then Uncle Cesaro told me you'd had a fire at home."

"Why don't you come over?" She gave instructions. "Sheba, the cat, is having her kittens tonight."

"Sheba the cat?" Robin sounded blank. "Oh, Tracy's cat."

"Actually I think she's more mine now. If she isn't Mariela's."

"Who's Mariela?"

"Just come over, Robin. Thing's are quite different here."

"Mother? I'm sorry." Robin hung up.

It occurred to her that she had just received one of the only apologies Robin had ever made since reaching puberty. Robin had seemed to feel that growing up meant that she never had to say she was sorry, never had to accept blame for anything and that never again would she admit any occurrence was her responsibility. If other people got hurt, that was their fault: that had been her attitude since fourteen.

What was wrong? She would find out soon. Yet she was smiling as she turned back to the corner holding the birth box. Her glance fell on Ali, forgotten, crouching on top of the refrigerator with eyes round and orange as wheels of cheddar cheese. He looked frightened. She realized no one had fed him for hours. She scraped some of the abundant leftovers from supper onto a saucer and handed it up to him. He gobbled all gratefully, still on the refrigerator. To the room in general she announced, "Well, that was my long estranged daughter, Robin, who's on her way over here. Finally."

Tom caught her gaze. "Now I meet this one."

"Or now I meet this one," Daria said. "I haven't seen Robin since Christmas."

"Another's coming." Sandra María announced. "That's a good mamá, come on and bear down." She was gently rubbing Sheba's belly. Sheba was braced against the side of the box. Something wet and slick was beginning to protrude. But it was not black: it was orange with faint tabby bars.

"Well, look at that," Daria said as she examined the newest kitten. "Now how did that one happen? It's a boy, Mrs. Sheba, it's a boy, but whose boy is it?"

"They could have recessive genes for tabby," Sandra María suggested. "If black is dominant."

"I like a scientific answer," Daria said. "I was thinking more about Fox, Annette's cat. Mariela, did you let Fox in?"

"Noooooo," Mariela said. "He came in himself. Through the back door. He opened it."

"I'll bet," Daria said. "Do you think we're done?"

Very, very gently Sandra María rubbed Sheba's belly. "Not so, I think. We have more to come."

"Imagine if we had children like that: four to six at a time, and at four months they're ready to hit the road," Daria said slyly.

Mariela's eyes got very large. "Would I have to leave? Would I go away to college like Tracy?"

"Have we sent kitties out to work?" Sandra María asked, stroking Mariela's black curls. "So the missing daughter comes home?"

"I hate to say this, but you have to be careful. Say nothing about SON. She's her daddy's girl, and she keeps his secrets rather than mine."

"What do you think is wrong?" Tom was making coffee for everybody. "Sylvia's problem? Which does by the way seem certain."

"I doubt that. Not Robin."

He cocked an eyebrow at her. "You don't like to admit your daughters have sex lives. Neither will I, when the time comes."

"Tracy certainly does. But while I'm sure Robin's been to bed with a couple of her male friends, she finds sex gross, as she told me once. She doesn't like anyone quite that close to her. It's too threatening, too messy."

"Don't sound so depressed." Tom put his arm around her. "She's coming to you of her own free will, finally. Can't you enjoy that?"

Daria considered. "Yes. How're we doing in the birthing business?"

"We got another on the way, but we seem to be getting bored with the whole business," Sandra María answered.

Sheba was lying with the three kittens at teat, not rising to help this one out. She looked up at Daria with a piteous interrogative mrew? This one was coming head first but very slowly. When it was finally out, Sheba showed no sign of interest. Perhaps tired of dealing with the first three, she lay still and did not lick the new one. Daria picked it up gently in its slimy wrap and presented it to her. Sheba gave a perfunctory couple of licks. Finally Daria gently ruptured the membrane and was about to present it to Sheba. The last afterbirth was emerging. Sheba slowly ate it. Then she turned to the final kitten as Daria knelt beside her, and ripped its umbilical cord, lying down with all the kittens now at teat. The last one was black, female and something was wrong. Daria bent closely. Its intestines protruded from its naval into a little sac. "Oh, no!" she said softly. "Mariela, would you get me some . . . some rubbing alcohol from my bathroom? Please. It's on the middle shelf."

"I'll get it," Sandra María said.

"Please, *no*," Daria said with emphasis. "Mariela can reach it. Stand on the closed toilet seat."

"Here I go! I can reach it!"

As soon as Mariela left the room, Daria carried the fourth kitten to the sink, ran warm water and held it under. Sandra María watched her horrified, and Tom tried to stop her. "What are you doing?"

"I can't save it," she whispered. "It's not operable. See?" She held out the kitten for an instant and then plunged it under. It was vigorous, unfortunately, but that kind of hernia was lethal. When the kitten finally hung limp under the water, she quickly put it in the garbage before Mariela came back, feeling doubly guilty. That was the birth defect they had feared, although the others seemed healthy and intact. "Don't all look at me that way," she protested. "Its intestines were all hanging out. It couldn't live!"

"Here's the rubbing alcohol," Mariela said proudly. "I know the bottle, right?"

"Actually this is witch hazel, but it's fine. Thank you." Officiously she washed her hands with the witch hazel. Sheba had fallen asleep with her three remaining kittens at teat. Daria hoped she would not realize when she woke that one was missing.

But Mariela could count. She frowned at the box. "What happened to the last kitty? Is it under her?"

"It died, baby," Sandra María said. "But the others are fine."

"It died? Where is it?"

"You don't want to see it," Daria said. "There was something wrong." Taking Mariela gently by the shoulder, she led her to the birth box. "Look at those others feeding! Which do you like best?"

"All of them! Poor Sheba looks wore out," Mariela was kneeling now. "It must be a lot of work."

Robin arrived soon afterward. She stood outside the screen door on the front porch calling plaintively, "Mother? Mother?"

Daria hurried through. "Robin, the door's open!"

"I didn't know if it was the right place." Robin walked in uncertainly, staring around.

In turn Daria drank her in, her lost daughter. Robin's beauty was in her coloring, although what she prided herself on was lack of flesh. Robin had Ross's hair, that bright red-gold, although lighter, finer, and his fair freckling skin; but the shape of her face was all Daria's, as heart-shaped as Daria's mother's. In childhood, Robin had been awkward, but years of athletics had given her a slow almost massive grace. She moved well but as if she were far bigger than she was.

Now Daria could read Robin's lack of ease as she stood first on one foot, than the other. She was still dressed in office clothes, a linen blazer and beige A-line skirt. "There isn't anything from home!"

"Mostly it all burned. But remember the trestle table? It's in the kitchen. There's the little Oriental that used to be in the front hall."

"Where's my camping gear? And my old books? My hockey gear?"

"Lovey, everything was burned. Everything in the basement."

"You don't have any . . . real furniture." Robin was looking around.

"Not yet," Daria said. "It will take a while."

Robin stared at her, her face twitching, jumpy with some hidden emotion. Then she burst out, "Daddy's rich now and you're poor."

Very tentatively she put her hand on her daughter's finely turned shoulder, as if afraid she might bolt. "Divorce is like that." She was moved by Robin's concern and wanted to hug her, but did not dare. "Soon this will be a duplex with the apartment above. The work has actually begun. Now come out to the kitchen—that's the most together room." She led Robin along with an arm gently embracing her back.

"Do you mind terribly living in a neighborhood like this?"

"I rather like it. I have more friends here already than I ever did in Lexington, friends who are mine and not just couples. And the shopping is the best I've had since I lived in Brookline—we're just over the border, actually." With regret, she decided not to rhapsodize over the fish market she had discovered, the Jewish bakery, the butcher, the Oriental food store, the little Turkish shop with eight kinds of caviar and twenty-two kinds of smoked fish, not the palaver to please her anorexic daughter. "Now that I'm not married, it was hard living in Lexington."

"Did people drop you?"

"Sure. They kept waiting for me to sell the house and let some real couple move in."

Robin was frowning. "I guess there are neighborhoods where a single woman is okay and neighborhoods where you make them nervous. I remember when we were apartment hunting . . ." Robin stopped and swung around. "Mother, Daddy didn't even ask me to his wedding. In fact he said it would be a little awkward. That's what he said! It would be a little awkward. Because his ugly wife is just eight years older than I am!" Robin walked into the kitchen still talking, staring at Daria in her outrage. Only then did she look around and take in the bystanders. "Who are these people?" she demanded.

"This is my roommate Sandra María. We started living together back in Lexington. We were burned out together. This is Mariela, her daughter."

Mariela lifted her hand up to shake. "You're Tracy's sister?"

"Tracy's been here?"

"Of course. But not too comfortably. Once we have the upstairs finished, it'll be nicer." She motioned to Tom. "And this is my friend. Tom. Tom Silver."

"Your friend?" Robin stared from one to the other in great puzzlement.

"He's her boyfriend," Mariela said helpfully. "I had to explain to Tracy too. This is my cat Sheba who is a mamá too and she just had babies and one of them died. There was something wrong. The daddy is on the refrigerator."

"Ugh. They look like little wet rats," Robin said.

"Have you had supper?" Daria asked.

Robin dismissed the food still spread on the table with a disdainful wave. "I couldn't eat now."

Sandra María stood with a sigh, unkinking her back. "I have to study now." She made a gesture behind Robin's back at Tom, waving good-bye.

Tom caught the gesture and turned to Daria in appeal. Then he thought better and said, "Here I go. Off to do something or other."

When Sandra María had cleared the kitchen for Daria, packing Mariela off to watch the battered old TV, slow tears began to run down Robin's face. Daria took her by the hand and sat her down. "What's wrong, lovey? You feel your father deserted you?"

Robin nodded. "I thought we were so close! Almost every day we ran together. He said I understood."

Daria handed her a paper napkin. "Did you have a fight with him?"

"No! But he stopped running with me as soon as he, you know, moved out and started living downtown. And I helped him move, and everything! He had one of Gail's pointers she gave him, and he used to call up and ask me to walk the dog for him. I had the key. But I started feeling as if the only times he called were when he wanted me to do something. Pick up his dry cleaning. Run errands for him. Walk his dog. Sign some papers. I don't even like that dog—he isn't a nice friendly doggy like Torte but this nervous thing that drives me crazy. Where is Torte?"

"He's dead, Robin. He died in the fire."

"That's awful! You should have let Daddy take him!"

"I begged Ross to take Torte. He wasn't interested."

"He said you wouldn't let him have Torte."

"Robin, I hate to say it, but he was lying. After Ross moved out, Torte wouldn't eat and he just lay around with his chin on his paws. I thought he'd die of loneliness. . . . But toward the end he was happy again. He adored Mariela."

"Who *are* these people?"

"Friends. Sandra María is a graduate student in public health."

"Everything's so different. Nothing's the way it used to be," Robin said in a tone of sodden despair. She had stopped crying but she sat slumped over the table. "Why did everything have to change?"

She felt like telling Robin that she was one of those who had encouraged Ross to change everything, but she bit back the words. "When you were saying he kept asking you to do favors, you mentioned signing papers?"

"Yeah, you know Daddy. Always lots of paperwork."

"But what kinds?"

Robin looked at her as if she had asked something totally rude. "How should I know? Daddy always has papers we witness, that kind of stuff."

"It wouldn't be some buildings he put in your name?"

"He does that. You know. It doesn't mean anything."

"Was he putting them in your name or taking them out?"

"I don't know, Mother, I never read that crap!" Robin scowled. Then she said reluctantly, "I think taking them out, because he said something about not wanting to worry me, which I thought was a big joke, because why should I worry about a bunch of papers? I remember seeing Gail's name on one of those things. Her maiden name, even though they had just got married and I was still angry about not being invited."

"Do you like Gail? How do you get on with her?"

"She talks about her dogs. But otherwise, it's all her dismal therapist. Her bitchy sisters. A bunch of people I don't know. What this one has that she doesn't have."

"Did you try to make friends with her?"

"I haven't seen her that much. Who would have thought Daddy would marry her? She's a physical wreck! He went on about how he needed independence and all the things he wanted to do. We were going to go places we'd both dreamed about. Then practically the day he got divorced, he got married again!"

"But, Robin, that's why he wanted the divorce. Didn't you know that? He's been involved with Gail since last summer at least."

"But . . . she isn't anybody! I tried so hard to please him! I've always been bringing him home trophies. Do you know how few women are in that executive training program? And then *her*—she doesn't do anything! She doesn't even have a job. She's nothing."

"She's rich."

"No, she isn't. Her family is rich. All she has is some income from a couple of trust funds. The dogs lose money. The rest she has to beg from her father or her uncle. I've heard her complaining about it." Robin blew her nose hard. "We were going to go skiing in Switzerland, that's what he said. Now he's moved into her house out there in Hamilton and if I call up, he has this tone of voice and he says, *What is it,* Robin? As if there had to be something major wrong for me to bother him." Robin got up and paced to the window, staring out blindly. "I suppose you hate me now?"

Daria pondered her answer. "To me you're still my baby, the child I raised. How could I hate you? I've been very hurt."

"You had Tracy."

"But I used to have both of you."

"It was so special with Daddy! When we ran together, I'd feel so proud. When people saw us, they knew we were father and daughter. How could he forget me so fast?"

"Robin, you and your father had a special closeness. Maybe you'll have it again, but I have no relationship with Ross anymore at all. I don't even have respect for him." She stared at her daughter, wondering how much she could tell her. She feared to presume too much tonight. "What you have to figure out with me is not how to get close to your father again, because that's none of my business. What you must work out with me, is how to be closer to me. How we can love each other."

Robin seemed embarrassed. Her cheeks flushed, she peered into the box of kittens as if expecting some answer from them. "How come you live with all these people? To pay the rent?"

"I own this building. I could live in the bottom apartment without going to the trouble and cost of making it a duplex and giving up the rent on the second floor. I like this arrangement."

"But you were happy the way things were. At least you acted happy."

"I don't think depression is a virtue. But everybody changes. Your father has changed incredibly."

She could feel Robin's gaze, a mixture of appalled curiosity and distress. "Daddy was always changing. He was up and down. He'd go in and come out like the sun. But you were always my mother. You were always the same."

Mac deigned to tell Daria, although at the core meeting rather than privately as she would have preferred, more of the hidden side of her family history as told by Lou. "Tony's the pivot. He's the one with the experience. He and Bernard, your uncle—"

"Barney, not Bernard." Mac was enjoying exposing her family to the group. She had not thought of her uncle Barney in years, an enormous man who had tried briefly to make it as a fighter and then worked as a bouncer down in a Combat Zone girlie club, a homely man with a big family, an overstuffed wife Amelia whom he adored, and big floppy white pet rabbits.

"They burned some restaurant another brother had in Salem—"

"Revere." What right had Mac to this ancient gossip? If Joe and Barney had burned that failing business, they hadn't hurt anybody. She felt defiant, her family raked back and forth across Mac's shiny mind. No tenants, no victims; and Joe had taken the money and followed her parents down to Florida.

"Because it was losing money. Your uncle asked the bartender to set the fire—pretending it came from emptying ashtrays into the trash. That gave Tony the idea later to hire some high school acquaintance from East Boston to torch the property you all owned there."

"So Patsy was right." Daria lost track of what Mac was saying, off on a fantasy of making all up to Patsy, turning the parking lot into a park. She had forgotten the parking lot in her settlement. She felt ashamed.

When she tuned back in, Mac was saying, "So Tony hired Lou to rewire that twenties-vintage fake Tudor he's living in, and a great association was born. Lou thinks they started burning earlier but they were using some kind of inferior talent. Lou had already burned several of his own buildings. The first building he torched for hire was one Tony and Ross owned in a section of Dorchester they'd expected to gentrify, but hadn't."

370

"Can we prove any of this?" Fay asked sharply. "Or is this all gossip?"

The sad consensus was that it was only Lou, with a police record, against the worthy well-connected developers. In his hospital greens, Elroy looked weary and not at all dapper. He sighed, speaking for them all. "I don't know. We been trying and trying. Still they pick us off. And we can't get out of the corner to land one solid blow."

Just before finals, Tracy did come home for a visit, at last. The floors were refinished upstairs and Sandra María had painted her own new room and moved in. Tracy's room downstairs was set up with the four-poster she had wanted and her old marble-topped dresser and her old stenciled chest. Daria had painted the walls the same peach color Tracy had selected for Daria's old office. She wanted it to be fixed up, totally the opposite experience of Tracy's last visit.

Tracy was openly astonished. "My room is super," she bubbled. "But the living room—when are we getting a real couch?"

"Soon, soon. Tracy, you sew much better than I can. Could you make curtains when you come home? The sewing machine survived the fire."

Mariela claimed Tracy and dragged her off to see, first the kittens, who were just opening round blue eyes. Then Mariela took Tracy on a grand tour, followed by an amused Daria. The back stairway was unusable so they had to go out the front door, up the steps and in the front door of the second story apartment. Daria had not moved yet, because it was still too noisy for her to work upstairs.

"This is going to be Daria's room," Mariela announced, swinging open the new door that had been installed to close off the former living room.

"Mama, you have the biggest room in the house."

"And why not? I'm the biggest woman in the house."

"This is Mamá's room. The walls are the color of my doll baby's hair who got killed in the fire." Mariela swung that door wide also. Sandra María's family had bought her a new bed. Her room was beginning to come together, like the house.

Daria watched Mariela closely. Night after night Sandra María and Daria met at her bedside, awakened at twelve, at two, at four by her screaming. She seemed to be collecting instances of death. Torte had died, Mr. Rogers the hamster had died, the baby kitten had died: would she die soon? she asked each of them daily.

"This room in between is going to be your mamá's office." Mariela opened that door, and then the one on the bedroom over the dining room. "And this is going to be Tom's room."

"Where did you get that idea?" Daria challenged her.

"He told me so."

"Mariela, he was teasing you." Daria glanced at Tracy.

"No, he wasn't." Mariela folded her arms, imitating Sandra María when she was laying down the law. "He said this is going to be his room and Marcus is going to live here too. So there."

Daria laughed a little hysterically. "This is all news to me!"

"Mama, he can't move in on you if you don't want him to," Tracy said indignantly. "You speak to him!"

"But I'm by no means sure I don't want him to," Daria said slowly.

"But, Mama!"

"Tracy, nothing will happen without a great deal of talking, believe me." As Mariela continued the tour, Daria hung back. To live with a man again, sharing decisions and chores and projects; but without sealing themselves hermetically into a couple. She could not resist wanting Tom there mornings, nights, weekends, casually there when she slept and when she woke, when she went on trips and when she returned. But she had learned how fragile the strongest ties could be. The closer someone came, the more he could hurt her and the larger the swath his going cut through her life. She wanted but equally she feared.

372

27

"CHICKEN with kiwi fruit. Sole with kiwi fruit—they mean flounder, of course. Salad of romaine, orange segments and kiwi fruit. Kiwi custard. Kiwi ice cream. It drives me insane!" Daria was crisscrossing her new bedroom tossing her clothing off as she paced. Tom lay on the enormous bed he had built for her, watching with a half smile. "It isn't that I don't enjoy the sweet morsels, but it's pure fad." Her blouse landed on the chair in front of her vanity. It had a greenish kiwi stain on the mauve silk, she noticed. "When I started off, it was truffles. That was how you made a dish elegant—truffled ham. Pheasant with truffles. Sole with white truffles." Her slip sailed after the blouse.

"How can you sit down and eat twelve meals?" He lay in tank top and khaki pants, his massive arms cocked behind his head.

"I just have about two bites." She sat down to get rid of her panty hose.

"And they all stand about and watch you eat, trying to judge the degree of your ecstasy by your expression?"

"If it's a teaching format, you comment aloud as you go. When it's a formal and even elegantly presented format like today, you keep a stiff face and write your comments. I'm cooked myself, anyhow. It's so humid!"

"If you're hot, why not turn on the air conditioner?"

"Air conditioner?" She swung back around. "What are you—" She saw it in the wall and ran to it.

"With the door open to your study, it'll cool both rooms. I didn't even have to buy the box. It was in the basement, ready to install in the wall. All I had to get was the air conditioner."

"I'm too sweaty to kiss you, even. Wait till I'm back from the shower."

"Do I look like I'm going anyplace? Nobody's home but us for once. We have the whole house to ourselves."

She had not said anything about an air conditioner, she hadn't even thought about one yet, and he had anticipated her need. She felt grateful, and gratitude for Daria was a sexy emotion. She liked being the one who brought back stories sometimes, who could carry home excitement and anecdotes without feeling guilty. Never with Ross had she felt equal. Why would the sense of equality with Tom free up her sexuality? She did not know why, although she could formulate many guesses as the freshening stream poured over her and washed away the sweat and cooking odors and sense of having been immersed to her neck in overrich sauces.

When she came back to her room, she was quick with energy, almost tormented by it: too much rich food in the middle of the day had made her drowsy at first. Now, thoroughly digested, it made her jumpy, over-energized. Something about Tom waiting for her was exciting. Whether he finally moved in or didn't, she wanted to keep this sense of herself as a separate active private person: not to live in the relationship as if in a house; not to refer whatever she did to him for approval or disapproval, for commendation or rejection.

She threw herself on top of him and made love, carried along by her energy. Between them was an ease in bed that she found excited her immensely. If she thought of something, such an impulse as she was experiencing now, she could try it out without dire punishment if her impulse did not ignite him. Firmly she held his hands above his head. Of course he was stronger than she, but the play force of the gesture seemed to excite him also. She faced over his body the massive headboard he had carved with crescent moons. Then she straddled him and kissed him from earlobe to hollow of throat, from the plum nipples with their surrounding aureoles of silky black hair down the slopes of his belly. Her fingers kneaded the great muscles of his thighs until she tantalized his standing purplish headed prick with her hair, with the caresses of her hanging breasts, the lightest brush of her lips, the faintest pressure of her teeth, before she let loose his hands and mounted him. A sense of permission between them allowed them to play. She had the sense of rediscovering some pleasure lost since childhood; sometimes she felt as if they were going deep into wordless mammalian physicality, the sense of good earthy body meeting good earthy body.

She dozed off in the crook of his arm and did not waken till twilight.

A door had been cut through one wall of Daria's new bedroom into the next room, now her office. Peggy was set up there with the files, a new cassette player for dictation with a foot pedal and headphone. Daria used the small recorder she carried in her purse more and more for notes, for letters, for travel and work-related expenses. She was far busier than she had been. Peggy was just finishing the manuscript while Daria had begun work on the mother-child book. She had become harder in her bargaining, for suddenly it all mattered far, far more.

In the past she had tended to turn down work that involved being out evenings, for she had not only to warn Ross far in advance but to arrange for Annette to feed him if he did not wangle a dinner invitation elsewhere. When her publisher put pressure on her to do an out-of-town gig, she cooked all his meals before she left and froze them. All the time Ross was running to the city the August before to make happy rendezvous with Gail, she was getting up at five-thirty to cook his supper and send it along in a picnic basket. What had he done with all those meals? Dumped them in some service station garbage can? But never had he been less than insistent on his due: a dinner from her cooked every night of his life. It would never occur to her to cook and freeze a meal for Tom before taking off for Philadelphia or Houston. He was a functioning adult; he could feed himself.

Her new bedroom, enormous and well lit by the bay window, was dominated by the huge bed Tom had built with its massive carved headboard. A shelf ran high above the cushions she had heaped there. On the floor was a six-by-nine, red-and-blue Hamadan carpet Cesaro had given her as a making up present, she suspected. Cesaro had become quite friendly again. "I have taken your advice to heart," he told her when he delivered the rug. "Rusty's accounts are with another agent. I have even reopened a previous inquiry into one of his old claims. . . . Your detective struck me as quite competent."

Tracy, home after finals, studied Daria's room with a touch of envy, as if in its deep golds and tones of scarlet, she read some possibility that had previously escaped her. "It doesn't look like your old room, Mama. That was light and airy . . . clean."

"Austere." Daria smiled.

The back stairway was still unusable. The former second floor kitchen was a general lumber room, full of tools, boards and sawdust. Her former bedroom downstairs was in the process of having a wall knocked down. All the bedrooms, however, were in order and kept their occupants busy improving them—all but the room that Tom might or might not move into, which stood with its door open like a question that asked itself whenever she walked along the central hall.

Endlessly they discussed his moving in; both flopped back and forth. It would be good for their relationship; it would be bad. They would become closer; they would fight more. His daughters would be upset; her daughters would be upset. It would be good for all their offspring. A few hot days reminded Daria that summer was coming and that meant the arrival in August of Tom's daughters. Sandra María was scheduled to get her degree in two weeks and after a short vacation would begin work with a VD clinic.

A couple of times Robin ate with them—or at least sat picking cautiously at the food. Robin was nervous with Daria's extended family, but she was also feeling lonely. One roommate was moving out to live with her boyfriend. The other had a steady friend with whom she spent many nights. Robin was shy with Daria, as if she had come to a decision that she did not know her mother as well as she had thought. Robin's tentativeness wounded Daria at first, but now she was reconciled to it, certainly an improvement on the open contempt that Robin had taken pains to act out toward her.

"But you and Tracy were always in the kitchen cooking up things,

376

talking about everybody, always so thick. If I came in, I'd just do things wrong."

"You were so impatient of mistakes, at least that's how it felt to me. If you didn't do something right the first time, you'd get angry." She rested her hand on Robin's shoulder. "Remember, I was as young as you are now when I had you. Almost exactly. And I was less mature at my age than you are—more naive, less experienced. I made a lot of errors. I wasn't so smart, then."

"My age?" Robin was struck by that. "And you had a baby. Why?"

"You know. I got pregnant and Ross wanted a baby. It seemed like a big adventure to me too."

"A boy. He wanted a boy," Robin said with her new bitterness. "Now he's got a whole new crack at it."

"You think they'll have children?"

"Mother! Didn't you know? Gail's pregnant."

She found she could not say anything. She felt kicked, kicked hard in the belly. Perhaps her womb contracted convulsively. She could only shake her head dumbly.

"I assume she was knocked up beforehand," Robin said sourly. "Isn't that his pattern? I think it's tacky. A baby at his age. I don't need a baby sister or baby brother. I think it's gross."

Automatic mothering came to her rescue. "I hope you didn't say all this to your father?"

"Why not? If he wants to make a fool of himself, why should I pretend? Gail's so used to training dogs, she'll probably walk it on a leash and train it to go after birds."

Robin was the only person she knew who was as ill-wishing about Ross's affairs as she was, because they had both been left. She had been left sooner; Robin had been abandoned the more recently. Tracy had been getting along so painfully with her father that perhaps she cared a shade less.

Tracy and Robin at first avoided each other, but just this weekend, Daria had noticed them willing to exchange information. Tracy was job hunting and returned home exhausted and depressed. She spent a lot of time with her boyfriend, and when she was home, she fussed over Mariela and the kittens, who were just beginning to venture from the box. Tracy lettered large signs in red Magic Marker on all the doors: WARNING IMPORTANT DO NOT STEP ON TINY TINY KITTENS OR LET THEM OUT. Daria and Tracy were sewing curtains and draperies together. Daria was trying to understand her daughter's attitude toward her boyfriend Scott: she did not seem passionately in love with him, as she had been with Nick, but she seemed intently interested. Daria was puzzled but did not want to pry too hard. Tracy had a great deal to become accustomed to this summer.

Sunday was the SON picnic and softball game in Ringer Park. The night before, Daria had made her special cold lemon chicken in vast quantities. Tom had made his hummus and his three-bean salad. As they woke in the morning, Tom hauled himself up and parted the curtains in fearful expectation: the sky was a hazy blue. Tracy went off to the beach with Scott, but Robin, surprisingly, came with her special bat and her old mitt.

With Tracy, Tom felt at ease. To please Tracy, he had only to listen; thus he had quickly become her confidant. She loved having a man to share her dates, her traumas, her misadventures. She could flirt with Tom in total safety. She could require from him the inside track on what men thought and felt, as if they were all of one mind. "Why do men want their friends to like you, but get mad when they do?" "Why do men insist on driving, even when they can't see straight?" Tom was better for Tracy than Ross had been in years. Daria could relax her defense of her daughter and coexist more gently.

Tom was slower to figure out how to interact successfully with Robin, but lately he had been showing her the work on the house in far greater detail than Daria would ever be willing to absorb. He had grown up around water, so Robin and he were planning to rent a sailboat to take out on the Charles the next weekend. He played backgammon in the evenings when Robin came to supper. Daria had not been aware either of them knew the game. "Mother! Everybody knows how to play backgammon," Robin said with something of her old scorn. Tom said his playing dated from the last year of his marriage, when Andy and he had

378

been searching for things they could do together that would not emphasize their difficulty in talking. Daria considered his being willing to play the game with Robin a gesture of immense goodwill.

They arrived early at Ringer Park—a rangy park crowning their hill between the various local institutions, the Jackson-Mann School, the boys' club, the hospitals. The local streets tended to run up to it and end. It did not offer the long view that Summit Park across Commonwealth spread out, where sometimes she and Tom, or the four of them with Mariela strolled on a mild evening. Sometimes when they were walking, she missed Torte freshly.

Ringer Park was a neighborhood possession, one side sloping down to the athletic field outside the school Mariela was again attending, enormous, redbrick and aluminum. The outfield was busy with pigeons and blackbirds, flapping up in great whistling flocks every time they were disturbed. The SON picnic was up on the hill, not all the way on the rocky crown where trees grew thickly but on the high grassy plateau, a tree or two for shade but plenty of space to spread out blankets. Already people were milling around, throwing Frisbees, sampling each other's provisions, admiring babies, tossing a ball around in anticipation of the SON softball game scheduled to start at one. The SON softball games were held Sunday afternoons, composed of teams varying in size from six to twenty players of ages ten to seventy. The two teams, the reds and the greens, were sorted out by means she had never identified, but Tom was always catcher for the reds.

It was hot for early June. Elroy, resplendent in white, the leanest, most elegant dandy on the hill, told Daria how pretty her sundress was. Tracy had picked it out. Tracy had taken over selecting Daria's clothes. Sylvia was glaring at Orlando as she sat on a blanket with her mother and younger sister. She refused to get an abortion and Orlando had dropped her. Now he was ostentatiously ignoring her, hanging around with a group of young people drinking beer. Tom was watching both of them, but when she asked him what he was thinking, he told her he was thinking of teaching Sylvia carpentry if she wanted to learn. "You feel responsible for them?"

Tom nodded. "In a way. I'll help her through it somehow."

Fay's son Johnny lay in the grass with his ghetto box against his ear, withering the green for a quarter mile. Fay called after Daria, "Hey, I hear Tom built you a bed big as a dance floor."

"She has standards to keep up," Sherry said, pale and undersea-looking as she hung limply over the back of her mother's wheelchair. Tom and Elroy had carried up Mrs. Sheehan and Mrs. Schulman, and then their chairs. "Lexington has come to Allston, ha!"

Being happily a food snob, she stuck to her own food and Tom's. Wearing a sundress and sitting in a patch of shade, nonetheless she was hot. She was not tempted by Fay's chicken salad, partially because she had contempt for anything made with commercial so-called mayonnaise with its sickly flavor, and partially because she had told Fay she was making her lemon chicken in great quantity and was annoyed that Fay had gone ahead with her own chicken dish, in equally great quantity. She did have a bite of Mrs. Schulman's challah, eggier than she was used to and braided in a circle. That was good, and she offered her compliments to the old woman in her wheelchair and at length extracted the recipe, writing it on a paper plate. Mrs. Schulman must knead the dough on a board across the arms of the chair. She avoided Sherry's hot dogs and potato salad, sure Sherry might be tempted to poison her.

The ball game went on forever. Robin singled to right in the second inning and had a home run in the fifth. She popped out to Mac in the seventh, but in that interminable inning, after Johnny hit a home run with two on, when Robin came up for the second time, she had slammed another line drive and brought Ángel in for a run.

It was midevening when everybody except Daria and Robin started throwing up. She was too frantic to think of calling anyone, when her phone rang. It was Mac. "I'm dying. We've been poisoned!"

Daria said pityingly, "I think it was the mayonnaise." Her old enemy. It could have been that potato salad, but she would bet it was Fay's chicken.

Nobody died or even went to the hospital, but everyone they knew was sick all night. It was fortunate they were controlling Lou, she thought, for the whole neighborhood could have been set afire. The next morning Mac called again. He was still sick and going over to Harvard Health; but he had an appointment with Lou at eleven. He had called everyone else in the SON core group. Those who had recovered sufficiently were at work and everybody else was in bed, as were Tom, Sandra María, Mariela and even Ángel, who was in Tracy's room laid out like a corpse, as if to move would bring back the frenzied vomiting.

Daria was annoyed to find out she had to meet Lou in a bar. She had never entered a bar alone in her life. She brought a large book to read and dressed drably. Nonetheless she walked past the entrance to Scanlon's twice before darting in.

At eleven the bar was mostly empty. The few patrons were at the bar itself, except for one old gentleman who sat nursing a hangover in a booth at the back, looking through the want ads of the *Globe* spread out on the scarred wood. She sat in the second booth, facing the door. When the bartender very leisurely came over, she said, "I'm waiting for a friend. Could I just have a cup of coffee?"

"Sure," he said amiably. "Regular or black?" He brought the coffee and left her alone with her review cookbook *Gladys Vandermeer's Stunning Desserts*. Daria considered that Gladys had a way of taking a simple and rather pure dish and tarting it up with elaboration that preened for the eye but confused the other senses. She always imagined Gladys's books aimed at women who would hand them to the cook and say, "Make twenty of that." Crème fraîche on everything this time, never mind the sour muck that usually resulted.

She forgot to look up. When she remembered, there was Lou loitering inside the door, about to take a place in another booth. "Lou!" she called.

He jumped, then came uncertainly forward. "Oh, Silver's lady. Mrs. Walker. What are you doing here?"

"Mac's sick in bed with food poisoning."

"Yeah? He going to be okay? I had an uncle died of that."

She was puzzled by how to speak to him, this man who had burned her house but to whom she was now linked in the pursuit of justice. "Mac will be fine by tomorrow."

"It was a lemon meringue pie did for my uncle. They look like something that could make you sick, all yellow." Lou ordered a draft beer and a hamburger. "I thought maybe you came to heft another brick at me, Mrs. Walker." He held up his bandaged hand. He was in his work clothes, jeans and a faded green tee shirt.

"I hope it doesn't hurt," she said politely, feeling ludicrous.

"I'm supposed to see Petris tomorrow. He's going to be teed off with me." Lou shook his long head self-pityingly.

"Tell him the patrols are still in force."

"Yeah, but I got to come up with something. He'll hire other talent."

"They're going to wire you again?"

Lou nodded morosely, patting his moustache with a paper napkin. "It wasn't my fault. I did what they told me. How many times I got to go through this?"

"I hope it works! Be careful to let Chuck Petris take the lead. If you suggest too much, it may be entrapment."

"Yeah, the assistant AG Bloomberg went on about that. But I got nothing to suggest anyhow. What am I going to tell him? He's getting antsy."

"So let him get antsy out loud." Daria had finished her coffee. In the mood of the rendezvous, feeling reckless, she ordered a beer—at eleven-thirty in the morning. In an offhand way, she was proud of herself. "After he's insisted enough, why not say you have this plan: you'll start a diversionary fire in the next street. Does he have a particular target he'd like hit? While the patrols are off watching that fire, you can set the other."

Lou finished his hamburger and sat tapping the plastic ketchup bottle, considering. "A mite risky, Mrs. Walker. You have to set up two fires. Some people might not go see the other. You have to haul all that kerosene around . . ."

"But would he buy it as an idea?"

"I'll knock it into shape." Lou waved his good hand dismissively and summoned another hamburger and another beer. "And I thought when I agreed with you people to talk to the AG, that would be that."

"They claim it doesn't make a good case. With you being offered a deal it's just your word against theirs. But if you have them on tape, they can't say you're lying."

"Well, if a jury won't believe me, Mrs. Walker, maybe they'll believe you in court." Lou grinned into his moustache, looking at her slyly from wide open light brown eyes.

"What do you mean?"

"You'll have to testify. Naturally." He was enjoying himself.

"Me? I can't testify against my husband. My ex-husband."

"Sure you can. You can testify against a husband, if you want to. They just can't make you. But they're sure going to subpoena you to be a witness against your ex, better believe it."

She was horrified. It had never occurred to her she would have to stand up publicly and relate all the details of her surveillance of Ross. She simply could not do it. She would explain to the AG. Then she pictured those busy extremely political men and she tried to imagine explaining anything personal. They could not ask that of her, they could not.

She realized Lou was speaking, sitting across from her aligning the hairs of his moustache with his finger and thumb as he asked, "So is Tony really your brother, Mrs. Walker?"

"He used to be. We're not speaking. He divorced me when Walker did."

"Tony's got class." Lou said. "I think Rusty envies him. Tony got a new wife and a baby, now your husband's trying the same thing. Only Tony's wife is a real fox. Whereas Rusty's new wife walks around like *Night of the Living Dead.* You know that movie? I see it sometimes when I'm killing time till I can do a set. They always put it on at midnight."

She was amused at the notion of Ross trying to keep up with Tony. Ross's eyes were fixed more on the Petrises, or perhaps on the Abbot-Wisbys themselves. "When did you meet Gail?"

"I know Rolly, her old man. I'm not lowlife, for all you people think. I'm a businessman. Sometimes they have properties they foreclosed on, they're stuck with. They give me a deal, a good mortgage. I take them on and I get them their money back one way or the other."

"You mean you rehab or burn—how does that help the bank?"

"They get their money out either way. The insurance company pays them before I touch a penny."

"You worked first for Tony, didn't you?"

"It isn't like I work for them. It's like I'm a consultant, Mrs. Walker, a specialist. I come in with my expertise to do a job, the way Mac says. Sure I work for Tony. In fact this week I'm doing a little piece for him."

She felt a spasm of fear, something spinning loose in her chest. "Oh yeah?" she asked casually, she hoped. "Tony's into the neighborhood just as heavy as Walker."

"Not in Allston! You think I wouldn't tell Mac if Tony was paying me to torch something in you guys' yard? No, not to worry. It's some spades in Dorchester. Off of Washington, near Girls' Latin."

"Tony has property in Dorchester?"

"Him and Rusty bought in there. Now they're getting out. It didn't turn the way they thought it would. You know, you win some, you lose some."

"Did you happen to mention this to Mac? Because I know he'd be fascinated."

"You think he'd want to come along? I can't use that kid Jay Jay anymore."

"Ask Mac." She tried to understand Lou: he was their tool now so he would not burn them, but it was asking a painter not to paint, an auto mechanic to lay down his tools, to expect Lou to abandon the arson business so quickly and blithely. She had a sour moment when she wondered if Mac would in fascination go along, but she knew she was libeling him.

When she was alone, she called the AG's office immediately and left a message for Bloomberg to call her back. In a couple of hours, she tried again. This time she told the secretary it was important. Finally at four-thirty when she called back, she was put on hold. She sat fuming while Peggy left and Tracy straggled in from job hunting and Sandra María came in with Mariela, toasty brown from a day out at Plum Island, and still Daria was holding the phone.

When Bloomberg, the assistant attorney general assigned to them, finally picked up the phone, he did not remember at first who Daria was. Of course. It took her five minutes to establish the situation, and all the while she felt as if rivulets of electric impatience were streaming through the phone. Bloomberg had a deep voice and he spoke as if addressing a crowd; she held out the phone away from her ear when he boomed replies to her. She had never seen him but imagined him as an ex-football end. When Bloomberg grasped what she was reporting about her talk with Lou, his reaction was succinct. "Shit," said Bloomberg.

"My sentiments, exactly. When he comes in with the Petris tape, maybe you could explain to him that arson counts in other neighborhoods too?"

"Your brother?" Bloomberg said after a pause. His voice was gentler.

"My brother. He kills by remote control."

"A by-product. We do have two possible murder charges in this matter. One, that kid. Two, the other body, never identified."

"Never? How could that be? I assume nobody cared up to this point."

"Mrs. Walker, you haven't looked at burn victims. It could even have been the arsonist. A hazard of the trade."

"I guess Lou's too skillful to be in danger."

"He thinks so. Let's see if he can manage a miniature mike and recorder this time."

28

At the moment Daria's family was in the confusing and overextended position of having two gardens some miles apart: the garden Sandra María and Daria had put in in Lexington, for spring crops—better prepared and with superior soil but overgrown with weeds—and the new garden in Allston, hastily dug but regularly weeded and watered, containing warm weather crops just coming into their own. Daria had gradually moved her day lilies; she was digging spring bulbs as the foliage browned. She was alarmed, then, when she received a phone call from Dorothy telling her that Ross was in the throes of selling the Lexington property to a builder who meant to demolish the old house at once, salvaging what he could, and erect a new house on the lot. Ross said if she came to Dorothy's office to sign the sales agreement that afternoon, he would write a check for the rest of the insurance money to the Allston Savings and Loan toward paying off the mortgage on Fay's building.

"I advise you to sign," Dorothy said. "It's proving hard to get the money out of him. This beats taking him to court for it."

Daria trekked down to sign. Dorothy waited for word from the bank that the check was deposited and then sent the papers back by messenger, and the arrangement was consummated.

The next morning, Daria left Peggy dictated instructions for the day's work and rushed to Lexington. If a builder was commencing at once, she had to dig what she could. She had borrowed Tom's van for the day. If she dug the rosebushes with enough soil on the roots, she might be able to save them. She was also horrified at the idea of leaving Nina's ashes in the yard of some new split-level. She had bought a dozen tall plastic buckets used for tofu from the health food store. She wished she could wait for the weekend, when she would have assistance, but she did not dare delay. A wrecking crew could arrive any moment, ending her opportunity.

She had come over often enough to the garden to make her practiced in ignoring the house. Today, however, as she pulled up, the doors of the still intact garage were open and Ross's Mercedes parked inside. Damn it. She considered simply driving off, but she could not abandon Nina's ashes. She sat in Tom's van staring morosely at the house. If at least one of her friends were with her, she would feel stronger. Meeting Ross was always an ordeal, but she could not allow him to thwart her. Knowing she was invisible in the van, she combed her hair and freshened her lipstick. Then tossing her leather feedbag purse over her shoulder, she got a shovel and the first several tofu buckets from the back of the van.

She began at one end of the rose bed with Frau Karl Druschki, a beautiful white hybrid perpetual with two of her flowers open, extremely vulnerable. She worked hard and steadily and within an hour had dug the last rose, Mr. Lincoln. She wished the hose were connected so that she could soak them before loading, but they would have to survive as they were, budded already. Fortunately the day was overcast, had drizzled, might again, an even oyster grey clammy and cool enough so that she was wearing a light jacket. Back in Allston the holes were dug and filled with manure, peat, and compost made in Lexington and moved a month before.

When she had finished, the empty bed yawned, a hole big enough for a grave although not as deep as they were traditionally dug. She sat in the grass grown tall and neglected, brooding on the trench. She saw Nina in the kitchen of the East Boston house, pushing her coppery brown hair back with her left hand as she stirred a sauce with her right, tasting, an expression of sensual concentration Daria could easily identify with.

She was so startled when Ross spoke—momentarily she had forgotten him—that she had to ask him to repeat, reluctantly rising and turning to face the house. He stood in the door to the kitchen. From the back the house looked almost intact. From the street, anyone could see that part of the roof was missing and the scorch marks were evident; but this side could almost fool the eye, except for the boarded-up windows and French doors.

"I asked if you were going to leave that gaping hole?"

She had forgotten how resonant and carrying his voice was. She must answer him. She could not, as she wished, simply turn her back. "The builders will make a mess anyhow. There won't be any landscaping left by the time they finish demolishing this and putting up a new house."

"I suppose you're right," he said reluctantly. A new highly polished leather attaché case leaned against his calf like a faithful dog. "What are you doing?"

"Digging up my mother."

"Oh." He shifted in the doorway. He seemed smaller to her than he had in the past. Perhaps she was used to Tom's size. Perhaps she merely experienced him as shrunken in stature. "An excellent idea. Can't have someone turning up bits of human bone. . . . Are you really planning to live in my house in Allston?"

"It's mine now." There was something rodentlike about the way he moved, in short rapid jerks. Surely his eyes had not used to bulge slightly. High blood pressure?

"That's beside the point. Why are you living there?"

"I like it. Why are you living in Hamilton?" She felt absurd bellowing at him from twenty feet, and besides, she saw Annette at her window peeking out. She picked up her purse and walked over.

"Why wouldn't anyone live in Hamilton, if they could? I presume you know I married Gail."

She felt weary of the exchange. "Sure. What are you doing here today? They say the criminal always returns to the scene of his crime."

"I had to leave you! Can't you see that yet? I was being smothered. I was choking to death."

"Actually I meant the arson. You know we have the proof."

"What you call proof is a matter of circumstantial evidence, and has only to do with whether or not arson was committed, not whether I committed it."

"As a lawyer, you know that evidence for arson is always circumstantial. And the usual proof of intent involves motive, as well as opportunity."

They stepped into the sad kitchen. All the old cabinets were present but everything else had been ripped out and hauled to Allston. She could sense in him a great eagerness to talk. She felt some fear at being alone with him, but Annette had seen them together and Ross was not a violent man. He could hire violence, but she could not imagine him performing it. Now he had her where he had wanted for months to get her, forced to listen to him, without lawyer, without friends. He was going to justify himself, she guessed. Casually she dropped her hand into her purse and discreetly fumbled with the buttons until she depressed record and play simultaneously. The little cassette recorder was quiet and would continue recording for half an hour. She could halt it by touching the pause button on the top.

"You don't understand! Gail is going to have a baby."

"That's your usual pattern—"

"It would have killed her," he rushed on over her interruption, "simply destroyed her, to have an abortion. We had to be married at once. She's a fragile, gentle woman, very sheltered. Vulgarity, brutality, scandal, noise, those things aren't something she just sloughs off."

"You're saying you tried to have me killed because Gail would be distressed to find herself pregnant out of wedlock?"

"You have a hard side to you, Daria. How can you imagine I tried to kill you?"

"You had . . . your arsonist disconnect the smoke alarms."

"I know nothing about what went on that night."

"How would he have known where they were—in the dark—if he wasn't following your instructions? No, you meant to kill me."

"Look at you. You're healthy as a cow. You needed the cash out of the house too, but you were being vindictive and holding me up." He glared around, his blue eyes glinting scorn. "You insisted on living in this pile."

"You hated the house," she said with abrupt insight. "You actually wanted to destroy it. It wasn't just for money."

"This ancient relic, sucking up money like a big yellow sponge!"

She sat down as comfortably as she could on the floor. The kitchen still smelled burnt, giving her a slight headache. "The house was too big and

I was too fat. The house was too old and I was too old. Both were too demanding—fascinating."

"Spare me the analysis. You forced me into it, Daria. You woudn't give me a divorce on terms I could live with, and you wouldn't put this monster on the market."

"Didn't get much out of your fire, did you?"

"Everything's sorted out. I'm refinanced, and although I'm hurting for the money you held me up for, I'm on a sound footing again."

"The pattern is interesting. I was pregnant, you were sure it was a son, and you insisted on saving me. Now Gail's pregnant, I'll bet you're convinced it's a son, and you're saving her."

"She's a sensitive person and she needs me. Far more than you had for years and years," he said with bitter resonance, facing her and braced against the cabinet. "You don't want to be really involved with a man. You just want to run around to women's clubs telling them how to make whipped cream desserts."

"How's Tony? You still in the burn and rehab business together?"

"You stopped liking Tony when he had the energy and willpower to change his life—"

"His wife, you mean."

"My detective said you had Gloria living here. You never wanted to be that thick with her till Tony left her. You saw the writing on the wall— if Tony could throw over a dead marriage and try again, so could I."

"You ought to be glad I took my new house off your hands. After little Bobbie Rosario died in your fire, you must have felt it was under some kind of curse. Or didn't you care at all?"

"They live like animals. If they took decent care of their children, no harm would come to them."

She chuckled theatrically. "I'd love to see how fast you'd get yourself organized, wakened by a raging fire in the dead of the night. If you're lucky. Smoke inhalation gets most people, as it did Torte. . . . Who do you think the other body was? You must know."

"What do you care about that old gossip? I did half the work fixing that house up, before you grabbed it. Still living on my tab."

"Gee, Ross, I don't remember sitting around getting high all those years. I thought I was having babies, raising our children, cooking, cleaning, doing the laundry, and working for real live green money. Guess I remember it wrong. . . . But living there I can't help wondering whose body that was."

"If you think you have ghosts, why don't you ask them?"

"So you and Tony are still partners?" Try another approach.

"I'm surprised at Cesaro. Never expected him to be sentimental about family." He studied her narrowly. "But he's causing me some small trouble at the moment, which I imagine you put him up to. Tony and I are not partners. You know my partners—Carl and Roger."

Both of them were glaring not really at each other but something the other symbolized. "Ross, remember the fairy tales I used to read the girls—"

"Terrifying and irrational. Sadistic. I objected but you—"

"Sometimes the ogre has an external soul. He's destroyed by capturing and killing that soul. But you made me be your external conscience, and you thought you'd be safer and more comfortable, if I could be destroyed."

"You've always liked to moralize daily life." He imitated a high-pitched voice. "Ross, the grass is *dying,* we must water it. Everything's a melodrama with you."

"For years I thought one value we had in common was to try to live a decent moral life, doing as little harm as possible. Living *carefully.*"

"Damn it, Daria, talking sense with you is a waste of time. You're just not in touch with reality. Everything is a fairy tale to you. I deal all day with land values, with urban blight, with mortgages, with profit and loss and lending rates, with variances and financing. You deal all day with chocolate mousse. If you never lifted another finger, who the hell would care? If men such as myself were stymied, the city would decay from within. Boston would rot into one huge festering slum filled with rats and welfare mothers breeding like hamsters."

She was sitting tucked in against the wall, imagining the little twin wheels turning in her purse. She would have liked to peek in to check that her little player was recording, but she did not want to risk calling his attention to it. She hoped her roses were surviving waiting for her to move them, but so long as Ross was giving vent to his compulsion to explain, to justify, to try to drag agreement or approval or absolution from her, she would sit and record. "You feel that you're improving neighborhoods, so it's all right to use fire as an eviction device. Especially since the condo law means you can't evict people fast enough."

"I haven't said anything like that." He turned from her sulkily, running his finger along the grime covered countertop. "You have fire on the brain. I'm trying to talk about the larger picture—but you've never been able to grasp that. You simply couldn't grow with me. You couldn't or you just wouldn't."

"Grow in what way?" She scuffled her feet and shut off the recorder. This part wasn't going to be any use. "Wasn't I always available to you? Didn't I put your dinner parties first—"

"I have a caterer to do that now," he said with morose satisfaction.

"When did I ever plead I was too busy to spend time with you as you did constantly with me?"

"I was busy! I'm trying to achieve something. It's a highly competitive field fraught with economic and sociological vectors that can make or break a project."

"So is cookbook writing, actually," she said with a giggle.

"Everyone created such a fuss, as if yours were any sort of real work. Taking something that every woman does as a matter of course and making a fetish of it. People begging your autograph. People fawning over you at parties. It brought out silliness in those I thought had better sense, like that fool Carl going on about the hands of genius. How long can anybody listen to that nonsense?"

She decided to turn the recorder on again. Her patience was running out. "Did you really think because you'd gotten miffed about the amount of attention people paid me and because your girlfriend was eager to marry, that you had a right to try to burn me alive?"

"If you'd moved when I asked you, instead of being stubborn, you wouldn't have been here at all."

"And you feel the same way about your tenants. Bobbie's parents wouldn't leave the third floor apartment—"

"You only moved there to annoy me. Let's see you run it into the ground. Let's see how you like being responsible for property. I'm not accountable to you any longer for what I do."

"Then why, Ross, are you having this conversation?"

His thin mouth opened and then shut. He said slowly, "You have to understand how hopeless it was."

"Why? Why should I understand?"

"You're blaming me for events that would never have occurred if you'd trusted me instead of running to that little mick shyster."

"She turned out to be a pretty good lawyer, didn't she?"

"I wouldn't say that." He spoke sharply. "In her position, with you for a client, I could have cleaned up. But I never handle divorces. It's a sordid business."

She found herself fighting a smile of amusement. Sordid? "What do you mean, with me for a client?"

"You know how to appear helpless and fluffy. When I met you, you acted innocent enough. But it's all a fake now."

"We each see the other as having changed into somebody else, having become a strange person with altered values, different needs "

"Exactly. And you couldn't grow with me. Now you see."

"I couldn't shrink with you is the way I see it. You're a moral pygmy, Ross."

"Hold onto your insults and sit on your fat fanny. Within three years, five on the outside, I'm going to be one of the most respected real estate investors and developers in this area. People will be courting me to sit on boards and lend luster to projects. I'd love to have you around to witness my progress, but you'll probably be mugged by one of those petty criminals you've grown fond of."

"Which of us has been thicker with petty criminals is up for debate. Or wouldn't you describe your torch as petty?"

"Your mind is petty. I'm clear financially, even if you managed to scalp me. At least I don't have to see this place again after today." He began to pace, glaring about.

"Why are you here, anyhow?"

"The contractor was supposed to meet me an hour ago. We're going over the salvage. Then I'm quit of it all."

"Ross, you were quit of it all the day you walked out. You just didn't want me to have the house."

He looked at her with a downward twist of his mouth. "Why should you have it? All that money, all that work down the drain. Down your maw. Everything to make you cozy!"

"I like to enjoy where I live and I'm beginning to again. I do think you're quite right that we belong apart."

He halted as if astonished. "You admit it! You admit I was right."

"You did unforgivable things, deceiving me, lying. And I'll never forgive you what you did to Torte and to this house and to Mariela—and to me."

"Who in hell is Mariela?"

"Think of her as another Bobbie." She realized suddenly that whenever she brooded on Bobbie's death she saw not that little boy, whom she had never met, but a more boyish Mariela lying dead.

"What flagrant sentimentality. If that kid had lived, what do you think he'd have grown up to be? One more junkie."

"When did you start thinking that you count more than other people? That because society pays you more than a taxi driver, you can use everybody up in your schemes?" She heard the recorder click off. The cassette was full.

"You're the same softheaded liberal you were when I had to marry—"

"Going to throw that at Gail, for the next twenty years? This is where I came in." She stood, dusting the seat of her pants. "Look around you. You made a mess. You're making one still."

"You're the mess in your old pants and carrying a load of dirt from one place to another and calling it your mother."

She walked out the open door. "For you, there'll be plenty of ashes. I'll stick to food and soil, and you persist with your cash and your ashes."

He stood in the doorway calling after her, "You can't see it even yet. You couldn't move up with me. You're happy with people like those troublemakers and bums. Daria, you won't let go of Eastie."

"Happy?" She nodded at him over the first bucket of rosebush as she heaved it up and staggered toward the van. "Absolutely. No, I've never let go of what I loved, while it had some good in it. But I sure am letting go of you. You may find out that the fires you order can burn your fingers too, by and by. So long, Ross."

29

BLOOMBERG was short, stocky, not at all fat but solidly built. His black hair was a mass of tight curls and he was boyishly handsome, with a little cleft in his chin and big brown eyes with lashes as long as Daria's. Being short and boyish in face, he scowled a great deal and affected a deep booming voice. From telephone contact Daria had built up a picture of him as bigger than Tom and about fifty, which she had trouble reconciling with the cute little satyr before her.

Lou's recording was gold and the case against Petris coming along fine.

"Mrs. Walker, I appreciate what you tried to do." Bloomberg twinkled at her. "Basically he fails to deny rather than admitting anything. As a confession, it's less use in court than to us privately. In essence, I suspect a jury would feel he admitted to having your house burned, but we're far more interested in pinning that kid's death on Walker. In that matter, he was too cagey to say anything we can sink our teeth into."

Tom said, "But he practically confesses to burning the Lexington house."

"Sure," Bloomberg roared, starting to light a cigarette and then glaring at Tom. He had agreed to refrain from smoking for the length of their morning meeting, but he clearly viewed it as extreme martyrdom and seemed angrier at Tom than at any arsonist. "But I'm not going after him on that. Truth is, you burn the house you live in for insurance, and half the time a jury thinks, why not? It's your house. It's hard to get them to convict, and I'm not wasting time with it. But the fire where the child was killed, that's mom and apple pie. We can bring that one in easy, if we can prove it. That's where we have to move against Walker. Murder in the commission of a felony. Conspiracy. On that a jury will convict."

"How about getting Petris to testify against the others?" Mac suggested. He seemed fascinated by Bloomberg, not even glancing at anybody else.

"I'd find that distasteful. We have to bargain with Ledoux, and that's smarmy enough. Petris is a big fish. I want the Kingsleys and I want Petris and I want Porfirio and I want Walker." Bloomberg fingered his Marlboros, glaring at Tom.

She had a moment of feeling bleakly detached from everyone else in the room. Walker, Porfirio, those were her names, her people.

"How about wiring Lou again?" Mac suggested. She noticed he had discarded his flannel shirt for the visit to the AG's office, replacing it with a button-down oxford cloth shirt and a rep tie.

"That's scheduled for his meeting with Porfirio tomorrow, but frankly his credibility won't persist ad infinitum. If he keeps delaying, we have the distinct possibility of one or all reaching the decision that Ledoux has lost his nerve. Then they'll simply hire somebody else and we'll have lost them."

Everybody sat glumly viewing the papers on Bloomberg's desk. "Maybe somebody we know could pretend to be a torch looking for work?" Fay suggested. Her hair was as usual freshly done and she had put on her best somewhat tight orange dress.

Mac snorted. "They wouldn't bite. It's like walking up to some respectable businessman and saying, Hey, any rival you want burglarized?"

"Actually they don't think it's the same, because prosecution for arson is so rare," Bloomberg said gloomily. "But that would be entrapment. Well, let's call in the rest of the Baker Street Irregulars. Now that we've picked up Jay Jay, I thought we'd just run everybody through their paces and see how it all hangs together. Ledoux and Jay Jay haven't seen each other. Dorsey," he said to his assistant, "bring in the folks. Ledoux is in 1020A and the kids are in 1014 and Lou's little helper in 1026. Get Ledoux first."

Lou ambled in nodding at everybody and greeting all by name, at his ease, with a smile for everybody. "Now, didn't I do right this time?"

Mac spoke first. "Lou, you did a terrific job for us. Couldn't have been better performed."

"And tomorrow you're meeting with Porfirio," Bloomberg boomed.

"You want me to wear that funny harness again? Christ, Mr. Bloomberg, listen to me. Tony's Italian. I'll end up in the Bay."

"My brother has no connection with the Mafia," Daria said crisply. "If he did, he wouldn't have to hire you to burn his buildings."

"Your other brother Cesaro, your older brother—" Bloomberg began.

"Cesaro isn't older, he just seems that way."

"He's proving most cooperative. He's reopened the case on your new dwelling. He's working with us."

"It's nice to know someone in my family will be out of jail when this is over," she said sourly.

Dorsey brought in Orlando, Sylvia, and the kid who had helped Lou in his recent burnings, Jay Jay, a school dropout now twenty. He was a skinny, gentle-looking kid with a slight limp or twist to his walk. He looked frightened, Daria was not surprised to notice. After Tom had surprised Lou and Jay Jay on the roof, Jay Jay had disappeared for a month. He had been picked up almost as soon as he came home.

Glancing at Lou, Jay Jay pouted. Then his eyes fixed dilated on Sylvia. Lou was staring at her too. Daria couldn't understand what about Sylvia upset them. Sylvia had that tough girl street veneer, but nothing about that should so rivet the attention of the two men. Bloomberg noticed too, his cleft chin jutting as if he smelled something. Sylvia was nervous today. This last hour was the first time she and Orlando had been in the same room since Orlando had dumped her when her pregnancy was confirmed. Daria wondered what they had been saying to each other when Bloomberg had closeted them both in a conference room together until he wanted them brought to his office. Sylvia was paying little attention to Lou or to Jay Jay. She kept her gaze fixed on Orlando and had not noticed how the others were observing her with what looked like fear.

Still glaring at Sylvia Lou burst out, "Now look here. I been playing a straight game with you guys. Don't try to pin that old mess on me."

Sylvia glared back, not understanding, Daria was sure, any better than she herself did what Lou was talking about. Mac started to speak but Bloomberg drowned him out, waving for everybody to shut up. "Well, Lou, it's up to you to explain it to us then. Let's everybody keep their mouths shut and let's hear Lou's side. Let's all listen with an open mind to everything he says."

"My side? I had nothing to with it. Jay Jay can tell you. Those bastards weren't paying but two hundred then. Walker gave Eddie a shitty two hundred. Eddie came to me and I told him what to do, but what do you expect from a kid doesn't know his ass from his useful parts?"

"Eddie? You mean Eduardo?" Sylvia burst out. "Where's my brother? Did you get him in some kind of trouble?"

Daria jumped up and put her arms around Sylvia, trying to keep her from saying more.

"Listen, my wife can tell you, that night was our fifteenth anniversary. I took her to Anthony's Pier Four. I dropped such a wad, I bet they remember me yet. Eddie came to me and said he was doing a job for Walker, and he knew I could tell him now. I told him okay, but he fucked up. That wasn't my fault. Ask Jay Jay!" Lou turned a glance of desperate appeal on the boy.

Sylvia pulled free of Daria. "Eduardo! Where is he? You know where he went!"

Bloomberg nodded to Dorsey. "Better take Miss Rodriguez out. I'm afraid we've all figured out where Eduardo is." When Sylvia, weeping and kicking, had been removed, he boomed on, "We'll get an exhumation order. Probably some way to identify him. Dental work? We better find out what dentist he went to."

Orlando, who had stood up and then sat down, stood again. "You're saying that Eduardo was the stiff in Daria's house, I mean before she moved in?"

"I think we can safely assume that. Right, Jaime?"

"Call me Jay Jay."

"Okay, Jay Jay. Orlando, you think you can get his family to figure out how to identify him?"

"Sylvia's mother's going to have a heart attack. She's been thinking he must be in trouble with the police or have somebody real tough after

398

him. See, he just disappeared. No letter, not even a postcard, nothing. It really got to Sylvia."

"But you'll talk to them for us?"

Orlando swallowed. He had been avoiding Sylvia and her family. If he talked to them, there was only one thing he could say, to start with. "It's going to kill her mother. Eduardo's the only boy she has."

Tom grinned. "But you can be like a son to them."

Bloomberg was shifting impatiently, patting his cigarettes. "Are you going to talk to them? Or are you scared? I don't want to send anybody official around the neighborhood yet."

"Why should I be?" Orlando squared his shoulders. "I'll talk to them."

Daria was not sure that Tom should have put that extra pressure on, but perhaps it was better for the kids to marry in spite of being too young than for Sylvia to have the baby alone. Perhaps Orlando simply wanted to be pushed. The pose of macho nonchalance he had assumed had left him no way back from the boys he hung with to Sylvia.

Lou wanted their attention. "Listen, you have to believe me. You have to make Jay Jay back me up. He knows I wasn't there. Walker was only paying two hundred. What do you get for two hundred? Some stupid kid who doesn't know the first thing about a successful set. He was supposed to arrange a little fire to scare out the tenants, just some smoke and water damage basically, so Walker could clear it and then rehab it for three condos. Instead he burned up himself and that little kid. Walker had to put in a whole new kitchen on the third floor and the second floor people never moved."

"I didn't do anything," Jay Jay said. "I just helped him carry the cans of gas. He got it on himself and he went up all at once. I didn't know what to do. He was screaming and the hall was burning. I didn't know what to do! I ran downstairs and then I pulled the fire alarm. I didn't know what else to do," Jay Jay kept repeating. "I didn't know!"

"Did you get paid by Walker or by Eduardo?" Bloomberg asked.

"By Mr. Walker. Eduardo brought me along to Saks by Walker's office and we met in the ties department. Mr. Walker, he was mad at Eduardo for bringing me. But Eduardo, see, he didn't want to pay me out of his money. He wanted Mr. Walker to pay me because he needed help carrying the stuff up. Also, like, he was a little scared. We practiced in a vacant lot, but that's different."

"I bet it is. You practiced setting fire to something?"

"Just a pile of junk. We went over to J.P.—Jamaica Plain—where we seen on the news there's been all these fires getting people out on the Orange Line. So we thought we could practice there. But these guys came up and asked us who we were and what we were doing in their neighborhood, and they kept following us. So we gave up and just burned that junk."

Bloomberg looked as if he wanted to groan. "Did Walker actually pay you?"

"He gave me twenty-five and he gave Eduardo a hundred. We were supposed to get the rest after."

"Did you ever receive the rest of what he owed you?"

"I was supposed to get fifty. That's what Eduardo promised and he talked Mr. Walker into it when we met at Saks in the ties. I stole a tie while they were arguing. Blue with dots and stuff. See, I'm telling you everything."

Bloomberg roared on with his massive patience. "Did Walker ever pay you the second twenty-five?"

"I was too scared to go to him afterward. Then I needed the money so bad I called him. He just hung up on me. At the office they'd say who is this calling and I was scared to give my name. I figured I'd never get the money. Besides, we didn't do it the way we were supposed to, and I figured Mr. Walker, he was mad at us about that."

"Okay, Jay Jay. Now Mr. Dorsey is going to take you in the next room and he's going to read you your rights and arrange about a lawyer and we're going to write down your statement. You just say everything you just told us and anything else you can remember. Just start at the beginning and go through it. You give us the help we need, and there's nothing to be scared of."

After Dorsey had taken Jay Jay out, Orlando cleared his throat diffidently, "Hey, what can they do to him? I mean, he's not all there. Eduardo felt sorry for Jay Jay for getting picked on all the time. He's a retard."

"He may be a little slow, but I think he's mentally competent." Bloomberg washed his hands together with a happy noise. "I think we just sewed up another of them. If you can come through with Porfirio tomorrow, Lou, I think we've got some reasonable cases."

"But you're not going to pin that little Bobbie mess on me."

"Never, Lou, never," Bloomberg roared. "You're our star witness. You're our sweetheart. You didn't know the kid would prove to have butterfingers. So after that they decided to pay for a professional?"

"Right. It scared the shit out of them, excuse me. That was late September. Walker comes to me and says, We need you, so what's your price? I'd done a little job or two for Tony—we practically live in the same neighborhood—so with us all being fellow property owners in the same bailiwick, it was natural for them to turn to me, once they got it together to pay a reasonable price."

"Lou, I'm going to give you some protection. We're going to be moving rather fast."

"I don't need protection."

"I think you do. I noticed you've put two of your buildings on the market. I don't want you to be thinking about a long vacation. You're our main man, Lou, and without you, no case. I believe it's time to start putting it all together. What I'm asking of you folks is that you lie low. No press conferences. No big meetings. No more amateur detective work. We've taken this over now and we're moving on it, and if you try anything ambitious, you're going to get in our way."

SON adjourned to Fay's kitchen to hold a postmortem over deli take-out, nobody quite able to go back to their day's work after the excitement of the morning. Orlando was simply delaying the visit to Sylvia's parents, but he and Sylvia were sitting side by side, as close as two kitchen chairs could be placed. Sylvia had been crying but she was also obviously happy, a balance that made her look brilliantly liquid, as if about to overflow with one or another emotion. Orlando looked serious and proud of himself.

Mac was slumped, button-down shirt unbuttoned and jacket hung crooked on the back of a kitchen chair, saying in dejection, "I thought

Lou was completely frank and open with me. That he never shared what he knew about that fire is a shock. I thought we had a full, open, trusting relationship."

"I dare say he's more open with you than with his wife." Daria said gently. "You mustn't expect miracles. He told you he didn't set that one, and it turns out he didn't."

"There was so much pressure on my brother," Sylvia said. "He wanted to be a success, and he couldn't even find a job. He'd been out of high school two years and he couldn't get work. He just wanted to support himself."

"I'm glad the Rosario family moved out of the neighborhood," Orlando said. "They might take it out on us." He and Sylvia were suddenly an *us,* Daria noted. Eduardo was his posthumous brother-in-law.

Tom helped himself to a beer. "I felt like a pariah this morning. Bloomberg would rather arrest me than the landlords. Charge: interfering with the addiction of an officer of the law. Anyhow, it's kiss off and good-bye, now."

Mac frowned. "They still need us."

"Do they?" Tom raised his brows mockingly. "They need Jay Jay. They need Lou. They may even need Daria. But the rest of us are on the shelf. Elections coming up. The AG belongs to a different faction from the governor."

"You give up too easily." Mac put his feet up on the table, leaning way back. "I say we'll still be cut in for a piece of the action."

Fay barked, "Get your big dirty feet off my kitchen table, Mac. A piece of the action! We're back to the comic books. Personally I'll be overjoyed to get out of the detective business. We have a lot of problems, and if we knock out arson, that's just one off the list. On to code violations. Trash. The deterioration of our park. Safety on the streets. Evictions. Roaches."

"We gave them their case," Mac mused. "We handed it to them on a platter. If they don't give us credit, we'll take our story to the media."

"Who wants credit—" Tom began.

"Yeah, give me cash any day." Fay crunched a pickle. "All we ever wanted was for the laws to be enforced against them too."

Tom smiled at Daria. "People around here know what we've been trying to do. I'd like more time to myself. We're going to be taking an apprentice into Aardvark and I'll have to be doing a lot of training."

"An apprentice?" Fay leaned forward, tapping his arm. "How about Johnny?"

"He's too young, Fay. This won't be a summer job."

Orlando was staring at Tom. "You got somebody for the job?"

Tom grinned. "I was thinking of Sylvia. I talked to her already."

Sylvia nodded.

"But she wants to be a nurse."

"Not anymore," Orlando said sourly.

Sylvia burst out: "Tom says we can still manage it. I'd make good money as a nurse. I talked to Eleni."

"I was thinking of you," Tom said to Orlando. "Interested?"

"Interested, man, interested? That's a joke. You want me to crawl and beg and have Masses said for it? You know they have me working in the store when there's no real need, just to give me some kind of job. But that's my bro Boz's, the store." Orlando looked hard and long at Tom. "Just when did you decide about this job?"

"I was considering it." Tom looked steadily back.

" 'Cause I'm going to do right by Sylvia and her family, huh?"

"You'll make a good carpenter. Don't you think so?"

"I always finish what I start," Orlando said portentously. He was still brooding. "I guess it was fair. But I didn't even know you were thinking along those lines, man."

"Just as well," Fay said. "You make a success of it, and maybe when Johnny's ready, Aardvark will take him on too."

"I don't want to." Johnny spoke from the floor where he was eating a sandwich beside his ghetto box. "I'm going to form my own group. Bandido and I been practicing and I wrote my first song."

"How does it go?" Sylvia asked.

"It isn't really finished yet, but it's got a great beginning," Johnny said with satisfaction. He stood up abruptly and belted out in his cracking voice:

"You left me all ay-lone, you left me flat.
You sent me spinning, you knocked me off my feet

Now you're running with another pack.
You left me like a dead dog in the street!

That's as far as I got."

"Beautiful," Fay said. "A love song, huh? It's real moving."

"I like it," Sylvia said. "I feel like that sometimes. You go work on it some more."

Orlando stood. "Time for us to pay a call on your mother."

Sylvia put her hands over her eyes. "She's going to take this hard. . . . You know, if a job like Tom's giving you had ever come through for Eduardo, he'd never have got mixed up with Walker." She followed him out.

Mac said reminiscently, tilting way back in his chair but leaving his feet off the table, "I recall wanting to be a rock star when I was in high school. I used to practice in the mirror."

"What happened?" Johnny asked. "How come you gave up?"

"I had all the right moves. The right faces. But I couldn't sing worth a damn. Even my own girlfriend couldn't stand listening to me." Mac sighed.

"A depressing story," Tom said. "So you gave up your dreams of glory and settled for Harvard."

"Politics is interesting up close," Mac said. "I expected to find it boring. I'll admit you're likely correct about the AG's motives, but I don't see how that necessarily excludes us."

"Oh yeah?" Fay rose and started clearing. "What are you going to run for?"

"Who knows?" Mac beamed. "There's a crude side to it, certainly, but I don't see that city politics should be harder to play than departmental politics. Bloomberg's bright, if a bit crude. I could learn something from him. I have everything I need for my thesis, but I can imagine an interesting study. . . ."

When Daria walked in to her house, the phone was ringing.

"Daria, listen, it's Gloria. Am I interrupting something?"

"Just arrived myself, actually. How are you, Gloria? Is everything all right?" The first thing she imagined was that Tony was not paying his child support.

"I just had the weirdest, I do mean weirdest phone call from your brother."

Since the divorce, Gloria referred to Tony in that manner.

This time Daria asked, to make sure, "Tony? Or Cesaro?"

"I will say Cesaro hasn't forgotten a Christmas or a birthday present for the kids. No, I mean Tony."

"What did he want?"

"He had this completely nutsola notion that I had moved in with you. He'd been trying to get ahold of me. Of course if he ever bothered exercising his visiting privileges with his own flesh and blood, he'd know where we're living. You'd think he'd notice it from the checks, but I guess his secretary mails them out."

"He thought we were living together?" Daria repeated, trying to keep herself from sounding amused.

"I don't know where he got such an idiot idea, believe me! Obviously he hasn't been in any closer touch with you than he has with me."

"I haven't had a conversation with Tony since Ross walked out. He took Ross's side. They're very thick."

"Cesaro told me and I'm so sorry. After all those years. And the two of you always seemed so solid. But Tony almost drove me crazy today. Honestly, it reminded me of when we were first together and he used to get jealous every time we went out in public together."

"What on earth did Tony want?"

"To ask a million stupid questions. None of them made sense."

"Well, like what? This is awfully mysterious."

"He kept asking about some group called the sons of something or other. The Sons of Allston, you know, like the Sons of Italy. And somebody who made me think of the Lone Ranger. Let me think. It was somebody Silver. He's absolutely gonzoed at Cesaro, by the way."

"Is he? Did he say why?"

"Something about insurance. You know those guys. But, Daria, it was the most ridiculous conversation. He hasn't spoken to me since Christmas! Now all he wanted to talk about was a bunch of people I'd never heard of and he kept saying I'd been living with you and why was I pretending I didn't know."

"Poor Gloria! You must have been upset."

"And then how Cesaro was screwing him—I'm quoting. Then he started bellowing in my ear about all the people who owe him favors and how we wouldn't succeed in bringing him down. What I want to know is, what's going on with him? Is Tony crazy?"

"If Tony calls you again, tell him to talk directly to me."

"But do you know what it's all about?"

"Vaguely. It has something to do with real estate."

"But, Daria, neither you nor me ever knew beans about that stuff. He got so angry at me he hung up."

"Why'd he get angry?"

"He kept asking all these questions and he wouldn't believe me when I tried to explain I didn't know what he was talking about. He kept saying you and Cesaro were out to get him. But that a lot of people owed him favors."

After Gloria hung up Daria felt apprehensive enough to call Bloomberg. It sounded as if Tony might be suspicious. Bloomberg was not in the office, but Dorsey assured her they were moving fast indeed.

30

A SECRET grand jury had been impaneled. Daria testified on a hot muggy Tuesday the last week in June. Since this was not a trial, the procedure was simpler than she had expected. Sandra María was on next with her charts on window shades and her graphs of neighborhood ownership, mortgage patterns and the incidence of fires. They both came home on the Green Line together to a dinner Tracy had volunteered to prepare. Tracy was working at a day camp for city children, doing simple music, drawing, storytelling. She had begun with great enthusiasm but was already growing a little tired of the massive baby-sitting operation on a low budget for sports and art supplies.

Scott ate with them. Afterward he and Tracy went out, and Sandra María and Daria cleaned up. Sandra María was ready to rehash the day's events in court, but Daria's attention was elsewhere. Scott was blond and rugged, except for a receding chin. Both his parents were in marketing research and lived in Ipswich. He did not have a summer job and every week he seemed a more leathery mahogany, his hair whiter, from six hours a day at the beach. "What does she see in him?" she demanded of Sandra María.

"Well, he's got a car and he's always available. He seems innocuous."

"I'm worried about her." Daria finished loading the dishwasher. "She's on the pill."

"I would hope so. We don't want any more births around here."

"That means she's sleeping with that bronzed coatrack. I'll wash."

Sandra María cocked her head. "She's not in love with him, I don't think." She picked up a dry towel.

"Then why?"

"What did she tell you?"

Daria fished around in the sudsy water for a knife she had just lost. "She didn't. I saw the pills on her dresser when I was cleaning her room."

"Daria! You just shocked me."

"Why?"

"Why are *you* cleaning *her* room?"

"I always clean it."

"Isn't she old enough to clean her own room?" Sandra María asked gently.

"She does, she does, but not as thoroughly as it ought to be."

"Daria, at her age you shouldn't be going into her room unless she asks you in. You know that!"

She wanted to lash out at Sandra María. She kept her back turned, scrubbing a frying pan as hard as she could with steel wool. She knew she was scratching the finish.

"Look at me. Daria . . ."

"Let's see how well you'll do when it's Mariela on the pill screwing somebody she shouldn't bother with!"

"You know you oughtn't to have been snooping. How lucky you are to have me as your private family therapist. Now look at me again, please."

Finally Daria turned, feeling she had been pouting. "I know I was being nosy, okay?"

The grand jury heard testimony all week and into the next. On Sunday Robin came to play softball. It had become her ritual, that she appeared Sunday morning and stayed till evening. The occasional softball games of previous years had solidified around Tom, Ángel and Robin and were now a regular feature of any Sunday when it didn't pour. Then Robin returned to the house for supper. If they were all going to a movie, she went; if they were hanging around the house, she hung with them until midevening, when she would return to her Back Bay apartment.

Tracy had not seen Ross since Christmas. Robin was the expert on Hamilton and described it to her mother and sister. "I've never been in the main house. It looks like something out of *Gone with the Wind,* all those white columns, with a lane of maples leading to it. But some menial has always met me and ushered me down another drive. They live in this stucco house from the twenties. There's a tall arbor vitae hedge between the house and the kennels, but what you can't see you sure can hear. They have their own tennis courts at the big house."

Even if Ross were an ax murderer, Daria reminded herself, he would still be Robin's father. She had said that Robin's and Ross's relationship was none of her business, and she must stick to that. Her daughters were engaged in a cautious rapprochement, tentative as Marcus and Ali. Robin was gruff with her sister. She did not seem to know quite how to come close, but Tracy was patient. Daria found it astonishing how muted and how soft and how patient Tracy could be as Robin circled her.

Clearly they both needed an affirmation of family from each other. Daria knew they talked over together their occasional jealousy of her new family, how Daria herself had changed and how they should regard those changes. One Sunday night, when Sandra María, Daria and Tom had all gone off to a SON meeting, Robin and Tracy smoked dope together and saw the ghost of little Bobbie, or so they swore, and certainly they were still giggling with fright when everybody got home.

"If Daddy goes to jail," Tracy asked at breakfast, "who'll pay my tuition? Will I have to quit school?"

"Never." Daria took her daughter's firm cool hands in hers. "I promise. As soon as the renovations are completed, I'll stop putting money into the house. I have a regular Friday night slot on the Channel Seven newsmagazine. I'll put that money aside for your tuition."

"We have to get you some dresses. You don't need to come along unless you want to. I know what fits you."

"Tracy, you seem very involved with this Scott."

"Don't worry about it. I'm not serious about him, but he's fine."

"You see a lot of him for somebody you're not serious about."

"This summer is tough enough without being madly in love. He's fun." Tracy pushed her curly auburn hair out of her eyes. "That's all I want from a man right now, Mama. It's really all I can handle."

The following Sunday was beyond hot into horrible. Daria shut herself in with her air conditioner turned as high as it would go. She ventured outside only to add cherry-wood chips to the little smoker in the yard, given her by the manufacturer for whom she was developing a booklet of recipes. Today she was trying a new marinade for salmon. She was alone, the others off at the park where Robin was now the regular pitcher for the reds. In midafternoon, the phone rang.

It was Bloomberg. "Mrs. Walker, this is it. I want you to know we've gathered a task force and at dawn we're going to pick up the men indicted. You're not to speak of this to anyone outside the core group of SON. Those whom I can reach, I'm calling. Nobody else is to know. It'll be all over the papers by tomorrow midday, but we don't want anyone skipping town tonight."

"Are you going to arrest my ex-husband?"

"We've been watching all of them since the indictments came down Thursday. We expect him to drive to the Beacon Street apartment this evening, as he's been doing. We plan to surprise him there early."

"Mr. Bloomberg, I testified before the grand jury. Am I really going to have to testify against my ex-husband at the trial?"

"If we didn't subpoena you, you better believe the other side would anyhow. And we need your testimony. You have to establish Walker's situation and the connection with Ledoux."

When her family came trickling in for supper, she had a difficult time keeping quiet. She did not so much mistrust Robin as want to shield her from the strain she herself was feeling. She was bound still across distance and distaste to Ross, implicated in his crimes and implicated in their punishment, if there were to be any punishment. She suspected that he might have suddenly flown off with his bride to some Caribbean island hospitable to refugees with money to spend. Ross had been lucky all his life. In a way he wouldn't recognize, he was even lucky they had not died in the fire, with Lou already under SON's surveillance. He was well-connected, certainly, and well-connected lawyers seldom went to jail.

She found casual conversation at supper beyond her. She excused herself by blaming the humidity. Robin scarcely noticed, high on having pitched a two-hitter in a game their side won 10 to 1, the most lopsided game of the year. Robin was talking of playing softball more seriously, of trying out for a women's team. Daria realized how depressed Robin had been all through June, by contrast to her animation tonight. Robin had been working at the insurance company for a year, but the promotion she expected had not come. She was beginning to suspect she was stuck in a dead-end, entry-level job. Now with her roommates moving out, she felt deserted. Daria said suddenly, "Robin, why keep that apartment? You could move in here for a while. Would you like that?"

Robin stared blankly. "Gee, Mom, that's sweet of you. But, no thanks. That would feel like a giant step backward. I like Back Bay and I like walking to work."

Wrong guess. She was relieved, even though she and Robin were closer now than at any time since her older daughter had entered high school.

As soon as Robin left, she described Bloomberg's call. "At last," Tom bellowed. "Let's break out the champagne!" He raised his arms over his head in triumph, like a prizefighter.

But Sandra María was looking hard at Daria. "I don't think so. We seem to have a case of the bad regrets."

"Not again!" Tom groaned. "He tried to kill you. What more does he have to do?"

"I don't want to talk about it." Daria got up. "I'm going upstairs. I have a headache."

She was lying on her bed facedown when she heard a soft knock, perhaps an hour later. "Sandra María? Come in."

The door opened. "It's me. Foot in mouth. Heart in hand. I came to apologize for terminal insensitivity." Tom waited just inside the door.

"Come in. I shouldn't have flounced up here like an injured adolescent." She rolled onto her back, sitting up to face him.

He had a way of looking at her sometimes so sweet and powerful, it made her feel as if she shone for him. "You're sad, peaches," he said softly, still poised in the doorway.

"Half blue, half jumpy. I don't even know if I dread more his being arrested or his getting away."

"What's happening is happening no matter what you hope. It's out of our hands." He held up a bottle. "I realize champagne is off-key, but how about some bourbon? That might help us through the night. You aren't going to sleep."

"I don't imagine I am." She sat up against a pile of pillows and motioned for him to shut the door and come in. The sight of him, dark and ruddy, black hair, a five-o'clock shadow darkening his cheek, his straight thick brows, the fiery glow of his skin red from the sun, his lips that always looked to her touched with wine, even in her funk pleased her. "One of the best things we have going for us is how we come back from being angry. Sit tight and I'll get ice and glasses. And Tom . . ." She paused on her way out the door. "This business of trekking back and forth is ridiculous. When we go sweeping out of the room in high dudgeon, it would be much more convenient if we had only to cross the hall to make up. Why don't you move in?"

"Should I really?" He put the bourbon on her vanity and stood facing it, looking at her in the mirror, their eyes meeting in the reflection above her row of perfumes and toiletries.

"Yes." She started to leave but paused and swung back, again meeting his dark gaze that was somber without being cold. She was struck that she had encountered in him anger, impatience, resentment, on occasion self-pity, but never coldness. "I do love you. I know it. I'm half surprised I have the sense and the resilience enough to do it, but yes, I love you."

31

THE arrests were a four-day wonder, the announcement by the attorney general all over the papers and the evening news, followed by indignant editorials and analyses of arson for profit. Then came the self-righteous repudiation by those arrested of the farcical and highly political nature of the roundup in an election year, the unscrupulous motives of the AG, the squalid self-interest of the tenants. Then the case dropped from the papers. Motions were brought by teams of defense attorneys and argued before judges. Trials were set, postponed, set again for September. The AG was eager to bring at least the first of the cases to court before the elections.

Gretta called when the news hit the papers. "I don't know whether to congratulate you or commiserate with you. Is revenge sweeter than alimony?"

"Oh, it was a lump settlement. But I worry about the girls' reactions."

"Does this have anything to do with that nasty fire you had?"

"I'd say so, but that's not what he's being indicted for."

"I always thought Ross was on the dull side. I'd never had him pegged as some sort of criminal mastermind." Gretta clucked. "Is it embarrassing?"

"More for his present wife, I'd imagine."

She realized she had mixed feelings about the trial. She dreaded having to testify, but there at last the truth would become evident. There she would come to grasp the essence of Ross and his actions. There she would see the pattern revealed. The critical fault was somewhere hidden, although she could trace it back most likely to the point when he had given up his public ambitions. Never had he said out loud, Well, people in cities get what they deserve, and since I have been driven from public life, a pox on them and I'll take whatever I can squeeze out. They don't deserve an honest defender; they deserve to be used and bled. They didn't appreciate me and now I'll show them. Or was that a fiction like all the other stories she had invented to try to make sense of what Ross had done and therefore what Ross had become? At the trial finally her questions would be answered.

SON was meeting little as the summer ripened. Elroy had gone to Monhegan Island on vacation. Sylvia and Orlando married and moved into Tom's old apartment. His share in the building had been bought out by the couple downstairs. Sylvia came to collect the orange and white kitten; Mr. Schulman stood at the back fence and received the first black female. The other had acquired a name, Cassis, and seemed to be staying.

Ali got into a fight. In the aftermath his hind leg swelled and he ran a high fever. After the abscess had been operated on, first he and then Sheba went in to be altered. "Three are enough to produce," Daria announced. "We have to leave room for a stray."

The renovations were finally completed, with Orlando on the crew learning. Even the living room was splendid since Tom moved in, bringing his couch, coffee table and good chairs. Daria told Robin, "The real reason I asked him to join us is so we could get rid of that doggy couch."

Sandra María put money down on a dining-room set. "Danish modern?" Daria groaned.

Sandra María crossed her arms and assumed a position of immovability. "Daria, I like it. It goes well with Tom's stuff. This is going to look different from your old house—it's going to look like all of us."

Daria realized that she had been used to a division of territory. Once in a while Ross had insisted that some gift from a client be displayed, but decoration had otherwise been her province. Now she had to learn to compromise, for she was not Mommy and did not always know best.

She was nervous not only about the trial to come, but more immediately about the impending arrival of Tom's daughters. Tom wanted her to travel to Vermont with them to his sister's farm. She had not decided. She could not take off all of August. Tom decided to keep the girls with them for the first week, to meet his new family and witness his new life. She wanted to see how she got along with his girls, how much they would resent her. She was much older than their mother, so that perhaps she would seem more like a grandmother to them.

Tom went alone to meet his daughters at Logan Airport. He told Daria he would probably take them out to eat. It was a quarter to ten when she heard him on the porch, his deep voice, dark and bittersweet, counterpointed with high queries. She did not want to be sitting in wait like a large spider, so she fled to the kitchen. Mariela had been persuaded reluctantly to bed, promised that she would meet Tom's daughters in the morning. Sandra María had tactfully retired to do some paperwork. "Let's not confuse them. They can meet all the rest of us tomorrow."

Daria had been half an hour dressing, with Tracy's help. She kept deciding she was too dressed up or too casual. Tracy, not in a mood to be tactfully absent, heard the voices too and stuck her head out her door, then dashed into the living room, while Daria was still pointlessly fussing in the kitchen. Daria had a moment of bad temper as if Tracy had preempted something; then she shook her head hard and ventured into the living room herself.

Rosa was tall for ten and Georgia about average for eight, so that Rosa seemed more than two years older than her sister. Unsmiling she shook hands with Daria. They both had dark curly hair like Tom's. Rosa was the prettier in spite of her solemnity and glasses too big for her oval face. She seemed also the more ill at ease, looking around suspiciously and then staring straight ahead as if determined to take no notice.

Georgia flung herself on the couch where Ali, Sheba and Cassis made a sandwich, Cassis in the middle with just her little head with the amber eyes wide open sticking up from the strong black curve of Ali's flank. Georgia exclaimed over them. "All black kitties. Are they yours?"

"They're mine," Tracy said. "But you can pet them. That's the father, the mother and their little girl."

"Where's Marcus?" Rosa demanded. "What did you do with Marcus?"

He was perched on the mantlepiece. He liked to be higher than the other cats. Daria thought he watched their family scene with a mixture of curiosity and envy, but he hissed if either adult approached too near. However, he had been found several times curled up with Cassis.

The cats took some of the awkwardness from the entrance, because Rosa fussed over Marcus and Georgia leaned over the others. Ali rolled to have his belly scratched. "Aren't you the darlings," Georgia pronounced. "What are we supposed to call you?"

Figuring out after a moment that the question was addressed to her, Daria was about to answer as Rosa cut in firmly, "Mrs. Walker, idiot!"

Daria said simultaneously, "You can call me Daria."

"Aunt Daria?" Georgia asked.

Rosa and Daria again spoke in unison, Rosa saying, "Don't be silly, she isn't our aunt," and Daria saying, "Aunt Daria or Daria, just as you like."

As Tom said upstairs later, "Georgia's going to be easy—she likes anybody who has animals. Andrea's allergic and the girls never have anything bigger than a goldfish. Rosa will come around too, you'll see."

The next day, Wednesday, they had to buy bathing suits. Tom told Daria that this happened every year, as if Andrea had so shaken the dust of the East Coast from her heels that she could not remember that in August people there went swimming. She never packed the girls' bathing suits. Every year Tom had to go with them to buy suits when they arrived. Daria stayed home with Peggy.

By Thursday, she could see that Georgia would indeed be easy. Georgia was a kid who, when dropped in water, swam. She liked variety. She was a little adventurer who charmed and was charmed. At eight, less pretty than her older sister, Georgia was far more conscious of the need to please and to please herself. She already had Cassis sleeping in her bed, seduced away from the parent cats. She already had Mariela following her about. She had sat in Ángel's lap and got him to photograph her with every one of the cats in succession: Ángel who had contempt for snapshots and only photographed Sandra María when he needed a human figure for perspective in some fascinatingly bleak urban landscape.

Rosa meantime withdrew behind a book or into the television. She had fixed programs she always watched and was alarmed not to find them on local stations or on at what she considered the wrong time. At home *Star Trek* reruns were aired regularly five days a week at five P.M., just before supper. Here they were only on Saturdays at seven. Immediately Boston plummeted to the bottom of the list of livable places for Rosa.

Her first response to anything new was to demand why it was that way. "Why do you grind the pepper? My mother buys it already ground in big square cans. It doesn't come out in those funny pieces."

The weekend passed bumpily. Georgia loved fried clams. Rosa said they squished in her mouth. Georgia loved the trip in Boston Harbor to visit the islands. Rosa gripped the railing and looked green. When they landed on Georges Island, she threw up on her shoes. Tom was beginning to take on a dogged, defeated look she imagined he must have worn the last years of his marriage. Rosa's face was set into a stubborn refusal to be entertained, wooed. Monday Tom took only Rosa with him while Georgia was promised time alone later and whisked off by Tracy for a day at camp, where she made a basket she displayed proudly at supper. Rosa was somewhat less unbending alone with Tom, he reported, but would not give full approval to anything from the Stoneham Zoo (the Fleishacker was better, which Tom freely admitted) to the swan boats in the public garden—for which Rosa felt she was too mature.

Rosa even resisted Mariela. She said she didn't want to spend her vacation baby-sitting. All the time she was home she toted Marcus around like a security blanket. He enjoyed that.

By Friday Tom was exhausted. Daria offered to take the girls into the studio with her while she taped her show for that night and for the next two weeks, which she had reluctantly agreed to spend in Vermont. When she asked him what he was going to do, he said he thought he would get back in bed with a bottle of bourbon and stay there.

She had a resigned hopeless feeling about the day, since once she got to the studio she could spare little time for the girls. She turned them over to Lena, the tall many-braided Black associate producer. At least they would get a nice lunch (if Rosa could be persuaded to eat) when the crew sat down. In order to film all stages, she customarily produced a dish four or five times, so they always had plenty to eat.

The first show was about how to make fast fresh tomato sauce and then easy entrées to use it on. The second concerned sauces for pasta that could be made in a hurry: pesto di basilico, primavera, carbonara. The third was on fast but elegant desserts made of late summer fruit. She had to have makeup reapplied twice, as she was sweating heavily under the hot lights. When they broke for lunch she ate with the girls and Lena, at the tables they set up near the door, behind the cameras. The girls seemed subdued, but Rosa was full of technical questions which Zed from the crew patiently answered.

She had to get used to this pace of taping several shows at once. Her segments having proved popular, she had renegotiated her contract and would be doing three shows every week in September. It was a long day's work. At supper she sat silent and weary. It wasn't until she noticed how happy Tom was looking that she realized Rosa was dominating dinner table conversation. Rosa was holding forth on television and how everything was done. "And then Daria made another big thing of spaghetti to put the bacon on and this one camera comes shooting up like the guy is driving a little golf cart. Two of the cameras are coming in on Daria from two sides. You see, this other guy is looking at the pictures from all the cameras on the row of monitors, and he's choosing which camera has the best shot. He's talking to them in their ears. And all this time Daria's carrying on just as if the camera wasn't leaning all over her like a crane."

She suddenly recalled Rosa had eaten lunch without a complaint. Tom's daughter had consumed spaghetti carbonara, two stuffed tomatoes and everything else in sight. If the food was on television, it must be okay. If Daria was on television, she must be okay, almost as good as Captain Kirk. Maybe they ate exotic food like that on the *Enterprise*. Suddenly her star had risen. Daria felt silly with relief.

On Sunday Tom waited till after the ball game to leave. It was a five hour trip to his sister's. Tracy was out with Scott; Ángel, Mariela and Sandra María were visiting her parents to celebrate her father's fiftieth birthday. Daria was glad Robin had stayed, but she was not at her best alone with her older daughter. She coped more smoothly when Tom was around. But after putting so much effort into Tom's children all week, she was determined to try hard tonight.

Robin seemed nervous too. Their relationship thrived in the matrix of others. "Now that Tom's living here, does Ángel want to move in?" Robin and Daria sat out on the new deck with their after dinner coffee.

"Not a chance. From time to time he tries to get Sandra María to move in with him. He has a loft in the South End where he has a darkroom and all his equipment and lights now. He's put as much money and work into that loft as we have into this whole house."

"The house came out really neat," Robin said with polite interest. "Don't care much about houses myself, but I thought this one was going to be grim. You know what Tracy says?"

"Tracy says a lot. What in particular?"

"She says it's really a women's house. A strong women's house. And that everybody likes that. That's why so many people hang around."

"Tom doesn't change that?"

"No, because he likes it that way too."

"What do you mean about people hanging around? The house was crowded this week just because Tom's daughters were staying."

"Don't you notice how people come in and out? Tracy's fascinated. One week she kept a log. She counted thirty-nine separate visits in one week by a total of twenty-one people." Robin picked at her sneaker sole idly. "She learned to do that in sociology."

"But your father and I entertained heavily—"

"You don't need anybody else to have a dinner party now. It's people coming to see you or Sandra María or Tom—just to pull up a chair and chew the fat or drop off a newspaper article or borrow something."

"I can't tell if you think that's good or what, Robin?"

"It's different. And you never had close girlfriends like Sandra María."

"What about Gretta?" She felt a pang of guilt. She was no longer communicating with her daily, giving bulletins. Gretta was breaking up with her friend and was again the one calling her in distress.

"Oh, Mother, you used to bitch all the time how she talked your ear off. It wasn't like you, you know, loved her or anything."

"That's true." Daria gripped the arms of her deck chair hard. "I do love Sandra María. And Mariela. Sandra María came into a part of my life that was empty."

Robin stirred. "It's getting dark. Let's go inside." She looked at her watch.

Reluctantly Daria left the mild soft air of the deepening twilight to follow her daughter to the cleared kitchen table. Robin said, "I saw Daddy yesterday."

"You did?" She felt a chill of apprehension. She also had to control a fear of betrayal. "How was it?"

"He called me up last week. Suggested we lunch Friday at a fish restaurant near his office. Then Friday A.M. he called me at work and said he couldn't make it. It'd have to be Tuesday. Then Monday he called and wanted it put off till Thursday."

"What did you think about his putting it off so many times?"

"Don't play shrink, Mother." Robin was picking toothpicks out of the shot glass they stood in and laying them in a neat row. She spent several minutes lining them up exactly. "I thought he didn't really want to do it."

"But then he met you?"

"I raised the ante. Told him I was busy the rest of the week. Said I'd drive out Saturday to Hamilton. Otherwise, it'd be a while, because I'd be very busy."

"Why did you do that?" She stared at her sunburned, self-possessed blond daughter.

"I was fed up. I wanted him to know he can't push me around. That's something I've always known about Daddy you never figured out."

"What exactly?" Daria watched her daughter, fascinated.

"That if he pushes you too hard, the best way to handle him is not to make him feel guilty, but to be even more outrageous. He respects that."

Daria sighed from her shoes. "Ross and I were always ill-suited."

"I often thought so," Robin said briskly. "I used to think you held him back. Now I see he cramped your style too."

"What did you think I held him back from?"

"Daddy's ambitious. He felt you didn't give him the support he needed. Then he used to complain about all the adventures he missed, except that now I think that was bullshit. He used to go on about all the things we'd do like taking a canoe down the Colorado or hiking the whole Appalachian Trail."

"Ross is no great hiker."

"When I was younger, I thought he was great at everything."

Younger did not end until a couple of months ago, Daria thought. "What was your father's response to your little ultimatum?"

"He fussed and said it was impossible. Then he called me back and said to come Saturday."

"I admit I'm terribly curious about how they live."

"He's just as curious about you."

"Really? He asked about me?"

"I'll get to that." Robin looked at her watch again, grimacing. Daria wondered if she was keeping Robin from something. "Saturday I took Tracy with me. I made her promise not to tell you till we could sit down together, once Tom took those little girls away and everything calmed down."

"You asked Tracy along? Without consulting Ross?"

"Sure." Robin thrust her chin out. "I didn't tell Tracy that. I told her he invited her and I thought she should come."

"But, Robin! That was a lot to take on. Was he awful to her?"

"Of course not, once she arrived. I know he's been rough on her. Tracy's felt hurt by his neglect. He's such a jerk around her anyhow. When he was making all that fuss about her doing it with Nick, I asked him one day, Daddy, what is all this, do you think I'm a virgin? He didn't even want to talk about it. He just pretended I hadn't said anything."

Daria had caught a surprising glimpse of a side of Robin previously hidden from her, a protective warmth toward her sister, whereas Daria had always been aware of their rivalry. "It's sweet of you to worry about Tracy. But don't you think it was a little risky?" She was not sure Ross was always capable of distinguishing between Tracy and herself.

"Maybe I wanted the company out there myself. Anyhow." Robin cleared her throat. "To answer your question, he skirted around it about an hour. Once he got started, he asked a lot of questions. Tracy was supposed to be back here before we had this conversation."

"I guess everybody would like documentary films of their ex's scene."

"He wasn't pleased with what we told him." Robin looked smug. "I think he kept trying to imagine . . . Hey is that Tracy?"

Tracy dashed in, tousled and radiant. She was coming quickly into a glowing ripeness of skin and hair that was close to beauty, set off tonight by a yellow sundress. Had she herself ever been that attractive? Daria wondered.

"I started telling her without you, asshole! You're an hour and fifteen minutes late."

"Robin, don't be compulsive. It isn't like a movie that starts at seven or you miss the first scene. He didn't want to bring me back so soon and I had to work him around." Tracy rummaged in the refrigerator for leftovers. "So what have you heard, Mama?"

"Robin was telling me about Ross asking questions."

Tracy rolled her eyes. "He kept wanting to hear you'd become a bag lady or ended up on the back ward of a mental hospital."

"He imagines this house is like a rooming house," Robin chimed in. "Nothing we said could get it across. It's too different from how you guys lived together and how they're living."

"So now satisfy my curiosity. Give me a home movie. Tracy, there's peach upside-down cake left in the breadbox."

Robin pursed her lips in disgust at the sight of the cake. "They're living in that stucco house they call The Little House. That means only six rooms. Ivy all over it. Sure, it's cute and quaint and all that."

Tracy barked and barked. "If you like that sound track. She's showing already and goes around all hunched over—"

"Daddy keeps offering me one of the puppies of what they call pet quality, not to be bred. But I'd rather have an ordinary dog like Torte who's sweet and friendly and relates to you, not off on a fit of his own."

Daria was controlling her reactions. She did not want her daughters seeing Ross; she did not want them out there in Hamilton. But she must keep those reactions to herself. Ross was still their father and they must make their own way with him.

Tracy was saying, "He's disgustingly proud of her being knocked up. I thought to myself I ought to go out and get pregnant and show him how easy it is, if he thinks it's such an accomplishment."

Robin said, "We kept calling him Daddy every two minutes, to bug him."

"But what do they do?" Daria asked. "Do they entertain a lot?"

"There's a hunt club, called some funny name—"

"The Myopia Hunt Club," Tracy put in. "They entertain there. Every other thing they say is, The Big House, The Little House. A lot of in-family politicking and scuffling for position among the sisters."

"But this indictment." Robin began lining up the toothpicks in four equal rows. "Daddy wanted to talk about that, and of course I absolutely won't!" Robin stopped arranging toothpicks and looked Daria in the eyes. "How dare he mention that to me?"

"Well, lovey, I suppose because he cares what you think of him."

"He said it was all lies. They were trying to use him to advance themselves politically, all the attorney general's minions he called them. I had to go home and look up that word."

"He's livid about you, Mama," Tracy said. "But we wouldn't let him go on about it."

"I'm sorry you're caught in the middle."

"I'm not in the middle." Robin began arranging toothpicks in a square, facing outward like little spikes. "I have nothing to do with that whole ugly mess."

"Is he scared, do you think?" Daria asked slowly.

"Him? No, he's angry," Robin said.

"He views it as a nuisance." Tracy kept cutting very thin slices of cake. She would cut as thin a slice as she could, eat it slowly, and then cut another equally thin. "I don't think he expects the trial to happen. He says they couldn't possibly convict. He kept saying he'd done nothing that isn't standard business practice."

Robin was adjusting her toothpicks head side out and narrow end in, around a perfect square. Daria decided this new design resembled covered wagons drawn up into a defense formation against attack. Robin mumbled, "That's when you said what you shouldn't have."

Tracy giggled. "I told him about Robin and me seeing little Bobbie's ghost. I didn't tell him we were stoned."

Robin was still lining up toothpicks. "That's when he took us out to the kennels and this time he tried to give *you* a puppy."

"Mama, Robin doesn't want to get involved. But I have to. After all, I live in this neighborhood now too. I want to sit down with you after Robin goes home tonight, and I want you to tell me exactly what you and Tom and all those people think Daddy did."

"Tracy, no one wants you involved. I got into it in spite of myself, to survive. But you don't have to."

Tracy pushed away the cake, her brows drawn into a frown. "I think I do have to know. It's my life too. He says you're doing this to wreck his new scene and that you're lying, I can hardly remember a time you lied to us. I have to know."

"Not in front of me." Robin rose. "I told him I didn't want to talk about it and I wouldn't listen. Then I went and played tennis with Gail's sister Flip. She's supposed to be this super tennis star, who was tenth seeded woman in some rinkidink tennis tourney a few years ago, but I beat her. Two sets out of three. Then Daddy came and started hinting it was time for us to hit the road."

"Hinting!" Tracy waved her hands. "He shooed us out. He dotes on Gail. He reminds me how he used to be sometimes with Torte when he'd just taught him some new trick. Gail's only got one trick but he's really into it. And they talk about the baby as *he* all the time."

Robin stood poised holding the back of her chair by the top. "You think they're kidding. It is a boy. They had it checked out."

"Robin, they probably did that because your father and I had a child with a serious birth defect. If they'd had those tests then, we could have learned how grave Freddy's problems were in time."

"Oh." Robin got that odd compressed expression her face wore when she had to remember Freddy. "I thought they just did it to find out if he finally struck it rich on the boy I was supposed to be. Honestly, around them Tracy and I felt like some banged up used cars that had been replaced, you know."

"I don't think I'd envy the child being born now," Daria said, "not from any point of view."

"And we got to have *you* for our mother," Tracy said, wagging her finger at Daria. "We got the best deal."

32

THE twelve days she spent in Vermont were awkward but pleasant. She got on well with his sister and her lover, fascinated to see Tom's features expressed in a robust, high-colored attractive woman. She did better on and off with Rosa, whom she actually preferred, as something sly and manipulative in Georgia rubbed against her grain. They could all manage together.

Nonetheless she was glad to come back to Boston ahead of them. She had two days at home to prepare for her first September taping. When Tom returned, it was to put the girls on a plane.

That night together in the bed he had built for her, they had a holiday feeling. The farmhouse bedroom had offered a morning view over its own fields toward low blue-green mountains gauzy with fog, but they never felt unheard. The old farmhouse seemed one room with partitions because of the way every sound carried. Their lovemaking was furtive, their conversations, whispered and truncated.

Now to lie making love at length and with all the cries and exclamations they wished and to talk and talk and talk was blissfully expansive, easy.

"The first bitter fight Andrea and I had—the first that couldn't be made up—was about day care." He was lying with his arms crooked behind his head. Although they had already made love, she could not stop caressing the barrel curve of his chest, playing with the pattern of hairs, his nipples. "I wanted day care where they'd meet a lot of different kinds of kids. I didn't want them growing up like the bratty, sophisticated hothouse flowers some of our friends had. Andy wanted a center that was connected with Harvard."

"I never had the girls in day care—Ross thought it would be bad for them. When I worked, my mother took them. Why would the center matter? Don't they all do about the same thing, at that age?"

"I didn't want the girls to grow up spoiled. Andy didn't want them to be without what she saw as absolutely essential advantages. I felt it was snobbery. After all, you don't learn particle physics in day care, so what the hell is the use of Harvard? For me it was important they be dealing with Black and Hispanic kids from their neighborhood before they were old enough to learn to be scared. For Andy there was a special track laid down from age three. We were both rock hard in conviction. We dug in and hated each other."

"So who won?" She was relieved that so long taboo a subject as his marriage had joined what could be discussed; but she also felt a chill rising along her spine she could not quite understand.

"Andrea. But I took it out on her, believe me." He shook his head with a sour grin. "Now they aren't really mine any longer."

"They adore you."

"But I don't make the big decisions or the little daily ones. I'm a major myth but a minor factor."

He's young, she thought, and he lost his children. He will want another family. Even if I weren't sterilized, I couldn't go through it all again. Eventually, no matter how well we communicate and how much we have together and how usefully we work in the neighborhood and how beautifully we make love, he will want children again and he will turn from me. She sighed. When he asked her what was wrong, she said only, "I'm tired. Let's turn out the light and go to sleep."

But she wasn't tired and she didn't sleep.

The trial had been going on for two weeks before what she imagined to be the trial actually got under way. There had been days of motions to dismiss and to discover and to change venue, followed by days and days of jury selection. Not until the morning of October 21 was Daria called to the stand. She had not been attending every day, as none of them could in fact. Always at least one observer from SON was present and reported to everyone else in the evening.

The night before her testimony, she lay awake. In the morning, she put on the simple blue jersey okayed by Bloomberg, who had coached her, rehearsed her and, playing defense attorney, had insulted and browbeaten her until she felt as if any actual scene today must be anticlimactic. Her stomach did not agree. As she rose to take the stand, she found herself dry-mouthed.

As she was sworn in, she remembered the first cooking demonstration she had given in a department store. Her hands had shaken so, looking into that ring of staring faces, she had poured gazpacho all over her new dress. After that she had learned to fake confidence and calm, a couple of years before she actually ever attained that state in public. Standing in the net of sharp gazes, hanging there in the crowded courtroom, she remembered too how her first time on television to push a cookbook, she had sautéed mushrooms to add to a beef dish and never in fact added them. She had almost passed out when she walked off the set and realized her error, but no one else noticed.

All that morning she testified. What the prosecutor was most interested in were the notes from Lou; how much she had known and how much she had been ignorant about in Ross's real estate dealings; her meeting with and gradual involvement in SON. She felt as if she had memorized a long recipe—a filled puff pastry, say—and was being quizzed on its minor points over and over. After Bloomberg had run her thoroughly and repetitiously through her paces, she was turned over to Ross's lawyer. Bloomberg had warned her she would be attacked as a lying and vengeful discarded woman.

She felt shy of looking at Ross. When she finally forced her gaze on him, she felt vertigo. But he was not looking at her. From that time on whenever she stole a glance at him, she saw him doing the same thing: leaning over the table busy with a pencil as if making notes. What she suspected he was really doing was what he used to do during boring phone calls or the very occasional PTA meetings he attended. He was probably drawing complex geometric shapes.

She had met the defense attorney Samuel Potter once and had actually danced with him at some tony function at the Union Club that Ross had managed to be invited to. She doubted if he remembered, for she might not have, except that he had such unpleasant cold dry hands and such a bloodless air, she had decided he was a vampire and had thought of him the rest of the night as Count Dracula, although he had none of the dark saturnine charm with which that character was often played. He was a New England vampire, grey-eyed, balding and tight-lipped with a voice just high of middle range and carrying, a sort of dry redolent amontillado sherry.

"Is it true as you stated you began reading your husband's mail and steaming open his letters secretly because you were interested in uncovering his relationship with another woman?"

"That's correct. I had accidentally seen the first note from Louis Ledoux when I was emptying wastebaskets, and I thought Lou was a woman's name."

"Mrs. Walker, isn't that still what interests you? Exposure of your former husband? Isn't it true that since you've lost Ross Walker, your sole interest is in discrediting him, punishing him?"

The prosecutor objected, but the judge said it was a permissible line of inquiry.

As if replaying a tape, the lawyer repeated the question. Daria's gaze kept straying to Gail in a beige dress, far more pregnant looking than she was supposed to be. "No, I wouldn't say that at all."

"I didn't ask you if you'd say it. I asked you if it's true."

"No. Anybody from SON will tell you I infuriated them by refusing to believe Ross Walker capable of arson until my own house burned and I barely escaped."

The attorney questioned her again and again on her testimony, trying to shake her version, trying to prove her wild in accusation and bent on revenge, a monster of jealousy. Daria had been coached by Bloomberg, but the attack was still hard to endure without reacting visibly. You must stay calm, he had ordered. Any sign of emotion and you'll seem hysterical. You must sound gentle and rational, he had warned her, and she did her best, although she knew her eyes must be sparking anger.

Too bad the glib attorney before her was dealing with a cookbook writer. Anybody who could describe accurately the process of deboning a leg of lamb or a turkey, or who could describe making a Saint Honoré cake or a terrine in crust from four kinds of meat and fowl, could with ease remember exactly what she had said in previous testimony and repeat accurately the third, the fourth, the fifth time.

"Revenge? But I was left in the lurch financially. My husband was not even paying our younger daughter's tuition at college, as he had promised. What he was offering as a divorce settlement, to give you some perspective, was less than twenty percent of what we finally agreed was my share of our mutual property."

"Do you want us to believe you spent what you admit were days and days trying to prove your husband a criminal, simply out of curiosity? You want us to believe you never sought revenge on your husband, whom you believed to be unfaithful, and who certainly wanted to marry another woman, but you just carried on weeks of research about him for the pure love of knowledge? Is that how you'd describe your activities?" Potter turned to the jury with a world-weary sigh. He invited them to share his skepticism and amusement.

"I wasn't trying to prove him a criminal, since I didn't believe him to be one. I was trying to find out exactly what we owned as husband and wife, in whosoever name it was listed."

"Who told you to play detective, Mrs. Walker? Who told you what to look for and where to look? Who were you reporting to, Mrs. Walker?"

"I was doing what all the books written for women undergoing divorce advise you to do. I was doing what my lawyer told me would be necessary to achieve a just settlement for myself and my minor daughter. Sandra María Roa Vargas taught me how to do the research, but I only went to her after my lawyer Dorothy Keough and my accountant found discrepancies in my husband's statements of financial worth."

"Are you telling us you were very rational as you sat there compiling this documentation? You're swearing you had no motive but financial gain?" Potter's face expressed astonished incredulity.

"I had no motive but financial justice. Our fair share." Daria knew she was lying, because she had cared even more for understanding Ross. Which would finally come with his testimony, when her ordeal was over.

"Yet you persisted, week after week, pursuing the history of buildings he had owned or partially owned?"

"Until I had what my lawyer said was necessary documentation. Then I stopped." She was staring at Gail again, because Gail's glare kept catching her eye. Gail fixed upon her with an aghast fascination, her lips pursed. Daria made herself look at Bloomberg instead.

"What did you think of your husband Ross Walker as you worked day after day to undermine him and to prove what you thought was information useful to the machinations of his tenants?"

"I felt distant from him. More and more distant. I came to understand how little I had known about what he did for money and what he was willing to do for money."

"And what were you willing to do for money, Mrs. Walker?"

"Objection."

"I withdraw that question," Potter said as if doing her an immense favor. He smiled tightly in the direction of the jury.

She felt as if she had been on the stand for ten hours. Yet when she was allowed to step down at last, it was only lunchtime. She felt clammy with sweat under her dress. When they filed from the courtroom, she hastened to the women's room and threw up. As she was washing her face, Gail came running in. Gail froze, her mouth opening and shutting. Daria wondered from the younger woman's expression if she thought Daria might be about to attack her. Daria nodded in awkward salutation. Seeing Gail up close, her spare body swollen in what had to be at least the eighth month of pregnancy, Daria had a sad vision of what she could only call the remorselessness of events. Gail had probably done little evil, if less good, in her life; now both her future and that of the child to be born would be stained by what Ross had done and what she in turn had done—and others, living and dead. Gail turned away pointedly and hurried into a booth, where she stayed locked in during the rest of the time Daria was repairing herself.

She could not eat lunch. She drank orange juice and tea. "On a diet," Bloomberg chided. "You women are always dieting." He was attacking a steak.

She kept thinking what she should have said. She had much more to tell the jury. Neither Bloomberg nor the defense attorney Potter had wanted her to talk about the Lexington arson, nor was it listed on the bill of indictment. Bloomberg viewed it as a red herring, an accusation that would distract the jury and never prove prosecutable. Yet Daria was sure if that fire had never occurred, she would not have been present today in the courtroom to testify against Ross. She wanted him brought to justice, but justice seemed more elusive the closer she came to the process supposed to deliver it.

For two weeks she had rehearsed her testimony. She had typed it out, studied it, gone over it aloud, practiced with Tom, practiced with Sandra María and finally with Bloomberg himself. Sitting in the restaurant with sounds of cutlery and crockery clattering around her, with the sweat cold on her and a dull pain in her stomach, she could not accept that her part was over. She had not been asked the right questions, not allowed to say what she desired, thrust into an arcane and rigid formula of questions and responses that had nothing to do with her experience. She wondered if she had seemed hysterical with the thirst for revenge, or if she had seemed contrariwise cold and unfeeling, hungry only for money.

"You did a fine job," Bloomberg roared. "You came across as a calm mature witness. Highly credible. At one point," he waggled his finger at her, "I thought you were going to lose it. Got mad, didn't you?"

"I got mad several times."

"No reason to show it. Gives them points."

"Will I get another chance to testify? There's so much I never got a chance to talk about."

"It went fine," Bloomberg said dismissively. "We're painting a picture of a man living a double life, financing his divorce through arson. You've done your part. We're building up to the big guns."

Tom found them in the restaurant. Bloomberg had asked him to appear by one o'clock, as first Sandra María and then Tom would take the stand next. Daria stirred herself from her self-absorption enough to notice that Sandra María was also too nervous to eat.

After lunch Sandra María presented her charts and graphs. Her voice was higher pitched than usual and she looked clumsy in a corduroy suit Daria had never seen before and doubted she would see again on her friend.

As Tom was testifying, she felt almost as nervous as she had when she was on. Since Daria had warned Bloomberg about Ross's attempt to smear Tom as a dangerous radical, his testimony was confined to reporting on his discovery of Lou and Jay Jay on the roof. Although Potter attempted to use Tom's background against him in cross-examination, Daria did not feel it carried much weight against the identification, also affirmed in her testimony. Potter did not question Tom about his relationship with Daria, as Bloomberg had thought he might. Perhaps Potter did not want any shading of his picture of Daria as a revenge-obsessed discard.

Mr. Schulman was next, to identify Lou and Jay Jay as perpetrators of attempted arson. Daria could plainly remember that Mr. Schulman had not in fact seen Jay Jay well enough to identify him, but by this time, Jay Jay and Mr. Schulman and Lou were all convinced that Mr. Schulman had recognized both of them as they fled. Although Potter attempted to cast doubt on Schulman's ability to catch sight of the men running in the middle of the night, Mr. Schulman was unshakable because he was totally certain by now of what he had seen. Daria was partly amused and partly disturbed. How often did that sort of false conviction overcome witnesses? Neither Jay Jay nor Lou wanted to challenge Mr. Schulman, for they were as persuaded as he was that he had identified them. Sometimes Daria suspected she was the only person who still remembered that Mr. Schulman had not gotten a good view. When she had said that to Tom, he had assured her that when Mr. Schulman saw Lou and Jay Jay again, of course he had recognized them.

At the very end of the court's day, Lou was sworn in. Somewhere he had acquired or been lent an Ivy League herringbone suit. The idea was no doubt to try to make him look as respectable as possible, to suggest that if someone this upright admitted to arson, then the jury could find it possible that Ross Walker was also guilty. He had only begun to testify about how he had met the defendant when court adjourned. Daria was sorry she would miss the next day, but she had to work. It would be Fay's turn.

Friday evening the day in court was retold over supper at Daria's in as much detail as Fay could muster. All day Lou had testified for the prosecution from his first meeting with Ross through his recent attempts to fulfill a contract to burn two of Ross's buildings. Monday Potter would have at him.

Daria was surprised to notice how glad she felt that a whole weekend

432

would pass before she or any of her friends must return to the courtroom. She felt as if she should attempt to go as often as possible, but she felt relieved to escape from the strict and peculiar formulae of the courtroom. She felt glad to escape Gail's prominent belly and baleful stare. She felt glad too to escape Ross's chilling presence, that man who had so recently been her own husband and who now felt as strange to her as if he spoke a Martian tongue and worshipped a Crab God.

She had finally invited Gretta to supper, but before the evening was well launched, she realized her timing was poor. Everybody really wanted to sit inertly around the living room staring at the television and drinking their way through a big bottle of Valpolicella. She had felt guilty for seeing little of Gretta since her move.

Gretta looked closely at Sandra María and launched into, "Oh, I adore Puerto Rico. It's my old stomping grounds. My husband and I used to fly down in February and stay at the Americana. Or the El San Juan."

"That isn't Puerto Rico any more than Disneyland is the U.S." Sandra María said, her brows drawing into a furrow and her eyes narrowing.

The evening bumped along from there. The living room emptied. Ángel and Sandra María found a pressing need to go out. Mariela was put to bed. As Tom tried to make conversation with Gretta, Daria remembered his stories about people at faculty parties asking him what department he was in and then telling him they'd built a fence or a shed themselves. Gretta, once she learned Tom was a carpenter, seemed only able to talk about renovations or cabinets. Everything about him was defined for Gretta by his job. He could not possibly have anything to say to her about politics or art or relationships.

After Tom retreated upstairs, Daria sat on with Gretta. By now Daria was yawning occasionally hoping that Gretta would go home soon. "I think it's marvelous really, Daria, your being able to take my advice and have an affair. It doesn't matter if you can't share your interests. It's still fun. But why on earth did you allow him to move in? That will cramp your style. I mean, you don't want to end up supporting him and eventually we all want to remarry. . . ."

* * *

433

Saturday Daria felt mildly depressed all day. Finally in the evening when they were alone in her room she began. "It worried me when you said you don't have enough influence over your daughters—"

"When did I say that?" He loomed up, dark eyes enormous with query.

"When we got back from Vermont."

"Two months ago?"

"Tom, you're younger than me. You'll want more children."

"I don't feel younger. Sometimes I feel older. Sometimes you mother me, sometimes I mother you."

"But I can't give you children."

"You think I want more? A whole second family?" He lay on his side facing her, hand on propped elbow. "I have one, thank you."

"You say you don't feel the girls are really yours."

"Of course they're mine. I just feel let down after they leave." He ruffled her hair with the flat of his hand. "What's this about? That in a couple of years, you think I'll sneakily turn into Walker?"

"Well, men change."

"Women don't? You've been changing yourself. What you're worrying about is stupid, peaches, made up. I never had this kind of intimacy with Andrea."

"You had some reason for marrying her." Gail's pregnant form lurked in her mind. Gretta was so sure Daria's relationship was temporary. Daria felt as if she were counting too much on Tom.

"Andy admired me because I was a big honcho in our little circle. I wanted her because she was the princess type, the kind who never looked at me in high school. Because she was pretty. Because at first, whatever I wanted, she wanted too. I deserved what I got."

"Divorce, you mean?"

"Divorce was hard, but that marriage was harder. The last years it was so bad I got used to being sore all the time—sore mad and sore hurt. Used to a high level of pain, like somebody living with a bad toothache."

"Why would having a bad marriage with Andrea mean you won't want children again with somebody else?"

"Because I want what I have. Our intimacy. I want more of that, not something else."

434

"You think without children sex is better?" She was thinking that for herself, sex with Ross had improved after children and then again after sterilization.

"It's a matter of being able to be truly alone. And I want your attention. I want us to go on talking the way we do. We're both people who've been deeply lonely without ever realizing it, in the middle of lives that seemed half overrun with people."

"But now that you have the kind of relationship you want, wouldn't it be natural for you to start wanting children?"

"Daria, if I get nuts for a kid we can adopt. As long as you don't insist on a white baby, you can find a kid. Okay?" He flopped onto his back.

"Do you ever think of moving out there to be near your girls?"

"What the hell is this, Fear Night? No. My visitation rights are specific. And I can't adjust to California. Strikes me like somebody who smiles constantly. I don't know what it all means out there."

"I have been scared. The trial doesn't help." In the curve of his arm, she curled against him, a slow relaxation flooding her muscles.

"Peaches, what you had with Walker, he went his way and you went yours. Don't you think if I started getting weird ideas, you'd be the first to know?"

"I had a letter from Tracy this morning. She's broken up with Scott."

"You ought to be pleased. He had the personality of a goldfish."

"I didn't think she really liked him."

"What's going on is that Tracy's trying to live less on a roller coaster. She wanted something calm, maybe even a little boring with Scott."

"You mean she's a born enthusiast and she's trying to fight that?" It was a quiet joy to talk about her children with him. She wondered how she had ever managed to bring them through adolescence with none of this kind of insight and involvement from Ross. Tom was a much better father to Tracy than Ross had been in years, even if Tracy cast him in an older brother role. "She tried so hard to be strong for me, I know it."

"She got a little scared." Tom settled her against him, her buttocks pressing into his belly, his arm against her breasts. "If you haven't noticed, Daria, we have rather a lot of children to worry about already."

33

Frost had blackened the tomato vines and the peppers. The kitchen surfaces were covered with green tomatoes, washed, sorted and halfway to their fate of storage in the basement or being pickled. Daria had taken out her woolens and packed away her light cottons. Tracy was dating a young poet who talked much of death and destruction. "He's much more real than Scott," she told Daria. "No, nobody up here pays attention to the trial. Walker is such a common name. You can tell me about it when I come home . . . or do you need me now?"

Daria assured Tracy she was doing fine. The experts droned on, Donald among them, talking about char factors and accelerants, showing their samples, photos and diagrams while the eyes of the jurors glazed over. She was waiting for the moment when Ross would stand before everyone and answer for his act, when at last she would comprehend what he thought about what he had done.

Mrs. Rodriguez—the mother of Sylvia and Eduardo—testified and the jurors woke up. Daria was angry at Bloomberg for putting Mrs. Rodriguez in front of everybody to stammer and sob. Sylvia and Orlando told their brief stories. Daria noticed how carefully Bloomberg had avoided letting out at this trial the tapes that would figure, she assumed, in the next, that of Petris and then of her brother. Then came Mrs. Rosario to describe the night of the fire that had killed her son.

She did not weep. She sat and spoke quietly; several times her voice died to inaudibility. She sat starkly rigid, for as the questioning brought out, she was still in a brace from a back injury that had crushed her vertebrae when she had leapt from the third floor window holding her baby. Her husband had rescued the infant from the flaming bedroom, suffering third degree burns in the act. She had taken the baby and jumped. Neither of them had been able to reach Bobbie, asleep in his bedroom near the head of the stairs. She had been wakened by someone screaming in the hall. The flames had already been fierce, cutting them off from both exits. As she had jumped she could still hear screaming. "I hear it yet," she said simply and almost inaudibly.

The defense brought in their own experts, their own detectives. The experts for the prosecution had claimed arson was proved; the experts for the defense denied that arson was even probable. Character witness after witness, respectable, eminent, mature, well-heeled, testified to the sterling virtue and probity of the accused. Instead of Mrs. Rodriguez and Mrs. Rosario with their broken English, the street voices of Sylvia and Orlando and Jay Jay, here were the voices of Harvard Business School, of the Rotary Club, of worthy charities and important institutions, all of which were supported, assisted, shored up by Ross Walker. Here were his law partners testifying to his success in attracting lucrative clients to their practice, his previous career of distinguished public service. The partners and Pierre also testified to his presence at dinner parties during the nights arson was supposed to have occurred. Pierre also swore that yes, he had known that the Walkers were having difficulties and that Mrs. Walker was disturbed over the breakup of the marriage. Bloomberg objected and the judge ruled that part of the testimony hearsay.

She stayed up late to leave work for Peggy so that she could attend the trial daily, now that Ross was about to testify. Finally Potter called Ross. Potter treated Ross gently, deferentially, as if apologizing moment by moment for subjecting a man of his caliber to such indignity as a trial. Ross looked lean and tan in a navy suit. Early in his life he had been told he looked well in blue—that it matched his eyes and set off his hair—and he had worn little else since. Browns, rusts, greens made him nervous, for he said they were too hard to match. How strange the things she knew about the man all gazes were now directed toward: how he liked his eggs, the boxer shorts and all cotton tee shirts he preferred, his

437

brand of hemorrhoid medicine, but not any longer how he saw right and wrong.

She was surprised as the initial questioning went smoothly on to find herself yawning. It was not tension but rather mild milk of magnesia boredom. She could no longer remember why she had loved him. Why him? She felt distance and some embarrassment. This cool estrangement felt worse than the hatred and howling bloody-mindedness that Ross and his lawyer attributed to her.

Who was he, tan, freshly shaved, in his well-tailored navy suit? Were they still connected at all, beyond their being caught in a sticky web of actions and reactions? She wanted to feel more. She felt guilty for her lack of excitement. She stared, trying to find in that long slightly fishy face—eyes bulging a little, weak chin—the man she had centered her life around. He was concentrating on the questions Potter asked, designed to show his civic-minded nature, his respectability, his good conduct, his worth. He paused and then dealt with each query deliberately. He was probably an impressive witness, sure of himself, in control, taking his time, sounding extremely precise and in command of the facts. The jury must believe him. Their fine resonant voices played in respectful turn, two lawyers in a duet of calm assurance. A cello and a viola. A counterpoint of dry amontillado and a fine cream sherry, their voices.

She heard him lie in that clear resonant voice with the ring of confidence, authority, probity, so that she half doubted her memory. He had been asking Daria for a divorce since the summer before. How could she have thought he had denied his affair well into December? She was a sick vengeful woman who had become immediately involved with SON upon her first encounter with them: she had invited them into the house and joined them at once in attempting to undo her husband. How could she have forgotten? Every statement issuing from his mouth sounded plausible. The edifice of lies stretched high, smooth and seamless, a wall of shining white marble. She felt sick. He would defeat them.

She was extremely angry as she left court that day. As she was using the women's room, once again Gail came in. This time Gail gaped at her in outrage. "You can't injure him, you . . . you!" Gail blurted out. "You'll see!" She dashed out without using the facilities.

Sunday Robin had her own complaint. "People are treating me like some kind of outcast! Like I'm a criminal. It's just awful. I feel so embarrassed. Why can't the media just let it go on if it must without making a fuss?"

"Robin, the trial doesn't get much airplay. The bust was much bigger. It's not on page one. It's buried halfway back in the papers."

"Everybody knows about it, everybody! I'm thinking of moving to New York."

"You don't have to run away." She tried to put her arm around Robin, but her daughter ducked away. "It isn't either of us on trial. We weren't in his confidence."

"I don't understand what's going on. I don't want to!" Robin stuck her chin out, looking like Ross. "Daddy calls me up and whines. He makes me sick."

"It's a hard situation for you, but it'll be over and nobody will remember it in six months except us."

"He makes it worse. At least you don't beg me to agree you're right all the time, when I just don't want to hear anything about the sticky mess."

Daria sighed. "Robin, if you want to look for a job in New York, I'll see if I can give you a little money. I don't have much, but let me see what I can do."

"I just can't stand everybody talking about it. I bet in New York, nobody cares about some dinky landlord case in Boston."

Monday Daria had to film her weekly segments, trial or no trial. This week she was talking about fall cabbage crops under the title "King Cole." Monday she prepared broccoli four easy ways; Wednesday's segment would be on cauliflower; Friday, red, white and savoy cabbages would be her subject.

Tuesday Ross was being cross-examined by Bloomberg. Bloomberg projected a wry amusement. He seemed almost condescending toward Ross, saying in his posture and voice and mannerisms, now, man to man, why don't we cut the nonsense and get down to facts? Enough of this pretending. We both know you're up to your chin in it.

Ross had never endured well being contradicted or argued with. That was why she had developed her habit of circumventing him, pussyfooting around his annoyance as if around some cleft in the earth from which clouds of steam and noxious vapors arose. As she watched she remembered that he had never practiced in the courtroom for one of his professors had advised him in school that he was not fitted for a career in forensic law. He had told Ross, as Ross had repeated to Daria with undiminished pique, that Ross lacked a winning style.

A winning style. Last Friday she would have said he had it, but that was under sympathetic and respectful questioning. But challenged, prodded, asked to refute the testimony of witness after witness, Ross showed annoyance. He looked and sounded petulant. "I'm sure I can't recall petty details of every conversation I engaged in six months ago. I had many business matters on my mind at the time."

"I'm sure you did. Could you have been annoyed enough that Eduardo Rodriguez had brought Jaime White with him to meet you, that some details of that conversation might have slipped your mind?"

"I had no such conversation," Ross snapped. "How can I remember something that didn't happen?"

"Isn't it true as Jaime White testified that you paid him twenty-five dollars in the tie department of Saks department store near your office?"

Potter objected. The judge overruled the objection. Potter turned to the jury with a look of disbelief. Look how they are harassing an honest man, he seemed to be saying silently. It was a pattern repeated again and again. Finally each time Ross would have to answer, as Potter suggested harassment.

"Mr. Bloomberg, I don't know these people. Owning buildings in a neighborhood doesn't mean I know the unemployed bums or the hoodlums who hang out on street corners."

"Mr. Walker, am I to understand that you are swearing to us that everybody is lying? Jaime White is lying. Louis Ledoux is lying. Daria Walker is lying. Mrs. Rodriguez, Mr. Schulman, the whole neighborhood is all joined in one big lie just to harass you. Do you expect us to believe that?" Bloomberg glanced at Potter, waiting for the objection, but Potter smiled like someone who has turned up exactly the card he awaited.

"It is a conspiracy, yes," Ross said with passionate conviction. "Run by those SON people. Helped by the spite of my ex-wife." He glared straight at Daria, one of the few times he had looked at her since the trial began. "Who's come here daily to gloat over me."

440

"Mr. Walker, are you aware your former wife is a Boston television personality?"

"I know she cooks on television sometimes."

"Are you aware she appears three times a week? Have you ever watched the program?"

"No."

"Are you aware she's well known as an author?"

"Of cookbooks."

"You don't approve of cookbooks, Mr. Walker?"

"I think they're silly."

"Might we presume you're aware that your wife has formed a close relationship with Mr. Silver?"

"I know about it."

"What did the detective you had watching Mrs. Walker just before your divorce report?"

"He said she was seeing that man. He also said she was spending a large amount of time with all the agitators from SON."

"To your knowledge, did your former wife ever hire a detective to watch you?"

"She hired a detective after the house in Lexington caught fire."

"Was that detective watching you or was he examining the rubble of the house for clues as to how the fire started?"

"That was the pretext."

"Did you see the detective's reports?"

"I saw some reports."

"Did Donald Lindsey carry out surveillance on you?"

"I suppose not."

"I would ask you, Mr. Walker, if you would not *suppose* if you were listening to another ex-husband talk about his former wife, if you wouldn't think that perhaps the husband was the one who exhibited jealousy and resentment?"

"Objection," Potter cried.

The objection was sustained and the jury was advised not to speculate on what the answer to that question might have been. Bloomberg was at his best with Ross. With the other witnesses, mostly he was establishing or questioning their stories. With Ross, he was setting him up in a subtle way she did not understand. He had a sense of Ross as prey that fascinated her. Under Bloomberg's questions, Ross fidgeted. He crossed his legs and uncrossed them. He scowled. He shifted in his chair. His voice dripped with sarcasm, grated with annoyance, rose in what Daria suspected had to be experienced by the jury as arrogance.

"I was merely conducting my business in a businesslike way," was the statement that stuck in her mind. It was uttered with conviction.

Bloomberg did not try to seem a gentleman conducting business with his peer in the jury's presence, as Potter did. Instead he took the jury into his confidence. He seemed to be saying to them, us regular guys, we know how it is.

"Those people," Ross said again and again, those agitators, those tenants, *those people*. "Those people don't take care of their children." "Those people leave trash on the stairs." "Those people create a fire hazard with their garbage and their drinking."

Daria began to see Bloomberg's strategy. What he regarded as the crux of the case was to persuade the jury that a man of Ross's standing could commit arson by proxy for convenience and profit. After the careful civic-minded lawyer and liberal businessman of Potter's gentle questioning, there emerged slowly another Ross Walker: one who could no longer sense how callous certain judgments sounded, how cold and distanced he seemed, how arrogance issued from him to hang like particles of ice in the courtroom air.

That day she realized she would never enter Ross's consciousness and understand. Whatever he said would be justification and lies, some mixture never to be sorted out. She would not be granted even his picture of himself. Nothing more would be attainable than a provisional guess. She felt as if she had been climbing an enormous mountain for months only to find at the top not the view she had imagined but simply fog and swirling clouds and rocks beneath her feet. No long view of the terrain covered would ever open up.

No climactic moment of truth arrived. Ross never changed his story: he was the victim of a conspiracy of riffraff, tenants, agitators, bums, neighborhood lowlife, masterminded by the malice of his divorced wife. He denied arson and he never stopped denying. Bloomberg could not shake Ross's account of himself. What Bloomberg destroyed was the character created by the rapport between Ross and Potter. The man who sat fidgeting, who grimaced with his thin lips, who arched his head back and glared, who showed how absolutely infuriating he found it to be challenged and interrogated publicly, was a man of high arrogance who did not consider himself accountable. Ross never contradicted his previous testimony. Only his icy contempt became more and more apparent as cross-examination proceeded. The two lawyers were dueling; neither could cripple the other. Feint and parry, feint and parry, the contest of wills and disparate styles went on.

Daria found the galleys of the seasonal cookbook waiting for her when she came home. She had to begin proofreading and correcting her way through the typeset book at once with Peggy and anybody else who could be pressed into reading aloud, because the difference in a recipe between 1 tsp. and 1 tbs. of salt was the difference between success and disaster. One line omitted could alter the results to high price garbage. Therefore she did not witness the final Thursday of the trial with the summations of Bloomberg and Potter. The jury went out before noon. She worked all day with Peggy.

Her family was still at supper, Sandra María trying to translate what she said was a funny joke she had heard in Spanish that afternoon, when the phone rang. Tom answered it. He exclaimed into the phone and then turned to the table. "That was Mac. The jury brought in their verdict—they convicted! Conspiracy to commit arson, defrauding an insurance company and manslaughter. The judge will pronounce sentence next week. Bloomberg's sure it'll be seven to ten years, anyhow."

At the impromptu party at Fay's that evening, she kept trying to read her own feelings. She felt a little guilty, although she could not decide if that was guilt by association, from having been long married to Ross, or guilt for having done her small but significant part in trying to bring him to justice.

"If only they could stop him from committing arson without putting him behind bars," she said softly to Tom. "I don't know how he'll survive prison."

443

"If he ever serves any time, it'll be soft time. They're not going to send him to Walpole," Tom answered just as quietly. He drew her aside, so they stood near a window on the street. "He'll sit in a cottage and write a book, like all the Watergate bozos. If there's money in it, he'll probably become an arson expert and go around lecturing."

"But he was found guilty of conspiracy to commit arson and manslaughter."

"He'll appeal. He's married the money to fight the case up through court after court. Nothing will happen to him for years. They'll fight it on technicalities. The AG wanted a conviction before the election and he just got it. With Walker down, he'll convict the others easier. But as for what's going to happen to those cases two years from now—"

Fay threw her arms around Tom's neck and kissed him. "It's my turn," she said to Daria. "You get to do this all the time."

Sandra María was holding a cranky Mariela, who was rubbing her eyes and pouting. "I'm not sleepy! I'm not sleepy!"

The nightmares had gradually abated, but Daria wondered sometimes if Mariela would ever in her life learn to go to bed willingly again. Sandra María grinned at Daria over her head. "Well, I am. I have to get up for work. And I thought you had school, minina mía." Sandra María poked Mariela's obstinately stiff arms into the sleeves of her coat.

Fay was kissing all the men and laughing jubilantly, so happy she shone as if she had sunburn. Sherry looked as if she would like to act that way, but did not dare. Orlando's older brother Boz was playing his conga drums along with a record and Orlando and Sylvia were dancing. Elroy asked Sherry to dance. She said she didn't know how, but he offered to teach her.

Daria felt an occasional rush of mutual delight, a sense of belonging to a group that was accomplishing some part of its purpose. Since the night Tom had caught Lou on the roof, there had been no fires in the neighborhood. Against all odds they had proved their case, opposed by far superior financing and resources. Something could be done: they had shown that to other neighborhoods in trouble when they seized their own opportunity to fight back. She felt herself part of a small but significant *We*.

Looking around the roomful of partying people, all of whom were good acquaintances and some of whom were friends, she realized that none here knew Ross except as a paper villain. She was free of him at last. He might in the future have some dealings with his daughters, although at the moment he was demonstrating his anger with Daria by once again withholding Tracy's tuition. She would put Tracy through college herself. One advantage of incurring that extravagant cost was never having to deal with Ross again. Robin's relationship with her father was independent of Daria and would continue without her help or hindrance. But Daria's own connection had ceased in court. That was her last meeting with Ross and it was over.

When everybody toasted victory, she sipped the cheap Spanish champagne Mac had bought to celebrate. There was something rancid, something wrongly sour in its oversweetness that made her shudder. The pleasures of revenge were overrated, she thought, or else she lacked the temperament to appreciate them. Furtively she felt a little sad. Something she was still convinced had originally been sound—her marriage—and someone she was still convinced had been a fine person, were contaminated and alien to her now. Daria Walker and Ross Walker, I now pronounce you woman and man, strangers to each other bodily, emotionally and in all your values and your lives unto death.

Tom slipped his arm around her shoulders. "Drink up, peaches. It's wet and cold and full of bubbles, anyhow. When your book comes out, we'll get you something better."

"You've already given me something better."

His hand tightened on her nape. "Oh, you did notice that?"

As Fay came around with the next bottle refilling glasses, she raised hers toward Tom, who stood at her shoulder in his lazy slumped pose with his lids half lowered, watching everything while pretending not to but always keeping an eye on her. He didn't save me, this one, she thought, not even from a burning house. I saved myself. No gratitude other than the daily appreciation of each other's small and middling contributions to the common good and the common pleasure binds us. And the private pleasure between us. I have my daughters, including Robin back and Tracy maturing nicely if bumpily, I have my work, I have my chosen new community, I have my house, I have my dear family, Tom and Sandra María and Mariela too. She realized she was doing it again, counting her blessings, proving to herself that she was happy. But I am, she thought, and maybe a better woman finally than I used to be, when I was Ross's, before I was my own.

MARGE PIERCY is the author of seven previous novels, including *Small Changes, Woman on the Edge of Time, Vida* and *Braided Lives*. She has written nine books of poetry including *The Moon is Always Female, Stone, Paper, Knife,* and *Circles on the Water*. With Ira Wood she coauthored the play *The Last White Class*. Her book of essays is called *Parti-Colored Blocks for a Quilt*.

Piercy was born in Detroit, and attended the University of Michigan and then Northwestern. She lived for the next fourteen years in Chicago, Paris, Boston, San Francisco and New York before sinking roots into the sandy loam of Cape Cod. She is married to the writer Ira Wood. They live in Wellfleet year round, although they also spend time regularly in Boston. Piercy travels all over the country giving readings, lectures and workshops.